# PRAISE FOR #1 *NEW YORK TIMES* BESTSELLING AUTHOR SANDRA BROWN

"[Brown] is a masterful storyteller, carefully crafting tales that keep readers on the edge of their seats." —*USA Today*

"Author Sandra Brown proves herself top-notch."
—Associated Press

"Sandra Brown has continued to grow with every novel."
—*Dallas Morning News*

"Brown's storytelling gift is surprisingly rare, even among crowd-pleasers." —*Toronto Sun*

"A novelist who can't write them fast enough."
—*San Antonio Express-News*

"Brown has few to envy among living authors."
—*Kirkus Reviews*

"A taut, seamless tale of nonstop action…A revel not to be missed." —*BookPage*

"Sandra Brown is a master at weaving a story of suspense into a tight web that catches and holds the reader from the first page to the last." —*Library Journal*

"Expect to be entertained." —*Denver Rocky Mountain News*

"Fast pacing and tricky plotting." —*Publishers Weekly*

"Brown's novels define the term 'page-turner.'" —*Booklist*

# THE CRUSH

## NOVELS BY SANDRA BROWN

*Seeing Red*

*Sting*

*Friction*

*Mean Streak*

*Deadline*

*Low Pressure*

*Lethal*

*Mirror Image*

*Where There's Smoke*

*Charade*

*Exclusive*

*Envy*

*The Switch*

*The Crush*

*Fat Tuesday*

*Unspeakable*

*The Witness*

*The Alibi*

*Standoff*

*Best Kept Secrets*

*Breath of Scandal*

*French Silk*

*Slow Heat in Heaven*

# THE CRUSH

## SANDRA BROWN

GRAND CENTRAL
PUBLISHING
NEW YORK BOSTON

Grand Central Publishing
Hachette Book Group
1290 Avenue of the Americas, New York, NY 10104
grandcentralpublishing.com
twitter.com/grandcentralpub

Originally published in hardcover by Grand Central Publishing in October 2002 First mass market edition: September 2003
Reissued: October 2017

Grand Central Publishing is a division of Hachette Book Group, Inc. The Grand Central Publishing name and logo is a trademark of Hachette Book Group, Inc.



ISBNs: 978-1-4789-4807-0 (mass market reissue), 978-1-4789-4808-7 (trade paperback reissue), 978-1-4555-4640-4 (ebook)

Printed in the United States of America

OPM

10 9 8 7 6 5 4

# THE CRUSH

# Prologue

Dr. Lee Howell's home telephone rang at 2:07 A.M.

His wife, Myrna, who was sleeping beside him, grumbled into her pillow. "Who's that? You're not on call tonight."

The Howells had been in bed barely an hour. Their poolside party had broken up around midnight. By the time they'd gathered up the debris and empty margarita glasses, stored the perishable leftovers in the fridge, and visited their sleeping son's room to give him a good-night kiss, it was nearing one o'clock.

As they undressed they had congratulated themselves on hosting a successful get-together. The grilled steaks had been only a little tough, and the new electric mosquito zapper had sizzled all evening, keeping the insect population to a minimum. All things considered, a good party.

The Howells had felt mellow but agreed that they were too exhausted even to think about having sex, so they'd kissed each other good night, then turned to their respective sides of the bed and gone to sleep.

Despite the shortness of time Dr. Howell had been asleep, his slumber, assisted by several margaritas, had been deep and dreamless. Yet when the telephone rang he was instantly awake, alert, and responsive, as years of conditioning had trained him to be. He reached for the phone. "Sorry, hon. A patient may have taken a bad turn."

She nodded grudging assent into her pillow. Her husband's reputation as an excellent surgeon wasn't based solely on his operating-room skills. He was dedicated to his patients and interested in their well-being before, during, and after their surgeries.

Although it was unusual for him to be telephoned at home in the middle of the night when he wasn't the doctor on call, it wasn't altogether rare. This inconvenience was one of the small prices Mrs. Howell was willing to pay for the privilege of being married to the man she loved who also happened to be in demand and well respected in his field.

"Hello?"

He listened for several moments, then kicked off the covers and swung his feet to the floor. "How many?" Then, "Jesus. Okay, all right. I'm on my way." He hung up and left the bed.

"What?"

"I've gotta go." He didn't turn on the lamp as he moved toward the chair where he'd left the pair of Dockers he'd been wearing earlier in the evening. "Everybody on staff has been called in."

Mrs. Howell came up on one elbow. "What's happened?"

Serving a busy metropolitan area, Tarrant General Hospital was constantly on alert to handle major disasters. The staff had been trained to provide immediate emergency treatment to victims of airplane crashes, tornadoes, terrorist attacks. By comparison this night's emergency was mundane.

"Big pileup in the mix-master. Several vehicles involved." Howell shoved his bare feet into a pair of Docksides, which he loved and his missus despised. He had owned those shoes for as long as she had known him and refused to part with them, saying the leather was just now molding to his feet and becoming comfortable.

"A real mess. A tanker trailer overturned and it's burning," he said as he pulled his golf shirt over his head. "Dozens of casualties, and most are being sent to our emergency room."

He strapped on his wristwatch and clipped his pager to the waistband of his slacks, then leaned down to kiss her. Missing her mouth, he caught her between nose and cheek. "If I'm still there at breakfast time, I'll call and update you. Go back to sleep."

As her head resettled into the pillow, she murmured, "Be careful."

"Always am."

Before he got downstairs, she had already fallen back to sleep.

* * *

Malcomb Lutey finished reading Chapter 3 of his newest science-fiction thriller. It was about an airborne virus that within hours of being inhaled turned the internal organs of human beings into a black, oily goo.

As he read about the unaware yet doomed blond Parisian hooker, he picked at the pimple on his cheek, which his mother had admonished him to leave alone. "That only makes it worse, Malcomb. Until you start picking at it, it's not even noticeable."

Yeah, right. The pimple was way beyond "noticeable." It was the current peak on the ever-evolving, knobby red mountain range that comprised his face. This severe, scar-producing acne had ushered in Malcomb's adolescence and for the past fifteen years had defied every treatment, topical or oral, either prescribed or purchased over the counter.

His mother blamed this chronic condition on poor diet, poor hygiene, and poor sleep habits. On more than one occasion she had hinted that masturbation might be the cause. Whatever her current hypothesis, it invariably suggested that Malcomb was somehow responsible.

The frustrated dermatologist who had valiantly but unsuccessfully treated him had offered up different, but as many, theories on why Malcomb was cursed with the facial topography of a Halloween mask. Bottom line: Nobody knew.

As if the acne weren't enough to keep his self-esteem at gutter level, Malcomb's physique was another misfortune. He was pencil thin. Supermodels who were paid to look undernourished would envy his metabolism, which seemed to have a profound aversion to calories.

Last but no less genetically dire was his kinky, carrot-colored hair. The fiery thatch had the density and texture of steel wool and had been the bane of his existence long before the onset of acute acne.

Malcomb's odd appearance, and the shyness it had bred, made him feel a misfit.

Except at his job. It was night work. And it was solitary. Darkness and solitude were his two favorite things. Darkness dulled his vibrant coloring to a more normal hue and helped to obscure his acne. Solitude was part and parcel of being a security guard.

His mother didn't approve of his career choice. She constantly nagged him to consider making a change. "Out there all by yourself night after night," she often said, tsking and shaking her head. "If you work alone, how're you ever going to meet anybody?"

*Duh, Mother. That's the point.* This was Malcomb's standard comeback—although he lacked the courage to say it out loud.

Working the graveyard shift meant fewer times he had to conduct a conversation with someone who was trying hard not to stare at his face. Working through the night also allowed him to sleep during most of the hated daylight hours when his hair took on the brilliance of a DayGlo orange Magic Marker. He dreaded the two nights a week he was off, when he had to endure his mother's harping about his being his own worst enemy. The recurring theme of her lectures was that if he were more open to people he would have more friends.

"You've got a lot to offer, Malcomb. Why don't you go out like other people your age? If you were friendlier, you might even meet a nice young lady."

Sure he would.

Mother scoffed at him for reading science fiction but *she* was the one living in a dream world.

His post at Tarrant General Hospital was the doctors' parking lot. To the other guards it was the least desirable post, but Malcomb preferred it. There wasn't a lot of activity at night. Business didn't pick up, so to speak, until early morning when the doctors began to trickle in. Most hadn't even arrived when he clocked out at seven in the morning.

However, this being a Friday night, there were more cars in the lot than on a weeknight. Invariably the weekend increased the traffic in the emergency room, so doctors came and went at all hours. Just a few minutes ago Dr. Howell had driven up to the gate and disengaged the arm with the transmitter he kept clipped to his sun visor.

Dr. Howell was okay. He never looked past Malcomb

as though he weren't there, and sometimes he even waved at him as he passed the guard shack. Howell didn't get all bent out of shape if the arm failed to disengage and Malcomb had to release it manually from inside the shack. Dr. Howell seemed like a regular guy, not snotty at all. Not like some of those rich assholes who acted so hoity-toity as they drummed their fingers on their padded steering wheels, impatiently waiting for the arm of the gate to rise so they could speed through as though they had someplace to be and something to do that was real important.

Malcomb read the first page of Chapter Four. As expected, the Parisian blond hooker succumbed mid-coitus. She died in the throes of agony and grotesque vomiting, but Malcomb's sympathies were with her hapless customer. Talk about a major bummer.

He turned the book facedown on the counter, straightened and stretched his spine, and sought a more comfortable position on his stool. As he did, he happened to catch his reflection in the window glass. The pimple was growing by the second. Already it was a monument of pus. Disgusted by his image, he focused his eyes on the parking lot beyond.

Mercury-vapor lights were strategically spaced so that most of the lot was well lighted. The shadows were deep only beneath the landscaping that formed its perimeter. Nothing had changed since the last time Malcomb had looked out, except for the addition of Dr. Howell's silver Beemer—third row, second car. He could see the gleaming roof of it. Dr. Howell kept his car in showroom condition. Malcomb would too if he could afford a set of wheels like that.

He returned to his novel but had only read a couple of paragraphs when something odd occurred to him. He looked toward Dr. Howell's Beemer again. His pale eyebrows furrowed with puzzlement. How had he missed Dr. Howell when he had walked past the shack?

In order to reach the sidewalk that led to the nearest employee entrance, one had to come within yards of the shack. It had become second nature for Malcomb to note when someone came past, either heading toward the building or returning to his car. There was a correlation. One either left the building and then shortly drove away in his car, or drove into the parking lot and then shortly passed the shack on his way into the building. Malcomb subconsciously kept track.

Curious, he marked his page and set the book beneath the counter next to the sack lunch his mother had packed for him. He tugged the brim of his uniform hat a little lower. If he were forced to talk to someone, even someone as easygoing as Dr. Howell, he didn't want to subject him to his unsightly face any more than necessary. The brim of his hat provided an extra layer of concealing shadow.

As he stepped from the shack's air-conditioned interior, he didn't notice any decrease in the outdoor temperature since making his last rounds. August in Texas. Almost as hot in the wee hours as at high noon. Heat from the asphalt came up through the rubber soles of his shoes, which made virtually no sound as he walked past the first row of cars, then the second. At the end of the third row, he paused.

For the first time since taking this job almost five years ago, he felt a prickle of apprehension. Nothing untoward had ever taken place on his shift. A couple months ago a guard in the main building had had to subdue a man who was threatening a nurse with a butcher knife. Last New Year's Eve a guard had been summoned to break up a fistfight between fathers over which of their newborns had been the first baby of the new year and therefore winner of several prizes.

Thankfully, Malcomb hadn't been involved in either incident. Reportedly they had drawn crowds. He would have been mortified by the attention. The only crisis he'd ever experienced while on duty was a dressing-down from a neurosurgeon who had returned to his Jag to discover that it had a flat tire. For reasons still unknown to Malcomb, the surgeon had held him responsible.

So far, his shifts had been luckily uneventful. He couldn't account for his uneasiness now. Suddenly his good friend Darkness no longer seemed as benevolent. He glanced around warily, even looking back behind him the way he'd just come.

The parking lot was as silent and still as a tomb—which at the moment wasn't a comforting analogy. Nothing moved, not even the leaves on the surrounding trees. Nothing appeared out of the ordinary.

Nevertheless, Malcomb's voice quavered slightly as he called out, "Dr. Howell?"

He didn't want to sneak up on the man. In a well-lighted room crowded with people, his face was startling to the point of being downright scary. If he were to come upon someone unexpectedly in the dark the poor guy might die of fright.

"Dr. Howell? Are you there?"

Receiving no answer, Malcomb figured it was safe to step around the first car in the row and check out Dr. Howell's Beemer, just to put his own mind at ease. He had missed him; it was as simple as that. When the doctor walked past he must've been concentrating a little too hard on what the blond hooker was doing to her john before she went into paroxysms of pain and started puking black gunk all over the guy. Or maybe he'd been distracted by the newest volcanic formation on his cheek. Or maybe Dr. Howell hadn't taken the paved path and instead had slipped through the shrubbery. He was a tall but slight fellow. He was slender enough to have squeezed through the hedge without creating much of a disturbance.

Whatever, Dr. Howell had slipped past him in the dark, is all.

Before rounding the first car in the row, just for good measure, Malcomb switched on his flashlight.

It was discovered later beneath the first car in the row where it had come to rest after rolling several feet. The glass was shattered, the casing dented. But the batteries would have done that annoying pink bunny proud. The bulb was still burning.

What was spotlighted in the beam of Malcomb's flashlight had frightened him more than anything he'd ever read in a science-fiction thriller. It wasn't as grotesque, bloody, or bizarre. But it was real.

# Chapter 1

Nice place you've got here."

"I like it." Ignoring the snide and trite remark, Wick dumped the pot of boiled shrimp into a colander that had never seen the inside of a Williams-Sonoma store. It was white plastic, stained brown. He didn't remember how he'd come by it, but he figured it had been left behind by a previous occupant of the rental house, which his friend obviously found lacking.

After the hot water had drained through, he set the colander in the center of the table, grabbed a roll of paper towels, and offered his guest another beer. He uncapped two bottles of Red Stripe, straddled the chair across the table from Oren Wesley, and said, "Dig in."

Oren conscientiously ripped a paper towel from the roll and spread it over his lap. Wick was on his third shrimp before Oren got around to selecting one. They peeled and ate in silence, sharing a bowl of cocktail sauce for dipping. Oren was careful not to get his white French cuffs in the horseradish-laced red stuff. Wick slurped carelessly and licked his fingers, fully aware that his sloppy table manners annoyed his fastidious friend.

They dropped the shrimp shells onto the newspaper that Wick had spread over the table, not to protect its hopelessly scarred surface but to keep cleanup to a minimum. The ceiling fan fluttered the corners of this makeshift tablecloth and stirred the spicy aroma of the shrimp boil into the sultry coastal air.

After a time, Oren remarked, "Pretty good."

Wick shrugged. "A no-brainer."

"Local shrimp?"

"Buy it fresh off the boat soon as it docks. The skipper gives me a discount."

"Decent of him."

"Not at all. We made a deal."

"What's your end of it?"

"To stay away from his sister."

Wick noshed into another plump shrimp and tossed the shell onto the growing heap. He grinned across at Oren, knowing that his friend was trying to decide whether or not he was telling the truth. He was a bullshit artist of renown, and even his best friend couldn't always distinguish his truth from his fiction.

He tore a paper towel from the roll and wiped his hands and mouth. "Is that all you can think of to talk about, Oren? The price of shrimp? You drove all the way down here for that?"

Oren avoided looking at him as he belched silently behind his fist. "Let me help you clean up."

"Leave it. Bring your beer."

A dirty table wasn't going to make much difference to the condition of Wick's house—which barely qualified as such. It was a three-room shack that looked like it would succumb to any Gulf breeze above five knots. It was shelter from the elements—barely. The roof leaked when it rained. The air conditioner was a window unit that was so insufficient Wick rarely bothered turning it on. He rented the place by the week, paid in advance. So far he'd written the slumlord sixty-one checks.

The screen door squeaked on its corroded hinges as they moved through it onto the rear deck. Nothing fancy—the plank surface was rough, wide enough only to accommodate two metal lawn chairs of vintage fifties style. Salt air had eaten through numerous coats of paint, the last being a sickly pea green. Wick took the glider. Oren looked dubiously at the rusty seat of the stationary chair.

"It won't bite," Wick said. "Might stain your suit britches, but I promise that the view'll be worth a dry-cleaning bill."

Oren sat down gingerly, and in a few minutes Wick's promise was fulfilled. The western horizon became striated with vivid color ranging from bloodred to brilliant orange. Purple thunderheads on the horizon looked like rolling hills rimmed with gold.

"Something, isn't it?" Wick said. "Now tell me who's crazy."

"I never thought you were crazy, Wick."

"Just a little nutty for shucking it all and moving down here."

"Not even nutty. Irresponsible, maybe."

Wick's easy smile congealed.

Noticing, Oren said, "Go ahead and get pissed. I don't care. You need to hear it."

"Well, fine. Thank you. Now I've heard it. How're Grace and the girls?"

"Steph made cheerleader. Laura started her period."

"Congratulations or condolences?"

"For which?"

"Both."

Oren smiled. "I'll accept either. Grace said to give you

a kiss from her." Looking at Wick's stubble, he added, "I'll pass if you don't mind."

"I'd rather you did. But give her a kiss from me."

"Happy to oblige."

For several minutes they sipped their beers and watched the colors of the sunset deepen. Neither broke the silence, yet each was mindful of it, mindful of all that was going unsaid.

Eventually Oren spoke. "Wick..."

"Not interested."

"How do you know until you've heard me out?"

"Why would you want to ruin a perfectly beautiful sunset? To say nothing of a good Jamaican beer."

Wick's lunge from the glider caused it to rock crazily and noisily before it resettled. Standing at the edge of the weathered deck, tanned toes curling over the edge of it, he tilted back his beer and finished it in one long swallow, then tossed the empty bottle into the fifty-gallon oil drum that served as his garbage can. The clatter spooked a couple of gulls who'd been scavenging on the hard-packed sand. Wick envied their ability to take flight.

He and Oren had a history that dated back many years, to even before Wick had joined the Fort Worth Police Department. Oren was older by several years, and Wick conceded that he was definitely the wiser. He had a stable temperament, which often had defused Wick's more volatile one. Oren's approach was methodical. Wick's was impulsive. Oren was devoted to his wife and children. Wick was a bachelor who Oren claimed had the sexual proclivities of an alley cat.

In spite of these differences, and possibly because of them, Wick Threadgill and Oren Wesley had made excellent partners. They had been one of the few biracial partnerships on the FWPD. Together they had shared dangerous situations, countless laughs, a few triumphs, several disappointments—and a heartache from which neither would ever fully recover.

When Oren had called last night after months of separation, Wick was glad to hear from him. He had hoped that Oren was coming to talk over old times, better times. That hope was dashed the moment Oren arrived and got out of his car. It was a polished pair of wing tips, not flip-flops or sneakers, that had made deep impressions in the Galveston sand. Oren wasn't dressed for fishing or beachcombing, not even for kicking back here on the deck with an Astros game on the radio and cold beer in the fridge.

He had arrived dressed for business. Buttoned down and belted up, bureaucracy personified. Even as they shook hands Wick had recognized his friend's game face and knew with certainty and disappointment that this was not a social visit.

He was equally certain that whatever it was that Oren had come to say, he didn't want to hear it.

"You weren't fired, Wick."

"No, I'm taking an 'indefinite leave of absence.' "

"That was your choice."

"Under duress."

"You needed time to cool off and get it together."

"Why didn't the suits just fire me? Make it easier on everybody?"

"They're smarter than you are."

Wick came around. "Is that right?"

"They know—everybody who knows you knows—that you were born for this kinda work."

"This kinda work?" He snorted. "Shoveling shit, you mean? If I cleaned out stables for a living, I wouldn't have to do as much of it as I did in the FWPD."

"Most of that shit you brought on yourself."

Wick snapped the rubber band he habitually wore

around his wrist. He disliked being reminded of that time and of the case that had caused him to criticize his superiors vociferously about the inefficiency of the justice system in general and the FWPD in particular. "They let that gang-banger cop a plea."

"Because they couldn't get him for murder, Wick. They knew it and the DA knew it. He's in for six."

"He'll be out in less than two. And he'll do it again. Somebody else will die. You can count on it. And all because our department and the DA's office went limp-dick when it came to a violation of the little shit's rights."

"Because you used brute force when you arrested him." Lowering his voice, Oren added, "But your problem with the department wasn't about that case and you know it."

"Oren," Wick said threateningly.

"The mistake that—"

"Fuck this," Wick muttered. He crossed the deck in two long strides. The screen door slapped shut behind him.

Oren followed him back into the kitchen. "I didn't come to rehash all that."

"Could've fooled me."

"Will you stop stomping around for a minute and let me talk to you? You'll want to see this."

"Wrong. What I want is another beer." He removed one from the refrigerator and pried off the top with a bottle opener. He left the metal cap where it landed on the wavy linoleum floor.

Oren retrieved a folder he'd brought with him and extended it to Wick, who ignored it. But his retreat out the back door was halted when his bare foot came down hard on the sharp teeth of the bottle cap. Cursing, he kicked the offender across the floor and dropped down into one of the chrome-legged dining chairs. The shrimp shells were beginning to stink.

He propped his foot on his opposite knee and appraised the damage. There was a deep impression of the bottle cap on the ball of his foot, but it hadn't broken the skin.

Showing no sympathy whatsoever, Oren sat down across from him. "Officially I'm not here. Understood? This is a complex situation. It has to be handled delicately."

"Something wrong with your hearing, Oren?"

"I know you'll be as intrigued as I am."

"Don't forget to pick up your jacket on your way out."

Oren removed several eight-by-ten black-and-white photographs from the folder. He held one up so that Wick couldn't avoid looking at it. After a moment, he showed him another.

Wick stared at the photo, then met Oren's eyes above it. "Did they get any shots of her with her clothes on?"

"You know Thigpen. He took these for grins."

Wick snorted acknowledgment of the mentioned detective.

"In Thigpen's defense, our stakeout house gives us a clear view into her bedroom."

"Still no excuse for these. Unless she's an exhibitionist and knew she was being watched."

"She isn't and she doesn't."

"What's her story?"

Oren grinned. "You're dying to know, aren't you?"

When Wick had surrendered his badge a little more than a year earlier, he had turned his back not only on his police career, but on the whole criminal justice system. To him it was like a cumbersome vehicle stuck in the mud. It spun its big wheels and made a lot of aggressive noise—freedom, justice, and the American way—but it got nowhere.

Law enforcement personnel had been robbed of their motivation by bureaucrats and politicians who quaked at the thought of public disapproval. Consequently the whole concept of justice was mired in futility.

And if you were the poor dumb schmuck who believed in it, who got behind it, put your shoulder to it, and pushed with all your might to set the gears in motion, to catch the bad guys and see them punished for their crimes, all you got in return was mud slung in your face.

But, in spite of himself, Wick's natural curiosity kicked in. Oren hadn't shown him these pictures for prurient purposes. Oren wasn't a Neanderthal like Thigpen and had better things to do with his time than to gawk at photographs of half-naked women. Besides, Grace would throttle him if he did.

No, Oren had a reason for driving all the way from Fort Worth to Galveston and, in spite of himself, Wick wanted to know what it was. He was intrigued, just as Oren—damn him—had guessed he would be.

He reached for the remainder of the photographs and shuffled through them quickly, then more slowly, studying each one. The woman had been photographed in the driver's seat of a late-model Jeep wagon; walking across what appeared to be a large parking lot; inside her kitchen and her bedroom, blissfully unaware that her privacy was being invaded by binoculars and telephoto lenses in the hands of a slob like Thigpen.

Most of the bedroom shots were grainy and slightly out of focus. But clear enough. "What's her alleged crime? Interstate transportation of stolen Victoria's Secret merchandise?"

"Uh-huh," Oren said, shaking his head. "That's all you get until you agree to go back with me."

Wick tossed the photographs in Oren's general direction. "Then you made the drive for nothing." He tugged again at the rubber band on his wrist, painfully popping it against his skin.

"You'll want to be in on this one, Wick."

"Not a chance in hell."

"I'm not asking for a long-term commitment, or a return to the department. Just this one case."

"Still no."

"I need your help."

"Sorry."

"Is that your final answer?"

Wick picked up his fresh beer, took a large swallow, then belched loudly.

Despite the smelly shrimp shells, Oren leaned forward across the table. "It's a murder case. Made the news."

"I don't watch the news or read the papers."

"Must not. Because if you had, you'd have sped straight to Fort Worth and saved me this trip."

Wick couldn't stop himself from asking "Why's that?"

"Popular doctor gets popped in the parking lot of Tarrant General."

"Catchy, Oren. Are you quoting the headline?"

"Nope. I'm giving you the sum total of what we know about this homicide. The crime is five days old and that's all we've got."

"Not my problem."

"The perp did the killing within yards of a potential eyewitness but wasn't seen. Wasn't heard. As silent as vapor. Invisible. And he didn't leave a trace, Wick." Oren lowered his voice to a whisper. "Not a fucking trace."

Wick searched his former partner's dark eyes. The hair on the back of his neck stood on end. "Lozada?"

Settling back in his chair, Oren smiled complacently.

# Chapter 2

Dr. Rennie Newton stepped off the elevator and approached the central nurses' station. The nurse at the desk, who was usually talkative, was noticeably subdued. "Good evening, Dr. Newton."

"Hello."

The nurse took in the black dress under Rennie's lab coat. "The funeral today?"

Rennie nodded. "I didn't take time to change afterward."

"Was it a nice service?"

"Well, as funerals go, yes. There was a large turnout."

"Dr. Howell was so well liked. And he'd just gotten that promotion. It's too awful."

"I agree. Awful."

The nurse's eyes filled with tears. "We—everybody on this floor—we saw him nearly every day. We can't believe it."

Nor could Rennie. Five days ago her colleague Lee Howell had died. Given his age, a sudden death from cardiac arrest or an accident would have been hard to accept. But Lee had been murdered in cold blood. Everyone who knew him was still reeling from the shock of his death as well as from the violent way he'd died. She almost expected him to pop out from behind a door and cry "Just kidding!"

But his murder wasn't one of the lousy practical jokes for which Lee Howell was famous. She had seen his sealed, flower-banked coffin at the church altar this morning. She had heard the emotional eulogies delivered by family members and friends. She had seen Myrna and his son weeping inconsolably in the front pew, making his death and the permanence of it jarringly real and even more difficult to accept.

"It will take time for all of us to absorb the shock," Rennie said in a tone both quiet and conclusive.

But the nurse wasn't ready to let the subject drop. "I heard the police had questioned everybody who was at Dr. Howell's party that night."

Rennie studied the patient charts that had been passed to her during the conversation and didn't address the implied question underlying the nurse's statement.

"Dr. Howell was always joking, wasn't he?" The nurse giggled as though remembering something funny. "And you and he fought like cats and dogs."

"We didn't fight," Rennie said, correcting her. "Occasionally we quarreled. There's a difference."

"I remember some of those quarrels getting pretty rowdy."

"We made good sparring partners," she said, smiling sadly.

She had performed two operations that morning before the funeral. Considering the circumstances, she could have justified rescheduling today's surgeries and closing her office this afternoon. But she was already in a time crunch due to a recent, unavoidable ten-day absence from the hospital, which had proved to be an awful inconvenience to her and her patients.

Taking another day off so soon after her return would have been unfair to those patients whose surgeries had been postponed once already. It would have placed her further behind and created yet another logjam in her scrupulously organized calendar. So she had elected to perform the operations and keep the appointments in her office. Lee would have understood.

Seeing the post-op patients was her last official duty of this long, emotionally draining, exhausting day, and she was ready to put an end to it. Closing the topic of her colleague's demise and funeral, she inquired about Mr. Tolar, whose esophageal hernia she had repaired that morning.

"Still groggy, but he's doing very well."

Taking the charts with her, Rennie entered the surgical recovery room. Mrs. Tolar was taking advantage of the five-minute visitation period that was permitted a family member once each hour. Rennie joined her at the patient's bedside. "Hello, Mrs. Tolar. I hear he's still sleepy."

"During my last visit he came awake long enough to ask me the time."

"A common question. The light in here never changes. It's disorienting."

The woman touched her husband's cheek. "He's sleeping through this visit."

"That's the best thing for him. No surprises on his chart," Rennie told her as she scanned the information. "Blood pressure is good." She closed the metal cover on the chart. "In a couple of weeks he'll feel like a new man. No more sleeping at a slant."

She noticed how dubiously the woman was gazing at her husband and added, "He's doing great, Mrs. Tolar. Everyone looks a little ragged fresh out of surgery. He'll look a thousand percent better tomorrow, although he'll be so grumpy and sore you'll wish he was anesthetized again."

"Grumpiness I can take, so long as he's not suffering anymore." Turning to Rennie, she lowered her voice to a confidential pitch. "I guess it's okay to tell you this now."

Rennie tilted her head inquisitively.

"He was skeptical when his internist referred him to you. He didn't know what to make of a lady surgeon."

Rennie laughed softly. "I hope I earned his confidence."

"Oh, you did. On the very first visit to your office you had him convinced you knew your stuff."

"I'm pleased to hear that."

"Although he said you were too pretty to be hiding behind a surgeon's mask."

"When he wakes up, I must remember to thank him."

The two women exchanged smiles, then Mrs. Tolar's expression turned somber. "I heard about Dr. Howell. Did you know him well?"

"Very well. We'd been colleagues for several years. I considered him a friend."

"I'm so sorry."

"Thank you. He'll be missed." Not wishing to have another conversation about the funeral, she returned the topic to the patient. "He's so out of it he won't really know whether or not you're here tonight, Mrs. Tolar. Try to get some rest while you can. Save your energy for when you take him home."

"One more visit, then I'll be leaving."

"I'll see you tomorrow."

Rennie moved to her next patient. No one was standing vigil at her bedside. The elderly woman was a charity case. She resided in a state-funded nursing facility. According to her patient history she had no family beyond one brother who lived in Alaska. The septuagenarian was doing well, but even after reviewing her vitals Rennie stayed with her.

She believed that charity went beyond waiving her fee.

In fact, waiving her fee was the least of it. She held the woman's hand and stroked her forehead, hoping that on a subconscious level her elderly patient was comforted by her presence, her touch. Eventually, convinced that the small amount of time she'd given the woman would make a difference, she left her to the nurses' care.

"I'm not on call tonight," she told the nurse at the desk as she returned the charts. "But page me if either of these patients takes a downward turn."

"Certainly, Dr. Newton. Have you had dinner?"

"Why?"

"Pardon me for saying so, but you look done in."

She smiled wanly. "It's been a long day. And a very sad one."

"I recommend a cheeseburger, double fries, a glass of wine, and a bubble bath."

"If I can keep my eyes open that long."

She said her good night and made her way toward the elevator. As she waited for it, she ground both fists into the small of her back and stretched. Being away, and for a reason not of her own making, had cost her more than time and inconvenience. Her pacing was still off. She wasn't yet back into the rhythm of the hospital. It wasn't always a regular rhythm, but at least it was a familiar one.

And just as she was beginning to get back into the swing of things, Lee Howell had been murdered on the parking lot she traversed each time she came to the hospital.

While she was still stunned from that blow, more unpleasantness had followed. Along with everyone who'd been at the Howell's house that night, she had been questioned by the police. It had been a routine interrogation, textbook in nature. Nevertheless, it had left her shaken.

Today she had seen Lee Howell buried. She would never quarrel with him again over something as important as OR scheduling or something as petty as whole milk versus skim. She would never laugh at one of his stupid jokes.

Taking all that had happened into account, it was an understatement to say that the past three weeks had amounted to a major upheaval in her routine.

This was no small thing. Dr. Rennie Newton adhered to rhythms and routine with fanatical self-discipline.

* * *

Her house was a ten-minute drive from the hospital. Most young professionals lived in newer, more fashionable neighborhoods of Fort Worth. Rennie could have afforded to live anywhere, but she preferred this older, well-established neighborhood.

Not only was its location convenient to the hospital, but she liked the narrow, tree-lined brick streets, which had been laid decades ago and remained a quaint feature of the neighborhood. The mature landscaping didn't look as though it had been installed yesterday. Most of the houses had been built prior to World War II, giving them an aura of permanence and solidity that she favored. Her house had been quaintly described as a bungalow. Having only five rooms, it was perfect for a single, which she was, and which she would remain.

The house had been renovated twice, and she had put it through a third remodeling and modernization before she moved in. The stucco exterior was dove gray with white trim. The front door was cranberry red with a shiny brass knocker and kick plate. In the flower beds, white and red impatiens bloomed beneath shrubbery with dark, waxy foliage. Sprawling trees shaded the lawn against even the harshest sun. She paid dearly for a professional service to keep the yard meticulously groomed and maintained.

She turned into the driveway and used her automatic garage-door opener, one of her innovations. She closed the garage door behind her and let herself in through the connecting kitchen door. It wasn't quite dusk yet, so the small room was bathed in the golden light of a setting sun that filtered through the large sycamore trees in her backyard.

She had forgone the suggested cheeseburger and fries, but since she wasn't on call tonight she poured herself a glass of Chardonnay and carried it with her into the living room—where she almost dropped it.

A crystal vase of red roses stood on her living-room coffee table.

Five dozen perfect buds on the brink of blossoming open. They looked velvety to the touch. Fragrant. Expensive. The cut crystal vase was also extraordinarily beautiful. Its myriad facets sparkled as only pricey crystal can and splashed miniature rainbows onto the walls.

When Rennie had recovered from her initial shock, she set her wineglass on the coffee table and searched among the roses and greenery for an enclosure card. She didn't find one.

"What the hell?"

It wasn't her birthday, and even if it were, no one would know it. She didn't celebrate an anniversary of any kind with anyone. Were the roses meant to convey condolence? She had worked with Lee Howell every day for years, but receiving flowers on the day of his funeral was hardly warranted or even appropriate given their professional relationship.

A grateful patient? Possibly, but unlikely. Who among them would know her home address? Her office address was the one listed in the telephone directory. If a patient had been so moved by gratitude, the roses would have gone either there or to the hospital.

Only a handful of friends knew where she lived. She never entertained at home. She returned social obligations by hosting dinner or Sunday brunch in a restaurant. She had many colleagues and acquaintances, but no friendships close enough to merit an extravagant bouquet of roses. No family. No boyfriend. No ex- or wanna-be boyfriends.

*Who* would be sending her flowers? An even more unsettling question was how the bouquet had come to be inside her house.

Before calling her next-door neighbor, she took a fortifying sip of wine.

The chatty widower had tried to become a chummy confidant soon after Rennie moved in, but as tactfully as possible she had discouraged his unannounced drop-overs until he finally got the message. They remained friendly, however, and the older gentleman was always pleased when Rennie took a moment to visit with him across their shared azalea hedge.

Probably because he was lonely and bored, he kept his finger on the pulse of the neighborhood and made everyone's business his own. If you wanted to know anything about anyone, Mr. Williams was your man.

"Hi, it's Rennie."

"Hey, Rennie, good to hear from you. How was the funeral?"

A few days ago he had waylaid her when she went out to get her newspaper. He had plied her with questions regarding the murder and seemed disappointed when she didn't impart the gory details. "It was a very moving service." In the hope of preventing more questions, she barely took a breath between sentences. "Mr. Williams, the reason I called—"

"Are the police any closer to catching the killer?"

"I wouldn't know."

"Weren't you questioned?"

"Everyone who was at Dr. Howell's house that night was asked for possible leads. To the best of my knowledge nobody had anything to offer." Instead of relaxing her, the wine was giving her a headache. "Mr. Williams, did I receive a delivery today?"

"Not that I know of. Were you expecting one?"

He was the only neighbor who had a key to her house. She had been reluctant to give him one, and it wasn't because of mistrust. The notion of someone coming into her home when she wasn't there was repugnant. As with rhythms and routine, she was a stickler for privacy.

But she had felt that someone should have a spare key in case of an emergency or to let in repairmen when necessary. Mr. Williams had been the logical choice because of his proximity. To Rennie's knowledge he had never abused the privilege.

"I was on the lookout for a package," she lied. "I thought it might have been delivered to you since I wasn't at home."

"Was there a notice on your door? A yellow sticker?"

"No, but I thought the driver might have forgotten to leave one. You didn't see a delivery truck parked at my curb today?"

"No, nothing."

"Hmm, well, these things never arrive when you're looking for them, do they?" she said breezily. "Thanks anyway, Mr. Williams. Sorry to have bothered you."

"Did you hear about the Bradys' new litter of puppies?"

Damn! She hadn't hung up fast enough. "Can't say that I have. As you know I've been out of pocket for a couple of weeks and—"

"Beagles. Six of them. Cutest little things you ever saw. They're giving them away. You should speak for one."

"I don't have time for pets."

"You should make the time, Rennie," he advised with the remonstrative tone of a parent.

"My horses—"

"Not the same. They don't live with you. You need a pet at home. One can make all the difference in a person's outlook. People with pets live longer, did you know that? I couldn't do without Oscar," he said of his poodle. "A dog or cat is best, but even a goldfish or a parakeet can ward off loneliness."

"I'm not lonely, Mr. Williams. Just very busy. Nice talking to you. Bye."

She hung up immediately, and not just to curtail a lecture on the benefits of pet ownership. She was alarmed. She wasn't imagining the roses, and they hadn't simply materialized on her coffee table. Someone had been here and left them.

She quickly checked the front door. It was locked, just as it had been that morning when she'd left for the hospital. She dashed down the hallway into her bedroom and checked under the bed and in the closet. All the windows were firmly shut and locked. The window above her bathtub was too small for even a child to crawl through. Next she checked the second bedroom, which she used as a study. Same there: nothing. She knew that nothing in the kitchen had been disturbed.

Actually, she would have been relieved to find a broken window or a jimmied lock. At least that element of this mystery would have been solved. Returning to the living room, she sat down on the sofa. She had lost all appetite for the wine, but she took another drink of it anyway in the hope it would steady her nerves. It didn't. When the telephone rang on the end table, she jumped.

She, Rennie Newton, who at fourteen had climbed the narrow ladder to the very top of her hometown water tower, who had put herself in peril by visiting practically every danger spot on the globe, who loved a challenge and never backed down from a dare, who wasn't afraid of the Devil, as her mother used to tell her, and who daily performed surgeries that required nerves of steel and rock-steady hands, nearly came out of her skin when her telephone rang.

Shaking spilled wine off her hand, she reached for the cordless phone. Most of her calls were work related, so she answered in her normally brisk and efficient manner.

"This is Dr. Newton."

"It's Detective Wesley, Dr. Newton. I spoke with you the other day."

The reminder was unnecessary. She remembered him as a physically fit and imposing black man. Receding hairline. Stern visage. All business. "Yes?"

"I got your number from the hospital. I hope you don't mind me calling you at home."

She did. Very much. "What can I do for you, Detective?"

"I'd like to meet with you tomorrow. Say ten o'clock?"

"Meet with me?"

"To talk about Dr. Howell's murder."

"I don't know anything about his murder. I told you that...was it the day before yesterday?"

"You didn't tell me that you and he were vying for the same position at the hospital. You left that out."

Her heart bumped against her ribs. "It wasn't relevant."

"Ten o'clock, Dr. Newton. Homicide's on the third floor. Ask anybody. You'll find me."

"I'm sorry, but I've scheduled the operating room for three surgeries tomorrow morning. To reschedule would inconvenience other surgeons and hospital personnel, to say nothing of my patients and their families."

"Then when would be a convenient time?" He asked this

in a tone that suggested he wasn't really interested in going out of his way to accommodate her.

"Two or three o'clock tomorrow afternoon."

"Two o'clock. See you then."

He disconnected before Rennie could. She returned the telephone to the end table. She closed her eyes and took deep breaths through her nose, exhaling through her mouth.

Lee Howell's appointment to chief of surgery had been a major blow. Since the retirement of the predecessor, she and Lee had been the leading contenders for the position. After months of extensive interviews and performance assessments, the hospital board of directors had finally announced their decision last week—while she had been conveniently away, a move she had thought ultra-cowardly.

However, when word of Lee's appointment reached her, she was glad she was away. The hospital grapevine would be circulating the news with the speed of fiber optics. By the time she had returned to work, the buzz had died down and she wasn't subjected to well-meaning but unwelcome commiserations.

But she hadn't escaped them entirely. A comprehensive write-up about his appointment had appeared in the *Star-Telegram.* The article had extolled Dr. Lee Howell's surgical skills, his dedication to healing, his distinguished record, and his contributions to the hospital and the community at large. As a consequence of the glowing article, Rennie had been on the receiving end of many sympathetic glances, which she had deplored and tried to ignore.

Basically, being chief of any department involved reams of additional paperwork, constant crises with personnel, and haggles with hospital board members for a larger share of the budget. Nevertheless, it was a coveted title and she had coveted it.

Then three days after the newspaper profile, Lee had

made headlines again by being slain in the hospital parking lot. Looking at it from Detective Wesley's standpoint, the timing would be uncanny and worthy of further investigation. His job was to explore every avenue. Naturally, one of the first people he would suspect would be Lee's competitor. The meeting tomorrow amounted to nothing more than a vigilant follow-up by a thorough detective.

She wouldn't worry about it. She simply wouldn't. She had nothing to contribute to Wesley's investigation. She would answer his questions truthfully and to the best of her knowledge and that would be the end of it. There was no cause to worry.

The roses, on the other hand, were worrisome.

She stared at them as though intimidation might cause them to surrender the sender's identity. She stared at them so long that her vision doubled, then quadrupled, before she suddenly pulled it back into sharp focus—on the white envelope.

Tucked deeply into the foliage, it had escaped detection until now. Being careful of thorns, she reached into the arrangement and removed the card from the envelope, which had been attached to a stem by a slender satin ribbon.

The hand with which she had established a reputation as an exceptionally talented surgeon trembled slightly as she brought the card closer. On it was a single typewritten line:

*I've got a crush on you.*

# Chapter 3

Uncle Wick!"

"Uncle Wick!"

The two girls rushed him like linemen intent on sacking the quarterback. Officially adolescents, they still had the exuberance of children when it came to showing affection, especially for their adored Uncle Wick.

"It's been ages and ages, Uncle Wick. I've missed you."

"I've missed y'all, too. Look at you. Will you please stop growing? You're going to get as tall as me."

"Nobody's as tall as you, Uncle Wick."

"Michael Jordan."

"Nobody who doesn't play basketball, I mean."

The younger, Laura, announced, "Mom finally let me get my ears pierced," and she proudly showed them off.

"No nose rings, I hope."

"Dad would have a cow."

"I'd have two."

"Do you think braces are ugly on girls, Uncle Wick? 'Cause I may have to get them."

"Are you kidding? Braces are a major turn-on."

"Seriously?"

"Seriously."

"Your hair's blonder, Uncle Wick."

"I've been on the beach a lot. The sun bleaches it out. And if I don't start using sunscreen I'm going to get as dark as you."

They thought that was hilarious.

"I made cheerleader."

"So I heard." He high-fived Stephanie. "Save a seat for me at one of the games this fall."

"Our outfits are kinda dorky."

"They are," her younger sister solemnly agreed. "Totally dorky."

"But Mom says guess again about making them shorter."

"That's right, I did." Grace Wesley joined them at the front door. Moving her daughters aside, she hugged Wick tightly.

When he released her, he whined, "Grace, why won't you run away with me?"

"Because I'm a one-woman-man kind of woman."

"I'll change. For you I'd change. Cross my heart I would."

"Sorry, still can't."

"Why not?"

"Because Oren would hunt you down and shoot you dead."

"Oh, yeah," he grumbled. *"Him."*

The girls shrieked with laughter. Over their protests, Grace shooed them upstairs, where chores awaited them, and ushered Wick into the living room. "How's Galveston?"

"Hot. Sticky. Sandy."

"Are you liking it?"

"I'm loving being a beach bum. Where's your old man?"

"On the phone, but he shouldn't be much longer. Have you eaten?"

"Stopped at Angelo's and scarfed a plate of brisket. Didn't realize how much I'd missed that barbecue till I took my first bite."

"There's chocolate pudding in the fridge."

"I'd settle for a glass of your iced tea."

"Sweetened?"

"Is there any other kind?"

"Coming up. Make yourself comfortable." Before leaving the room, she turned back and said meaningfully, "Sure is good to have you back."

"Thanks."

He didn't correct her. He wasn't *back* yet and didn't know if he was coming back. He had only consented to think about it. Oren had an interesting case cooking. He had asked for Wick's professional opinion. He was here to help out his friend. That was all.

He'd yet to darken the door of PD headquarters, and he didn't intend to. He hadn't even driven past it or felt a nostalgic yearning to do so. He was here as a favor to Oren. Period.

"Hey, Wick." Oren bustled in. He was dressed for home in knee-length shorts, sneakers, and a University of Texas T-shirt, but he was still all cop; a case binder was tucked beneath his arm. His pager was clipped to his waistband. "How was your drive up from Galveston?"

"Long."

"Don't I know it." Oren had made the round trip the day before. "Get checked into the motel all right?"

"Is that rathole the best the FWPD can afford?"

"Oh, and you left such luxurious accommodations in Galveston."

Wick laughed good-naturedly.

"Grace take care of you?"

"In the process." She came in with two tall glasses of tea and set them on coasters on the coffee table. "The girls said for Wick not to dare leave without saying good-bye."

"I promise I won't. I'll even tell them a bedtime story."

"A clean one, I hope," Grace said.

He shot her his most wicked grin. "I can edit as I go."

"Thanks for the tea," Oren said. "Close the door behind you, please."

This was a familiar scene. Before moving to the coast, Wick had often spent evenings at the Wesleys' house. It was a happy house because Grace and Oren's happiness with each other permeated the place.

They'd met in college and married upon graduation. Grace was a student counselor and vice-principal at a public junior high school. With each year her responsibilities increased and became more complicated, but she never failed to have a hot evening meal for her family and mandated that everyone be there for it.

Their home was noisy and active with the girls and their friends trooping up and down the stairs, in and out of the kitchen. Neighbors stopped by with or without an invitation, knowing they'd be welcome. The house was as clean as a U.S. Navy vessel but cluttered with the trappings of a busy family. When Grace was at home, chances were very good that the washing machine would be chugging. Reminder notes and snapshots were stuck to the refrigerator with magnets. There were always cookies in the cookie jar.

Wick had been a guest so often he was considered one of the family and pitched in when it came time to do the dishes or take out the garbage. He teased Grace about doing her best to domesticate him. The joke wasn't far off the mark.

Following dinner and cleanup, it had been his and Oren's

habit to seclude themselves in the living room to discuss troublesome cases. Tonight was no exception.

"I've got a video I want you to see." Oren inserted a tape into the VCR, then carried the remote control back to the sofa and sat at the opposite end from Wick. "Recorded this afternoon."

"Of?"

"Dr. Rennie Newton."

The video picture came on the screen. It was a wide shot of an interrogation room. Wick had watched a hundred such video recordings. The camera, he knew, had been mounted on a tripod situated behind Oren. It was aimed at the chair occupied by the individual being questioned. In this case it was the woman in the photos Oren had shown him yesterday.

Wick was surprised. "She's a doctor?"

"Surgeon."

"No shit?"

"I called her after leaving your place. She came in for questioning today."

"In connection with the Howell homicide?" Once he had agreed to come to Fort Worth, Oren had given him the basic facts of the case, scarce though they were.

"She agreed to being videotaped, but she also brought along her attorney."

"She's no fool."

"No. In fact she was . . . well, you'll see."

Dr. Newton's lawyer was standard issue. Height, average. Weight, average. Hair, white. Suit, gray pinstripe. Eyes, wary and cunning. It took only one glance for Wick to assess him.

He then directed his attention to Dr. Rennie Newton, who didn't come even close to standard issue. In fact if someone had ordered him to conjure a mental picture of a surgeon, the woman on the tape would not have been it. Not in a million years.

Nor was she typical of someone being questioned about a felony offense. She wasn't sweating, nervously jiggling her legs, drumming her fingers, biting her nails, or fidgeting in her seat. Instead she sat perfectly still, her legs decorously crossed, arms folded at her waist, eyes straight ahead and steady, a portrait of composure.

She was dressed in a cream-colored two-piece suit with slacks, high heels in a tan reptile skin, matching handbag. She wore no jewelry except for a pair of stud earrings and a large, no-nonsense wristwatch. No rings on either hand. Her long hair was pulled into a neat ponytail. He knew from the surveillance photos that when it was down, it reached the middle of her back. Pale blond, which looked as genuine as the diamonds in her earlobes.

Oren stopped the tape. "What do you think so far? As a connoisseur of the fairer sex, your first impression."

Wick shrugged and took a sip of tea. "Dresses well. Good skin. You couldn't melt an ice cube on her ass."

"Cool."

"We're talking frostbite. But she's a surgeon. She's supposed to be cool under pressure, isn't she?"

"I guess."

Oren restarted the tape and they heard his voice identifying everyone present, including Detective Plum, the second plainclothesman in the room. He provided the date and the case number, and then, for the benefit of the tape, asked Dr. Newton if she had agreed to the interview.

"Yes."

Oren plunged right in. "I'd like to ask you a few questions about the murder of your colleague Dr. Lee Howell."

"I've already told you everything I know, Detective Wesley."

"Well, it never hurts to go over it again, does it?"

"I suppose not. If you've got a lot of spare time on your hands."

Oren stopped the tape. "See? There. That's what I'm talking about. Polite, but with a definite attitude."

"I'd say so, yeah. But that's in character too. She's a doctor. A surgeon. The god complex and all that. She speaks and folks sit up and take notice. She isn't accustomed to being questioned or second-guessed."

"She had better get accustomed to it," Oren mumbled. "I think there's something going on with this lady."

He rewound the tape to listen again to her saying, "If you've got a lot of spare time on your hands."

On the tape, Oren gave Plum a significant glance. Plum raised his eyebrows. Oren continued. "On the night Dr. Howell was murdered, you were at his house, correct?"

"Along with two dozen other people," the attorney chimed in. "Have you questioned them to this extent?"

Ignoring him, Oren asked, "Did you know everyone at the party that night, Dr. Newton?"

"Yes. I've known Lee's wife for almost as long as I've known him. The guests were other doctors with whom I'm acquainted. I'd met their spouses at previous social gatherings."

"You attended the party alone?"

"That's right."

"You were the only single there."

The lawyer leaned forward. "Is that relevant, Detective?"

"Maybe."

"I don't see how. Dr. Newton went to the party alone. Can we move on? She has a busy schedule."

"I'm sure." With a noticeable lack of haste, Oren shuffled through his notes and took his time before asking the next question. "I understand it was a cookout."

"On the Howells' terrace."

"And Dr. Howell manned the grill."

"Do you want the menu, too?" the attorney asked sarcastically.

Oren continued looking hard at Rennie Newton. She said, "Lee fancied himself a gourmet on the charcoal grill. Actually he was a dreadful cook, but nobody had the heart to tell him." She looked down into her lap, smiling sadly. "It was a standing joke among his friends."

"What was the reason for the party?"

"Reason?"

"Was it an ordinary Friday night cookout or a special occasion?"

She shifted slightly in her chair, recrossed her legs. "We were celebrating Lee's promotion to chief of surgery."

"Right, his promotion to head of the department. What did you think of that?"

"I was pleased for him, of course."

Oren tapped a pencil on the tabletop for a full fifteen seconds. Her gaze remained locked with his, never wavering.

"You were also under consideration for that position, weren't you, Dr. Newton?"

"Yes. And I deserved to get it."

Her attorney held up a cautionary hand.

"More than Dr. Howell did?" Oren asked.

"In my opinion, yes," she replied calmly.

"Dr. Newton, I—"

She forestalled her lawyer. "I'm only telling the truth. Besides, Detective Wesley has already guessed how I felt about losing the position to Lee. I'm sure he regards that as a motive for murder." Turning back to Oren, she said, "But I didn't kill him."

"Detectives, may I have a private word with my client?" the lawyer asked stiffly.

Unmindful of the request, Oren said, "I don't believe you killed anyone, Dr. Newton."

"Then what am I doing here, wasting my time and yours? Why did you request this"—she gave the walls of the small room a scornful glance—"this interview?"

Oren stopped the tape there and consulted Wick. "Well?"

"What?"

"She denied it before I accused her of it."

"Come on, Oren. She's got more years of schooling than you, me, and Plum there added up. But she didn't need a medical degree to guess what you were getting at. Driving a herd of longhorns through that room would have been more subtle. She got your point. Any dummy would have. And this lady doesn't strike me as a dummy."

"She and Dr. Howell had a history of quarreling."

"So do we," Wick said, laughing.

Oren stubbornly shook his head. "Not like they did. Everybody I've talked to at the hospital says she and Howell respected each other professionally but did not get along."

"Love affair turned sour?"

"Initially I posed that question to everyone I interviewed. I stopped asking."

"How come?"

"I got tired of being laughed at."

Wick turned and quizzically arched his eyebrow.

"Beats me," Oren replied to the silent question. "That's the reaction I got every time I asked. Apparently there were never any romantic fires smoldering between them."

"Just a friendly rivalry."

"I'm not so sure it was all that friendly. On the surface, maybe, but there might have been a lurking animosity that ran deep. They were always at each other's throats for one reason or another. Sometimes over something trivial, sometimes major. Sometimes in jest, and sometimes not. But their disagreements were always lively, often vitriolic, and well known to hospital staff."

As he mentally sorted through this information, Wick absently popped the rubber band against his wrist.

Oren noticed and said, "You were wearing that yesterday. What's it for?"

"What?" Wick looked down at the rubber band circling his wrist as though he'd never seen it before. "Oh, it's...nothing. Uh, getting back, was Howell's appointment gender based?"

"I don't think so. Two other department heads at Tarrant General are women. Howell got the promotion Newton felt she deserved and probably thought she had sewn up because of her seniority status. She'd been affiliated with the hospital for two years before Howell joined ranks."

"She would resent the hell out of that."

"Only natural that she would."

"But enough to bump him off?" Staring at the static picture on the TV screen, Wick frowned with a mix of skepticism and concentration. He motioned with his chin for Oren to restart the tape.

On it, Oren asked, "Did you go straight home following the party, Dr. Newton?"

She gave a clipped affirmative.

"Can anyone corroborate that?"

"No."

"You didn't go out again that evening?"

"No. And no one can corroborate that either," she added when she saw that he was about to ask. "But it's the truth. I went home and went to bed."

"When did you hear that Dr. Howell had been killed?"

That question caused her to lower her head and speak softly. "The following morning. On television news. No one had notified me. I was stunned, couldn't believe it." She laced her fingers together tightly. "It was horrible to hear about it that way, without any warning that I was about to receive terrible news."

Wick reached for the remote and paused the video. "It appears to me she was really upset about it."

"Yeah, well..." Oren gave a noncommittal harrumph.

"Have you asked the widow about their relationship?"

"She said what everyone does: mutual respect, but they had their differences. She said Howell actually got a kick out of pestering Dr. Newton. He was a jokester. She's all business. She was a good foil."

"Well there you go."

"Maybe Dr. Newton thought his getting that position was one joke on her too many."

Wick stood up and began to pace. "Recap the facts for me."

"On the homicide? According to Mrs. Howell, the party broke up about midnight. They were in bed by one. The house phone rang at 2:07. She's definite on the time because she remembers looking at the clock.

"Dr. Howell answered the phone, talked for several seconds, then hung up and told her he was needed at the hospital, said there'd been a major freeway accident with multiple casualties.

"He dressed and left. His body was found beside his car in the doctors' parking lot at 2:28. That's when the 911 came in. Which was just long enough for him to make the drive from home. The security guard had seen Howell drive in minutes earlier, so he was popped the moment he got out of his car. His wallet was intact. Nothing taken from or off his car.

"Cause of death was massive hemorrhaging from a stab wound beneath his left arm. The murder weapon was left in the wound. Your average filleting knife. The manufacturer says they haven't produced wood hilts in twelve years, so this knife could've come from anywhere. Grandma's kitchen, flea market, you name it. No prints, of course.

"The blade went through Howell's ribs clean as a whistle and burst his heart like a balloon. Best guess is that he was attacked from behind, probably around the neck. Reflexively he reached up, the assailant stabbed him with his left hand. It happened like that," he said, snapping his fingers. "Whoever did him knew what he was doing."

"Like another doctor?"

Oren shrugged.

"Yesterday you mentioned a potential eyewitness."

"The parking-lot security guard. One..." Oren opened the binder and scanned a typed form until he located the name. "Malcomb R. Lutey. Age twenty-seven."

"Did you check him out?"

"Considered and eliminated as a suspect. He called in the 911. Scared shitless, and he wasn't faking it. Threw up four times while the first officers on the scene were trying to get information out of him.

"Hasn't missed a day of work since he's had the job. Works holidays. Has never caused anybody any trouble. Not even a traffic ticket on record. Yes-sirred and no-sirred everybody. Kind of a geek. Take that back. He's a full-fledged geek."

"He didn't see or hear anything?"

"Like I told you, Wick, nothing. Once this kid stopped hurling chow, he cooperated fully. Nervous as hell, but Mom was responsible for that. Scary old bat. She made me nervous too. Believe me, he's not our man."

"And the freeway accident?"

"No such accident occurred. Everyone on the hospital staff denies calling Howell. Telephone records indicate that the call originated from a cell phone."

"Let me guess. Untraceable."

"You got it."

"Male or female?"

"The caller? We don't know. Dr. Howell was the only one who spoke to him. Or her."

"What does the wife get by way of an estate?"

"Plenty. Howell was insured to the hilt, but the missus came into the marriage with money of her own and stands to inherit more when her daddy passes."

"Good marriage?"

"By all accounts. They were trying to have another kid. There's one seven-year-old boy. Ideal American family. Churchgoers, flag-wavers. No drug abuse or alcoholism. He made small wagers on his golf games and that was the extent of his gambling. Not even a hint of marital infidelity, and especially not with his colleague Rennie Newton."

Oren rattled the ice in his glass, shook a cube into his mouth, chomped on it noisily. "The doc never had a malpractice suit filed against him. No outstanding debts. No known enemies. Except Rennie Newton. And I've just got a gut feeling about her, Wick."

Wick stopped pacing and looked at Oren, inviting him to elaborate.

"Don't you think it's a bit tidy and damn convenient that her rival gets popped within days after he's appointed to a position she wanted?"

"Wild coincidence?" Wick ventured.

"I could concede that except for the phone call that put Howell in that parking lot in the middle of the night. Besides, I don't believe in coincidences that wild."

"Me neither. I was playing devil's advocate." He sank back into the cushions of the sofa and placed his hands behind his head. He stared into the TV at the surgeon's calm face, which was freeze-framed on the screen. "Stabbing?

True, she'd know right where to stick you to make it fatal, but I dunno." He frowned. "Just doesn't seem like something this lady would do."

"I don't think she did it herself. Somebody did it for her."

Wick turned and looked hard at his former partner. "Lozada is into knives."

"On occasion."

"But he once used a flare gun."

Oren made a face. "Jesus, was that a mess."

Body parts of that victim had been discovered floating over several acres of Eagle Mountain Lake. Lozada had also used a tire tool once to bash in a skull. That hadn't been a contract kill, as were most of his murders. That poor bastard had just pissed him off. Of course they could never prove that he had committed any of these crimes. They just knew it.

Wick came off the sofa again and moved to the fireplace. He looked at the pictures of Stephanie and Laura on the mantel. Then he went to the window and peered through the blinds. He ambled back to the mantel before returning to the sofa. "You think this Dr. Newton hired Lozada to eliminate her competition? Or had Lozada kill him out of spite? Is that basically it?"

"It's his kind of kill. Silent. Quick. Leaving the weapon."

"I'm not disputing that, Oren. It's her involvement I have a problem with." He gestured toward the TV. "She's a surgeon with a good reputation and no doubt a six-figure income. She seeks out a scumbag—that we all know Lozada to be no matter how fancy he dresses himself up—and hires him to kill her colleague? No way. Sorry, but I ain't buying it."

"What? She's too educated? Too well dressed? Too clean?"

"No, she's too...dispassionate. I don't know," Wick said

impatiently. "Is there any evidence of a connection between her and Lozada?"

"We're looking."

"That means no."

"That means we're *looking,*" Oren stressed.

Wick expelled a deep breath. "Right. Lozada could be having meetings with the pope and we'd be the last to know. He's slippery as owl shit."

"The doctor could be just as slippery, just as deceptive. She spends the majority of her time at the hospital, but nobody—and I mean no one—seems to know much about her personal life. They say she keeps to herself, keeps her private life private.

"That's why everyone laughed at my question about hanky-panky between her and Howell. If she dates at all, nobody knows about it. She's a loner. An excellent surgeon," he stipulated. "On that everybody agrees. Generally she's very well liked. She's friendly enough. Kindhearted. But she's aloof. *Aloof.* That's a word I heard a lot."

"You need more," Wick said.

"I agree."

Reaching into the breast pocket of his shirt, Oren withdrew a slip of paper and laid it on the sofa cushion that separated him and Wick.

"What's that?"

"Her address."

Wick knew what that implied, what Oren was asking of him. He shook his head. "Sorry, Oren, but you haven't convinced me. What you've got on her is thin. Way too thin. Speculation at best, and nothing substantive. Certainly nothing concrete. There's no just cause for—"

"You heard about Lozada's most recent trial, right? Or is your head buried too deep in Galveston sand?"

"Sure I heard. Capital murder. Another acquittal," Wick said bitterly. "Same song, tenth verse. What of it?"

Oren leaned forward and spoke in a stage whisper. "The jury that acquitted him... ?"

"Yeah?"

"Guess who was forewoman."

# Chapter 4

Wick wore running shorts, a tank top, and athletic shoes. If he bumped into a nosy neighbor, he could always pretend to be a jogger who was looking for a place to take a leak. That might not go over well, but it was better than the truth: that he was doing his cop friend a favor by illegally breaking into a suspect's house for the purpose of obtaining information.

To make the guise believable, he ran several laps around the city park a few blocks away from Rennie Newton's house. By the time he vaulted the fence that separated her backyard from the rear alley, he had worked up a plausible sweat.

From several houses down came the hum of a lawn mower. Otherwise the neighborhood was quiet. They'd picked this time of day for him to break in. It was too early for most people to be returning home from work and too hot for stay-at-homers to be doing outdoor chores or activities.

He went up her back steps and unzipped the fanny pack strapped to his waist. From it he removed a pair of latex gloves and slipped them on, which he might have difficulty explaining to a nosy neighbor in the I'm-just-taking-a-leak scenario. But better a neighbor than a judge with an indisputable fingerprint match. Next he took his MasterCard from the zippered pouch. In under three seconds the back door was unlocked.

With Oren's final warning echoing through his mind—"If you get caught I never heard of you"—he slipped inside.

Rarely was Wick stunned into silence and left without a clever comeback. But last night, when Oren had told him about Rennie Newton's recent jury duty, it was several moments before he found his tongue, and all it could manage was an ineloquent, "Huh."

Oren had baited him and knew he had him hooked.

Now inside the former juror's house, he paused to listen. They hadn't expected a security system. Oren had checked city records for the required registration. No such registration was on file, and no electronic beep alerted Wick now that a system had been breached.

All that came back to him was the hollow silence of an empty house. For almost a week Dr. Newton had been under police surveillance. They knew she lived alone, and Oren had said you could set your clock by her schedule. She didn't return for the day until after making evening hospital rounds. According to him, there was rarely more than twenty minutes' variance in her ETA.

The back door had placed Wick in the kitchen, which was compact and spotlessly clean. Only two items were in the sink: a coffee cup and the coffeemaker carafe. Each held an inch of soapy water.

In the drawer nearest the stove, cooking utensils were lined up like surgical instruments on a sterile tray. Among her knives was a filleting knife. It had a hilt made of some synthetic material that matched the others in the set.

Inside the bread box was half a loaf of whole wheat, tightly resealed and clamped. Every opened cereal box in the pantry had the tab inserted into the slot. The canned vegetables weren't alphabetized, but the neatness of the rows was almost that extreme.

The contents of the refrigerator indicated that she was a conscientious eater but she wasn't a fanatic weight watcher. There were two half-gallon cartons of ice cream in the freezer. Of course, the ice cream could have been for a guest.

He checked the drawer in the small built-in desk and found a laminated list of emergency telephone numbers, a ruled notepad with no doodles or notes, and several BIC pens, all black. Nothing personal or significant.

Through a connecting door he entered the living room. It could have been a catalog layout. Cushions were plumped and evenly spaced along the back of the sofa. Magazines were in neat stacks, the edges lined up like a deck of cards. The TV's remote control was squared up with the corner of the end table.

"Jesus," Wick whispered, thinking about the condition in which he'd left his shack in Galveston. When he'd left his motel room this morning it looked like it had sustained storm damage.

Midway down the short hall was a small room she obviously used for a home study. He hoped it would prove to be a treasure trove of information and insight into this woman. It didn't. The titles of the medical books on the shelves were as dry as dust. There were a number of atlases and travel-guide books, a few novels, mostly literary, nothing racy, certainly nothing to suit his unsophisticated reading taste.

On top of the neat desk her mail had been separated into two metal baskets, one for opened, the other for unopened. He scanned the ho-hum contents of both. In the deeper drawer of the desk he discovered an expandable file of receipts—a labeled compartment for each month. He looked through them but did not find a paid invoice for a contract killer tucked into the accordion folds.

It was in her bedroom that he received his first surprise. He stood on the threshold, giving it one swift survey before assimilating it more slowly. By comparison, this room was messy. This room wasn't occupied by a surgeon. It was lived in by a person. By a woman.

He had expected to find a bed that would meet military standards, one you could bounce a quarter off of. But, oddly, the bed had been left unmade. He moved past it to the window, where he knew Oren and Thigpen could see him from the second-story window of a house two houses down and behind Rennie Newton's. He gave them the finger.

Turning back into the room, he began his search with her bureau drawers. Undies were folded and stacked, panties in one drawer, bras in the one below it. She had divided the non-frilly from the frilly.

When she opened those drawers, he wondered what determined her selection. Daytime, nighttime? Work, play? Did her mood dictate which stack she chose from, or vice versa?

He rifled through the garments, looking underneath for keepsakes, letters, photographs that would give him a hint into the personality of Rennie Newton. Was she a woman who would link up with a noted criminal, as Oren suspected?

His search of the bureau drawers yielded several scented sachets but no clues. Nor did her closet, which was as neatly arranged by category as her lingerie drawers. He found nothing in shoe boxes except shoes.

He moved to her nightstand. A fitness magazine had been left open to an article about exercises one could do throughout the day to relieve neck tension. The cap on a bottle of body lotion hadn't been securely replaced. He picked up the bottle, sniffed. He didn't know one flower from another, but it said gold leaf and hydrangea, so he supposed that was what it was. Whatever, it smelled good.

Taking the cordless phone from its stand, he listened to the dial tone. It wasn't the broken tone indicating messages on her voicemail. As long as he was here he wished he had a bug to plant, but Oren had nixed the suggestion.

"We'd need a court order, and no judge is going to give us one until we can show probable cause."

"We could learn a lot by monitoring her calls."

"It's illegal."

Wick had laughed. "So's breaking and entering. We can't ever use anything I find in there."

"Yeah, but it's different."

He failed to see the difference but Oren was adamant, and it was Oren's show. He replaced the telephone in the recharger and opened the nightstand drawer. Inside he found a box of stationery, still wrapped in clear cellophane, unused. There was also a tear sheet from a newspaper. He took it out of the drawer and unfolded it.

It was an obituary page. One of them was for Eleanor Loy Newton. Daughter Rennie was listed as her only survivor. He recognized the name of the town on the masthead. Dalton, Texas. Carefully refolding the sheet, he replaced it in the drawer.

As he did, he noticed a small white triangle barely visible beneath the box of unused stationery. He picked up the box. Under it lay a small card with only one line typed on it: *I've got a crush on you.*

It was unsigned, unaddressed, and undated, making it impossible to know if Rennie Newton had received it or if she had considered sending it before changing her mind. It looked like a gift-enclosure card. Had it accompanied a gift she'd received recently, or was it a keepsake from a high school beau, a former lover, last Saturday's one-night stand? It obviously held some significance for her or it wouldn't be in her nightstand drawer along with her mother's obituary.

Curious, but not criminal.

He replaced the card exactly as he'd found it and went next into the adjoining bathroom. He located a damp towel in the clothes hamper along with a pair of boxer shorts and a ribbed tank top. Her sleeping attire last night? Probably. A recent girlfriend had preferred comfy over sexy. Actually he had thought the comfy was pretty damn sexy.

An array of bath salts and gels was lined up on a shelf above the tub. And they weren't just for show. They'd been used often. The room smelled flowery and feminine. The tub was spanned by a wire rack, a resting place for a scented candle, a sponge, a razor, and a pair of reading glasses. She liked to lounge in the tub. But alone; it wasn't large enough for two.

Inside the mirrored medicine cabinet he found her toothbrush and a glass, a tube of toothpaste rolled up from the bottom—he didn't know anybody who actually did that—and mint-flavored dental floss. There was an assortment of cosmetics and night creams, a bottle of aspirin, and a blister-pack of antacid tablets. No prescriptions. Under the sink were rolls of toilet tissue and a box of tampons.

He stepped back into the bedroom and for a long time stood looking at the unmade bed. The pale yellow sheets were rumpled and the duvet was half on, half off. Unless he was very wrong, Rennie Newton not only bathed alone, she slept alone. At least she had last night.

* * *

"Took you long enough," Oren said when Wick rejoined them in the second-story room of the stakeout house.

"Yeah, what were you doing in there all that time, trying on her panties?"

That from Thigpen, whom everyone called Pigpen because that was what he looked like. He was crude and sloppy and, in Wick's opinion, unforgivably stupid.

"No, Pigpen, I stopped on my way back for a blowjob. Your wife says to pick up bread on your way home."

"Asshole. We got pictures of you flipping us the bird. Very professional, Threadgill."

"I stoop to the level of the people I'm with."

"I'm gonna add that photo to my gallery." Thigpen hitched his thumb toward the wall where he had taped the more revealing eight-by-tens of Rennie Newton.

Wick glanced at the pictures of which Thigpen was so proud, then angrily grabbed a bottle of water and twisted off the lid. He drank all of it before taking a breath.

"Well?" Oren asked.

Wick sat down and toed off his running shoes. "In a word?"

"For starters."

"Neat. As a pin. Obsessively clean."

He described the kitchen, living room, and study. Of the bedroom he said, "It wasn't quite as tidy. The bed was unmade but everything was in its place. Maybe she was in a rush this morning before she left for the hospital." He itemized what he'd found in the nightstand drawer.

"Was the card in an envelope?" Thigpen asked.

"I told you, no. It was a plain white card. Small. One typed line."

"She's from Dalton," Oren confirmed when Wick told them about the newspaper obituary. "Grew up there. Her father was some bigwig cattleman and businessman.

Community leader. An iron in every fire. She was an only child."

"With no living relatives, apparently. She was listed as her mother's only survivor." Which would explain why she had an unopened box of stationery, Wick thought. Who would she write to?

"Did you find anything to indicate—"

"An alliance with Lozada?" Wick asked, finishing Oren's question for him. "*Nada.* I don't think she has a relationship of any kind with anybody. Not one single photograph in the place, no personal telephone numbers scribbled down. Our lady doctor appears to live a very solitary life."

When he paused, Oren motioned for him to expand. "Definitely no sign of a masculine presence, criminal or otherwise. No men's clothing in her closet or drawers. The only razor in the bathroom was pink. One toothbrush. No birth-control pills or condoms or diaphragm. She's a nun."

"Maybe she's a dyke."

"Maybe you're a cretin," Wick fired back at Thigpen.

Oren looked at him strangely, then turned to the other detective. "Why don't you knock off early today?"

"Don't have to ask me twice." Thigpen stood and hiked up his slipping khakis, which rode well below his belly. Giving Wick a sour look, he grumbled, "What's your problem, anyway?"

"Don't forget the bread."

"Fuck you."

"Thigpen!" Oren looked at him reprovingly. "Report back at seven tomorrow morning."

Thigpen shot Wick another annoyed look, then lumbered down the stairs. Neither Wick nor Oren said anything until they heard the front door of the empty house close, then Oren said, "What *is* your problem?"

"I need a shower."

His answer didn't address the question, but Oren let it go for the time being. "You know where it is."

As bathrooms went, it was sadly lacking. The towels they'd brought in were hardly worth the bother. They were cheap and small and didn't absorb. Wick had contributed soap he'd pilfered from his motel room. There was no hot water. But his bathroom in the Galveston house was no great shakes either. He was accustomed to an unreliable hot-water heater. He barely noticed the absence of amenities.

The vacant house was a perfect location for the department's surveillance of Rennie Newton since it afforded a clear view of both her backyard and the side driveway of her home. The house had been in the process of being remodeled when a dispute arose between the contractor and the non-resident owner. The squabble had turned nasty and was now in litigation.

FWPD had asked both parties if the house could be used, and both had agreed to it, for a small stipend. Its being a construction site made it easy for them to come and go dressed more or less as tradesmen and craftsmen, and to carry in supplies and equipment without attracting unwanted attention from neighbors who were used to having houses in their neighborhood undergoing renovation.

Wick emerged from the bathroom and rummaged in the duffel bag he'd brought along so he would have a change of clothes. He dressed in a pair of jeans and a souvenir T-shirt from an Eagles concert he had attended in Austin years before. He raked back his wet hair with his fingers.

Oren had taken up Thigpen's post at the window. He gave Wick a critical glance over his shoulder. "Strange uniform for a cop."

"I'm not a cop."

Oren merely grunted.

"I guess beer is against house rules."

"Thigpen would rat us out. There're Cokes in the ice chest."

Wick got one, popped the top, and took a long swallow. "Want one?"

"No thanks."

He kicked his running shoes in the general direction of the duffel bag and dropped into a chair. He took another long pull on the soda can. Oren was regarding him closely, watching every move. Finally Wick said, "*What?*"

"What did you find inside her house?"

"I told you."

"Everything?"

Wick spread his arms and raised his shoulders in an innocent shrug. "Why would I hold out on you?"

"Because of your dick."

"Excuse me?"

"For a white woman the doc's pretty good-looking."

Wick laughed, then said, "Okay. So?"

Oren gave him a look that spoke volumes.

"Do you really think...ach." He swatted down Oren's surmise, shook his head, looked away. When he came back to meet Oren's unflinching gaze he said, "Look, if she's in cahoots with Lozada, it doesn't matter to me if she's Helen of fucking Troy. In heat. I want that bastard, Oren. You know I do. I'll use whoever I have to, do whatever it takes to get him."

Far from being reassured, Oren said softly, "Which is the second reason you might withhold information from me."

"I don't follow."

"Don't turn this into a personal vendetta, Wick."

"Who came knocking on whose door?"

Oren raised his voice to match Wick's. "I brought you in because I need a good man. Someone with your instincts.

And because I thought you deserved to be in on this after what happened between you and Lozada."

"Is there a point floating around in there somewhere?"

Oren wasn't put off by his surliness. "Don't make me sorry I involved you." He subjected Wick to a stare as stern as his warning. Wick was the first to look away.

Oren always played by the rules. Wick found rules restrictive, and he seldom abided by them. It was that difference that usually caused them to clash. It was also what each admired most about the other. While Oren often chided Wick for his recklessness and casual approach to regulations, he admired his audacity. Wick rebelled against rules, but he respected Oren for upholding them.

Oren went back to watching Rennie Newton's house. After a short silence, Wick said, "One thing I thought was curious. In her closet. Lots of blue jeans. Not designer shit. Worn ones like mine." He rubbed his hand over the denim that time and a thousand washings had bleached and softened. "Three pair of western boots, too. I didn't expect that."

"She rides."

"Horses?"

"It was in her bio. The *Star-Telegram* had an extensive file on her. I asked them for a copy of everything. Dr. Newton's been in the newspaper numerous times. Charity events. Community involvement. Doctors Without Borders."

"What's that?"

A manila folder was lying on the table. Oren picked it up and dropped it into Wick's lap. "Do your own research. Grace is holding dinner for me."

He got up, stretched, reached for a roll of architectural drawings he was using as props, and headed for the staircase. "We didn't finish the video last night. It's there if you want to watch it, but don't let it distract you from keeping an eye on the house."

"I'd like to see the rest of it. Might pick up something."

Oren nodded. "My pager will be with me. Call if anything out of the ordinary happens."

"Like Lozada showing up?"

"Yeah, like that. I can be here in ten minutes. See you in the morning."

"Is there any food?"

"Sandwiches in the minifridge."

The stairs creaked beneath Oren's weight. After he left, the house fell silent except for the occasional groan of old wood. The empty rooms smelled like the sawdust left over from the uncompleted renovation. Most would consider it an unpleasant place in which to spend a night, but Wick didn't mind. In fact, he had volunteered for the night shift. Oren needed to be with his family. Thigpen, too. Although Wick imagined that Mrs. Thigpen would probably prefer him to be away as much as possible.

He picked up the binoculars and checked Rennie Newton's house. She wasn't home yet. He used the opportunity to check the small refrigerator and found two wrapped sandwiches. Tuna salad. Turkey and Swiss. He selected the turkey and carried it back with him to the table near the window. He put the tape into the combo VCR and monitor, then settled back to watch the video as he ate his sandwich.

The recording started playing at the point where Oren had stopped it the night before. On the video Oren said, "Dr. Newton, did you recently serve on the jury that acquitted an accused killer, Mr. Lozada?"

Her lawyer leaned forward. "Where's the relevance, Detective?"

"I'll get to it."

"Please do. Dr. Newton has surgical patients waiting for her."

"It could become necessary for another doctor to take over her responsibilities."

"Is that a threat that I might be detained?" Rennie Newton asked.

Oren sidestepped the direct question by saying, "The sooner you answer my questions, the sooner you can go, Dr. Newton."

She sighed as though finding the proceedings extremely tedious. "Yes, I served on the jury that acquitted Mr. Lozada. You must know that or you wouldn't have brought it up."

"That's right, I do. In fact I've interviewed all eleven of your fellow jurors."

"Why?"

"Curiosity."

"About what?"

"It struck me that Dr. Howell's murder looked like a contract kill. His killer didn't rob him. We can't isolate any other motive. Fact is, his only known adversary was you."

Taken aback by that statement, she exclaimed, "Lee and I weren't adversaries. We were colleagues. Friendly colleagues."

"Who quarreled constantly."

"We had disagreements, yes. That's hardly—"

"You were a friendly colleague of his who recently let a contract killer back onto the streets."

"Mr. Lozada's crime was *alleged,*" the attorney said in typical lawyer fashion. "Which has no bearing on this matter one way or the other. Dr. Newton, I insist you say nothing more."

Wick fast-forwarded through the argument that ensued between the attorney and Oren, who evidently persuaded the lawyer that it would be in his client's best interest to answer the questions. Cooperation with an investigation went a long way with the FWPD, and so forth. Wick knew the drill. He'd used it a thousand times himself.

He restarted the tape in time to hear Oren say, "All the other jurors told me you were for Lozada's acquittal from the get-go."

"That's incorrect," she said with remarkable calmness. "I wasn't *for* acquittal. Not at all. I believe Mr. Lozada was probably guilty. But the prosecuting attorney didn't convince me beyond a reasonable doubt. Because of that, and the charge we received from the judge, I couldn't conscientiously see him convicted."

"So it was a matter of conscience that drove you to persuade the other eleven to vote for acquittal."

She took a deep breath and let it out slowly. "As forewoman, it was my duty to see that every facet of the case was explored. It was a heinous crime, yes, but I encouraged the other jurors not to let their emotions overrule their pledge to uphold the law, even though it may be imperfect. After two days of deliberation each juror voted according to his own conscience."

"I think that sufficiently answers your questions." Once again her lawyer stood up. "That is unless there's another totally unrelated subject you wish to chit-chat about, Detective Wesley."

Oren agreed that at this point he had nothing further to ask, and switched off the recorder, ending the tape.

As it rewound, Wick recalled the last conversation he and Oren had had about the case the night before.

"Lozada seemed to make a . . . a connection with her during the trial," Oren had told him.

"Connection?"

"A lot of people noticed it. I asked the bailiff if there was a juror Lozada had especially played to and he said 'You mean the forewoman?' First thing out of his mouth, and I hadn't even mentioned Dr. Newton. The bailiff said our boy stared at her throughout the trial. Enough to make it noticeable."

"Doesn't mean she stared back."

Oren gave him one of his noncommittal shrugs that paradoxically said a lot.

"I'm not surprised Lozada would single out an attractive woman and stare at her," Wick had continued. "He's a creep."

"He's a creep who looks like a movie star."

"Of *The Godfather* maybe."

"Some women get off on that dangerous type."

"Speaking from experience, Oren? I promise not to tell Grace. Details. I want details. The really juicy ones." He had annoyed his friend further by giving him a lascivious wink.

"Cut it out."

It was then that Grace had joined them. She asked what Wick was laughing about, and when he declined to tell her, she reminded him that the girls wouldn't settle for the night until they got their story. He wove them a tale about a sassy rock star and her handsome, dashing bodyguard whose physical description strongly resembled him. He and Oren had no further conversation before he left.

After removing the videotape from the player, he decided to eat the tuna sandwich too. It tasted fishy and old, but he ate all of it, knowing he'd get nothing more until morning. He was dusting crumbs off his hands when he saw a Jeep wagon swing into Rennie Newton's driveway.

He yanked up the binoculars but barely got a glimpse of her before the car rolled into her garage. Less than thirty seconds later the light in her kitchen came on. The first thing she did was slide the strap of her oversized handbag off her shoulder and lower it to the table. Then she pulled off her suit jacket and tugged her shirttail from the waistband of her slacks.

Crossing to the fridge, she took out a bottle of water, uncapped it, and took a drink. Then she twisted the cap back on and stood at the sink, her head down. Wick adjusted the focus on the binoculars. Through the window above the sink, she appeared close enough to touch. A loose strand of hair trailed alongside her cheek and fell onto her chest.

She rolled the cold water bottle back and forth across her forehead. Her expression, her body language, her posture indicated profound weariness. She *should* be tired, he thought. It had been a long day for her. He knew. He had been there when her day began.

# Chapter 5

Rennie leaned against the counter and rolled the bottle of cold water across her forehead. It had been years since deep-breathing exercises were necessary for her to regain her calm. Years, but she hadn't forgotten how terrifying it felt not to be in absolute control.

For the last three weeks her life had been in disarray. The disintegration of her carefully structured life had begun with the jury summons. The day after receiving it through the mail, she and a group, including Lee Howell, had been gathered in the doctors' lounge. When she told them about the summons, they had groaned collectively and commented on her rotten luck.

Someone suggested that she claim to have young children at home.

"But I don't."

"You're the sole caretaker of an elderly parent."

"But I'm not."

"You're a full-time student."

She hadn't even acknowledged that suggestion.

"Throw the damn thing away and ignore it," another advised her. "That's what I did. Figured it would be worth the fine, no matter how steep, if I didn't have to appear."

"What happened?"

"Nothing. They never follow up on those things, Rennie. They run hundreds of people through there each week. You think they're going to take the time and effort to track down one no-show?"

"I would be the exception. They'd throw me in jail. Use me as an example to those who try and dodge their civic responsibility." Thoughtfully, she twirled the straw in her soft drink. "Besides, that's what it is. A civic duty."

"Please." Lee groaned around a mouthful of vending-machine potato chips. "It's a civic duty for people who have nothing better to do. Use your work to get you off."

"Work is not an exemption. That's printed in bold letters on the summons. I'm afraid I'm stuck."

"Don't worry about it," he said. "They won't choose you."

"Wouldn't surprise me if they did," another male colleague had chimed in. "My brother's a trial lawyer. Says he always tries to seat at least one good-looking woman on every jury."

Rennie returned his wink with a scathing glare. "And what if the lawyers are women?"

His smile collapsed. "Didn't think of that."

"You wouldn't."

Lee dusted salt off his hands. "They won't choose you."

"Okay, Lee, why not? You're just itching to tell me why I'd be an unsuitable juror, aren't you?"

He counted off the reasons on his nimble surgeon's fingers. "You're too analytical. Too opinionated. Too outspoken. And too bossy. Neither side wants a juror who could sway the others."

That was one argument Rennie would have gladly let

Lee win. She had been the second juror picked from forty-eight candidates, and then she'd been voted forewoman. For the following ten business days, while paperwork mounted and her patient load got backlogged, her time had belonged to the State of Texas.

When it ended, her relief was short-lived. Through the media, the verdict had been criticized by the district attorney's office. Nor had it won the approval of the average citizen, Dr. Lee Howell being one.

He had voiced his opinion at that Friday night cookout. "I can't believe you let this joker off, Rennie. He's a career criminal."

"He's never been convicted," she'd argued. "Besides, he wasn't on trial for previous alleged crimes."

"No, he was on trial for executing a prominent banker, one of our fair city's leading citizens. The prosecutor was asking for the death penalty."

"I know, Lee. I was there."

"Here they go," said one of the other guests who'd gathered around to eavesdrop on what was sure to be a heated debate. "The staunch conservative and the bleeding-heart liberal are at it again."

"We jurors were informed going in that the DA was asking for the death penalty. That wasn't the reason we voted to acquit."

"Then how was it that you twelve decided to let this creep walk instead of giving him the needle? How could you believe for a second that he was innocent?"

"None of us believed that he was *innocent.* We voted him *not guilty.* There's a difference."

He shrugged his bony shoulders. "The distinction escapes me."

"The distinction is reasonable doubt."

"If it doesn't fit, you must acquit. That bullshit?"

"That bullshit is the foundation of our judicial system."

"She's on a roll now," someone in the background said.

"The so-called evidence against Mr. Lozada was entirely circumstantial," she said. "He could not be placed at the scene of the crime. And he had an alibi."

"A guy he probably paid to lie for him."

"There were no eyewitnesses. There were—"

"Tell me, Rennie, did all the jurors put this much thought into their decision?"

"What do you mean?"

"I mean that you're Miss Precision. You would've lined up all the facts in a neat little row, and God forbid that you take the human element into account."

"Of course I did."

"Yeah? Then tell me this, when you took that first vote, before you even began deliberation, how many voted guilty and how many not guilty?"

"I won't discuss what happened in that jury room with you."

He glanced around the ring of faces as though to say, "I knew it." "Let me guess, Rennie. You—"

"I deliberated the case once, Lee. I don't want to do so again."

"You were the conscientious objector of the group, weren't you? You led the charge for acquittal." He stacked his hands over his heart. "Our own Dr. Rennie Newton, crusader for the freedom of career criminals."

The argument ended there with their listeners' laughter. It was the last verbal skirmish she and Lee would ever have. As always, they'd parted friends. As she said good night to him and Myrna, he'd given her a quick hug. "You know I was only teasing, don't you? Of all the jurors who ever sat on any trial, you would work the hardest at getting it right."

Yes, she had tried to get it right. Little had she known what an impact that damn jury summons, the trial, and its outcome would have on her personally. She had counted on it being an inconvenience. She hadn't counted on it being catastrophic.

Did Detective Wesley really consider her a suspect?

Her lawyer had dismissed her concerns. He said because the police had absolutely no clues, they had thrown out a wide net and were interrogating everyone with whom Lee Howell had any interaction, from hospital orderlies to his golfing buddies. At this point everyone was suspect. Insinuation and intimidation were standard police methods, the attorney assured her. She shouldn't feel that she'd been singled out.

Rennie had tried to reassure herself that he was right and that she was overreacting. But what her lawyer didn't know was that when it came to being questioned by police, she had a right to be a little jittery.

Wesley's interrogation had been in the forefront of her mind this afternoon when the hospital board of directors invited her to join their weekly meeting and offered her the position tragically vacated by Dr. Lee Howell.

"I appreciate your consideration, but my answer is no thank you. You had months to consider me before, and you chose someone else. If I accepted now, I would always feel as though I were your second choice."

They assured her that Dr. Howell had received only one more vote than she and that none of them thought she was an inferior candidate.

"That's not the only reason I'm declining," she'd told them. "I admired Dr. Howell professionally, but I also regarded him and Myrna as friends. To benefit from his death would feel...obscene. Thank you for the offer, but my answer is no."

To her surprise, they refused to accept that answer and pressed her into thinking it over for a day or two more.

While flattered and gratified by their persistence, she was now faced with a difficult decision. She had wanted the position and knew she was qualified, but it would feel wrong to get a career boost from Lee's death.

Wesley was another factor to take into account. Were she to assume the position he considered a motive for murder, his suspicions of her involvement might be heightened. She wasn't afraid of his finding anything that would implicate her. There was nothing, absolutely nothing, connecting her to Lee's murder. But before Wesley determined that, she would be put through a rigorous police investigation. *That* was what she feared and wanted to avoid.

With all this weighing on her mind, her head actually felt heavy. Reaching back, she slid the coated rubber band from her hair and shook out her ponytail, then massaged her scalp, pressing hard with her fingertips.

She had performed four major surgeries before lunch. The waiting room outside the operating room had been filled with anxious friends and family not only of her patients, but of other patients.

Immediately following each operation, she had come out to speak briefly with the patient's loved ones, to report on the condition of the patient, and to explain the procedure she'd done. For some she was even able to show color photographs taken during the surgery. Thankfully all the patients' prognoses had been good, all the reports positive. She hadn't had to break bad news to anyone today.

Thanks to her able staff, things had gone smoothly in her office this afternoon. Rounds at the hospital had taken a little longer than usual. She had the four post-op patients to see, and three more to brief before their scheduled surgeries tomorrow morning. One had to be sweet-talked into his preop enema. The frazzled nursing staff had given up. After Rennie talked to him, he surrendered quietly.

Then, just before she left for the day, she had received the telephone call.

The reminder caused her to shudder. Quickly she finished the bottle of water and tossed it into the trash compactor. She rinsed out the soaking carafe of the coffeemaker, then prepared it for tomorrow morning and set the timer. She knew she should eat something, but the thought of food made her nauseous. She was too upset to eat.

She left her handbag on the table—she didn't think she had the strength to lift it—and turned off the kitchen light. Then, as she started toward the living room, she paused and switched the light back on. She had lived alone all her adult life, and this was the first time she could remember ever wanting to leave the lights on.

In her bedroom she switched on the lamp and sat down on the edge of her unmade bed. Ordinarily it would have bothered her that she hadn't had time to make her bed before leaving that morning. Now that seemed a trivial, even silly concern. An unmade bed was hardly worth fretting about.

With dread, she opened the drawer of her nightstand. The card was beneath the box of stationery her receptionist had given her last Christmas. She had never even broken the cellophane wrapping. Pushing the stationery box aside, she stared down at the small white card.

She had been making notations on the charts of her post-op patients when the duty nurse had informed her that she had a call. "Line three."

"Thanks." She cradled the receiver between her cheek and shoulder, leaving her hands free to continue the final task of a very long day. "Dr. Newton."

"Hello, Rennie."

Her writing pen halted mid-signature. Immediately alarmed by the whispery voice, she said, "Who is this?"

"Lozada."

She sucked in a quick breath but tried to keep it inaudible. "Lozada?"

He laughed softly, as though he knew her obtuseness were deliberate. "Come now, Rennie, we're hardly strangers. You couldn't have forgotten me so soon. We spent almost two weeks together in the same room."

No, she hadn't forgotten him. She doubted that anyone with whom this man came into contact would ever forget him. Often during the trial his dark eyes had connected with hers across the courtroom.

Once she had begun to notice it she had avoided looking at him. But each time her gaze happened to land on him, he'd been staring at her in a way that had made her uncomfortable and self-conscious. She was aware that other jurors and people in the courtroom also had noticed his unwelcome interest in her.

"This call is highly inappropriate, Mr. Lozada."

"Why? The trial's over. Sometimes, when there's an acquittal, defendants and jurors get together and have a party to celebrate."

"That kind of celebration is tasteless and insensitive. It's a slap in the face to the family of the murder victim, who still have no closure. In any event, you and I have nothing to celebrate or even to talk about. Good-bye."

"Did you like the roses?"

Her heart skipped several beats, then restarted, pounding double-time.

After dismissing every conceivable possibility, it had occurred to her that he might have been her secret admirer, but she hadn't wanted to acknowledge it even to herself. Now that it had been confirmed, she wanted to pretend that she didn't know what he was talking about.

But of course he would know better. He had placed the roses inside her house, making certain she would receive them, leaving no margin for error. She wanted to ask him how the hell he had gotten inside her home but, as Lee Howell had pointed out to her, Lozada was a career criminal. Breaking and entering would be child's play to a man with his arrest record.

He was incredibly intelligent and resourceful or he couldn't have escaped prosecution for all his misdeeds, including the most recent murder for which he'd been tried and that she fully believed he had committed. It just hadn't been proved.

He said, "Considering the color of your front door, I guessed red might be your favorite."

The roses hadn't been the color of her front door. They'd been the color of the blood in the crime-scene photos entered as evidence and shown to the jury. The victim, whom it was alleged that Lozada had been hired to kill, had been choked to death with a garrote, something very fine yet so strong that it had broken the skin of his throat enough to bleed.

"Don't bother me again, Mr. Lozada."

"Rennie, don't hang up." He said it with just enough menace to prevent her from slamming down the telephone receiver. "Please," he said in a gentler voice. "I want to thank you."

"Thank me?"

"I talked to Mrs. Grissom. Frizzy gray hair. Thick ankles."

Rennie remembered her well. Juror number five. She was married to a plumber and had four children. She seized every opportunity to bore the other eleven jurors with complaints against her lazy husband and ungrateful children. As soon as she learned that Rennie was a physician, she had run down a list of ailments she wanted to discuss with her.

"Mrs. Grissom told me what you did for me," Lozada said.

"I didn't do anything for you."

"Oh, but you did, Rennie. If not for you, I'd be on death row."

"Twelve of us arrived at the verdict. No one was singly responsible for the decision to acquit you."

"But you led the campaign for my acquittal, didn't you?"

"We looked at the case from every angle. We reviewed the points of law until we unanimously agreed on their interpretation and application."

"Perhaps, Rennie," he said with a soft chuckle. "But Mrs. Grissom said you argued my side and that your arguments were inspired and... passionate."

He said it as though he were stroking her while he spoke, and the thought of his touching her made her skin crawl. "Don't contact me again." She had slammed down the telephone receiver but continued to grip it until her knuckles turned white.

"Dr. Newton? Is something wrong? Dr. Newton, are you all right?"

Drops of perspiration beaded on her face as though she were performing the most intricate and life-threatening surgery. She thought she might throw up. Taking a deep breath through her mouth, she let go of the telephone receiver and turned to the concerned nurse.

"I'm fine. But I'm not going to take any more calls. I'm trying to wrap up here, so if someone wants me, tell them to have me paged."

"Certainly, Dr. Newton."

She had quickly completed her chart notations and left for home. As she walked across the familiar doctors' parking lot, she glanced over her shoulder several times and was reassured by the presence of the guard on duty. She'd heard that the young man who had discovered Lee's body was taking some time off.

On the drive home, she kept one eye on the road and another in the rearview mirror, half expecting to see Lozada following her. Damn him for making her feel paranoid and afraid! Damn him for complicating her life when she had finally gotten it exactly as she wanted it.

Now as she stared at the hateful little card in her nightstand drawer, her resentment increased. It made her furious that he dared speak to her in sexual overtones and with implied intimacy. But it also frightened her, and that was what she hated most—that she was afraid of him.

Angrily she closed the nightstand drawer. She stood up and removed her blouse and slacks. She wanted a hot shower. Immediately. She felt violated, as though Lozada had touched her with his sibilant voice. She couldn't bear to think about his being here inside her house, invading her private space.

Worse, she felt a presence here still, although she told herself that was just her imagination, that it had been thrust into overdrive. She found herself looking at every object in the room. Was each item exactly as she'd left it this morning? The cap on her body lotion was loose, but she remembered being in a hurry this morning and not replacing it securely. Was that the angle at which the open magazine had been left on the nightstand?

She told herself she was being silly. Nevertheless, she felt exposed, vulnerable, watched.

Suddenly she glanced toward the windows. The slats of the blinds were only partially drawn. Moving quickly, she snapped off the lamp and then went to the windows and pulled the louvers tightly closed.

"Damn him," she whispered into the darkness.

In the bathroom, she showered and prepared for bed. When she turned out the light, she considered leaving it on, but only for an instant before deciding against it. She wouldn't give in to her fear even to that extent.

She had never been a coward. On the contrary, her courage when she was a child had caused her mother to wring her hands with concern. As a teen, her bravery had escalated into deliberate recklessness. In recent years she had traveled to war- and famine-plagued corners of the world. She had defied despots and raging storms and armed marauders and contagious disease in order to provide medical treatment to people in desperate need of it, always with little or no regard for her personal safety.

Now, inside her own bedroom, lying in her own bed, she was afraid. And not just for her safety. Lozada posed more than a physical threat. Detective Wesley had mentioned his trial, had insinuated...

"Oh my God."

Gasping, Rennie sat bolt upright. She covered her mouth and heard herself whimper involuntarily. A chill ran through her.

Lozada had tried to impress her with a lavish bouquet of roses in a crystal vase. Personally delivered. What else had he done in an attempt to curry her favor?

The answer to that was too horrible to consider.

But obviously the homicide detective had considered it.

* * *

Wick opened another Coke, hoping it would wash away the unpleasant aftertaste of the tuna sandwich. Rennie had retired for the night. It had been thirty-two minutes from the time she got home until she had turned out her bedroom light. Not long. No dinner. No leisure activity. Not even a half hour of TV during which to unwind after a hard day.

She had spent some of that thirty-two minutes at the kitchen sink, appearing to be lost in thought. Wick saw her shake her hair loose and massage her scalp. She'd had the aspect of someone weighted down by a major problem, or suffering a severe headache—or both.

Which didn't surprise him. She'd worked her ass off today. He had arrived at the family waiting room at seven that morning, knowing the day began early in the OR. Nobody questioned his being there. It was assumed that he belonged to one of the families who had set up temporary camp with magazines and cups of vending-machine coffee. He chose a chair in the corner, pulled his straw cowboy hat low over his brow, and partially hid behind an edition of *USA Today.*

It was 8:47 A.M. before Dr. Newton made her first appearance.

"Mrs. Franklin?"

Mrs. Franklin and her retinue of supporters clustered around the surgeon. Rennie was dressed in green scrubs, the face mask lying open on her chest like a bib. She wore a cap. Paper slippers covered her shoes.

He couldn't hear what she was saying because she kept her voice at a confidential pitch to ensure the family's privacy, but whatever she said made Mrs. Franklin smile, clasp her hand, and press it thankfully. After the brief conference, Rennie excused herself and disappeared through the double swinging doors.

Throughout the long morning she had made three other visits to the waiting room. Each time she gave the anxious family her full attention and answered their questions with admirable patience. Her smiles were reassuring. Her eyes conveyed understanding and compassion. She never seemed to be rushed, although she must have been. She was never brusque or detached.

Wick had found it hard to believe that this was the same guarded, haughty woman on Oren's videotape.

He had stayed in the OR waiting room until his stomach started rumbling so loudly that people began looking at him askance. The crowd had thinned out too, so the tall cowboy sitting all alone in the corner with a newspaper he'd read three times was beginning to attract attention. He had left in search of lunch.

Oren thought he'd been sleeping through the day in his dreary motel room. He hadn't told him about going to the hospital. Nor did he tell him that after grabbing a burger at Kincaid's he had staked out Rennie Newton's private office. It was located near the hospital on a street that had formerly been residential but had been given over largely to medical offices.

The limestone building was new looking and contemporary in design, but not ostentatious. The office had done a brisk business all afternoon, with patients going in and coming out at roughly fifteen-minute intervals. The parking lot was still half full when Wick left to go break into her house.

Yeah, Rennie had put in a full day. To reward herself she'd drunk a bottle of water. That was it. When she moved out of the kitchen, she had switched off the light, then turned it back on almost instantly, which he thought was strange.

She had left that light on when she went into the bedroom, where she sat slumped on the edge of the bed, loose hair falling forward. Her whole aspect had spelled dejection. Or terrible trouble.

Then she'd done another strange thing. She had opened

her nightstand drawer and, for the next several minutes, stared into it. Just stared. She didn't take anything out or put anything in—she just stared into it.

What had she been looking at? he wondered. He concluded that it had to be the enclosure card. What fascination could an unopened box of stationery hold for her? Her mother's obituary might be something she would read occasionally, maybe in remembrance of her. But he was putting his money on the card. And that made him damn curious about its origin and significance.

Eventually she had closed the drawer and stood up. She'd unbuttoned her blouse and pulled it off. She was wearing an unadorned bra. Maybe the sheer lacy ones were reserved for the days when she didn't perform four surgeries. Or for the man who had sent her the card.

Next she had removed her slacks.

That was when Wick had realized he was holding his breath and admonished himself to resume breathing normally—if such a thing were possible. Could any heterosexual man breathe normally when he was watching a woman take off her clothes? He didn't think so. He didn't know of one. The question might warrant a scientific study.

Conducting his own test, he had inhaled deeply, then exhaled an even stream of carbon dioxide.

And in that instant, almost as if she had felt his breath against her bare skin, she looked toward the windows with alarm. Immediately the bedside lamp was extinguished. A vague silhouette of her appeared momentarily at the windows, then the slats of the blinds were closed tightly, blocking her from sight.

The light in her bathroom had come on and remained on for ten minutes, long enough for her to bathe using one of the scented gels. She might've used the pink razor, too. She'd probably brushed her teeth and rolled the tube of toothpaste up from the bottom before replacing it in the cabinet above the sink that had not one single water spot.

Then the house had gone dark except for the light in the kitchen. Wick surmised that she had probably gone straight from her bath to bed.

And now, after thirty-two minutes, she was probably sleeping between the pale yellow sheets, her head sunk deeply into the down pillow.

He remembered that pillow. He had stared at it for a long time before peeling off the latex gloves and lifting it from the bed. He'd held it close to his face. Only for a second, though. Only for as long as any good detective would.

He hadn't told Oren about that, either.

# Chapter 6

It was the best Mexican restaurant in Fort Worth, making it, in Lozada's opinion, the best restaurant in Fort Worth.

He came here only for the food and the deferential service he received. He could have done without the trio who strolled among the tables strumming guitars and singing Mexican standards in loud but mediocre voices. The decor looked like the effort of someone who had run amok in a border-town curio shop, buying every sombrero and piñata available.

But the food was excellent.

He sat at his customary table in the corner, his back to the wall, sipping an after-dinner tequila. He'd have shot anyone who offered him one of those frozen green concoctions that came out of a Slurpee machine and had the audacity to call itself a margarita.

The fermented juice of the agave plant deserved to be drunk straight. He favored a clear *añejo,* knowing that what made a tequila "gold" was nothing but caramel coloring.

He had dined on the El Ray platter, which consisted of enchiladas con carne, crispy beef tacos, refried beans, Spanish rice, and corn tortillas dripping with butter. The meal was loaded with carbohydrates and fat, but he didn't worry about gaining weight. He'd been genetically gifted with the lean, hard physique that people joined health clubs and sweated gallons of perspiration to acquire. He never broke a sweat. Never. And the one time in his life he had lifted a dumbbell he had brained someone with it.

He finished his drink and left forty dollars cash on the table. That was almost double the amount of his bill, but it guaranteed that his table would be available anytime he came in. He nodded good-bye to the owner and winked at a pretty waitress on his way out.

The restaurant was located in the heart of the historic Stockyards area. Tonight the intersection of Main and Exchange Streets was thronged with tourists. They bought trashy Texas souvenirs like chocolates shaped as cow patties or rattlesnakes preserved in clear acrylic. The more affluent were willing to pay handsomely for handmade boots from the legendary Leddy's.

The tantalizing aroma of mesquite-smoked meat lured them into barbecue joints. Open barroom doorways emitted blasts of cooler air, the smell of beer, and the wail of country ballads.

The streets were congested with every kind of vehicle from mud-spattered pickup trucks to family vans to sleek European imports. Bands of young women and groups of young men prowled the wooden sidewalks in search of one another. Parents had pictures of their children taken sitting atop a bored and probably humiliated longhorn steer.

Occasionally one could spot an authentic cowboy. They were distinguished by the manure caked on their boots and the telltale circle worn into the rear pocket of their Wranglers by the ever-present tin of chaw. They also regarded their counterfeits with an unconcealed and justifiable scorn.

The atmosphere was lightheaded, wholesome, and innocent.

Lozada was none of those.

He retrieved his silver Mercedes convertible from a kid he'd paid twenty dollars to car-sit and drove up Main Street, across the river, and into downtown. In less than ten minutes he left his car with the parking valet, crossed the native-granite lobby of Trinity Tower, and took the elevator up to the top floor.

He had bought the penthouse as soon as the renovated building became available for occupancy. Like most of the buildings in Sundance Square, the exterior had been left as it was to preserve the historic ambience of the area. The interior had been gutted from the foundation up, reinforced to meet current building codes—and, hopefully, to withstand tornadic winds—and reconfigured for highrise condo living.

After buying the expensive floor space, it had cost Lozada another two million dollars to replicate the apartment he had admired in *Architectural Digest.* This financial setback was earned back in only three jobs.

He let himself in and welcomed the quiet, cool serenity of the condo after the festive confusion of Cowtown. Indirect lighting cast pools of illumination on the glossy hardwood floors that were softened only occasionally with sheepskin area rugs. Every surface was sleek and polished—lacquered wood, slate, and metal. Much of the furniture was built-in, crafted from mahogany. The free-standing pieces were upholstered in either leather or animal pelts.

The main feature of his living room was a large glass tank situated atop a knee-high pedestal of polished marble. The tank was eight feet square and a yard deep. This unusual display was the only deviation from the apartment he'd seen in the magazine. It was a necessary addition. Inside the tank, he had created an ideal habitat for his lovelies.

The temperature and humidity were monitored and controlled. To prevent them from killing each other, he saw to it that they had enough prey on which to feed. Presently the tank contained five, but he had had as many as eight and as few as three.

They didn't have names; that would have been ridiculous, and nobody would ever accuse Lozada of being ridiculous. But he knew each of them individually and intimately and occasionally took them out and played with them.

The two *Centruroides* he had smuggled out of Mexico himself. He'd had them less than a year. The one that had been living with him the longest was a female of the common Arizona species. She hadn't been hard to come by, nor was she valuable, but he was fond of her. She had borne thirty-one young last year, all of which Lozada had killed as soon as they had climbed off her back, thereby declaring their independence from her. The other two in the tank were rarer and deadlier. It was hard not to be partial to them because they had been the most difficult and expensive to obtain.

They were the finest scorpions in the world.

He paused to speak to them, but he didn't amuse himself with them tonight. Ever the businessman, he checked his voicemail for messages. There were none. At the wet bar in the living room, he poured another *añejo* into a Baccarat tumbler and carried it with him to the wall of windows that provided a spectacular evening view of the river, for which the building was named, and the neighboring skyscrapers.

He raised a mock toast to the Tarrant County Justice Center. Then he turned in the opposite direction and raised his glass in a heartfelt salute to the warehouse across the railroad tracks.

These days the building housed a business that customized RVs and vans. But the corrugated-tin structure had been vacant twenty-five years ago when Lozada had committed his first murder there.

Tommy Sullivan had been his pal. He'd had nothing against the kid. They'd never spoken a cross word to one another. Fate had just put Tommy at the wrong place at the wrong time. It was during the hot summertime. They were exploring the empty warehouse for lack of something better to do. Boredom had placed them there and boredom had gotten Tommy killed.

Tommy had been walking several steps ahead of Lozada when it suddenly came to him how easy it would be to grab Tommy from behind, reach around his neck, and jab his pocketknife into his friend's jugular.

He'd done it just to see if he could. Tommy had proved he could.

He'd been smart to attack from behind because Tommy had spouted blood for what seemed like forever. It had been a challenge to keep it off him. But overall, killing Tommy had been incredibly easy. It had been just as easy to get away with it. He'd simply walked to Tommy's house and asked his mom if Tommy was at home. She told him no, but he was welcome to come inside and wait; Tommy was bound to show up sooner or later.

So Lozada had passed the time after killing Tommy playing Tommy's stereo in Tommy's room, in delicious anticipation of the hell that was about to break loose inside Tommy's house.

A knock interrupted Lozada's fond recollections. Out of habit, he approached the door cautiously, a switchblade flattened up against his wrist. He looked through the peephole and, seeing a familiar uniformed woman, released the lock and opened the door.

"Turndown service, Mr. Lozada?"

Living in the building came with perks, including the

parking valet, the concierge, and twice-daily maid service. He motioned her inside. She went into his bedroom and set about her chores. Lozada refreshed his drink and returned to a chair near the window, setting his switchblade on the table within reach. He stared down at the movie marquee across the street, but none of the featured film titles registered with him.

His mind was on the telephone conversation he'd had with Rennie Newton earlier that evening. He smiled over her poor attempt at playing hard to get. She truly was adorable.

The maid approached him. "Do you want me to draw the drapes, Mr. Lozada?"

"No, thanks. Did you leave chocolates on the pillow?"

"Two. The kind you like."

"Thank you, Sally."

She smiled down at him and then began undoing the top of her uniform. He had never solicited personal information from her. In fact, he wouldn't even know her name if she hadn't volunteered it. She had been eager to tell him that this housekeeping job was strictly temporary. Her ambition was to become an exotic dancer in a men's club.

She had the tits for it, maybe. But not the ass. Hers was as broad as a barn.

When she began to dawdle playfully over the buttons of her uniform, he said, "Never mind that," and pulled her between his thighs, pushing her to her knees.

"I could give you a lap dance first. I've been practicing in front of a mirror. I'm good, even if I do say so myself."

By way of answer, he unbuckled his belt and unzipped his trousers. She looked disappointed that he didn't want to see her performance, but she applied herself to pleasing him. She unbuttoned his shirt and spread it open. She fingered the tattoo on his chest. A bright blue dagger with a wicked blade appeared to be spearing his nipple. Tattooed drops of blood spattered his ribs. "That gets me so hot." Her tongue, as quick and agile as a snake, flicked the tip of the dagger.

He had gotten the tattoo when he was sixteen. The tattoo artist had suggested he get his nipple pierced at the same time. "With this dagger, a ring through your nipple, that'd look cool, dude."

Lozada remembered the fear in the man's eyes when he had grabbed him by his Adam's apple and lifted him off his stool. "You think I'm a fag?"

The guy's eyes bugged. He'd choked out, "Naw, naw, man. I didn't mean nothin' by it."

Lozada had gradually released him. "You'd better do a fucking good job on those blood drops or it'll be your last tattoo."

By now Sally's avid mouth had worked its way down to his crotch. "Condom," he said.

"I don't mind."

"I do."

He never left DNA evidence. Nail clippings were flushed down the toilet. He shaved his entire body every day. He was as hairless as a newborn, except for his eyebrows. Vanity prohibited him from shaving them. Besides, without the eyebrow, the scar wouldn't be as noticeable, and he wanted that scar to show like a banner.

Thankfully he had a perfectly formed cranium. It was as smooth and spherical as a bowling ball. Add to that his olive complexion and he looked very handsome with a bald head. He used a handheld vacuum on his bed and dressing table twice a day just in case dry skin was sloughed off. He'd had his fingerprints burned off years ago.

From the experience with Tommy, he'd learned that a victim's blood could be troublesome. He had been afraid that someone would ask to see his pocketknife, and he wasn't sure that he'd been able to scrub away all the blood. No one ever considered him a suspect, and eventually he'd gotten rid of the knife, but from there on he tried to leave the weapon at the scene. He used common, ordinary things—nothing exotic, recently purchased, or traceable to him. Sometimes his hands were the only weapon necessary.

He had a social security number. Like a good citizen he paid taxes on the income he earned from a TV repair service. An old rummy who'd been drunk since they invented televisions ran the place for him. It was in a bad neighborhood where few bothered to have a broken TV repaired. They simply went to a good neighborhood and stole a newer one. Nevertheless it was a legitimate, if not very lucrative, business.

His real source of income left no trail an IRS auditor—or officer of the law—could follow.

Sally ripped open the foil packet with her large teeth. "You must be awful rich. Having this place. That sweet Mercedes."

He loved his possessions, even more now than before he had languished for eight months in the Tarrant County jail while awaiting trial. That taught one to appreciate the finer things in life.

Of course those months had also cost him revenue. But he wasn't worried. He had been well paid for the job on the banker.

His money was tucked away in interest-bearing accounts in banks all over the world, places he'd never been or intended to go. He could retire anytime he wanted and live very well for the rest of his life.

But retirement never occurred to him. He didn't do what he did for the money. He could make money any number of ways. He did what he did because he was good at it and liked doing it. He *loved* doing it.

"Those scorpions sorta creep me out, but I love your apartment. You've got awesome stuff. That bedspread is real mink, isn't it?"

Lozada wished she would shut up and just suck him.

"Are you as dangerous as people say?"

He grabbed a handful of her dyed black hair and yanked her head up. "What people?"

"Ouch! That hurts."

He twisted her hair tightly around his fist, pulling it tighter. "What people?"

"Just the other girls who work here in the hotel. We were talking. Your name came up."

He looked into her eyes but could see no signs of treachery. She was too stupid to be a paid informant. "I'm only dangerous to people who talk about me when they shouldn't." He relaxed his hand.

"Jeez, no need to get so touchy. It was just girl talk. I had bragging rights and wanted to brag." She grinned up at him.

If only she knew how repugnant that smile was to him. He despised her for her stupidity and coarseness. He would have liked to hurt her. Instead he pushed her face back into his lap. "Hurry up and finish me."

She was here only because she was convenient. He could always get a woman. Women were easy to come by. Even attractive ones would do anything for a little of his attention and a fifty-dollar tip.

But the easy ones weren't the kind of woman he wanted. He wanted the kind he'd never had before.

In school he'd been a punk who ran with a rough crowd. He was always in trouble either with school officials or the police, or both. His parents weren't interested enough to care. Oh, they complained about his bad behavior but never really did anything to correct it.

His baby brother had been born with a severe birth defect. From the day his parents brought the baby home from the hospital, Lozada might just as well have ceased to exist, because in his parents' hearts and minds he had. They devoted themselves exclusively to his little brother and his special needs. They'd assumed that their handsome, healthy, precocious older son didn't have any needs.

Around age four he had gotten angry over their neglect, and he'd never stopped being angry at them for favoring baby brother over him. He learned that being disobedient won him a little of Mommy and Daddy's attention, so he did every mischievous and mean thing his young mind could devise. He had been a hellion as a boy, and by the time he became a teenager he was already a murderer.

In high school the popular girls didn't date guys like him. He didn't use drugs, but he stole them from the dealers and sold them himself. He went to illegal cock fights rather than the Friday night football games. He was a natural athlete but didn't play team sports because he couldn't play dirty and where was the thrill in playing by the rules? Besides, he would never have sucked up to an asshole with a whistle who called himself Coach.

The popular girls dated guys who proudly wore their letter jackets and would go on to UT or Southern Methodist and major in business or law or medicine, like Daddy. The desired girls went steady with the boys who drove BMWs to the country club for their golf lessons.

The girls who dressed well and participated in all the extracurricular activities, the classy girls who held school offices and were members of academic clubs, avoided him, probably fearing they would be compromised if they so much as looked twice.

Oh, he had turned their heads all right. He'd always been good-looking. And he had that element of danger about him that women couldn't resist. But his raw sexuality scared them. If he looked at one too long, too hard, too suggestively, she got the hell away from him. He could never get near the nice girls.

Nice girls like Rennie Newton.

Now *there* was a classy woman. She was all the women he'd ever wanted wrapped in one beautiful package. Each day of his trial he couldn't wait to get into court to see what she would be wearing and how her hair was styled. Several times he'd detected a light floral scent and knew it must be hers, but he never got close enough to be certain.

Not until he entered her house. It was redolent with the fragrance. Recalling the essences of her contained in the rooms she occupied made him shiver with pleasure.

Mistaking the reason for it, the maid tightened her mouth around him. He closed his eyes and envisioned Rennie Newton. He fantasized that it was she bringing him to climax.

As soon as it was over, he told the girl to go.

"Don't you wanna—"

"No." The sight of her heavy breasts disgusted him. She was a pig. A whore.

Validating his thought, she ran her hands down the front of her body and swayed to silent music. "You're the best-looking guy I've ever been with. Even this is cute." She reached up and touched the scar, still pink, that bisected his left eyebrow. "How'd you get it?"

"It was a gift."

She looked at him stupidly. Then she shrugged. "Okay, don't tell me. It's still sexy."

She stretched upward, and when he realized she was about to kiss his scar, he shoved her away. "Get out of here."

"Well excuse me for breathing."

Before she could get to her feet, he clamped his fingers around her jaw like a vise, holding it so tightly that her lips became scrunched and protruding. "The next time you talk about me with anybody, *anybody,* I'll come find you and cut out your tongue. Do you understand?"

Her eyes were wide with fear. She nodded. He released her. For a large girl she surprised him by how quickly she could move. Maybe she had a future as an exotic dancer after all.

After she was gone, he mentally replayed his telephone conversation with Rennie. He conjured up the pitch of her voice and the cadence of her speech until he could almost hear it.

The moment he had spoken her name, she had known who was calling. How silly of her to pretend she didn't. She had told him not to call her again, but that, too, was posturing. That was just the surfacing of a nice girl's innate wariness of the bad boy, and he didn't mind that. In fact, he had enjoyed hearing the trace of fear.

His experience with women was vast, but it was also limited in the sense that all had been mindless encounters for the sole purpose of sex. He was tired of that. Picking up women and going home with them could be tedious, especially when they wanted to cling. And he hated whining.

Paid whores came with their own set of nuisances. Meeting them in hotel rooms, no matter how upscale, was a tawdry proposition. It was essentially a business transaction, and inevitably the whore believed she was boss. He'd had to kill only one for insisting that she was in charge; they usually submitted to his superiority before it came to that.

Besides, whores were dangerous and couldn't be trusted. There was always a chance that the police were using one in an entrapment setup.

The time had come for him to have a woman who was of his own caliber. It was the one area of his life that was deficient. He owned the best of everything else. A man of his standing deserved a woman he could show off, one other men would envy him for.

He had found that woman in Rennie Newton.

And she must be attracted to him, or why would she have argued so passionately for his acquittal? If he'd had a mind to, he could already have satisfied their physical longing for each other. He could have waylaid her at any time and, if she had put up some bullshit female resistance, eventually subdued her. After he had fucked her a few times, she would've come to the understanding, as he had, that they were destined to be a couple.

But he'd wanted to take a more subtle approach. She was different from all the others; she should be wooed differently. He wanted to court her as a woman like her would expect to be courted. So even before the trial was over he had set out to learn who this glorious creature was and whether she had any enemies. Through his sly attorney the information had been easily obtained.

Killing that other doctor had been almost too easy. It wasn't a sufficient demonstration of his affection. Before calling Rennie, he had felt the need to follow that up with something that would better convey the depth of his feelings for her. Thus the roses. They had struck the perfect romantic note.

He finished his tequila. Chuckling softly, he thought of Rennie's rebuff. Actually, he was glad she hadn't been swept away by these preliminary overtures. Had she given in too soon and too easily, he would have been disappointed in her. Her spirit and air of independence were part of her attraction. To a point, of course.

Eventually she would need to be taught that what Lozada wanted, Lozada would have.

# Chapter 7

Wick approached the table where Lozada was having breakfast. "Hey, asshole, the glare reflecting off your head is blinding me."

Lozada's fork halted midway between his plate and his mouth. He looked up with anger-controlling slowness. If he were surprised to see Wick, he gave no indication of it, but rather treated him to an unhurried once-over. "Well, well. Look who's back."

"For about a week now," Wick said cheerfully.

"Is the Fort Worth Police Department so hard up they invited you to rejoin their miserable ranks?"

"Nope. I'm on vacation."

Wick pulled a spare chair from beneath the corner table, turned it around, and straddled it backward. Other customers in the hotel's dining room would think him rude, but he didn't care. He wanted to get under Lozada's skin. If the tic in the other man's cheek was any indication, he was succeeding.

"Say, those pancakes look good." He dipped his finger in the pool of maple syrup on Lozada's plate and licked it off. "Hmm. Right tasty."

"How did you know I was here?"

"I just poked my head out the window and followed the stench."

Actually, this hotel coffee shop was known by the department to be one of the killer's favorite breakfast places. The son of a bitch had never kept a low profile. In fact, he jeered at his would-be captors from the driver's seat of his fancy car and the panoramic windows of his penthouse—material luxuries that gave the cops all the more reason to despise him.

"Are you having something, sir?"

Wick turned toward the young waitress who had approached the table. "Fun, darlin'," he said, sweeping off his cowboy hat and placing it over his heart. "Just having a little fun here with my old friend, Ricky Roy."

Lozada despised his first two names and hated being addressed by them, so Wick used them whenever an opportunity presented itself. "Have you two met?" He read the waitress's name off the plastic tag pinned to her blouse. "Shelley—pretty name, by the way—meet Ricky Roy. Ricky Roy, this is Shelley."

She blushed to the roots of her hair. "He comes in here a lot. I know his name."

In a stage whisper, Wick asked, "Is he a good tipper?"

"Yes, sir. Very good."

"Well now, that's nice to hear. And somewhat surprising. See, actually, Ricky Roy has very few redeeming qualities." He tilted his head thoughtfully. "Come to think of it, being a good tipper might be his only redeeming quality."

The waitress divided a cautious look between them that eventually landed on Wick. "Would you like some coffee?"

"No thanks, Shelley, but you're a sweetheart for asking. If I need anything I'll let you know." He gave her a friendly wink. She blushed again and scuttled away. Coming back around to Lozada, he said, "Now, where were we? Oh, yeah, long time no see. Sorry I missed your trial. Heard you and your lawyer put on quite a show."

"It was a waste of everybody's time."

"Oh, I agree. I surely do. I don't know why they would bother with a trial for a sack of shit like you. If I had my way, they'd skip the folderol and you'd go straight to death row."

"Then lucky for me my fate isn't up to you."

"You never know, Ricky Roy. One day soon it just might be." Wick flashed him a wide grin and the two enemies assessed one another. Eventually Wick said, "Nice suit."

"Thank you." Lozada took in Wick's worn jeans, cowboy boots, and the hat he had set on the table. "I could give you the name of my tailor."

Wick laughed. "I couldn't afford him. Those look like expensive threads. Business must be good." He leaned forward and lowered his voice. "Whacked anybody interesting since that banker fellow? I'm itching to know who hired you for that one. His daddy-in-law maybe? Heard they didn't get along. What'd you use on him, anyway? Piano wire? Guitar string? Fishing line? Why not just the old one-two with your trusty blade?"

"My breakfast is getting cold."

"Oh, sorry. I didn't mean to stay so long. No, I just stopped by to say hello and let you know I was back in town." Wick stood up and reached for his hat. He turned the chair around and pushed it back into place. Then he leaned across the table as far as he could reach and spoke for Lozada's ears alone. "And to let you know that if it's the last thing I do, I'm gonna carve my brother's name on your ass."

* * *

"I'm not sure that was a smart move, Wick."

"It did my heart good."

"In fact, I'm certain it was a dumb move."

Wick had miscalculated. Oren hadn't found the account of his meeting with Lozada funny. Not in the slightest. "Why's that?"

"Because now he knows we're watching him."

"Oh, like that's a shocker," Wick said sarcastically. "He knows we're always watching him." He'd been irritable to start with, and Oren's disapproval wasn't helping his mood. He lunged from his chair and began to pace. He snapped the rubber band against his wrist.

"That slick-headed bastard doesn't care if we've got a whole division watching him twenty-four seven. He's been mooning the police department and the DA's office every day of his career. I wanted him to know that I hadn't forgotten what he did, that I was still after him."

"I can appreciate how you feel, Wick."

"I doubt that."

At that Oren got pissed, but he bit back a retort and remained calm. "You shouldn't have placed your personal feelings above the investigation, Wick. I don't want either Lozada or Rennie Newton to get wind of our surveillance. If they were involved in Howell's murder—"

"He might've been. She wasn't."

"Oh. And you're sure of this how?"

Wick stopped pacing and made an arrow of his arm to point out her house two lawns away. "We've been watching her for a whole friggin' week. She does nothing except work and sleep. She doesn't go out. Nobody comes to visit. She doesn't see anyone but the people she works with and her patients. She's a robot. Wind her up and she does her job. When she runs out of juice, she goes home, goes to sleep, and recharges."

The second-story room of the vacant house was uncomfortably warm. They'd had the electricity turned on so they could operate the central air-conditioning system, but it was antiquated and inefficient against the brutal afternoon heat.

The room seemed to Wick to be shrinking around him, and the schedule was as confining as the room. Couple his claustrophobia with Oren's stodgy adherence to the rule book and it was enough to drive him nuts. The investigation had turned stale. It was tiresome, and boring to boot.

"Just because we haven't seen them together doesn't mean they're not communicating," Oren said. "Both are too smart to do anything publicly. And even if they haven't made contact since Howell's murder, that doesn't mean they didn't conspire."

Wick threw himself back into the chair, his temper momentarily spent. Dammit, Oren was right. Dr. Newton could have hired Lozada to take out her rival before the police got suspicious and started watching her. It would have required only one phone call. "Have her phone records been checked yet?"

"All were numbers she calls regularly. But you wouldn't expect her to use her home phone to arrange an assassination." Oren sat down across from him. "Okay, enough of this BS. Out with it. What's bugging you?"

Wick pushed back his hair, held it off his forehead for several seconds, then lowered his hands. "I don't know. Nothing." Oren gave him a paternal I-know-better look. "I feel like a goddamn window-peeper."

"Surveillance work like this has never bothered you before. What's making this time different?"

"I'm out of practice."

"Could be. What else? You miss the beach? Salt air? What?"

"I guess."

"Uh-huh. It's more than homesickness for that swell place you have down there in Galveston. You look to me like you're about to claw out of your skin. You're restless and edgy. What's the matter? Is it because this investigation involves Lozada?"

"Isn't that enough?"

"You tell me."

Wick gnawed on the inside of his cheek for several moments, then said, "It's Thigpen. He's a goat."

Oren laughed. "And he speaks so highly of you."

"I'll bet."

"You're right. He thinks you're a jerk."

"Well at least I don't stink. This whole house reeks of those godawful onion sandwiches he brings from home. You can smell them the minute you open the door downstairs. And his butt crack sweats."

Oren's laughter increased. "What?"

"Yeah. Haven't you ever noticed the sweat stains on his pants? It's disgusting. And so are these." Again, he came out of his chair like a circus performer shot from a cannon. He was across the room in three strides, yanking the photographs off Thigpen's "gallery" wall.

He crumpled them and tossed the wadded pictures onto the floor. "How juvenile can you get? He's got the mentality of an adolescent pervert. He's crude and stupid and…" Oren was gazing at him with a thoughtful frown. "Shit," he muttered and returned to his chair.

Wick lapsed into a sulky silence and stared out the window at Rennie's house. Earlier she had gone for a run through her neighborhood. As soon as they saw her strike off down the sidewalk, Oren had rushed downstairs and followed her at a discreet distance in his car.

After doing five miles she returned, breathing hard and sweating through her tank top. According to Oren, she had done nothing on the outing except run. "The lady's fit," he'd said.

She hadn't gone out again. Because of the outdoor glare on the windowpanes, it was difficult to see anything inside her house except occasional movement. After nightfall she had started drawing her blinds closed.

Wick sighed. "All right, maybe I shouldn't have approached Lozada. But it was hardly a red alert. He knew I would come after him one day. I swore I would."

Oren was contemplative for another several moments, then said, "I think he did Howell."

"Me too."

He had read the completed report as soon as it was available. The CSU had done its detail work, but the crime scene had been as sterile as the victim's operating room. They had no cause for searching Lozada's condo or car, and even if they did, they would find nothing that connected him to the crime. Experience had taught them that.

"He's a fucking phantom," Wick said. "Never leaves a clue. Nothing. Doesn't even disturb the air when he moves through it."

"We'll get him, Wick."

He gave a curt nod.

"But by the book."

Wick looked at Oren. "Go on and say it."

"What?"

"You know what. What you're thinking."

"Don't put thoughts in my head, okay?"

"You're thinking that if I'd played by the book, we would've had him three years ago. For Joe."

The fact was indisputable, but Oren was too good a friend to say so. Instead, he smiled ruefully. "I still miss him."

"Yeah." Wick sat forward and planted his elbows on his knees. He dragged his hands down his face. "So do I."

"Remember that time—you'd just graduated from the academy. Wet behind both ears. Joe and I were staking out that illegal gambling parlor on the Jacksboro highway. Coldest night of the year, freezing our nuts off. You thought you'd be a good rookie and surprise us with a pizza."

Wick picked up the story from there. "I showed up in a squad car, marked you for damn sure. Joe didn't know whether to horsewhip me for blowing your cover or eat the pizza before it got cold." He shook his head with chagrin. "Y'all never let me live that one down."

Joe and Oren had attended the police academy together and shortly after their graduation had been made partners. Joe had been with Oren when both his daughters were born. He'd waited with Oren through anxious hours when Grace had a cyst in her breast biopsied. He'd traveled with him to Florida to bury his mother. Oren had cried with Joe when the woman he loved broke their engagement and his heart.

They had trusted each other implicitly and entrusted one another with their lives. Their bond of friendship was almost as strong as the one Wick and Joe had shared as brothers.

When Joe was killed Oren had assumed the role of Wick's big brother, and later his partner, although each acknowledged that no one would ever fill the void that Joe had left in their lives.

Almost a full minute of thoughtful silence elapsed before Oren slapped his thighs and stood up. "If it's all right with you, I'm gonna shove off."

"Sure. Tell Grace thanks for the ham and potato salad. It'll go down good tonight after all those lousy sandwiches. Give the girls hugs."

"Sorry you have to spend your Saturday night here."

"No problem. I—" He stopped, remembered something, glanced at his watch. "What's the date?"

"Uh, the eleventh. Why?"

"Nothing. Just lost track of my days. You'd better move along. Don't want Grace to get pissed at you."

"See you tomorrow."

"Yeah, see ya." Wick slumped down in his chair and stacked his hands on the top of his head, trying to look casual and bored.

He waited until he heard Oren's car pull away, then he scooped up his keys and followed him out. He climbed into his pickup and drove past Rennie's house. No signs of her. No hint of her plans for the evening. What if his hunch was wrong? If it was, and Lozada paid a call to her house tonight, Oren would have his head on a pike by daybreak.

But he was going to gamble that he was right.

* * *

He made it to the church with three minutes to spare. He jogged from the parking lot toward the sanctuary and barely made it into a seat in the last row before the steeple bells tolled the hour of seven.

Upon leaving the surveillance house, he'd driven like a madman to the nearest mall, entered the department store at a dead run, and had thrown himself on the mercy of a haberdasher who was looking forward to the end of his long Saturday shift.

"Forgot the damn thing until half an hour ago," Wick explained breathlessly. "There I am at the Rangers game, having a cold beer and a chili dog, and it hits me." He smacked his forehead with his palm. "Left the game, and wouldn't you know it? For once the Rangers were leading."

So far the elaborate lie had moved the haberdasher to do nothing except sniff in boredom. Some embellishment was required. "If I don't go my mom'll never forgive me. Her back went out last Thursday. She's laid up popping muscle relaxers and fretting over missing this thing. So I shot off my big mouth and said, 'Don't worry about it, Mom. If you can't go, I will.' I hate like hell to break a promise."

"How much time do you have?"

Ah! Everybody had a mom. "An hour."

"Hmm, I just don't know. You're awfully tall. We don't keep that many longs in stock."

Wick flipped out his credit card and a fifty-dollar bill. "I'll bet this you can find something."

"A challenge," said the haberdasher as he pocketed the fifty, "but by no means impossible."

With the assistance of a tailor who muttered deprecations in an alien dialect while he marked the needed alterations, they outfitted Wick for the occasion, including a pale blue shirt and matching necktie.

"The monochromatic look is in." Apparently the haberdasher had determined, as Lozada had, that he needed some fashion guidance.

While the suit pants were being hemmed and the jacket nipped in at the waist, Wick went into the mall and had his boots shined. Luckily he'd worn his black ostrich pair today. Next, he located a men's room and wet his hair. He combed it back with his fingers. Time didn't allow for barbering.

Now, as he settled into the pew, he didn't believe anyone would guess that he'd been assembled for the affair in under sixty minutes.

The ceremony began with the seating of the mothers. Next came the bridesmaids decked out in dresses the color of apricots. Everyone stood for the bride's grand entrance.

Wick used the advantage of his height to search as many faces as he could. He was on the verge of thinking he'd gone to a hell of a lot of trouble and expense for nothing when he spotted her about a third of the way down the sanctuary. Best he could tell, she didn't have an escort.

He stared at the back of her head for the duration of the ceremony. When it concluded, he kept her in sight as the guests filed out of the church and returned to their cars for the drive to the country club. He was glad to see that her Jeep wagon joined the procession headed toward the reception.

The wedding invitation had been among her opened mail the day he'd searched her house. He'd read it, memorized the day, time, and place, thinking that the information might come in handy. When Oren mentioned this being Saturday night, it had sparked his memory. He had taken a chance on Rennie attending the wedding and had made an instantaneous decision to watch her up close rather than from afar through binoculars.

When he arrived at the country club, he opted to park himself and take his keys with him rather than turning his pickup over to a valet. It was faster, and he wanted to be inside the club ahead of Rennie. The haberdasher had called the bridal department of the store and arranged a wrapped gift for him. He carried it in with him and left it on the table draped in white fabric.

A pretty young woman was attending the guest book. "Don't forget to sign it."

"My wife already did."

"Okay. Have fun. Bar and buffet are already serving."

"Great." And he meant it. He had feared it might be a seated dinner, in which case there would be no place card with his name on it and he would be forced to leave.

But he didn't go to either the bar or the buffet. Instead he took up a position against the wall and tried to remain as inconspicuous as possible. He saw Rennie the moment she entered the ballroom, and for the next hour, he tracked her every move.

She chatted with anyone who engaged her, but for the most part she stood alone, an observer of the festivities more than a participant. She didn't dance, ate sparingly from the buffet, declined the wedding cake and champagne, preferring instead a glass of clear liquid on the rocks with a lime twist.

Wick gradually made his way toward her, keeping to the fringes of the crowd and avoiding the principals of the bridal party lest one of them introduced himself and asked to whom he belonged.

Rennie was concluding a conversation with a couple, backing away from them with promises of another dinner date soon, when Wick saw his opportunity.

He put himself in her path; she bumped into him.

Coming around quickly, she said, "Oh, I'm so sorry. Please excuse me."

# Chapter 8

No problem." Wick smiled and nodded down at her hand. "You're the one who got wet. Allow me?"

He took her glass from her and signaled a waiter, who not only took away the glass but also provided napkins for her to use to dry her hands. "Thank you," she said to Wick when the waiter moved away.

"You're welcome. Let me get you another drink."

"I'm fine, really."

"My mom would disown me if I didn't." Mom again. "Besides, I was about to get one for myself. Please." He motioned toward the bar.

She hesitated, then gave a guarded nod of assent. "All right. Thank you."

He steered her toward the bar and when they reached it, he said to the bartender, "Two of whatever the lady is having."

"Ice water with lime, please," she told the young man. Then she glanced up at Wick, who was tugging on his ear and smiling with chagrin.

"And here I thought I was being so suave by letting you order for me."

"You're under no obligation to let the order stand."

"No, no, ice water is just what I wanted. Tall, cold, and refreshing. August weddings are thirsty work." The bartender slid the two glasses toward him. Wick passed one to her and then clinked the glasses together. "Don't drink it too fast or it'll go to your head."

"I promise I won't. Thanks again."

She stepped away so other guests could get to the bar. Wick pretended not to recognize a brush-off line when he heard one and fell into step beside her. "I wonder why January and February aren't the big wedding months?"

She looked at him with misapprehension. He didn't know if she was surprised he hadn't taken the hint and left her alone or if she was confused by the random question.

"What I mean is," he rushed to say, "why do so many couples get married in the summer months when it's so blasted hot?"

"I'm not sure. Tradition?"

"Maybe."

"Convenience? Those are vacation months. That makes it easier for out-of-town guests to attend."

"You?"

"From out of town?" Her hesitation wasn't long, but long enough to be noticeable. "No, I live here."

Although she didn't look all that interested, he told her he also was a local. "Are you here on behalf of the bride or the groom?"

"The groom's father and I are colleagues."

"My mother is second cousin to the bride's mother," he lied. "Something like that. Mom couldn't come but felt that someone from our branch of the family... You know how these things go."

She began moving away from him again. "Have a nice time. Thanks again for the ice water."

"My name's Wick Threadgill."

She stared down at his extended right hand, and for several seconds he believed she wasn't going to take it. But then she reached out and clasped it, firmly, but only for an instant before withdrawing. It didn't give him time to register much except that her hand was colder than his, probably from keeping a death grip on her water glass, which she had done since he handed it to her at the bar.

"Did you say Wick?"

"Yes. And I haven't got a speech impediment."

"That's an unusual name. Is it short for something?"

"No. Just Wick. And you?"

"Rennie Newton."

"Is that short for something?"

"*Doctor* Rennie Newton."

He laughed. "Pleased to meet you, Dr. Rennie Newton."

She glanced toward the exit as though locating the nearest escape route should the need for one arise. He got the feeling that at any moment she was going to bolt, and he wanted to keep the conversation going for as long as possible.

Even if she hadn't been the subject of a homicide investigation he would be curious. If they'd met innocently, he would still want to know why a woman who appeared sophisticated was this damned nervous over carrying on a conversation with a stranger in the harmless environment of a wedding reception with hundreds of people around.

"What kind of doctor?" he asked.

"Medical."

"Do you specialize?"

"General surgery."

"Wow. I'm impressed. Do you do trauma surgery? Shootings, stabbings, the kind of stuff you see on TV?" The kind of stuff that landed your rival colleague in the morgue?

He watched for telltale signs of guilt in the incredibly green eyes, but if she was an accomplice to that crime her eyes didn't give her away.

"Mostly it's scheduled, routine procedures. I sometimes get a trauma case if I'm on call." She patted her beaded handbag. "Like tonight. I've got my pager."

"Which explains your teetotaling."

"Not even a champagne toast when I'm on call."

"Well, I hope there won't be any emergencies that call you away tonight." His tone of voice, and the manner in which he was looking at her, made his meaning unmistakable. And his unmistakable meaning made her unmistakably uncomfortable.

Her smile faltered. Barriers went up all around her like laser beams around a treasured museum piece. If he ventured too close he would trip them and set off all kinds of alarms.

A drum roll drew their attention to the front of the bandstand, where the bride was preparing to toss her bouquet to a group of eager young women all jostling for the best position. Wick stood slightly behind Rennie and to her right. He had read the reactions of enough women to know that his nearness was unsettling to her. Why? he wondered.

By now most women would have either: (A) flirted back and let him know that she was available for the rest of the evening; (B) informed him of a boyfriend who unfortunately couldn't attend the wedding but to whom she was committed; or (C) told him to get lost.

Rennie was in a category of her own. She sent mixed signals. She was still here, but she'd taken cover behind a do-not-touch, don't-even-think-about-it demeanor that was as daunting as a convent wall.

Wick was curious to know how much pressure he could

apply before she cracked. So he inched even closer, close enough to make his presence impossible to ignore without actually touching her.

After the bouquet toss, the groom went down on bended knee to slide a frilly garter off his bride's extended leg while several young men reluctantly shuffled forward to form a tight group, hands in pockets, shoulders hunched.

"Ah, the difference between the sexes clearly demonstrated by this simple wedding tradition." He leaned down and slightly forward in order to speak directly into Rennie's ear. "Notice the men's level of anticipation compared to that of the women."

"The men look like they're going to the gallows."

The groom threw the garter. A young man was forced to catch it when it hit him in the forehead. One of the bridesmaids squealed and rushed out to embrace him. She covered his blushing face with kisses.

"I've got a drawer full of those things," Wick said.

Rennie turned. "That many?"

"I always had the advantage of height."

"Anything to show for them?"

"A drawer full of garters."

"All those garters wasted? Maybe your height was a disadvantage."

"I never thought of it that way."

The band launched into a crowd-pleasing song. Other guests began making their way to the dance floor, but they eddied around Rennie and Wick because neither of them moved.

"*Doctor* Newton, huh?"

"That's right."

"Dang the luck."

"Why?"

"I'm healthy."

She lowered her gaze to the Windsor knot of his monochromatic necktie.

"Are you here with anyone, Dr. Newton?"

"No."

"Me neither."

"Hmm."

"Dance?"

"No thank you."

"Another ice water?"

"No. Thanks."

"Is it a breach of etiquette to leave the reception ahead of the bride and groom?"

She raised her head quickly, met his eyes. "I believe so."

"Rats."

"But I think I've had all the gaiety I can stand."

Grinning, Wick nodded her toward the nearest exit. As they wended their way through the crowd, his hand rode on the small of her back and she made no effort to dislodge it.

The parking valets were lounging against the columns on the wide portico. One sprang forward as soon as he and Rennie came through the door. "I parked your car right over there, Dr. Newton. Easily accessible like you asked."

"Thank you."

She opened her handbag for a tip, but Wick was the faster draw. He pressed a five-dollar bill into the young man's palm. "I'll walk Dr. Newton to her car. No need to bring it up."

"Uh, okay, thank you, sir. Keys are in it."

Her smile for the obliging valet froze into place. She allowed Wick to guide her down the wide brick steps toward the tree-shaded VIP parking lot, but her posture was as rigid as an I-beam. Her lips barely moved when she said, "You shouldn't have done that."

Yep, she was pissed. "Done what?"

"I pay my own way."

"Pay your own...What? The tip I gave the valet? Getting to walk you to your car was well worth the five bucks."

By now they had reached her Jeep. She opened the driver's door and tossed her handbag inside, then turned to face him. "Walking me to my car is all that five-dollar bill bought you."

"Then I guess going for coffee is out of the question."

"Definitely."

"You don't have to give me an answer right away. Take your time."

"Stop flirting with me."

"I only asked you to have coffee, not—"

"You've been flirting since I apologized for bumping into you. If you expected anything to come of it, you've wasted your time."

He held up his hands in surrender. "All I did was tip a valet for you. I only meant to be gentlemanly."

"Then thank you for being a gentleman. Good night." She got into the car and pulled the door closed.

Wick immediately reopened it and leaned in, putting his face inches from hers. "Just FYI, Dr. Newton, if I'd been flirting you'd know by now that I think your eyes are sensational, and that I'll probably have a real dirty dream about your mouth. Have a nice night."

He closed the door soundly, then turned and walked away.

* * *

From the vantage point of his car, which was parked half a block down and across the street from the country club, Lozada saw Rennie emerge from the wide double-door entry of the club. She was wearing a dress of some lightweight summer fabric that clung to her figure, stirring his desire.

When she stepped out from beneath the second-floor balcony the setting sunlight struck her blond hair and made it shimmer. She looked fantastic. He noticed the grace with which she walked. She would—

"... the *fuck* is this?"

Lost in his fantasies, he hadn't paid any attention to the man walking alongside Rennie. When he suddenly recognized the rangy physique and realized who her companion was, he could barely restrain himself from leaving his car, crossing the street, and murdering Wick Threadgill then and there.

It was bound to happen eventually. He was going to have to kill that smart-mouthed motherfucking cop, so why not sooner rather than later? Why not right fucking now?

Because it wasn't Lozada's style, that was why. Crimes of passion were for amateurs with no self-control. While he would enjoy having the matter of Wick Threadgill finally and satisfactorily settled, he had better things to do than spend the rest of his days on death row, exhausting appeals until they finally ran out and then having the state put a needle in his vein for killing a cop.

If Wick hadn't screwed up, Lozada probably would be awaiting execution for killing his brother Joe. Lozada knew that that mistake still chafed Wick. It must drive him crazy to know that his brother's murderer was living well in a penthouse, wearing hand-tailored suits, driving expensive cars, eating, drinking, fornicating—living free thanks to him.

Lozada fingered the scar above his eye and snickered. He was too clever to react in the heat of the moment as Wick had. Others made mistakes like that, but not Lozada. Lozada was a pro. A pro without equal. A pro didn't lose his head and act without thinking.

Besides, when he finally got around to killing Wick Threadgill, the anticipation of it would be half the fun. He didn't want to take him out now, quickly, and deny himself the pleasure of planning it.

However, as he watched the cop walking close to the woman he would soon possess, he gripped his car's steering wheel as though he were trying to pry it off its mounting.

What the hell was his Rennie doing with Wick Threadgill?

The initial shock of seeing them together gave way to concern. This was a disturbing turn of events. Threadgill had interrupted his breakfast this morning and he was at a wedding reception with Rennie tonight? Coincidence? Not likely.

What was Wick's interest in Dr. Rennie Newton? The role she'd played in his recent trial? Or was it something to do with the Howell murder case that remained unsolved? Lozada wouldn't have known her plans for this evening if he hadn't seen the wedding invitation the day he went snooping through her house after delivering the roses. How had the cop known where she would be tonight? Had Wick also been snooping in her house?

These were troubling questions.

But the one possibility that really nagged him, that made him see red, that caused heat to rise out of his hairless head, was that Rennie might be in league with the police. Had they somehow discovered his attraction to her? Had Threadgill and company enlisted her help to try to trap him?

Oh now, he would hate that. He really would. Having to kill her for betraying him would be a waste of a good woman.

He watched with increasing suspicion as Threadgill leaned down into her car, then straightened up and shut the door. She backed out of her parking space, turned out of the country-club parking lot, and drove right past Lozada without noticing him. Her eyes were on the road straight ahead, and she wasn't smiling. In fact, she looked angry. Threadgill's parting words must've made her mad. He was a wiseass with everyone else, he probably was with women, too.

Lozada started his car and executed a tight U-turn. He followed Rennie home. She went in alone. Parking farther down the block, he watched her house for hours. She didn't leave again. Neither Threadgill nor anyone else showed up there.

It was after midnight before Lozada began to breathe easier. His suspicions about Rennie receded. There was a logical explanation for why she'd been with Threadgill. Perhaps he had been investigating her in connection with the Howell murder. It was well known that she and Howell had had their differences. Fort Worth's finest would have learned that. Being questioned by a cop at a social event would have made her angry, which explained why she'd looked pissed when she drove away from the country club.

Satisfied that he'd reached the correct conclusion, he picked up his cell phone and dialed her number.

# Chapter 9

Wick trudged up the stairs in the dark. Carrying his new suit jacket and the department-store shopping bag in one hand, he yanked on his necktie with the other. By the time he reached the stuffy second-floor room his shirt was hanging open and his belt was unbuckled.

From the country club he had trailed Rennie into her neighborhood. He didn't turn down her street, but took another route to the stakeout house, which put him there about the same time she pulled into her garage.

He went straight to the window and looked through the binoculars. He toed off his boots and peeled off his socks.

Rennie passed through her kitchen without stopping and disappeared through the doorway leading into the living room.

Wick shrugged off his shirt.

The light in Rennie's bedroom came on. Like him, she seemed to have found her clothes confining. She stepped out of her shoes—high-heeled sandals, he remembered—and then reached behind her neck for the zipper of her dress.

Wick kicked out of his trousers.

Rennie pulled her dress off her shoulders, worked it past her hips, then stepped out of it.

Wick stood stock-still.

Sexy undies tonight. Pale lavender. Mere suggestions of raiment that made her look more naked than nakedness. Fabric as sheer as breath. Totally inadequate, but damned effective.

She replaced the sandals on a shelf in the closet and hung her dress on the rod, then went into the bathroom and closed the door.

Wick closed his eyes. He leaned against the windowpane to cool his forehead on the glass. Had he actually groaned? He was salivating. Jesus, he was becoming Thigpen.

Leaving the binoculars on the table, he took a bottle of water from the small refrigerator. He didn't come up for air until he'd drunk it all. Still keeping an eye on her house, he groped inside the shopping bag until he located the jeans he'd worn into the department store. He pulled them on but left his shirt in the bag. It was too damn hot up here to be fully dressed.

"What's wrong with that freaking air conditioner?" he complained to the empty darkness.

Seeing Rennie come from the bathroom, he grabbed the binoculars. She had swapped the fantasy lingerie for a tank top and boxers, which actually held their own against the fancier stuff but disabused Wick of the notion that she might be waiting for a lover to arrive.

For the wedding she had worn her hair pulled back and wound into a bun at her nape. Now it was hanging long and loose. It was a coin toss which he liked best. Both served their purpose. One looked like a professional woman. One looked like a woman, period.

She rubbed her arms. Chilled? Or nervous? She glanced at the window and when she realized that the blinds were open, she quickly extinguished the light. Definitely nervous.

Wick exchanged the regular binoculars for a pair of night-vision ones. He could now see Rennie standing at the window and peering through the open slats of the blinds. She turned her head from side to side slowly, as though searching all corners of her dark backyard. She tested the lock on the window, then she drew the cord that shut the blinds. A few seconds later she reopened them.

Was that a signal to someone? he wondered.

She stood there for several minutes more. Wick kept the binoculars on her, but occasionally swept the yard with them, looking for movement. Nobody scaled her back fence. Rennie didn't climb out the window. Nothing happened.

Eventually she backed away. Wick refocused the binoculars. He could see her turning down her bed. She lay down and pulled the sheet up as far as her waist. She plumped her pillow beneath her head, lifted her hair to fan out behind her, then rolled onto her side, facing the window. Facing him.

"Good night, Rennie," he whispered.

* * *

The phone awakened her. She switched on her nightstand lamp and automatically checked the time. It was nearly one o'clock. She'd been asleep over three hours. When she was on call she tried to sleep when she could, never knowing when a night would be cut short.

She could almost count on being interrupted on a Saturday night when the emergency room stayed busy trying to patch up the damage that human beings inflicted on one another. When the patients outnumbered the surgical residents, or a case required a surgeon with more experience, the one on call was asked to come in.

She answered ready to respond. "Dr. Newton."

"Hello, Rennie."

Instinctively she clutched the sheet against her chest. "I told you not to bother me again."

"Were you sleeping?"

How had Lozada obtained her home number? She had given it only to a very few acquaintances and the hospital switchboard. But he was a career criminal. He would have ways of finding even an unlisted number. "If you continue to call me—"

"Are you lying on your pale yellow sheets?"

"I could have you arrested for breaking into my house."

"Did you enjoy yourself at the wedding?"

This question silenced her. He was letting her know how close he was. She envisioned him smiling the complacent smile he'd worn throughout his trial. It had made him appear relaxed and unconcerned about the outcome, even a little bored.

On the surface his smile had seemed benign, but to her it signaled an underlying evil. She could imagine him wearing that gloating smirk as his victims breathed their last. Knowing that he had discomfited her, he would be smiling it now.

"I liked the dress you wore," he said. "Very becoming. The way that silky fabric swished against your body, I doubt anyone was looking at the bride."

Following her wouldn't be difficult for him. He had disarmed a sophisticated security system and choked the banker to death in his home while his wife and children slept upstairs.

"Why are you watching me?"

He laughed softly. "Because you are so watchable. I looked forward to seeing you every day of that dreary trial and missed you at night when I could no longer see you. You were the one bright spot in the courtroom, Rennie. I couldn't take my eyes off you. And don't pretend you were unaware of my attention. I know you felt my eyes on you."

Yes, she had felt him watching her, and not only at the trial. She also had sensed it in the past few days. Maybe knowing that he had been inside her house was making her imagine things, but sometimes the sensation of prying eyes was so strong she couldn't have mistaken it. Since the day she got the roses, she hadn't felt alone in her own home. It was as though someone else were always there.

Like now.

She switched off the lamp and moved swiftly from the bed to the window. Earlier she had decided to leave the blinds open, thinking that if Lozada was out there watching her, she wanted to know it. She wanted to see him, too.

Was he out there now, looking in? Feeling exposed, her arms broke out in gooseflesh, but she forced herself to stand at the window while she searched the dark, neighboring houses and the deep shadows of her own yard, which lately had seemed sinister.

"I wasn't flattered by your constant staring during the trial."

"Oh, I think you were, Rennie. You just don't want to admit it. Yet."

"Listen to me, Mr. Lozada, and listen well," she said angrily. "I disliked your staring. I dislike these telephone calls even more. I don't want to hear from you again. And if I catch you following me, there'll be hell to pay."

"Rennie, Rennie, you don't sound at all grateful."

She swallowed hard. "Grateful? For what?"

After a significant pause, he said, "For the roses, of course."

"I didn't want them."

"Did you think I would let a favor go unreturned? Especially a favor from you."

"I didn't grant you a favor."

"Ah, I know better, Rennie. I know more than you think. I know a lot about you."

That gave her pause. How much did he know? Although she realized she was playing right into his hands, she couldn't stop herself from asking, "Like what?"

"I know that you wear a floral fragrance. And that you're never without a tissue in your handbag. You prefer your right leg to be crossed over your left. I know that your nipples are very sensitive to air-conditioning."

She disconnected and threw the cordless phone across the room. It landed on her bed. Covering her face with both hands, she paced the width of her bedroom and breathed deeply through her mouth, trying to stave off the nausea that threatened.

She could not let this maniac continue to terrorize her. Apparently he had developed a sick infatuation for her and was conceited enough to believe that she would reciprocate it. He wasn't only homicidal, he was delusional.

In medical school she had studied enough required psychology to know that he was the most dangerous kind of criminal. He believed himself invincible and therefore would dare to do anything.

Reluctant as she was, ever, to be involved with the police, this couldn't continue. She must report it.

She retrieved her phone, but before she could dial 911, it rang. She froze. Then she remembered to check the caller ID, which she had failed to do before. Recognizing the number, she took a stabilizing breath and answered on the third ring.

"Hey, Dr. Newton, this is Dr. Dearborn in Emergency. We've got a car-wreck casualty. Male. Early thirties. We're doing a CAT scan now to check the extent of his head injury, but there's a lake of blood in his abdomen."

"I'll be right there." Just before hanging up, she remembered. "Dr. Dearborn?"

"Yeah?"

"My code number, please?"

"Huh?"

The security measure had been implemented after Lee Howell was called out on a phony emergency. "My code—"

"Oh, right. Uh, seventeen."

"Ten minutes."

* * *

The instant Wick's bare, wet foot made contact with the tile floor, someone knocked on his motel-room door. "Shit." He stepped from the shower, reached for a towel, and wrapped it around his hips. He hoped to get to the door and put on the chain lock before the housekeeper used a passkey to let herself in.

As though knowing that he was working a graveyard shift every night, she timed cleaning his room within minutes of his return each morning, when he was ready only for a shower and sleep. He thought she might even be on the lookout for him. One of these dawns he might let her catch him bare-assed. Maybe that would cure her bad timing.

"Come back later," he shouted as he stamped across the room.

"This can't wait."

Wick opened the door. Oren was on the other side of it, a white paper sack in his hand, a manila envelope under his arm. He looked as glum as a bulldog.

"Uh-oh. Another hemorrhoid flare-up?"

Oren thrust the sack at him as he pushed his way into the room. "Doughnut?"

"Krispy Kreme?"

"You particular?" Someone knocked; Oren turned. The punctual maid was at the threshold with her cart. "Go away," he barked and slammed the door.

"Hey, I live here, remember?" Wick said.

"You said she was a pest."

"But now she might not come back all day."

"Like you're Mr. Clean."

"Jeez, you're in a foul mood. Take a load off." He motioned Oren into the room's only chair. "I apologized for waking you up last night. You told me to call if anything happened, so when something happened, I called. When I saw Rennie Newton rolling out of her garage, I didn't know she was going to the hospital for an emergency.

"Did my call interrupt something? You and Grace dancing the horizontal tango? She put fresh batteries in the vibrator? What? Or maybe Grace wasn't in the mood. Is that why you're so grumpy this morning?"

"Shut up, Wick. Just shut up." Glowering, Oren took back the sack and plunged his hand inside, coming up with a doughnut.

Laughing at his ill-tempered friend, Wick dropped his towel and pulled on a pair of boxers. He reached for the sack, got himself a glazed doughnut, took a bite that demolished half of it, and said around the mouthful, "No coffee to go with it?"

"Tell me about last night."

He swallowed. "I already did. The doctor got a call a little after one. She left her house within two minutes of getting the call. I nearly broke my goddamn neck running down those dark stairs while trying to get my boots on. Caught up with her on Camp Bowie three blocks from her house. Followed her straight to the hospital. She was there until five-ten. I followed her home. That's where she was when I turned it over to Thigpen. Who, by the way, showed up fifteen minutes late this morning."

Oren tossed him the manila envelope. He caught it against his bare chest. He finished the doughnut and licked the sugar off his fingers before opening the envelope and sliding out the eight-by-ten photographs.

There were four of them. He studied them one by one, then held one up to Oren. "This one's pretty good of me even though it's not my best side."

Oren snatched back the black-and-whites and threw them on the table beside his chair. "That's all you've got to say?"

"Okay, you caught me. I'm busted. What do you want me to say? Congratulations, Detective. Outstanding police work. Or do you want me to kneel and beg forgiveness? Kiss your ring? Kiss your ass? What?"

"What the hell were you doing, Wick?"

"Undercover investigation of a suspect."

"Bullshit." Oren picked up the most compromising photo. It was a rear shot of Wick and Rennie outside the country club walking toward her car. He was looking down at her and his hand was pressed against the small of her back. "Don't insult me."

Wick stewed under his accusatory glare. Finally he said, "We weren't getting anywhere by watching her house, were we? I've been sitting around for a week doing absolutely nothing. I've trimmed my fingernails three times for lack of anything else to do. I've sat so long my ass is growing as wide as Thigpen's. So I thought that maybe, if I exercised a little initiative, I could do us some good."

"By hitting on a suspect?"

"It wasn't like that."

"No? Then you tell me, Wick, what was it like? What was it like to be up close and personal with Dr. Rennie Newton?"

To avoid Oren's incisive glare, he reached into the bag for a second doughnut. "She's an ice maiden. She takes to being touched no better than a rattlesnake. In fact, she hissed at me."

"You touched her?"

"No. That," he said impatiently, pointing to the telltale photo, "and a handshake were the extent of touching. She showed her fangs when I tipped the parking valet."

"He'll give you back your five."

Wick looked at Oren, shook his head with disbelief, snorted, "He was *ours*? That pimply kid?"

"Rookie. Good with a camera. One of those fountain pen–looking things."

"That explains how you got the photos. How'd you know she was going to the wedding?"

"We didn't until she checked in with the hospital. She stopped by there on her way to the church. We hustled. By the time she reached the reception we had this guy in place."

"Why didn't you tell me all this?"

"Well, now, see, I tried. I even went back to the house to explain where she was going and to tell you that I had someone else covering her, just in case you wanted to take a break, go out for a good dinner, maybe see a movie. I was feeling bad about you being cooped up on a Saturday night. Imagine my surprise when I discovered the house empty and you nowhere to be found."

"I was buying a suit."

"Conveniently, your cell phone was turned off."

"There was a sign at the church asking that cell phones and pagers be turned off before entering the sanctuary."

"It doesn't vibrate?"

"Yeah, but... It..." For once he couldn't think of a plausible excuse or lie. So he took another tack. "I don't know why you're so upset, Oren. I minded my manners. Didn't have a single drink at the reception. I even took a set of steak knives to the happy couple. Nobody there would've guessed I wasn't invited." He finished his doughnut, then stretched out on his back on the bed and bunched the pillows beneath his head. "No harm was done."

Oren looked at him hard for a few moments. "As I sit here, I'm trying to decide whether to continue this conversation, or get up and walk out and to hell with you, or come over there and knock the shit out of you."

"You're that pissed? Because I spent twenty minutes, a half hour tops, with Rennie Newton?"

"No, Wick. I'm upset because I saw you fuck up once. And you fucked up huge. And now you've made me real scared that you're about to fuck up again. Huger than before."

Wick saw red. "Don't let the door hit you in the ass on your way out, Oren."

"Oh no, I'm not leaving. You need to be reminded what that mistake cost you. You think I don't know what that rubber band around your wrist is for?"

"It's a habit I've taken up."

"Yeah, right." It looked to Wick like he still might hit him. "For those of us who care about you—God knows why—it hurt to watch the disintegration you went through after what happened.

"It's a credit to your stamina that you stayed on the force another two years before you took leave. Looking back, I see how dangerous you were to have around and to be around. Don't you remember all that crap, Wick?"

"How could I forget it with you reminding me of it all the damn time?"

"I'm reminding you because I don't want you to make the same kind of mistake again."

"I'm not!"

"The hell you're not!"

Wick jackknifed into a sitting position. "What? Because I went to a wedding reception and shared a glass of water and some polite conversation with a suspect? Come on, Oren."

Wick's anger wasn't directed at his friend so much as it was at the accuracy of what he was saying. If Wick had followed procedure three years ago, they could have had Lozada for Joe's murder. He was breaking with procedure again—blatantly by leaving the surveillance house and approaching Rennie Newton at the wedding reception, and not so blatantly by failing to tell Oren about the telephone call she had received last night. The first call, the one that had upset her.

At least she had appeared to be upset when she rushed to her window with phone in hand and peered out into the darkness as she talked. The call, whatever its nature, had left her distressed. Was it fear, frustration, or anguish that had caused her to throw the telephone down onto the bed, cover her face with her hands, and give every appearance of a woman on the verge of unraveling? After that call she'd been totally different from the calm, cool, and collected woman who had capably rejected him only a few hours before.

Who the hell had called? Friend? Foe? Lover? The person who wrote "I've got a crush on you" on that small white enclosure card? Whoever it was had rocked her world. Oren needed to know about it.

But Oren had barged in here like a fire-breathing evangelical laying out all his transgressions for review, so he wasn't feeling very obliging toward his friend right now.

Anyhow, that's how he rationalized not sharing everything he knew. Some of it could wait until both had cooled off.

While he'd been processing this, Oren had been looking at him as though waiting for an explanation for his behavior. "I'm a free agent on this case, Oren, remember? You recruited me to help out. So okay, I'm helping out. In my style."

"Just make sure your 'style' helps and doesn't hurt my case."

"Look, my tan is beginning to fade. I miss the sound of the surf. I even miss scraping gull shit off my deck. I'd just as soon return to the beach, hang out, go after that shrimper's sister, and forget you ever came knocking. So if you don't want my help anymore, please just say so."

Oren regarded him closely for several moments, then shook his head. "And give you an excellent excuse to go after Lozada alone? Uh-huh. No way." He stood up, gathered the photographs, and extended them down to Wick. "Want these for your scrapbook?"

"No thanks. The encounter was unremarkable."

Oren grunted. "You've never had an unremarkable encounter with a woman." He stuffed the pictures back into the envelope, picked up the sack with what remained of the doughnuts, and on his way out, said, "See you this evening. Have a good sleep."

"Oh, I will."

He had no intention of sleeping.

# Chapter 10

"What're you havin', hon?"

Wick closed the laminated menu and looked across the lunch counter at the waitress. *They must breed them like this somewhere and ship them all to Texas,* he thought. Bleached hair was stacked into an intricate tower. Eyebrows appeared to have been stenciled on with a black crayon. Fluorescent pink lipstick was bleeding into the smoker's lines radiating from her thin lips, which had formed a wide smile for him.

"What do you recommend?"

"You Baptist or Methodist?"

"I beg your pardon?"

"This is Sunday. The Baptist go back to church tonight, so I don't recommend the Mex'can platter for lunch. Heartburn and gas, ya see. They're better off stickin' to the chicken-fried steak, pork chops, or meat loaf. But the Methodist can skip the evenin' service without fearin' hellfire and damnation, so they're fine with hot and spicy."

"What about us heathens?"

She gave his arm a playful slap. "Had you pegged for one the minute you sauntered in. I said to myself, nobody that good-lookin' can be a saint." She propped her hand on her hip. "Anything we got and you want, you can have."

Winking at her, he said, "I'll start with the chicken-fried steak."

"Gravy with that?"

"You bet. Extra on the side."

"My kinda man. The Sunday plate lunch comes with your choice of strawberry shortcake or banana pudding."

"Can I let you know?"

"Take all the time you need, sugar." She glanced at the neon wall clock. "It's past noon. How 'bout a beer while that steak's fryin'?"

"Thought you'd never ask."

"If you need anything else, just holler for Crystal. That's me."

The Wagon Wheel Café was typical of small-town Texas. Situated two miles off the interstate highway on the outskirts of Dalton, the restaurant served hearty breakfasts twenty-four hours a day. Truckers from everywhere knew the place by name. The coffee was always hot and fresh, the beer always cold. Almost everything on the menu was deep-fried, but you could get a sixteen-ounce T-bone grilled any degree from still mooing to charred.

The restaurant catered to the after-church crowd on Sundays and to the sinners on Saturday nights. The Rotary and Lions Clubs met in its "banquet" room, and adulterous lovers rendezvoused in its gravel parking lot.

The booths were upholstered in red vinyl and each had a mini jukebox linked to the vintage Wurlitzer in the corner, which was bubbling even on this Lord's day. There was a counter with chrome stools for folks in a hurry or parties of one, like Wick.

Diners seated at the counter had a view into the kitchen—too good a look and it could spoil your appetite.

But as the sign outside boasted, "Open Since 1919...And We Ain't Kilt Nobody Yet."

The game schedule for the high school football team was taped to the cash register and the civic baseball team's first-place trophy for '88 stood next to a dusty jar in which contributions were collected for the local SPCA.

Wick's beer tasted good after the hot, three-hour drive from Fort Worth. The miles had put him at a safe distance from his friend's advice against making up his own rules of law enforcement as he went along. To Wick's way of thinking, proper procedure put a crimp in creative flow. Rules for just about anything were kept in his personal "major pain in the butt" file.

Everything Oren had said was right, of course, but he didn't dwell on that.

He did justice to the steak, which was fork-tender beneath the crispy breading. He decided on the banana pudding. Crystal poured him a complimentary cup of coffee to go with it.

"First time in Dalton?"

"Yeah. Just passing through."

"A good place to pass through."

"Looks like a nice town. Lots of civic pride." He used his spoon to point at the posters taped to the front windows announcing upcoming local events.

"Oh, I guess it's as okay as anywhere," Crystal said. "When I was a kid I was bent on leaving soon as I could, but, you know." She shrugged philosophically. "Married this sorry-ass because he looked a little like Elvis. He up and left soon's the third kid came along. Life got in the way of my big plans to seek my fortune somewhere else."

"So you've lived in Dalton your whole life?"

"Ever' fuckin' day of it."

Wick laughed, then took a sip of coffee. "I knew a girl

in college who hailed from here. Her name was... hmm... something unusual. Regan? No. Ronnie? Hell, that's not it either, but something like that."

"Your age?"

"Thereabout."

"You don't mean Rennie Newton, do you?"

"That was it! Rennie. Yeah, Rennie Newton. Did you know her?"

She snorted with disdain. "Was she a good friend of yours?"

"Knew her by sight, that's all."

"That's a surprise."

"How come?"

"Because Rennie made it her life's ambition to know every man around." One of the oily eyebrows arched eloquently. "You were one of the few men that never *knew* her—if you get my drift."

He did. But he was having trouble reconciling Crystal's drift with what he knew of Dr. Rennie Newton, the ice maiden. "She got around?"

"That's a nice way of putting it."

"What's the un-nice way?"

That was all the encouragement Crystal needed. She leaned across the counter and spoke softly. "That girl screwed everything in pants and didn't care who knew it."

Wick stared at her blankly. "Rennie Newton? She put out?"

"And then some, honey."

The grin he forced felt stiff. "Son of a gun."

"The way guys talk among themselves, I would've thought you'd know her reputation."

"Just my rotten luck, I guess."

Crystal patted his arm consolingly. "You were better off. Believe me."

"She was bad news, huh?"

"She was an okay little kid. Then about the ninth grade, about the time she blossomed, you might say, she turned bad. Soon as her woman parts started showing up real good, she learned how to use 'em. She just went hog wild. Tore her mama up, the way she slutted around.

"One day I was standing right here behind this very counter filling the ketchup bottles and heard all this racket outside. Rennie came blazing past in the new red Mustang convertible her daddy had given her. She was honking her horn and waving to one and all—nekkid as a jaybird. On the top anyway.

"Seems her and some friends were out swimming at the reservoir. Their horseplay got a little rowdy. One of the boys stole the top of Rennie's swimsuit and wouldn't give it back, so Rennie said she'd teach him not to mess with her. She told him she was gonna drive straight to his daddy's insurance office and tattle on him, and damned if that's not what she did. Went sashaying in there, walked right past a secretary and into that man's private office. Bold as brass. Wearing nothing but her bikini bottoms and a smile. You ready for more coffee?"

Wick's mouth had gone dry. "I'll take another beer."

Crystal checked on two more customers before bringing him back another long-neck. "Be glad you never got tangled up with that one," she said. "You married?"

"No."

"Ever?"

"Nope."

"Why not? You're sure cute enough."

"Thanks."

"I've always been partial to blue eyes."

"The Elvis look-alike?"

"Hell, yes. Had 'em bright as headlights. Turns out that's

about all he had goin' for him." She gave Wick an experienced appraisal. "But you're the whole package, honey. I reckon you have to beat the women off with a stick."

"Naw, I've got a nasty temper."

"I'd take the temper if the baby blues came with it."

He gave her the abashed aw-shucks-ma'am grin she probably expected. After another sip of beer, he said, "I wonder what happened to her."

"Rennie?" Crystal used a damp cloth to swipe some spilled sugar off the counter. "I heard she became a doctor. Can you beat that? Don't know whether to believe it or not. She never came back to Dalton after her folks packed her off to that fancy boarding school up in Dallas. I guess after what happened they wanted to wash their hands of her."

"Why? What happened?"

Crystal didn't catch his question. Instead she smiled at an old man who hobbled up to the counter and took one of the stools near Wick's. He was wearing a plaid cowboy shirt with pearl snap buttons and blue jeans, both starched and ironed as stiff as boards. As he sat down, he removed his straw hat and set it on the counter, crown down—the proper way.

"Hey, Gus. How's life treatin' you?"

"Same as yesterday when you asked me."

"What'chu havin'?"

He looked over at Wick. "Been ordering the same goddamn meal for twenty years and she still asks."

"Okay, okay," Crystal said. "Chili cheeseburger and fries," she called out to the cook, who had been catching a break now that the after-church crowd had thinned.

"And one of those." Gus nodded toward Wick's beer.

"Gus is one of our local celebrities," Crystal told Wick as she uncapped a beer bottle.

"Not so you'd notice," the old man grumbled. He took the bottle from her and tilted it to his tobacco-stained lips.

"Rodeo bull rider," Crystal said proudly. "How many years were you a national champion, Gus?"

"A few, I guess."

She winked at Wick. "He's modest. He's got more of those champeen belt buckles than Carter has liver pills."

"That many broken bones, too." The old man took another long drink of his beer.

"We were talking about Rennie Newton," Crystal said. "Remember her, Gus?"

"I may be all bent and broke near in two, but I ain't brain-dead." He looked over at Wick again. "Who're you?"

Wick extended his right hand across the vacant stools separating them. It was like shaking hands with a cactus. "Wick Threadgill. On my way to Amarillo. Killing some time before hitting the road again. Seems I knew one of your local girls."

Crystal moved down the counter to slap menus in front of two young men who had come in and greeted her by name. When she was out of earshot, Gus turned on his stool toward Wick. "You knew the Newton girl?"

"In college," he said, hoping that Gus wouldn't ask which institute of higher learning they had attended.

"You gonna take offense at straightforward man talk?"

"No."

"Some do these days, you know. Everybody's gotta be politically correct."

"Not me."

The old man nodded, sipped his beer. "That little gal was one of the finest-looking two-legged animals I ever clapped eyes on. One of the most spirited, too. 'Course she wouldn't've looked twice at a mangled old fart like me, but when she was racing, everybody stopped to watch. She got the blood of all the young bucks pumping hot and thick."

"Racing?"

"Barrel racing."

*Barrel racing?* The Rennie Newton he knew used a ruler to stack up her magazines. He couldn't imagine her competing in a rodeo event. "I didn't know she participated."

"Hell, yeah, son. Every Saturday night April through July, Dalton holds a local rodeo. Ain't much of one on a national scale, but to folks around here it's a pretty big deal. Almost as big as football.

"Anyhow, cowboys would stack up three deep to watch Rennie race. Never showed an ounce of fear. No, sir. I saw her throwed off her horse twice. Both times she got right up, dusted off that saucy butt, climbed right back on.

"The cowboys used to say it was the way she rode that made her thighs so strong." He winked his crinkled eyelid. "Don't know myself, as I never had the pleasure of getting between them, but them that did said they ain't never had it that good."

Wick grinned, but his fingers had formed a death grip around his beer bottle.

"But that was cowboy talk," Gus said with a shrug. "We're all big liars, so it's anybody's guess as to who was talking from experience and who was talking out his ass. I figure a lot more tried than actually got to enjoy. All I know is, that little filly kept T. Dan good and riled, and that was fine by me."

"T. Dan?"

The old cowboy fixed a rheumy, wary gaze on him. "You didn't know her at all, did ya?"

"No. Not at all."

"T. Dan was her daddy. A son of a bitch of the worst sort."

"What sort is that?"

"Y'all doing all right?" Crystal had returned after preparing cherry Cokes for the two young men at the end of the counter.

Wick said, "Gus was telling me about T. Dan Newton."

"He hasn't been dead near long enough to suit most people around here," she said with a dry laugh.

"What did he do to piss everybody off?"

"Whatever he damn well felt like," she replied. "Just for example, tell him about your beef with him, Gus."

The old cowboy finished his beer. "T. Dan hired me to break a horse for him. He was a good horse but a mean bastard. I broke him, trained him, but wound up with a busted anklebone. T. Dan wouldn't pay for my doctor bill. Said it was my own fool fault that got me hurt. I'm talking about a lousy seventy-five dollars, which was chicken feed to somebody with T. Dan's bankroll."

"He was good at making money but bad at making and keeping friends," Crystal said.

"It sounds like the whole family was rotten to the core," Wick said.

"If you ask me, the town's well rid of 'em." Gus scratched his cheek. "Wouldn't mind seeing that gal take another spin around those barrels, though. Just thinking about it has got me horny. You got plans tonight, Crystal?"

"In your dreams, old man."

"What I figured." With what looked like a painful effort, Gus got off his stool and hobbled over to the jukebox.

Wick finished his beer. "Thanks for everything, Crystal. It's been great talking to you. You take credit cards?" Before signing the tab, he added a hefty tip and enough for an extra beer. "Uncap another long-neck for Gus. My compliments."

"He'll appreciate it. Never knew him to turn down a free drink."

Trying to appear nonchalant, he said, "Earlier you said that Rennie's parents had sent her to boarding school. What was the final straw for them? Why did they want to get rid of her?"

"Oh, that." Crystal pushed a slipping bobby pin back into her pile of hair. "She killed a man."

# Chapter 11

"Excuse me?"

"You heard right, Oren. She killed a man."

"Who?"

"I don't know yet."

"When?"

"Don't know that either."

"Where are you?"

"Headed back."

"From?"

"Dalton."

"You went to Dalton? I thought you were going to bed and sleep the day away."

"Do you want to hear this or not?"

"How'd you find out that she killed a man?"

"Crystal told me."

"Am I supposed to know who Crystal is?"

Wick recounted most of his conversation with the waitress in the Wagon Wheel. When he finished, Oren said, "Was she credible, you think?"

"As the FBI. She's lived there all her life, knows everybody in town. The café is the epicenter of the community. Anyway, why would she lie?"

"To impress you?"

"Well, I *was* impressed, but I don't think that's why Crystal told me."

"Then for kicks?"

"I don't think so. She isn't the type who'd lie for recreation."

"Well, she's your friend, not mine. I'll have to take your word for it. Did she know you're a cop?"

"I'm not a cop."

"Jesus," Oren muttered. "Did she know or not?"

"No."

"Then why was she divulging all this information to a total stranger?"

"She thought I was cute."

"Cute?"

"That's what she said. But I don't think Gus was all that keen on me." Wick smiled, imagining Oren silently counting to ten.

Finally he said, "You're going to make me ask, aren't you?"

Wick laughed, then repeated almost word for word his conversation with the retired bull rider. "Rennie Newton fanned his embers, but he hated her old man. According to your research, T. Dan Newton was a successful businessman, right?"

"And community gadabout."

"Even so, he wasn't the town's favorite son. Gus called him a 'son of a bitch of the worst sort,' which, in policemen's vernacular, probably translates to somewhere in the vicinity of cocksucker."

Oren ruminated on all that, finally saying, "Rennie Newton was a wild child? Promiscuous?"

"Both said our Rennie was hot to trot."

"The gossip about her could've been exaggerated. Once a girl's reputation goes bad it only gets worse."

"Gus conceded that," Wick said.

"In any case, it sure as hell doesn't match Dr. Newton's present image."

"Sure as hell doesn't."

"So who is this woman?" Oren asked in frustration. "What's the reality and what's the pose? Will the real Rennie Newton please stand up?"

Wick had nothing to contribute. He was more bumfuzzled than Oren. He'd been subjected to a brush-off that still stung. To get that good at rebuffing a man's attention she must've had lots of practice, which was contradictory to what he'd heard today.

Oren said, "The talkative Crystal didn't give you the lowdown on the murder?"

"What murder?"

"She killed a man, Wick."

"We don't know it was a murder. It could've been a hunting accident, an errant tennis serve, a boating mishap, or—"

"Or maybe she screwed some poor bastard into a coronary. Did you check with the local police?"

"I don't have a badge so I couldn't go waltzing in and start asking questions about a killing when I didn't even know the nature of the crime—if indeed it was a crime. I didn't know the victim's name or when the incident occurred."

"Newspaper files?"

"It's Sunday. A high school kid was babysitting the phone, but the offices were closed. Ditto on government offices and the courthouse."

"Public library?"

"Closed for remodeling. Books could be checked out at the bookmobile parked on Crockett Street, but no research material was available."

Oren sighed with frustration.

"I couldn't press Crystal for more information," Wick continued. "I was still experiencing the concussion from her bombshell when the city's baseball team trooped in. They were fresh from practice, hot, thirsty, demanding beer and burgers. Crystal had her hands full.

"Besides, if I'd continued talking about a girl I was supposed to have had a passing acquaintance with years ago, Crystal might have turned suspicious and clammed up. Gut instinct told me she wouldn't have taken such a shine to me if she'd known I was a cop."

"You're not a cop."

"Right. That's what I meant."

"What about the old man? That Gus. Did he have anything else to impart?"

"He'd started talking to a clone of himself about the good ol' days on the rodeo circuit. I couldn't very well interrupt and ply him with more questions."

"Maybe you didn't want to hear the answers."

"What's that mean?"

"Nothing."

Wick did a ten-count of his own. For the last couple days Oren had been casting out these tidbits of bait. Wick recognized them for what they were and refused to bite. Oren wanted to know whether or not he was attracted to Rennie Newton, regardless of her possible involvement in a homicide. It wasn't a subject he cared to discuss, or even self-analyze.

"I tried to learn more, Oren. I drove around Dalton to see what I could see, but it was futile. As soon as I get back to Fort Worth I'll go online and see what I can find, but I didn't bring my laptop—"

"Got it, got it," Oren said. "You did all you could."

"Thank you."

After a long silence, Oren said, "So what do you think?"

"About what?"

"Her, Wick. Dammit! Who are we talking about?"

"Hell, I don't know what to think. We need to find out what this 'killing' amounted to."

"Except a dead man, you mean."

Wick's patience slipped another notch, but he kept his voice even. "Until we know the facts surrounding that, we shouldn't jump to any conclusions."

"She took a life." Oren said it as though that were enough for him, and it probably was. He had unshakable criteria for right and wrong and didn't assign much importance to mitigating circumstances.

"She saved two this morning," Wick said quietly.

"You trying to make me feel bad?"

"No, I just think that's a more-than-fair equation. It's at least good enough to give her the benefit of the doubt, isn't it?"

The silence became as strained as the tired muscles in the back of Wick's neck. He was going on twenty-four hours without sleep and five hours of driving, and he was beginning to feel it. "Look, Oren, I need to grab a few z's before my shift tonight. Can you cover the first two hours?"

"If you'll do me a favor first."

"Like what?"

"You're on Interstate Twenty, right? West of Fort Worth?"

"Yeah. Not quite to Weatherford."

"Good. You won't need to backtrack."

"Where am I going?"

* * *

Rennie nudged the gelding's flanks and he obediently picked up his gait. She had bought him as a colt three years ago and had spent hours training him to respond to the merest squeeze on the reins, the flexing of a leg muscle, the pressure of her heels. Of the five horses in her stable, he was probably her favorite because he was so intelligent and responsive. When she was riding bareback, like today, they moved virtually as one even without a bit and reins. He made it effortless, which was what she needed this afternoon.

The emergency spleenectomy in the wee hours had been tricky. The injury was severe and had left the organ the consistency of raw hamburger. It literally fell apart in her hands when she tried to remove it.

But she had removed it successfully and repaired the patient's other internal injuries. Since his head wounds hadn't caused any permanent damage, he would live and recover. His frantic wife and parents had wept with gratitude for her saving his life.

The ruptured appendix that followed had been easy by comparison, but it was no less gratifying to give good news to the patient's anxious husband.

In her mailbox at the hospital was a letter from the board of directors putting into writing the offer they had extended to her earlier in the week and reiterating their hope that she would accept the chief of surgery position.

She had also received a note from Myrna Howell thanking her for the floral arrangement she had sent to Lee's funeral. She had concluded by urging Rennie to accept the post made available by her husband's death. "Lee would be pleased," she had said.

Rennie was still conflicted over that decision. The letter from the board and Myrna's note had eliminated her reservation in regard to benefiting from Lee's untimely death, but she couldn't dismiss Detective Wesley's suspicions.

This morning she had done her job well and had prolonged the lives of people who might have died. She was being courted for a position she wished to accept. She should feel exhilarated, able to enjoy a Sunday afternoon temporarily free from pressing responsibilities and serious decisions.

But she found it impossible to relax because of the call she had received last night from Lozada.

His intrusion into her life had upset her sense of order and was affecting a major career decision. How could she possibly accept the board's offer knowing that if she did, Wesley would investigate her more thoroughly? And if the detective ever discovered that Lozada was contacting her…

Damn him! He gave her the creeps and made her skin crawl. He had never actually touched her, but his voice had a tactile quality that made her feel as though he were stroking her with every word he spoke.

Why in heaven's name had he chosen her to be the object of his affection? She certainly hadn't encouraged him by look, word, or deed. Quite the opposite. Usually her disdain worked on even the most diehard would-be suitor. Around the hospital and within associated circles, she knew of her reputation for being cold and distant. Spurned men, both married and single, talked about her in unflattering, sometimes ugly, terms. She accepted the nasty gossip as a price she must pay for being left alone.

But Lozada was different. He wasn't going to be easily discouraged.

Angered by the thought, she gave the gelding's flanks another nudge and he surged into a full gallop. He ran as though he had only been biding his time until he received the subtle command. Now that she had given him permission, he applied his powerful muscles to the function they had been created for.

His hooves thundered across the dry ground, creating a

trailing cloud of dust. He had always run with heart, but this afternoon he seemed to be galloping with more determination than normal. Her fingers meshed in his mane. The hot wind scoured her cheeks and tore off her hat. She let it go.

Astride a horse running full out was the only time she felt completely free. For a short while she could outdistance the bad memories she could never completely abandon.

Out of the corner of her eye she noticed movement and turned her head to see a pickup truck on the road on the other side of the barbed-wire fence. The driver was keeping the truck even with her. Now she understood the gelding's desire to gallop. He was pitting his own speed and stamina against that of a man-made machine.

She had never raced this horse before. Maybe she should have. Maybe he felt cheated. Maybe he wanted to prove himself to her. Maybe she should prove herself to him.

"Okay, boy. You've earned this."

She bent low over his neck and pressed him with her knees. Immediately she felt a burst of renewed energy. He nosed ahead of the pickup. The truck accelerated. The gelding pushed himself, gained on the truck.

Rennie laughed out loud. It was his race. All she did was hang on, and, God, it felt great.

They ran at a full gallop for at least three minutes, staying nose-to-nose with the sporting pickup. Ahead, Rennie saw her house and barn taking shape. In sixty seconds they would be at the fence. Now she should begin slowing him down gradually so she could pull him to a full stop, dismount, and open the gate.

But she was reluctant to forfeit. Lozada's telephone call had left her feeling afraid and vulnerable. She needed to prove she wasn't afraid of anybody or vulnerable to anything. Never, ever again.

Besides, how could she cheat her horse out of a victory

when he'd been trying his hardest to win? "Are you game?" He seemed to understand. He sped up, marginally, but she could feel it in the muscles of her legs. "Okay, then. Let's do it."

Her heart was thudding in rhythm to his hoofbeats. She thrilled to the danger of it. She tightened her grip on the coarse hair of his mane. She sensed the pickup beginning to fall behind, but that didn't deter either her or the gelding. They had already won, but they needed to do this.

"Here we go."

She leaned into him and he went airborne. He cleared the fence with a yard to spare and landed hard but gracefully on the other side. Again, Rennie laughed out loud.

It was the crashing sound that caused her to pull back hard on the mane and bring the gelding around in a tight spin. The pickup had come to rest just beyond her gate. It was enveloped in a dense cloud of dust.

As the dust began to clear, she saw that the driver hadn't allowed for the loose gravel on the road. Probably he had braked too quickly. The lighter rear end had spun around and slammed into the metal gatepost. The post was intact. The damage to the truck remained to be seen. But it was the driver Rennie was concerned about.

She slid off the gelding and ran toward the gate. "Are you all right?" The gate was on a track. She rolled it open and ran to the driver's side of the cab. "Sir?"

His head was lying on the steering wheel and at first she thought he'd been knocked unconscious. But when she touched his shoulder through the open window, he groaned and gradually sat up. He pushed back his cowboy hat and removed his sunglasses. "You are no good for my ego, Dr. Newton."

She actually recoiled in surprise. It was the man from the wedding reception. "What are you doing here?"

"Losing a race." He nodded toward the gelding. "That's some horse." Then he looked at her. "Some rider, too. You lost your hat back there."

"I'm not believing this!" she exclaimed angrily. "How did you get here?"

"Interstate Twenty, then north on the Farm to Market Road."

She gave him a withering look.

"Okay, I nosed around till I found you."

"*Nosed* around?"

"At the hospital. I can't believe you were riding that fleet-footed son of a gun bareback. Do you always do that? Isn't it dangerous?"

"Not as dangerous as being tracked down by a total stranger. Nobody at the hospital would give out personal information."

He unfastened his seat belt, opened his door, and climbed out. "I'm not a *total* stranger, but you're right. I lied. I got the information off the Internet. You own this place. There're records. Property-tax rolls and such. I called the hospital and when they told me you weren't on duty today, I thought just maybe I'd catch you out here." He shrugged. "I needed a Sunday drive anyway."

As he talked he had walked to the rear of his pickup to assess the damage. He hunkered down and inspected the vertical dent on the rear panel. It was about eight inches long and half an inch deep, and the paint was scratched. The truck seemed to have sustained no more damage than that.

He ran his finger down the dent, then dusted off his hands as he stood up. "They should be able to buff that right out."

"Mr.—"

"Wick."

"I gave you—"

"A snowball's chance in hell."

"So why did you come here?"

"I had nothing to lose."

"Time. You've got time to lose. So let me save you some, Mr. Threadgill." His eyebrows shot up. He was obviously impressed that she remembered his name, and she wondered why she did. "I'm not in the market for..."

When she hesitated he leaned forward expectantly.

"Anything," she said. "A date. A... Whatever you had in mind, I'm not interested."

"Are you married?"

"No."

"Engaged?"

"I'm nothing and don't want to be."

"Huh. Is this aversion a general thing, or is it me in particular you don't like?"

"What I *like* is my privacy."

"Hey," he said, spreading his arms at his sides. "I can keep a secret. Try me. Tell me a secret and see if I don't carry it to my grave."

"I don't have any secrets."

"Then let me tell you some of mine. I've got some dillies."

He had a slightly crooked front tooth that added to the mischievousness of his smile, which he probably thought was disarming. "Good-bye, Mr. Threadgill." She turned her back on him and started for the gate. After going through, she slid it closed with a decisive clang of metal.

"Hold up. One more second?"

He was good-looking and charming, and he knew it. She'd had to deal with his type before. Cocksure and arrogant, they believed that no one, especially a woman, could resist them.

"Please, Dr. Newton?"

She wasn't nearly as furious as she pretended to be or should have been. In spite of her determination not to turn around, she did. "What?"

"I wanted to apologize for that parting remark last night."

"I don't even remember it," she lied.

"About your mouth and the dirty dream? That was out of line."

That wasn't a cocksure and arrogant thing to say, and the disarming grin had disappeared. At least on the surface he seemed sincere. Besides, if she made a big deal of the remark, he might think it had gotten to her. It had. A little. But she couldn't let him know that.

"Apology accepted."

"I was... Well, whatever—it was uncalled for."

"Maybe I overreacted to your tipping the valet."

He approached the gate slowly. "Maybe we ought to give it another shot."

"I don't think so."

"What could it hurt?"

She turned her head away and squinted into the distance. To anyone else this wouldn't have been a monumental decision. To her it was equivalent to leaping off the crest of a mountain in an unreliable hang glider.

When her eyes came back to him, he was staring straight at her. And though there was no longer a teasing glint in his eyes, they were unnerving nonetheless.

*What could it hurt?* Maybe nothing, or only everything. In any case it wasn't worth the risk. Which made it all the more surprising when she heard herself say, "There's an ice-cream parlor on the square."

"In Weatherford?"

"I was thinking of stopping there once I've finished my chores, on my way back. You could meet me there."

"I'll help you with the chores."

"I'm used to doing things for myself."

"I believe that," he said solemnly. Then he turned and set off at a jog down the road.

"Where are you going?"

He called back, "To get your hat."

# Chapter 12

It took an hour and a half for her to complete her chores. First she walked the gelding around the paddock to let him cool down, then led him into a barn. The rustic exterior was deceptive. Wick knew little about stables, but this one looked state of the art.

"I've got first-class horses," she said in response to his compliment. "They deserve a first-class home."

He was no expert judge of horseflesh, either, but he didn't have to know a lot to recognize that these were impressive animals. Rennie rubbed down the gelding, slowly and methodically, talking to him lovingly the whole while. Wick stood beside her as she combed the horse's long mane.

"He seems to understand what you're saying to him."

She took umbrage. "Why wouldn't he?"

"I didn't know horses had language skills."

"Mine do." Eyes shining with affection and pride, she ran her hand over the gelding's smooth coat. "At least with me."

"Then that's probably a talent of yours, not the horse's."

She turned to respond, but apparently felt they were

standing too close. Ducking beneath the gelding's head, she moved to the other side. Undeterred, Wick followed. "Does this English-speaking wonder have a name?"

"Beade."

"Unusual. Does it have any significance?"

"I like the sound of it."

"You don't elaborate much, do you?"

"No." Then she looked at him and they laughed. "You ask a lot of questions."

"I have a curious nature. Do you race Beade often?"

"Only when he's challenged by a pickup truck."

She moved away then, but glanced back at him over her shoulder and it was as close as she'd come to flirting. Or maybe she was dead serious and it only looked like flirting because of her tight jeans and the long blond braid that hung down her back from beneath the straw cowboy hat that he'd jogged a mile to retrieve. Maybe it looked like flirting to him because he wanted it to.

After all the feed buckets had been filled and she had said a personal good-bye to each of the horses, she led the way from the barn to the house. She excused herself to go inside.

"You can enjoy the porch swing."

"Exactly what I had in mind." Rather than make an issue of not being invited inside, he sat down in the swing and gave it a push. "Take your time."

"If Toby shows up, tell him I'll be right out."

"Toby?"

But she had disappeared inside and Toby remained a mystery until a few minutes later, when a man drove up in a rattletrap pickup. He climbed out of the cab and paused there to stare at Wick before coming up the front steps onto the porch. Wick wouldn't have been surprised to hear the ring of spurs.

He was tall and barrel-chested. Gray hair curled beneath his sweat-stained cowboy hat. When he removed his sunglasses, his deep-set eyes reminded Wick of the badass lawmen in classic Westerns. He curbed his impulse to say "Howdy, Marshal." Somehow he didn't think Toby would appreciate the humor.

"Where's Rennie?"

Not much of a greeting, was it? "Inside. If you're Toby, she said for you to wait, that she'd be out soon."

He sat down on the porch rail, propped a size-twelve Lucchese boot—no spurs—on his opposite knee, folded his arms over his chest, and made no bones about staring at Wick.

"Nice day," Wick offered.

"If you say so."

Okay, Toby hated him on sight. Why?

After a lengthy silence that was broken only by the squeaking chain of the porch swing, the old man asked, "You live around here?"

"Fort Worth."

He snorted as though Wick had replied "I live in Sodom, just this side of Gomorrah."

"Hello, Toby." Rennie emerged from the house and joined them on the porch.

Toby came to his feet and whipped off his hat. "Rennie."

"How are you?"

"Doin' good. Everything meet with your approval?"

"You ask me that every time I come out, and the answer is always the same. Everything is perfect." The way she smiled at him would've made a jealous man murderous. Wick was afraid to define the spark it kindled in him. "Did you meet Mr. Threadgill?"

"We hadn't got quite that far." Wick stood up, extended his hand, and said his full name.

"Toby Robbins." He seemed reluctant to shake hands, but he did. His hand felt even rougher than Gus's. His palm was spiky with calluses.

"Toby owns the neighboring ranch," Rennie explained. "He looks after the horses for me. Sometimes it's a week or more between my trips out here."

"Then you're a good man to have around."

Toby ignored him and addressed Rennie. "The vet came out this week and gave them all a good goin' over. No problems that he could see."

"I hadn't spotted any, but I wanted to be sure. Thank you for arranging his visit. Will he be mailing me a bill?"

"He left it with me." He removed an envelope from the breast pocket of his shirt and passed it to her.

"Thanks. I'll take care of it tomorrow." She stuffed the envelope into her shoulder bag. "Any more signs of the bobcat?"

"Not since he got that calf a few weeks back. Hopefully we scared him off. I think one of my shots might've wounded him. Maybe he crawled off and died or just moved on to friendlier hunting territory."

Wick wouldn't have thought the man capable of smiling, but he did and Rennie returned it. "I hope you're right."

"He's a big cuss," Toby continued. "Big as I've ever run across, but I think we've seen the last of him."

"Well," Rennie said, "we were just about to leave."

"Don't let me hold you up. House secured?"

"I locked up on my way out."

Toby motioned for her to precede him, and the three of them filed down the porch steps. "Anything special you want me to do this week?" he asked.

"I can't think of anything offhand. If I do I'll call you. Just take good care of the horses for me."

"You bet."

"Say hello to Corinne."

"Will do." He tipped his hat to her and shot Wick a look that made his balls shrivel, then replaced his sunglasses, climbed back into his truck, and drove away.

Rennie gave the house and barn a wistful glance, then announced, "I'm ready."

* * *

The ice-cream parlor was doing a summer Sunday afternoon business. When one of the small wrought-iron tables became available, Rennie held it for them while Wick stood in line to place their order for two hot fudge sundaes. As he carried them back to the table he was thinking that between Crystal's banana pudding and this sundae he would probably gain several pounds today.

They were well into the ice-cream confections when Rennie asked, "Do you experience panic attacks?"

Coming out of the blue like that, the question stunned him. "Pardon?"

She gave a quick shrug. "I noticed the rubber band around your wrist. It was there last night, too."

"Oh. That. It's a, uh, just an old habit. Can't remember when I took up wearing it or why."

She nodded, but she was regarding him closely. "Sometimes people who suffer acute anxiety are urged to wear a rubber band around their wrist. If they feel a panic attack coming on, they can pop the rubber band. Sometimes that halts the false signal being sent to their brain that they're in mortal danger. It wards off the panic."

"Huh. I didn't know that."

They finished their sundaes in silence. When she was done, she pulled a napkin from the dispenser in the center of the table and blotted her lips. If one could will the dreams he had, Wick would have willed having a dirty dream about her mouth. That would be something to look forward to.

"What made you think I might own property outside the city?" she asked.

"Last night when I walked you to your car I saw a saddle in the back."

"I could've been a member of a riding club."

"You could've been a Canadian Mountie, too, but I didn't think so."

"You're very clever."

"Thanks. But probably not as clever as I think I am."

"That was going to be my next observation."

Her smiles transformed her face. Unfortunately, she didn't smile very often. All afternoon he'd been looking for evidence of the audacious barrel racer who slept around and had all the studs in Dalton standing three deep to catch a glimpse of her. He hadn't seen any. Other than the attire. The jeans did in fact make her butt look saucy, but that's the only aspect of her that came across as such.

What had happened to that wild, reckless girl? he wondered. And who was this tightly contained woman who'd taken her place? He was interested to know what had caused such a dramatic transformation. Rennie was a puzzle he wanted to solve whether or not she was Lozada's client.

His mystified stare must have made her uneasy, because suddenly she declared, "I need to be going."

"How come?"

"I have things to do."

That was what she said. What her expression telegraphed was *None of your damn business.*

He groped for something else to talk about so she wouldn't bolt. "How many acres do you have out there?"

"Two hundred and twenty."

"Ah, that's nice. A good place to escape from the grind."

"What do you do, Wick?"

Well, he'd made some headway. She was still seated, and she had asked him a question about himself, and she had finally called him by his first name. "Computer software."

"Sales?"

"And design."

"Hmm."

"What?"

"Just an observation."

"What?" he probed.

"I can't see you confined to a desk all day working on computer software."

"Very insightful. My job is boring as hell."

"Then why don't you do something else?"

"I'm in the process of looking. I guess you could say I just haven't found my niche yet."

"You don't know what you want to be when you grow up?"

He laughed. "Something like that." Scooting his empty dish aside, he propped his arms on the table. "You seemed sad when you left today. You must really like being out there on the ranch."

"Very much. I love the house."

From what he could see, he could understand why. She had a pleasing place in Fort Worth, but this house appealed to him more. It was a typical two-story ranch-style home with a native stone and cedar exterior and a deep porch running the length of it. Casual but classic. And a lot of house for one person.

Or was it occupied by only one person? Maybe Toby looked after more than the horses. Wick had assumed the mentioned Corinne was Mrs. Robbins, but she could be an elderly aunt or a wire-haired terrier.

"Have you known Toby and Corinne long?"

"Yes."

"Do they have children?"

"Three. Just had their fifth grandchild."

Good. They were a pair, and it was doubtful that Grandpa Toby was a sleepover at Rennie's ranch house. "Aren't you afraid to stay out there by yourself?"

"Why would I be afraid?"

He raised a shoulder. "A woman alone. Remote location."

She hastily gathered up her shoulder bag and scooted back her chair. "People are waiting on the table. Anyway, it's time I got back to Fort Worth. Thanks for the sundae."

She made for the exit. Wick nearly mowed down a family of four in his rush to follow her out. By the time he reached her Jeep, she was sliding into the driver's seat.

"Hey, slow down. What'd I say?"

"Nothing."

"Then why the sudden split?"

"I need to get back, that's all."

"Rennie, Olympic sprinters don't move that fast. What's wrong?"

She jammed her key into the ignition, then turned to him, eyes blazing. "Your insinuation that I need protection."

"I insinuated no such thing."

"Were you hoping for an invitation to come out and *protect* me?"

"I was making conversation. You're reading a bunch of crap into an innocent question." They wrestled over control of the door. "Listen, if we're talking about fear, let's talk about mine."

"Yours?"

"Yeah. You scare the hell out of me." She stopped tugging on the door and looked at him for an explanation. "You're richer than me, smarter than me." He glanced down at the door handle. "Nearly as strong as me, and I'm afraid you could probably beat me in a foot race."

She ducked her head and he saw a trace of a smile. He pressed the advantage. "Have dinner with me, Rennie."

"What for?"

"Well, for one thing, as soon as this sundae wears off I'll be hungry."

"The sundae *was* my dinner."

"Okay, we don't have to eat. We could go to a movie. Take a walk. Anything. I'd just like to spend time with you."

She turned the key in the ignition and started the motor. "Good-bye, Wick."

"Wait a minute." He added a soft "Please," which stopped her from reaching for the door again. "Why are you always rushing away from me?"

"I told you. I'm not—"

"I know, I know, you're not in the market. Do you see somebody?"

"Yes."

*Don't let it be Lozada,* he thought.

"Patients," she said. "I see patients."

"You have dinner with them every night?" He gave her his best sad-puppy-dog smile, but it didn't earn him even one of her half-smiles.

She turned away and stared through the windshield for several ponderous moments. "You're very engaging, Wick."

"Thanks. But...?"

"But things should have stayed where we left them last night."

"That was nowhere."

"That's right."

"Well, I wasn't content with that."

"You'll have to be. I tried to make it clear then. I'm telling you again now. I can't, I won't, see you again. There would be no point." Turning back to him, she added, "And I won't change my mind."

He searched her eyes for a long time. Finally, he extended his hand toward her face.

She whispered, "Don't."

But he didn't touch her. He lifted a strand of hair from her cheek and tucked it beneath her hat. His fingers lingered there just above her ear for several seconds before he withdrew his hand. Softly he said, "I'll follow you home, see that you get there safely."

"I don't want you to do that."

"I already know where you live."

"You won't be invited in, Wick."

"I'll follow you home."

He backed away and closed her car door. She drove off without even a wave. Nevertheless he kept his promise. He followed her all the way home and when she rolled her car into her garage, he tooted his horn twice as his good-bye.

* * *

She called the hospital to check on her post-op patients and was told that the doctors on call had nothing untoward to report. The spleenectomy patient's condition had been upgraded from fair to good. He was doing well.

Following that call, she was officially off duty for the remainder of the night. Ten minutes later she was soaking in a tub of hot bubble bath. She breathed deeply and focused on relaxing, but when she closed her eyes she saw an image of Wick Threadgill and smiled in spite of herself. It was impossible not to like him. She liked him more than she had liked anyone in a very long time.

That was why she would never see him again.

Her capacity for romance had ceased to exist. It had died along with Raymond Collier that fateful afternoon in her father's study. She had killed that part of herself as surely as Raymond had been killed.

Or had it died? Maybe it had only been successfully suppressed.

She had denied common yearnings so effectively and for so long that she had convinced herself those yearnings no longer existed for her. What was natural for most women didn't apply to her. She didn't need love and romance. She didn't need anyone or anything in her life except her work. Work was what she desired, so work was what satisfied her. That had been her mantra, her anthem.

It had begun to ring hollow.

Her resolve never to marry and have a family had seemed courageous in her twenties. Now she wondered. Had she spited only herself when she made that decision? Over the years the line between independence and loneliness had become so fine that there was now little distinction between the two.

This man, this lanky Wick Threadgill with the long legs and unruly blond hair, had stirred longings that she had thought long dead. She hadn't wanted to say goodbye to him this evening. She liked his company but feared what she felt when he looked at her in that certain way.

His kisses were probably as potent as his smiles. Not that she would have allowed a kiss. But it would have been nice, when he replaced that loose strand of hair, to have turned her head ever so slightly and to have rested her cheek against his hand. Just for a moment. Just to—

Her telephone rang.

She sat up, scattering mounds of bubbles across the surface of her bathwater. Maybe it was Wick. He was just arrogant enough, persistent enough, to try again.

But it could also be Lozada.

The caller ID registered no number. She hesitated, then cleared her throat and answered.

"Rennie, are you all right?"

# Chapter 13

Lozada thrilled to the sound of her light, rapid breathing. Only fucking or fear caused a woman to breathe like that. He would enjoy it either way with Rennie.

"Why are you calling me again when I specifically told you not to?"

"I was worried about you, Rennie," he said. "I'm calling to make certain that you're all right."

"Why wouldn't I be?"

"Because of the company you keep."

He hadn't been able to believe his eyes when she'd arrived home followed by Threadgill in his pickup truck. He could dismiss their meeting at the wedding reception as bizarre coincidence. But two days in a row? It stunk to high heaven of police tactics.

Threadgill had given two short honks of his horn as he drove away. The only reason the bastard was still alive was because he hadn't gone inside the house with Rennie. But where had they been? How long had they been together? An hour? All day? What had they been doing?

Lozada had considered several ways he could kill Wick Threadgill. Which method would inflict the most pain? He wanted Threadgill's death to be painful, yes, but it must transcend normal pain. He also wanted the death to be ignominious. He didn't want to leave Wick Threadgill a martyr, a dead hero.

He couldn't repeat what he'd done to his brother Joe. That would be unoriginal, and Lozada was known for his creative flair. He would devise something unique, something special. Perhaps he would incorporate one of his scorpions. The fear factor alone would be ingenious.

However it came about, killing Wick Threadgill would be his masterpiece, the hallmark of his career. He must take his time and think about it very carefully.

Of course, if Threadgill had gone inside with Rennie, he would have been forced to act immediately, killing them both. Threadgill for his poaching. Rennie for her infidelity.

It had then occurred to him that she might be entirely innocent. What if she were unaware that Threadgill was a cop? Threadgill could be using her in hope of getting to him. That was what he'd wanted to believe. To make certain of it, he'd placed this call.

"I don't know what you're talking about, Mr. Lozada," she said. "Furthermore, I don't care."

"I don't approve of your friends."

"I don't give a damn what you approve or disapprove. For the last time, *leave me alone.*"

"I don't like your keeping company with cops."

Her silence was sudden and total, indicating surprise.

"I especially don't like your spending time with Wick Threadgill. He's a loser, Rennie. Unworthy of you. Unworthy of us."

A few seconds ticked past. When she spoke, her voice was thin. "Wick...? He's a...?"

Lozada's grin spread wide. He'd been right. She hadn't known. "Poor darling. I thought you knew."

* * *

"Then what happened?"

"I've told you. About a dozen times." Wick rubbed his eyes. They were scratchy from lack of sleep.

"Tell me again."

"After we left the barn, she went into her house. I was not invited inside."

"Do you think somebody else was in there?"

"I never saw anyone else. There were no other cars around. I have no reason to believe anyone was inside, but I couldn't swear to it. Okay?"

"Why didn't she invite you in?"

"Common sense would be my guess. She had only met me once. Briefly. And I show up at her place in the country with some half-baked explanation about how I tracked her down? If I were a woman I wouldn't have invited me in."

"Good point. Go on."

"I have a question," Thigpen said. "Did you see any weapons around?"

Wick snapped his fingers. "Now that you mention it, she was packing an Uzi in the pocket of her jeans."

Thigpen muttered a disparagement. Oren gave Wick a retiring look and motioned for him to continue. "I forgot where I left off."

"She went in. You stayed out."

"Right. Then this old man shows up. Toby Robbins. Big, robust dude." He recounted his and Rennie's conversation with the rancher. "He seemed very protective of her and suspicious of me. Kept looking at me funny."

"You're kinda funny-looking."

Thigpen was making himself hard to ignore, but Wick was determined to ignore him. He had hoped that by the time he arrived Thigpen would have left for the day and that he would have to tell his story only to Oren. No such luck.

He also noticed that the photographs of Rennie he had removed from the wall had been smoothed out and replaced. He didn't acknowledge their return. He refused to give the slob the satisfaction.

"Is the FWPD going to pay for the damage to my truck?" Wick asked, changing the subject. "The cost of having it fixed will be just below my deductible. You watch."

Oren dismissed the dent with a negligent wave. "When I sent you there I asked you to scout out the place. I didn't know it would wind up being a date."

Wick rolled his eyes. "We have differing opinions on what constitutes a date. I didn't know I was going to see her. The race just sorta happened and things progressed from there. I went with the flow. I wasn't into it for fun."

*Liar, liar. Pants on fire,* Wick thought to himself. He had very much enjoyed watching Rennie attend to her horses. Whatever else she might be, or whatever else she might have done, or whoever else she was involved with, when it came to those animals, it was a mutual love affair. That was the only time Wick had seen her looking completely happy and relaxed.

He hadn't minded the earthy smell of the stable. The merest scent of horse flesh stirred the latent cowboy spirit in every Texan. The hay had been fresh and sweet-smelling. And the sight of Rennie riding bareback hadn't exactly been hardship duty. But he didn't dare expound on that.

He said, "I don't consider grooming a bunch of horses a date."

"You went for ice cream."

"At a place where they play Donny and Marie and wear red-and-white-striped shirts. Hardly candlelight and wine. And still not my idea of a date."

"It's not a date unless he gets laid."

"Thigpen!" Oren rounded on him. "Shut up, okay?"

Wick was on his feet, fists tightly clenched. "At least I *can* get laid, Pigpen. How your wife can find your dick underneath all that flab is a mystery to me. If she even wants to look for it, which I seriously doubt."

"For the love of God, will the two of you cut it out!" Oren barked. "We've got work to do here."

"Not me. I'm outta here."

"Wick, wait!"

"I've been up for hours, Oren. I'm tired."

"I know you're tired. We're all tired. No need to get nasty."

"I passed nasty a long time ago. I haven't slept in... Hell, I can't even remember when I last slept. I'm going to my home away from home and sleep till this time tomorrow. See ya."

"He was her father's business partner."

The simple statement halted Wick. It also deflated him. He dropped back into the metal folding chair, flung his head back, closed his eyes. Even though he had a strong intuition about what the answer would be, he asked, "Who was her father's business partner?"

"The guy our lady doctor whacked."

Again disregarding Thigpen, Wick opened his eyes and looked at Oren, who nodded somberly. "I spent a few hours this afternoon in our downtown library. I had to go back several years to find the story, but it made even our newspaper."

"The really juicy ones usually do," Thigpen remarked. "And this one's really juicy."

Oren shot him another warning glance before turning back to Wick. "His name was Raymond Collier. He was shot and killed in T. Dan Newton's home study. Present at the scene was sixteen-year-old Rennie."

Sixteen? Jesus. "And?"

"And what?"

"What were the details?"

"Scarce and sketchy," Oren said. "At least in the *Star-Telegram.* I can't really start researching it until tomorrow. I didn't want to call Dalton PD until I could talk to somebody in a carpeted office. I don't want this to filter out through the rank and file. If word got around that she was under investigation, it could backfire on us." He studied Wick for a moment. "I don't suppose she opened up and talked about any of this with you."

Wick waited for several seconds to see if Oren was serious, and when he determined that he was, he laughed. "Yeah. I think it came up when she was trying to decide between strawberry or hot fudge." Oren frowned his displeasure. Wick said tiredly, "No, she didn't open up and talk about anything that happened when she was sixteen."

"Did she mention Lozada?"

"No, Thigpen, she did not mention Lozada."

"The trial? Her jury duty?"

"No and no."

"You spent hours with her. What'd you talk about all that time?"

"Primates and how some are still evolving. In fact, your name came up."

"Wick," Oren said in a chastening tone.

Wick exploded. "He's a moron. Why would she mention Lozada?"

"Why don't you just tell us what you talked about?"

"Her horses. Her place. How much she likes it out there. My boring job in computer software. Nothing. Chitchat. Stuff. Stuff people talk about when they're getting to know one another."

"But it wasn't a date." Thigpen snorted like the hog he was.

Wick sprang up from his seat again. "I don't need this shit."

Oren shouted over him. "I'm only trying to get your impressions of this suspect."

"All right, you want my impressions? Here's the first. She's not a suspect. I think her association with Lozada stopped the minute the judge banged the gavel to end the trial. And speaking of Lozada, has anybody been watching *him*?"

"His Mercedes was in his building's parking garage all day," Thigpen reported.

"Whatever," Wick said. "Keeping this surveillance on Rennie Newton is a waste of time. It's stupid and pointless. She doesn't look like a murderer. She doesn't act like a person who's just knocked off her colleague. What has she done that's the least bit suspicious? Nothing. Not a damn thing. It's been business as usual since we started watching her.

"Meanwhile, while we've been sitting here playing pocket pool to keep ourselves alert enough to monitor everything she does, whoever did knock off Dr. Howell is laughing up his sleeve at us because he got away with it. You asked for my impressions. Those are them."

"You want Lozada as much—no, *more*—than I do."

"Goddamn right I do," Wick shouted. "But she's got nothing to do with Lozada."

"I'm not ready to concede that."

"That's your problem." He scooped up his hat.

"You're leaving?"

"Good guess."

"For home?"

"Right again."

"To Galveston?"

"Tell Grace and the girls good-bye for me."

"Wick—"

"See ya, Oren."

He turned toward the staircase but was drawn up short. Rennie was standing on the top step.

Oren and Thigpen spotted her at the same time. Thigpen muttered something that Wick couldn't hear for the roaring in his ears. Oren, who ordinarily stood tall and proud, lowered his head like a kid whose mother had caught him with a dirty magazine. The stuffy atmosphere became even more claustrophobic, the stale air too thick to inhale.

Her eyes moved from one of them to the other, landing on Wick.

He took one step toward her. "Rennie—"

"You lying son of a bitch."

He decided that for now silence was his best defense. Besides, he felt they deserved her fury.

She crossed the room and raised the night-vision binoculars to her eyes, looking in the direction of her house. Wick discerned a slight sagging of her shoulders, but it lasted only until she returned the binoculars to the table and came around to face them. That was when she saw the photographs Thigpen had taped to the wall, the ones of her in various stages of undress.

Her lips parted silently and color drained from her face, but again her initial reaction was quickly replaced by righteous outrage. "Which of you has the highest rank? Who is responsible for this?"

"I am," Oren replied. "How did you know we were here?" He looked suspiciously toward Wick.

Wick returned a look that said *You know me better than that.*

Interpreting the exchange, Rennie said, "I assure you that Mr. Threadgill was a master of deceit. You can be very proud of him, Detective Wesley."

"Then how did you know—"

"It's my turn to ask questions," she snapped. "What possible explanation do you have for watching my house?"

"You left us with a lot of unanswered questions about Dr. Howell's homicide."

"And you expected to find answers to those questions by spying on me?"

"We thought we might, yes."

"Did you?"

"No."

"Have you also been eavesdropping on my telephone calls?"

"No."

"Spying on me at work?"

"To some extent," he admitted.

"You have invaded my privacy in the most despicable way. Your superiors will be hearing from my attorney first thing tomorrow morning."

"My superiors approved this surveillance, Dr. Newton."

"This isn't surveillance. This is window-peeping. This is—" She threw a disgusted glance at the photos, then, too angry to continue, headed for the stairs. "You'll be hearing from my lawyer."

She jogged down the stairs.

"Well it's hit the fan now."

Wick wasn't interested in Thigpen's editorial. He rushed down the staircase behind Rennie and caught up with her on the sidewalk in front of the house. He hooked his hand around her bicep to stop her. "Rennie."

"Let go of me."

"I want to explain." She tried to wrest her arm free, but he wouldn't release her. "Listen, I need to say this."

"I'm not interested in anything you have to say."

"Please, Rennie."

"Go to hell."

"I'm not proud of myself."

She stopped struggling and looked up at him. She gave a brittle laugh. "Oh, but you should be, Officer Threadgill. You played the role of the handsome stranger so convincingly. But then I wasn't much of a stranger to you, was I? You knew me from the pictures on your wall in there."

"I don't blame you for being mad at me."

"Don't flatter yourself." She jerked her arm away from him. Her eyes blazed. "I don't care enough about you to be mad at you. You aren't important enough to make me mad. I just wish I had never met you. And I don't want to see you again. Not by accident. Not by design. Never."

Wick didn't try to detain her. He watched her turn and jog away. He continued watching until she disappeared around the corner.

# Chapter 14

He felt like getting drunk.

To accomplish this unambitious mission, he'd chosen a bar in Sundance Square. In this popular watering hole, Wick sat hunched over his second or so Wild Turkey.

This bar wouldn't have been his first choice. He would have preferred a seedier tavern where the drinks were stiffer, the music sadder, and the customers unhappier. But this lively hangout was right across the street from Trinity Tower, where Ricky Roy Lozada lived like the fucking millionaire that he'd become by killing for hire.

Lozada's affluence contributed to Wick's misery, and heaping one misery onto another somehow seemed appropriate and warranted tonight.

Because of the proximity of Lozada's luxury digs combined with his overall feeling like shit, Wick estimated that it was going to take a couple more bourbons before he started feeling even a little bit better.

"Hey, cowboy, how come you're drinking alone?"

The young woman who plopped down on the stool beside his had dyed black hair and a red T-shirt with YOU BET YOUR ASS THEY'RE REAL spelled out in letters of silver glitter.

"I'll warn you right now, miss, I'm not good company tonight. That's why I'm drinking alone."

"Try me. I'll bet I can stand your company."

Wick shrugged and signaled the bartender. She ordered a bourbon on the rocks like his. She thanked him for the drink. "I'm Sally."

"Pleased to meet you, Sally. I'm Wick."

"So, why the long face, Rick? You have a fight with your significant other?"

He didn't correct her on his name. "In a manner of speaking."

"That sucks."

"Tell me."

"What was it over?"

"Our falling out? I did something dumb. Lied by omission. Lost trust. You know."

"Guys do that," she said with the resignation borne of experience. "How come, I wonder."

"Nature of the beast."

"Must be, 'cause you're all the same." She took a big slurp from her drink and tried to lighten the mood with a smile. "Change of subject. What do you do?"

"When?"

"For work, silly."

"Oh. You guessed it. I'm a cowboy."

"Really? I was just joking. You're a gen-u-wine cowboy?"

"Um-huh. Just this afternoon I was working in the stable with horses, hay, currycombs. All that stuff."

In his mind he was comparing the Rennie who had so lovingly groomed her horses to the one who had soundly rebuked a trio of Fort Worth's finest. Dr. Newton could not only skillfully wield a scalpel, she could slash with words just as effectively. He cleared his mind of these images and, playing turnabout, asked Sally what she did for a living.

"I'm an exotic dancer." She gave him a wicked smile and executed a move that caused the shiny letters to shimmy.

Wick wasn't impressed, but he let her believe he was. No sense in two people feeling like shit. "Wow."

Flattered, she giggled.

"Where do you perform?"

Her smile faltered. "Well, see, I'm not actually performing yet. I'm still auditioning. Right now I'm working at this temporary job. Over there. Cleaning condos." She nodded toward the high-rise.

Wick's instincts were stronger than the bourbon. His mind instantly sprang to attention. Trying to keep his sudden curiosity from showing, he smiled at her. "Let me know when you get hired to dance. I'd like to see you sometime."

She laid her hand on his thigh. "Maybe I could give you a private show? On the house."

"Where? Over there?" He hitched his thumb toward the high-rise. "Do you live there?"

"Oh sure." She snorted. "Like I could afford it."

"Man, I've always wanted to go inside that place." He gave the facade of the building a wistful glance. "See if it's as fancy as it looks."

"Oh, it's fancy all right. Only rich people live there."

"Like who?"

She took a wary glance around. "I'm not supposed to talk about the residents. If we're caught talking about the people who live in the building, we get canned, no questions asked."

"Oh, sure. I understand."

"It's a privacy thing."

"Right." He turned toward the TV behind the bar and

pretended to have a sudden interest in *The Magnificent Seven,* which was playing silently.

"But you look trustworthy." Sally nudged his knee with hers beneath the bar. Regaining his attention, she leaned close enough for him to hear her whisper and to feel the weight of her breast against his arm. "You know the race-car driver?"

Wick named a NASCAR driver who he knew lived in Fort Worth. Sally nodded vigorously. "Ten-B."

"Honestly? What's he like?"

"Nice. But that wife of his?" She made an ugly face. "A bitch royale."

"Any other celebrities?"

"One of the Cowboys lived there through last season, but he moved after he got traded. And there's some old lady on the fifth floor who used to be on *Dallas,* but I don't know her name or what part she played."

"Hmm." He pretended that his interest had waned again and glanced at the closeup of a stoic Yul Brynner. The breast got heavier against his arm and Sally's hand inched a little closer to his crotch.

"Did you see on the news where that guy just beat a murder rap?"

Wick kept his expression impassive. "Murder rap? I don't think so. How long ago?"

"Couple of weeks. His name is Lozada."

"Oh, yeah, I think I remember seeing something about that. You know him?"

She scooted so far toward him he couldn't imagine how she was managing to stay seated on her own stool. "Me and him are…close. His condo is on the floor where I work. The penthouse floor. I'm in his place all the time. And not just to clean." She raised her eyebrows suggestively.

"You're kidding, right? A murderer?"

*"Shh."* Again she glanced around nervously. "He got off, remember?" Then she giggled and added, "Now *I* get him off."

"Come on." Wick guffawed.

"I swear."

He lowered his voice to a conspiratorial whisper. "Does he do it different from, you know, regular guys?"

She considered the question seriously before answering. "Not really. Pretty much the same. We've only balled a few times. Mostly he just likes for me to blow him. And this is kinda weird." She moved closer still. "He doesn't have any hair down there."

"Why, what happened to it?"

"He shaves it."

Wick let his jaw drop. "Get out!"

"I swear."

Wick looked at her with feigned respect and awe. "And you're this guy's girlfriend?"

"Well, not officially." She cast her eyes down and trailed a finger along his arm. "I mean, he's crazy about me and all. He's just not the type that shows his feelings, you know?"

"Have you ever seen him with any other women?"

"No."

"Any ever come up to his fancy apartment?"

"No."

"Are you sure?"

"Well, yeah. And I would know. I pay attention to detail. There's never been a trace of another woman in the place and believe me, I check things out while I'm cleaning. I'm always on the lookout for one of those damn scorpions. If one ever got out I would freakin' shit."

"Scorpions?"

Wick knew about Lozada's fascination with them, but it chilled him anew to hear Sally tell about the climate-controlled tank. "I keep my eyes open when I'm in there."

"What about his phone?"

"His phone?"

"You ever answer it for him?"

"Are you serious? I'd be fired for sure. Besides, he only uses a cell."

"Have you ever heard him talking on it?"

"Once, but I didn't hear what he was saying."

"So you don't know if he was talking to a woman?"

She withdrew slightly and gave him an odd look. "Hey, what is this?"

He smiled and patted the hand still resting on his thigh. "Just trying to help you out, Sally. Looking for signs that the guy is seeing someone else. But it sounds to me like you've got no competition."

She snuggled closer. Both breasts were propped on his forearm now. "You're cool, Rick. Would you like to go to my place? I've got booze."

"Hey, I don't want this Lozada character after my ass."

"I see other guys too."

"I thought you liked him."

"I do. He's good-looking and wears the coolest clothes."

"And he's rich."

"For sure."

"Then what's the problem?"

"Well, he... scares me a little."

"He doesn't hit you, does he?"

"No. Well, sorta. I mean, he doesn't actually hit, but like the other night, he warned me not to talk—"

"Wick, what the hell are you doing?"

Wick swiveled around. Oren was standing behind them, glowering.

Sally, glowering back, asked crossly, "Who's this?"

"My partner. Oren, meet Sally."

"Did you say partner?"

"That's right."

"You're a *fag*?"

Her screech drew the attention of nearly everyone in the bar. Even Steve McQueen seemed to do a double take from the TV screen. Sally dismounted the stool with a hop that caused the breasts, of which she was so proud, to bounce like a pair of water balloons. She stamped away on her platform heels.

"I'd still like to see you dance sometime," Wick called after her.

"Bite me," she hollered back.

Oren grabbed him by the back of his collar and practically dragged him through the exit. Once they were outside, he gave Wick a shove that nearly sent him sprawling. "I've been looking all over town for you."

Wick spun around. "You push me again, Oren, and you'll regret it."

Oren looked ready not only to push him, but to slug him. "I've had every cop on the force on the lookout for your truck."

"What for?"

"Because I didn't trust you not to do something stupid." Oren took several heavy breaths as though forcibly tamping down his anger. "What's the matter with you, Wick?"

"Nothing."

"Nothing my ass. You're sulky, edgy, disagreeable. Argumentative. Defensive. Thigpen was right on when he called you a jerk."

"Then why don't you and Thigpen get together and suck each other's dicks. I'm going home."

Oren grabbed him by the shoulder and, heedless of Wick's warning, pushed him backward against the wall. He held him pinned there with one strong forearm across his chest. Oren's first beat had been in a tough neighborhood rife with gangs and drugs, but he was just as tough as the criminal offenders and had come to be respected and feared by the meanest of the mean. He and Joe.

"This time I'm not going to let you get away with copping an attitude. That's too easy. You've got a bee up your butt, and I want to know what it is. If Joe were here—"

"But he isn't," Wick shouted.

"If he were," Oren shouted back, "he'd pound it out of you."

"Leave me the hell alone." Wick pushed him aside, knowing he could do so only because Oren allowed it.

"Is it her?"

Wick turned. "Who?"

Oren shook his head, looked at him with a mix of aggravation and pity. "She's bad news, Wick. A whore dressed up in a doctor suit."

"She's not."

"You heard so yourself. From those people in Dalton. She fucked—"

Wick took the first swing, but the last Wild Turkey had finally kicked in. It hampered his speed and his aim. Oren caught it in the shoulder, which was padded with plenty of muscle. Oren's fist caught Wick on the chin, which wasn't padded with anything. He actually heard his skin split. Felt the blood spurt.

Mercifully, Oren grabbed him by the front of his shirt before his knees gave way. He pulled him close and held him face-to-face. "A few days before he was shot, Raymond Collier's wife filed for divorce. She cited adultery. Guess who was named correspondent."

Before he heaved up the bourbon on a public sidewalk, Wick pushed away from Oren, turned, and headed toward the parking lot where he'd left his pickup, which had apparently been spotted by a tattletale cop. It hadn't been that hard for Oren to find him.

"Wick!"

He stopped, then came around and aimed a threatening finger at Oren. "If you ever talk about her like that again..." He was breathing hard. Gasping, in fact. He couldn't deliver the warning with the impetus he wished. He had to get out of there, fast. So he settled on "Just don't, Oren. Just don't."

"You shouldn't be driving, Wick. Let me take you to the motel. Or to my house."

Wick turned away and kept walking.

* * *

From the driver's seat of an SUV parked in a metered slot on the street, Lozada watched the scene play out between Wick and Joe Threadgill's former partner, Oren Wesley. He was too far away to hear what they were saying, but the exchange was angry.

To Lozada's delight, they actually swapped punches. This was better than he ever could have anticipated. Dissension within the ranks. Strife between good friends. Everybody close to Wick Threadgill was pissed at him. Perfect.

Earlier he'd had the pleasure of revealing Wick's profession to Rennie. While she was still trying to assimilate that, he had added the *furthermore.* Furthermore, the FWPD had her under surveillance.

Earlier, after Wick had left her with those two cute blasts of his horn, Lozada had trailed him around the block to a house that was supposedly under reconstruction. Since he had been the object of surveillance himself, he knew the signs: three cars parked out front, including Wick's pickup. Building materials scattered around but no evidence of actual work being done. An empty Dumpster in the front yard. These were stage props, the police department's clumsy attempts to put one over on Lozada. How absurd of them to think they ever could.

"They're watching you from a house on the street behind yours," he had told Rennie.

"You're lying."

"I wish I were, my dear."

"Why would they be watching *me*?"

"I suppose because of your murdered colleague."

Coldly, she said, "I don't believe you."

But she had. Within seconds of hanging up on him she had left her house at a jog and run around the block straight to the other house. She was inside for several minutes before emerging, visibly upset, with Threadgill on her heels.

Neither of them paid any attention to the SUV parked nearby. There were no records of his ownership of this car. The police didn't know to look for it. They followed his Mercedes, and he tolerated that. But when he didn't want to be followed he drove this SUV.

He had been parked within eavesdropping distance of the conversation during which Rennie told Wick she never wanted to see him again. God, what a sensational sight—his Rennie telling off Wick Threadgill, in terms that even a dimwitted cop like him could understand.

From his observation point Lozada felt the heat waves of anger coming off her. It gave him an erection. If she made love with even a fraction of that heat she was going to be well worth the trouble.

She had returned home. Lozada had wanted nothing more than to join her there and begin phase two of his seduction, but his focus was, of necessity, Threadgill. He had followed him as far as the bar, where he had no doubt gone to drown his sorrows.

Poor Wick, Lozada thought now as he watched him storm away from Wesley. First he'd been put down by Rennie, now by his longtime friend. The cocky bastard didn't look so cocky anymore.

A sudden knocking on the passenger window of his SUV caused him to react reflexively. Less than an eyeblink later, the barrel of a small pistol was aimed at Sally Horton's astonished face.

"Jesus, it's just me," she exclaimed through the window glass. "I thought it was you, but I wasn't sure. What're you doing parked out here?"

Lozada wanted to snuff her right then for drawing attention to him. Wesley was still across the street, talking to one of the policemen who patrolled Sundance on bicycle.

"Get lost."

"Can't I join you?" she whined.

Lozada stretched across the console and opened the passenger-side door. He would rather have her inside than yelling at him through the window. She climbed in. "Where's your Mercedes? Not that this isn't cool too." She ran her hand over the glove-soft leather upholstery.

Lozada was watching Wesley. She followed his gaze. "He's gay."

He looked at her. "What?"

"He's a fag."

Wesley was a family man. It was Lozada's business to know these things. Wesley had a wife and two daughters. "What makes you think he's gay?"

"This guy I met in the bar? He bought me a drink, and we were getting along pretty good, when that man there comes along. Mad as hell. Turns out they're partners."

She had been talking to Threadgill? He had bought her a drink? "Was the other guy black too?"

Sally shook her head. "Blond and blue-eyed. A cowboy. Tough-looking, but cute."

Threadgill.

"I'm not into being a fag hag, I don't care how cute the guy is." She reached across the console and stroked his fly. "Say, that gun of yours really turns me on. And so does your pistol." She laughed at her own asinine joke.

"What did you talk about?"

"Me and the cowboy? I told him about my dream to become a dancer. And then I told him about this guy I like, who likes me." She winked. "Wonder who?"

Lozada forced himself to smile. "It wouldn't be me, would it?"

She squeezed him playfully. "And he said—"

"The cowboy?"

"Yeah, he said that since there weren't any women coming in and out of your place, that I probably didn't have any competition. What do *you* say?"

Lozada reached across and fingered her nipple through the ridiculous T-shirt. "How did he know there were no women coming in and out of my place? Did he ask?"

"Yeah, but I told him—" Suddenly she stopped, looked at him apprehensively, changed course. "I didn't tell him shit. You asked me not to talk about you, so I didn't. I mean, not by name."

"Good girl." He tweaked her, hard enough to make her wince. "You know, you've got me really hot."

"Hmm, I can tell."

"Let's go somewhere more private."

"We can do it here."

"Not what I have in mind, we can't."

* * *

Rennie looked at her bedside clock. It was after 3 A.M. and she was still awake. She was due at the hospital at 5:45. She fluffed her pillow, straightened the sheet that had become twisted around her restless legs, and closed her eyes, determined to clear her mind long enough to fall asleep.

A half hour later she gave up. She went into her kitchen, filled her electric kettle with water, and plugged it in. She assembled the fixings for tea, but her coordination was shot, her motions clumsy. She dropped the lid of the tea canister twice before she was able to replace it properly.

"Damn him!"

But exactly which "him" she was referring to, even she wasn't sure. Wick Threadgill or Lozada. Take your pick. They were tied for first place on her shit list. Detective Wesley was a close second.

She had every intention of making good on the threat she had issued. Wesley's superior would be hearing from her attorney. Either he could arrest her or he could leave her alone. But she would not live under a cloud of suspicion for a crime she had neither committed nor knew anything about.

The five dozen roses were the returned "favor" to which Lozada had referred. Anything else was unthinkable.

He frightened her. He was a criminal. He was creepy. He was persistent and, she feared, patient. He would continue the phone calls until she put a stop to them. The problem was, she didn't know how.

Reporting him to the police would be the normal course of action, but she was reluctant to do that now. She had waited too long. Telling Wesley this far after the fact would validate, and could even increase, his suspicion. She would eventually be cleared of any involvement in the crime that had cost Lee his life, but in the meantime…

It was that "in the meantime" that she must avoid. The incident in Dalton would be resurrected and—

The kettle screamed. She quickly unplugged it and poured the boiling water over the tea bag. Carrying the steeping cup into her living room, she switched on the television set and sat down in a corner of her sofa, tucking her legs beneath her. She channel surfed, trying to find any programming that would take her mind off her troubles with Lozada and keep her from thinking about Wick.

She had lied about not being mad. She *was* mad. Furious, in fact. But she also had been hurt by him, and that was the most unsettling part of this whole thing—knowing that she still could be hurt. She had believed herself immune to caring that much. Obviously she'd been wrong.

She had discouraged him at every turn, but her rejection hadn't deterred him. She had begun to admire his tenacity, and she was flattered by his obstinate pursuit. In all honesty, she had been glad he turned out to be the driver of the racing pickup. When he pushed back his hat and drawled "You are no good for my ego, Dr. Newton," she'd felt an unmistakable flutter of excitement.

But he wasn't a dogged suitor at all, only a detective hot on the trail of a suspect.

His betrayal had been a wake-up call. Time had eclipsed hurtful memories. Years had dulled the pain of deep emotional wounds. Resolves had begun to diminish in importance. Wick's double-cross had been a cruel reminder of why she had made those resolutions. She was back on track now, more resolute than before. She should thank him for that, she supposed.

But she wasn't grateful for his making her experience feelings and sensations she had long denied herself. She hated him for making her miss them, for making her yearn to explore them. With him.

She set her half-finished tea on the coffee table and settled more deeply into the cushions. When she closed her eyes, she relived how grand it had felt yesterday afternoon being astride Beade. The sun and wind hot against her skin.

The exhilaration of speed. The feeling that she could outrun anything. Freedom.

Had she known then that Wick was driving the pickup, she probably would have felt even happier. He made her smile, laugh even. That crooked front tooth—

The telephone awakened her.

# Chapter 15

Wick got away from Oren with no time to spare. He climbed into his pickup—it seemed to take an hour for the parking-lot attendant to tally his charge—and drove to the edge of downtown. He parked on a deserted side street and then, for the next few minutes, tried to convince himself that he wasn't about to die.

Repeatedly he popped the rubber band against his wrist, hard, but it didn't stop the false signals of imminent death from whizzing toward his brain. He'd never had much faith that a rubber band could work that kind of miracle. It would be like using a bull whip to halt a runaway freight train. But the doctor had recommended it, so Wick had humored him and started wearing it.

His fingers and toes tingled. Numbness crept up his legs and through his hands into his arms. The first time he experienced that temporary paralysis, he took it as proof positive that he had a brain tumor. He had learned that it was symptomatic of nothing except a shortage of oxygenated blood in his extremities due to hyperventilation.

He opened his glove box and took out the brown-paper lunch sack he carried with him. Within seconds of breathing into it, the tingling abated, the numbness receded, and feeling returned.

But his heart was pumping as though he had come nose-to-nose with a cobra poised and ready to strike. He was drenched with sweat. Although he knew he wasn't dying, it sure as hell felt like he was. For five hellish minutes his reason and his body went to war. His reason told him he was suffering a panic attack. His body told him he was dying. Of the two, his body was the more convincing.

He had been having dinner out with friends when he was seized by his first. Midway through the meal it had slammed into him. He hadn't seen it coming. There was no warning. He didn't just begin to feel bad and then gradually get worse.

One second he was fine, and the next a wave of heat surged through him and left him trembling. Immediately he was dizzy and nauseated. He excused himself from the table, rushed into the men's room, and was stricken with violent diarrhea. He shook like he had a palsy, and his scalp felt like it was crawling off his head. His heart was beating like a son of a bitch, and though he was gasping, he couldn't suck in enough breath.

He had believed wholeheartedly that whatever the hell had made him suddenly sick was going to kill him. There and then. He was going to die on the floor of that public restroom. He had been convinced of that as he'd never been convinced of anything in his life.

Twenty minutes later he was strong enough to stand, to wash his face with cold water, to excuse himself from the group of friends. He felt lucky to be leaving the restaurant alive—as wrung out as a dishcloth, but alive. He'd gone home and slept for twelve hours. The next day he was weak but otherwise fine. He figured he'd been gripped by a vicious strain of flu, or maybe the marinara sauce he'd been eating was toxic.

Forty-eight hours later it had happened again. He woke up in his own bed. No nightmare. Nothing. He'd been sleeping soundly when he abruptly awoke, in abject terror of dying. His heart was hammering. Sweat poured from him. He was gasping for air. Again he'd had the tingling in his extremities, the crawling scalp, and the absolute conviction that his time on earth was ending.

This had taken place shortly after all the shit with Lozada had gone down. The assassin was thumbing his nose at the department in general and at Wick in particular. And now he'd been stricken with a terminal disease. That was his take on the situation when he made an appointment with an internist.

"You mean I'm just crazy?"

After putting him through a battery of tests—neurological, gastrointestinal, cardiological, you name it—the doctor's diagnosis was that he suffered from acute anxiety disorder.

The doctor was quick to tell him he wasn't crazy and to explain the nature of the syndrome.

Wick was relieved to learn that his illness wasn't fatal, but the cause was imprecise and that bothered him. He wanted a quick fix and was disheartened to learn that it usually didn't work that way.

"You may never experience another one," the doctor told him. "Or you may have them periodically for the rest of your life."

Wick studied the subject, researched it, exhausted the material available. While he hated to think of thousands of others suffering as he did, he was comforted to know that his symptoms were common.

For a while, he saw a therapist weekly and took the prophylactic medication that was prescribed. Finally, though, he persuaded both doctors, and himself, that he was cured.

"I'm over it," he told the psychologist. "Whatever triggered the attacks—and it was a combination of things—has passed. I'm good to go."

And for the past ten months he had been. That was how long it had been since his last panic attack. He'd been fine. Until tonight. Thank God it wasn't a severe one, that it had been short-lived. He'd recognized it for what it was and had talked himself through it. Maybe the rubber band had helped after all.

He waited five minutes more to be certain it had passed before he began driving again. He took an entrance ramp onto the west freeway and drove with no particular destination in mind. In fact, his mind was empty except for thoughts of Rennie Newton. Surgeon. Equestrian. Lolita. Killer.

His panic attack might have been precipitated by hearing that, at sixteen, she'd been involved with a married man. Her father's business partner no less, probably much older than she. She had been a teenage home-wrecker.

That jibed with Crystal's description of a teenage hell-raiser. A girl who would drive around town bare-breasted would also sleep with her father's partner, destroy his marriage, and probably laugh about it later.

Dalton's moral majority would be outraged by such behavior. Throw into the mix the fatal shooting of her father's business partner and it was little wonder that her parents had said good riddance when they sent her to boarding school.

But all that was incongruous with the woman Wick knew. Granted, he'd been in her company all of two times, but from what he had observed, he believed he had a fair grasp on her character.

Far from a party girl, she had the social life of a monk. Rather than flaunting her sexuality, she shrank from being touched, going so far as to say "Don't" when he would have touched her cheek.

Now, was this the behavior of a femme fatale?

He couldn't reconcile the two Rennie Newtons and it was making him nuts, and for reasons that had nothing to do with the Lozada connection and Howell's murder. His objectivity had flown, and Oren knew it. That's why Oren was monitoring his activities, tracking him like a damn bloodhound.

But he couldn't really be angry at Oren. Okay, he was pissed that he'd hit him so hard, and he was dead wrong about Rennie. But Oren was doing his job. He had recruited Wick to help him do it, and instead he had added a complication.

Suddenly he realized that his driving hadn't been as aimless as he had thought. He was on the street where he had grown up. He guessed his subconscious had directed him here. Maybe he needed to touch home base, get grounded again. He pulled the pickup to a stop at the curb in front of his family's house.

He had sold it after Joe was killed. It would have seemed like a sacrilege to live there without Joe. He didn't know if the couple who'd bought it from him still lived here or if it had exchanged hands since then, but the present owners were good trustees. Even in the dark he could tell the place was well-kept.

The Saint Augustine was clipped and neatly edged, the shrubbery pruned. The shutters had been painted a different color, but he thought his mother would approve it. Her rose bed on the east side still flourished.

He could hear his father saying, "You boys should be ashamed of yourselves."

"Yes, sir."

"Yes, sir."

"Your mother prides herself on those roses, you know."

"It was an accident," Wick mumbled.

"But she had asked you not to play ball near her rose bed, hadn't she?"

Wick had been going out for a pass thrown by his older brother. The football had landed in the rosebushes—and so had Wick. By the time he had thrashed around to extricate himself, he'd broken off the branches of several plants at ground level. His mother had cried when she saw the irreparable damage. When their father got home from work, he had laid into them.

"From now on, play football on that vacant lot down the street."

"There're fire ants on that lot, Dad," Wick had said.

"Will you just shut up?" Joe hissed.

"Don't tell me to shut up. You're not my boss. You're no Joe Namath either. If you'd hadn't thrown the damn ball—"

"Wick!"

When their dad used that tone of voice he and Joe knew it was wise not to say anything more. "This weekend the two of you will clean out the garage and scrape out the gutters. No friends can come over, and you can't go anywhere. And if I hear any complaining, quarreling, or cussing," he said, looking directly at Wick, "you'll have it even worse next weekend."

Wick smiled at the memory. Even then Joe had shown self-restraint and had known when to keep his mouth shut—lessons Wick had yet to learn.

Many memories had been made inside that house. His mom had made major events of holidays and birthdays. A variety of cats and dogs, two hamsters, and one injured mockingbird had been their beloved pets. He'd fallen from the pecan tree in the backyard and broken his arm, and his mom had cried and said it could've been his neck. The day Joe got his first car, he had let Wick sit in the driver's seat while he pointed out its features.

Parties had been held for each of their school commencements and then again when they graduated from the police academy. Their parents had been proud of them. Wick figured his dad had bored his Bell Helicopter coworkers with stories of his boys, the policemen.

There were some sad memories too. Like the day his parents had told them about his father's cancer. By then he and Joe were living separately in apartments, but they came home frequently for family get-togethers.

They had been gathered around the kitchen table, eating chocolate cake and regaling Mom and Dad with cop stories, which they always edited so as not to cause them too much worry, when their father had turned serious. His mother had become so upset she had had to leave the room, Wick recalled.

Two years into her widowhood, a teenage driver ran a stop sign and hit her broadside. The EMTs said she had died instantly. At the time Wick had railed at the injustice of losing both parents so close together. Later, he was glad his mother hadn't lived to see her firstborn slain. She had thought the sun rose and set in Joe. If that car accident hadn't killed her, having to bury him would have, and it would have been much more painful.

His darkest memory was of the night Joe had been taken from him.

After their mother's death, they had moved back into the house together. That night he had been entertaining a group of friends. It was a boozy, noisy crowd, and he had barely heard the doorbell above the blaring music. He was surprised to see Oren and Grace standing on his threshold.

"Hey, who called the fuzz? Is the music too loud?" He

remembered raising his hands in surrender. "We promise to be nice, Officer, just don't haul us off to the poky."

But Oren didn't smile, and Grace's eyes were wet.

A slam-dunk of realization, then, "Where's Joe?"

He had known before asking.

Wick sighed, gave the house another poignant look, then let his foot off the brake and drove slowly away. "Enough of Memory Lane for one night, Wick ol' boy."

The city slept. There were few other vehicles on the streets. He wheeled into the motel parking lot, got out, locked his pickup, trudged to his door, and let himself in.

The room smelled musty. Too many cigarettes, too many occupants, too many carryout meals. Disinfectant couldn't penetrate the layers of odors. He turned on the air conditioner full blast to circulate the stale air. The bed, sad and sagging as it was, looked inviting, but he needed a shower first.

Even at this hour of the morning the hot water ran out before he could work up a sufficient lather, but he didn't rush. He let the cold water stream over his face and head for a long time, washing away the aftereffects of the panic attack. Besides, he was beginning to like cold showers, and just as well. It seemed that he and ample hot water were never going to be roommates.

The moment he switched off the faucets, he heard the noise in the bedroom. "Goddammit," he muttered. That maid must have radar. But this was ridiculous. It was... He checked his wristwatch. 4:23. The manager was going to hear about this.

Angrily he snatched a towel off the bar and wrapped it around his waist, then yanked open the door and barged through.

She was lying on his bed, faceup. The silver letters on her T-shirt glittered in the glare of the nightstand lamp. It also reflected in her open eyes and shone garishly on the two neat holes in her forehead.

He sensed movement behind him but didn't have time to react before an iron forearm was clamped down on his Adam's apple. He was punched hard in the back just above his waist. It caused his ears to ring and the room to tilt.

"You can blame yourself for her, Threadgill. Think about that as you die."

The punch started hurting like hell, but it jump-started his conditioned reflexes. He tried to throw off the arm across his throat. At the same time he jabbed his elbow backward. It connected with ribs, but not with any significant thrust. He repeated the movements and aimed for his assailant's kneecap with his heel. Or thought he did. He wanted to. He tried, wasn't sure he did.

Jesus, he hadn't realized he was so out of shape. Or had the panic attack been worse than he thought? It had left him as weak as a newborn kitten.

"Mr. Threadgill?"

His name echoed out of a hollow distance. It was followed by repeated knocking.

"Fuck!"

The arm across his neck let go. When it did, his knees buckled and he went down, landing hard on the smelly carpet. Pain rocketed through his skull. Jesus Christ, that hurt!

Oblivion rolled in like a dense fog. He saw it coming, welcomed it.

* * *

Rennie rushed from the doctors' parking lot into the emergency room.

"Number Three, Dr. Newton."

She tossed her shoulder bag to the desk attendant.

"Watch this for me, please." She ran down the corridor. There was a lot of activity in Room Three, numerous personnel, all busy. A nurse was standing ready with a paper gown for her. She pushed her arms through the sleeves and pulled on a pair of latex gloves. As she adjusted a pair of clear goggles to cover her eyes, she said, "Tell me."

The ER resident said, "Forty-one-year-old male, stab wound in the back, lower right side. Object still buried to the hilt."

"Kidney?"

"Almost certain."

"Pressure's down to eighty," a nurse said.

Other nurses and an intern called out other vital information. The patient had been intubated. He was being transfused with O-negative blood and was getting Ringer lactate solution through an IV. He'd been rolled onto his side so she could inspect the wound. The handle of what looked like a screwdriver extended from it.

"His abdomen's swelling. He's got a bellyful of blood."

She looked for herself and determined there was no need to do a peritoneal lavage or CAT scan. The patient was bleeding out internally.

"Pressure's dropping, Doctor."

Rennie assimilated the barrage of information within thirty seconds of her arrival. A nurse hung up a wall phone and shouted above the confusion, "OR is ready."

Rennie said, "Let's go."

As she turned away she happened to glance at the patient's face. Her wordless cry momentarily halted everyone surrounding the gurney.

"Dr. Newton?"

"You okay?"

She nodding, saying gruffly, "Let's move." But nobody did. "Stat!" That galvanized them. The gurney was wheeled into the corridor. She ran alongside. The elevator was being held open for them. They had almost reached it when someone shouted her name.

"Wait up!"

She stopped, turned. Detective Wesley was running toward her.

"Not now, Detective. I've got an emergency on my hands."

"You're not operating on Wick."

"Like hell I'm not."

"Not you."

"This is what I do."

"Not on Wick."

The gurney had been rolled inside the elevator. She motioned the emergency team to take it up. "I'll be right there." The elevator doors closed. She turned back to Wesley. "He's in shock and he could die. Soon. Do you understand?"

"Dr. Sugarman is on his way. He'll be here in five minutes."

"Sorry, haven't got it to spare, Detective. Besides, I'm a better surgeon than Sugarman and have more trauma experience. A patient needs me, and I'll be damned before I'll let you stop me from saving his life."

She held his stare for ten seconds before turning away and rushing toward the elevator that had been sent back down for her.

* * *

"The girls are all right? You're sure?"

"Oren, you asked me that ten minutes ago. I called the house. They're fine."

He took Grace's hand and rubbed the back of it. "Sorry."

"It's okay." She slipped her arm across his shoulders.

"The policewoman you sent over was cooking breakfast for them. Another officer is watching the house. They're fine." She massaged his neck. "I'm not so sure about you."

"I'm okay." He pushed himself off the waiting-room sofa. "What could be taking so long? He's been in surgery for hours."

"That could be a good sign."

"But what—"

"Are you Detective Wesley?"

He spun around. A nurse in green scrubs approached. "Dr. Newton sent me to tell you that she would be out in a few minutes. She asked you to wait."

"What about Wick? The patient? What about him?"

"Dr. Newton will be out soon."

She turned and went back through the double doors. Grace reached for Oren and pulled him back down beside her. He covered his face with his hands. "He's dead or she would have told us something."

"She didn't tell us anything because that's not her job."

"He's dead. I know it."

"He's as strong as an ox, Oren."

"It's Joe all over again."

"No it's not."

"The only difference is that when I found Joe he was already dead."

"It's not Joe. It's not the same."

"I wasn't there for Joe, and I wasn't there for Wick."

"You weren't responsible for what happened to either of them."

"If Wick's dead—"

"He isn't."

"If he is, Grace, I'll have let Joe down. He would've expected me to take care of his brother. Watch over him. Protect him from something like this."

"Oren, stop it! Don't do this to yourself. You can't take the blame for this."

"I *am* to blame. Weren't for me, Wick would still be in Galveston. Safe. Not dying on that fucking motel-room floor." His voice cracked with emotion. "He asked me if that place was the best the police department could do. I told him to stop his bellyaching, that he'd slept in worse, and that it was several rungs up from that dump he'd been living in. Jesus, Grace, I can't take this. I swear I can't."

"Wick is *not* dead."

"How do you know?"

She smiled at him gently. "Because he's too ornery to die."

He wanted to believe it, but Grace was a professional counselor. That was what she did all day, every day. She earned her living from knowing good things to say in bad situations. But even if they were platitudes, he was glad she was here beside him, saying the things he wanted and needed to hear.

It was another twelve minutes before Dr. Newton came through the double doors. The sight of her wasn't encouraging. She looked like a battle-scarred soldier who'd lost the battle.

She had pulled on a lab coat, but it didn't hide the bloodstained tunic of her scrubs. Strands of hair damp with sweat trailed from beneath her cap. Her eyes were ringed with dark circles, and she looked like she could stand a hot meal or two.

She didn't prolong their suspense. As she approached, she said, "He survived the surgery."

Oren expelled a deep breath and hugged Grace tightly. She pressed her face into his chest and whispered a prayer of thanksgiving. They held each other that way for several moments. He finally released Grace and wiped his eyes.

Grace extended her hand to the surgeon. "I'm Grace Wesley."

"Rennie Newton."

"Thank you, Dr. Newton."

After the two women shook hands, Dr. Newton handed Oren a plastic bag containing a bloody Phillips screwdriver. "I'm the only one who touched it."

Then she pushed her hands into the pockets of her lab coat and went straight to business. "The wound was deep. The solid part of his right kidney was penetrated. The organ was repaired and should heal without any adverse effect to his renal system.

"He also suffered some muscle damage. I called in our orthopedic specialist. He did an outstanding job of repairing the muscle. He'll be available for consultation later today if you wish."

"He lost a lot of blood," Oren said.

She nodded. "Once I found the main source of the bleeding—a severed artery—I was able to direct the blood flow back to the kidney. Fortunately we got to him when we did. Otherwise, he might have lost the organ or died of exsanguination."

If they'd waited on Sugarman he might not have survived. That was what she was telling him. Oren asked when they could see him.

"Right now, if you like. Come with me."

She turned and they followed. Grace must have sensed the underlying animosity between them. She gave him a quizzical look and mouthed, *What's going on?*

He shook his head. Later he would explain to her the intricacies of the situation. Once he did she would understand why his conversation with the doctor was polite but stilted.

She led them through two sets of automatic sliding doors into the surgical ICU. "He's still under heavy anesthesia, and I should warn you that he doesn't look very good. Something happened to his face."

"He fell on it." Dr. Newton stopped and looked back at him, her eyes wide, revealing more feeling then she'd shown thus far. "He was attacked from behind," he explained. "Apparently when his assailant let go of him, Wick collapsed and landed hard on the floor facedown. That's how the paramedics found him." He was too ashamed to tell them that he was responsible for busting open Wick's chin.

"The orthopedist X-rayed his face," she said. "His cheekbone wasn't broken, but he's... well, you'll see."

She motioned them into one of the units. Grace, who was braver than he, went directly to the bed, took one look at Wick, and began to cry. Oren hung back, but he could see well enough. His first reaction was to curse beneath his breath.

Wick lay on his left side, propped up in that position by a body pillow. The right side of his face, the one visible, was so badly swollen and bruised that he was hardly recognizable. Both eyes were closed but he couldn't have opened his right one if he had wanted to—it was that swollen. A breathing tube was taped to his lips. The cut on his chin seemed inconsequential compared to the other injuries, but that was the one that caused Oren to grimace.

"We're giving him antibiotics through his IV to prevent infection, although there's nothing to indicate that the bowel was punctured, which would have complicated his condition considerably," Dr. Newton explained in a voice that sounded mechanical and detached again. "He has a catheter. There was blood in his urine initially, but it's cleared."

"That's a good sign, right?" Grace asked.

"Definitely. His heart is strong, pulse steady. We're keeping a tight check on his blood pressure. We'll be taking him off the respirator as soon as he regains consciousness. Naturally he'll be sedated for pain. His good physical condition helped him survive and it will help him recover. He'll remain in ICU for several days, and I'll continue to watch him closely, but his prognosis is good."

The three stood and stared at him in silence for a couple more minutes, then Dr. Newton motioned them out. "Is there someone who should be notified? Does he have a family? We didn't know if there were someone we should call."

"Wick isn't married," Grace said, answering before he could. "He has no family."

Dr. Newton's hands disappeared once again into the pockets of her lab coat, delving deep, as though she were trying to push her fists through the bottom seams. "I see."

"Is there anything we can do for him?"

She gave Grace a wan smile. "Presently, no. Once he's released, he'll need someone with him for at least a week. He'll require a lot of bed rest. Until then, our capable nursing staff will take good care of him. By late tomorrow I'll allow him to have visitors, but only on a limited basis."

Oren said, "Unfortunately, Dr. Newton, *I* can't allow him to have visitors. He was the victim of a crime. He's also a key witness."

"To what?"

"Murder."

# Chapter 16

A young woman was in the room with Wick when he was attacked," Wesley said. "She was dead at the scene."

Rennie schooled her features not to show any reaction. It wasn't easy. Mistrusting her voice, she only nodded.

"The CSU is going over the room now. The motel housekeeper, who'd been a nuisance until this morning, saved his life. She came into Wick's room with her passkey. If she hadn't interrupted when she did, he would have died too."

"Did she see who did it?"

He shook his head. "The bathroom window was left open. We figure he climbed out just ahead of her coming in. She had knocked first. He was scared off."

"So she can't give you a description."

"Unfortunately, no. And motel rooms are hell to gather evidence from because hundreds of people come and go through them."

"Footprints outside the window?"

"Blacktopped alley. So far, we have no clues. But hopefully our techs will find something useful."

"What about that?" she asked, pointing to the bagged screwdriver.

"We'll get what we can from it."

Rennie wanted to ask him if he had any suspects in mind but was afraid of what his answer would be.

"As soon as Wick wakes up, I'll need to question him, find out what he knows," he said.

"I understand, but keep in mind that he fought for his life last night. He'll need rest. I don't want my patient to be agitated."

"I wouldn't do anything to jeopardize Wick's recovery," he said irritably.

"I'll trust you not to. Now, I must excuse myself. I have another operation scheduled in half an hour."

"But you look exhausted," Grace exclaimed.

"I just need some breakfast." She smiled at Grace Wesley, whom she had liked instantly, then turned back to the detective. "Obviously you and Mr. Threadgill are more than professional associates."

"Friends. Virtually family."

"Then I'll leave word with the ICU nurses that if you call they're free to give you an update on his condition."

"I would appreciate that consideration. Thank you."

"You're welcome."

Grace Wesley thanked her again for saving Wick's life.

The detective said a clipped "I'll be in touch," then punched the Down button on the elevator.

Rennie went back into Wick's cubicle and asked the nurse if he had shown any signs of coming around. "He's moaned a couple of times, Doctor. That's all."

"Please page me when he does. I'll be in the OR, but as soon as he wakes up I want to know about it."

"Of course, Dr. Newton."

Before leaving, she gazed down at her patient, but curbed the impulse to brush a wayward strand of hair off his forehead.

* * *

She showered in the locker room and put on fresh scrubs, then went to the cafeteria on the ground level. She had a breakfast of scrambled eggs, toast, and orange juice, but she ate it only because she needed fuel, not because she wanted it or enjoyed tasting the food.

Back on the surgical floor, she reviewed her next patient's charts and spoke to her briefly. "Your oncologist and I agree that the tumor is contained. Once that section of bowel is removed, your prognosis is very good."

The woman thanked her groggily as the anesthesiologist administered the heavy sedative into her IV.

Rennie scrubbed methodically. It felt good to be performing a task that was familiar and routine. Her carefully organized life had slipped out of her control. Ever since she heard about Lee's murder, ever since the appearance of the roses in her living room, nothing had been in order.

But, she thought as she scrubbed ruthlessly between her fingers, she could get back that control. All she needed to do was focus on her work. Work was her handle on life. Get a grip on her work and she had a grip on her life.

In the operating room, she was slicing through adipose tissue on the patient's abdomen when the assisting resident surgeon said, "Heard you had some excitement around here this morning."

"Our Dr. Newton is a regular heroine," said the scrub tech.

Rennie, whose mind was on her task, asked absently, "What are you talking about?"

"It was all over the news this morning."

Rennie glanced at the anesthesiologist, who'd spoken from his stool behind the patient. "What was on the news?"

"How you saved the cop's life."

The resident said, "Threadgill's brother died in the line of duty a few years ago. You prevented him from doing the same."

"Except that this Threadgill wasn't on duty at the time," said one of the circulating nurses.

"I don't know anything about him," Rennie said coolly. "Suction, please. I responded to an emergency, that's all."

"According to the news, the girl was beyond help," the anesthesiologist remarked.

The talkative resident picked up the story. "I heard straight from the paramedics who responded to the 911 call that she was found in the cop's bed. Apparently whoever attacked Threadgill killed her first."

"Jealous boyfriend?"

"Or husband."

"Could be. The way they've pieced it together, Threadgill was in the shower."

"Speaking for myself," the resident quipped, "I always have a cigarette first. Then shower. What about you, Betts? Do you smoke after sex?"

"I don't know," replied the circulating nurse. "I've never looked."

Everyone laughed.

The scrub tech bobbed her eyebrows above her mask. "If this cop looks anything like the picture they printed in the newspaper, I'd say the girl died smiling."

"Could we please get back to business here?" Rennie snapped. "What's her pressure?"

The anesthesiologist replied in a subdued, professional tone. Rennie's brusqueness had quelled the joking. She kept her head down, her concentration focused on the surgery. But when her pager chirped, she asked the circulating nurse to check it for her.

"It's surgical ICU, Dr. Newton."

"Would you call them, please?"

She listened as the nurse placed the call. "Okay, I'll tell her." She hung up.

"Threadgill's waking up."

"Thanks."

Although she sensed the raised eyebrows above the masks, no one dared to comment. From there the talk related only to the procedure they were performing. Finally Rennie withdrew her hands and nodded for the assisting surgeon to clip the last internal suture. She probed the area with her gloved finger to make certain all the sutures held. "Looks good."

"Perfect," he said. "Excellent job, Dr. Newton."

"Thank you. Would you mind closing up for me?"

"Your wish is my command."

"Thanks. Good job, everyone."

She peeled off her bloody gloves and pushed through the door, knowing that as soon as it closed behind her she would be the topic of speculative conversation. Let them wonder, she thought.

She reported the satisfactory results of the operation to the patient's anxious family, then hurried to the locker room, took a second shower, and reached the ICU just as the nurse was urging Wick to cough up his breathing tube.

He suffered the choking sensation all patients did, but eventually the thing was out. "Now, that wasn't so bad, was it, Mr. Threadgill? You did real good."

He moved his lips but the nurse couldn't hear him, so she leaned down close. When she straightened up, she was chuckling. "What did he say?" Rennie asked.

"He said, 'Get fucked.' "

"You don't have to tolerate that from him."

"Don't worry about it, Doctor. I've got a husband and four sons."

Rennie took her place at Wick's bedside. "Wick, do you know where you are?"

He grunted an unintelligible reply. She placed her stethoscope on his chest and listened for several moments. "You're doing fine."

"Thirsty."

"How about some ice chips?" She looked across at the nurse, who nodded and left on the errand. "We'll start you out on ice chips, Wick. I don't want you to drink anything yet and get nauseated."

He grunted again and was struggling to open his right eye, unaware that it was swollen shut. He would be groggy and disoriented for hours yet. "How's the pain, Wick? I can increase the dosage of your pain medication." He mumbled something else she couldn't interpret. "I'll take that as a yes."

The nurse returned with the cup of crushed ice and a plastic spoon. "Give him a few spoonfuls every time he wakes up." She made the necessary notations on his chart. Before leaving she said, "I'll be either here or at my office. Page me if there's any change."

"Certainly. Oh, Dr. Newton, I think he wants to speak to you."

Rennie returned to Wick's bedside. He groped for her hand. Despite the IV port that was taped to the back of his hand, his grip was surprisingly strong. She leaned down close. "What is it, Wick?"

He whispered only one word.

* * *

"Lozada."

Detective Wesley frowned at her from the other side of his cluttered desk. "Anything else?"

"Just that. 'Lozada,' " Rennie repeated.

"When was this?"

"Around noon today."

"And you're just now telling me?"

"I had to sort it out first."

"Sort what out?"

Other personnel in the Criminal Investigation Division appeared to be going about their business, but Rennie was aware that she was an object of curiosity. "Is there someplace we can talk more privately?"

Wesley shrugged and indicated for her to follow him. He led her into the same room where the interrogation had been videotaped. They sat in the same seating arrangement. She didn't particularly like the implication that she was once again being placed in a defensive position, but she didn't remark on it. Instead she immediately resumed the conversation.

"Could that mean it was Lozada who attacked Wick last night?"

"Oh, you think so?"

She felt her cheeks turn warm. "Apparently that's not a news flash to you."

"Hardly, Doctor."

"May I ask you a question?" He shrugged with indifference. "What is it about me that rubs you the wrong way?"

He shifted in his chair. "Nothing."

"That's not true. You've disliked me from the get-go. Why?"

"Why don't you just tell me what's on your mind, Dr. Newton? What did you 'sort out' this afternoon?"

"The day of Lee Howell's funeral, I received a bouquet of roses. This was the enclosure card."

She opened her handbag and took out a plastic bag in which she'd placed the small white card. It was the second piece of evidence she had collected that day, although she tried not to think about having to pull the screwdriver from Wick's back.

Wesley took the bag from her, looked at the card, and read the single typed line, but his reaction wasn't what she had expected. In fact, he didn't react at all. His expression remained unchanged.

"Evidently this comes as no surprise to you, either."

"I didn't know it had accompanied a bouquet of roses sent to you the day of Howell's funeral."

"But you recognize the card, don't you? How could you? It's been..." She stopped, looked at him aghast. "You weren't content just to watch my house—you searched it. You did, didn't you?"

"Not me."

She sat back as though pushed by an invisible hand. "Wick."

Wesley said nothing.

Her head dropped forward. She stared at her hands, which no amount of cream or lotion could keep moisturized because of the antiseptic soap she scrubbed with.

Wick had been inside her house, rummaging through her drawers, going through her things. Before or after they'd met? she wondered. Although it didn't matter. Her privacy had been violated, and, worse, Wick had been the one who'd violated it.

After a brief but strained silence, she raised her head and looked at Wesley. "The card came from Lozada. He personally delivered the roses. He broke into my house and left them for me to find."

"How do you know?"

"He told me."

"Told you?"

"He's called me several times. I've asked him not to. I've insisted that he leave me alone. But he keeps calling."

"And says what?"

"Read the card, Detective. He developed a crush on me during his trial. He stared at me constantly, every moment he was in the courtroom. To the point where it became noticeable and embarrassing. Apparently he's now deluded himself into thinking that I reciprocate his romantic interest."

"Because of the verdict?"

"I suppose. Who knows why? He's crazy."

He harrumphed. "Lozada is a lot of things, but crazy isn't one of them." He watched her for a moment. "Why are you telling me all this now?"

"I'm afraid that he killed Dr. Howell. I think he learned that Lee was named chief of surgery over me, so he killed him as a favor for me. He told me he wanted to return the favor I did him."

"By acquitting him?"

"A twelve-person jury acquitted him."

His deep shrug said *If you say so.* "Go on."

"Lozada is the one who told me about your surveillance. He's been watching me too. He saw Wick follow me home yesterday afternoon. I guess Lozada followed him around the block to the stakeout house. Then he called me. He enjoyed telling me that my newfound friend is a cop."

"Wick would argue that."

"What do you mean?"

"Never mind. Why didn't you tell us about Lozada last night when you confronted us?"

"Because I didn't want you to think what you're thinking."

"Which is?"

"That I'm in cahoots with Lozada!" she exclaimed. "That is what you're thinking, isn't it? You think I contracted him to kill Lee. And now…now Wick. That's why you objected to my operating on him."

"You were angry at us. At Wick in particular."

"So you think I called this paid assassin, who just so happens to have a crush on me, and instructed him to stab Wick in the back with a screwdriver?"

Wesley stared at her impassively. He was a seasoned policeman with years of experience. Confessions came in all forms. No doubt he thought she was unburdening herself of guilt.

"If that's your allegation, it's too absurd even to deny," she said.

"Then what are you doing here?"

"After Wick spoke Lozada's name, everything became clear. I saw things as you've been seeing them. Lee gets a promotion I wanted. He gets killed. I told Wick I never wanted to see him again. An attempt is made on his life. When it crystallized in my mind, I came straight here, only stopping at home long enough to retrieve that card."

"Why did you save it?"

"I'm not sure. I destroyed the roses. Maybe I saved the card because I thought I might need...proof."

"Meaning that from the beginning you suspected Lozada of killing Howell."

"No. It wasn't until a few days after Lee's funeral, after I received the roses, that Lozada called me for the first time. He asked if I had enjoyed them. I didn't know until then who had sent them."

He gave her a retiring look. "Come now, Dr. Newton."

"I swear I didn't."

"You didn't have an inkling?"

"All right, possibly. Subconsciously. I knew of no one else who could or would have broken into my house."

"Yet when you learned it was Lozada, you still didn't contact me. Why not?"

"Because of the tone of the interrogation you conducted

in this room. I was afraid it would confirm your suspicions of my involvement."

"You had information that might have led to Lozada's arrest and you failed to come forward with it."

"Which was a mistake."

"Why didn't you come running to me waving that card and saying 'I think I know who murdered my friend and why'?"

"I could have been terribly wrong. I could have impeded your investigation, sent you down the wrong path."

"No, I don't think that's it, Dr. Newton. I think you hoped that we would solve the mystery of Dr. Howell's murder all by ourselves. Without your help. Isn't that right?" His eyes probed hers. "You didn't want your name attached to a man's violent death." After a meaningful pause, he added, "A second time."

"Ah." She lowered her head again, but only for an instant, then met his incisive gaze defiantly. "You know about Raymond Collier."

"Some. Want to tell me more about it?"

"You've got your resources, Detective, and I'm sure you'll put them to good use."

"You can count on it." He crossed his arms over his chest and tilted his head. "There is something that puzzles me. I'm wondering how you got seated on that jury. Didn't the lawyers question the prospective jurors, ask if there were any arrest records? Weren't you sworn to tell the truth?"

"Raymond Collier's death was a tragic accident. I don't have a police record. And during voir dire nobody asked if I had been involved in an accidental shooting when I was a minor."

"Well that was convenient, wasn't it?"

She stood up. "I can see you neither value nor want my help."

"On the contrary, Dr. Newton. It's been an enlightening conversation."

"Will you arrest Lozada now?"

"When I get my hands on enough evidence to back up an arrest and indictment."

"What do you mean *when*? This morning my hands were soaking in all the evidence you need. Wick's blood. And I've handed you the weapon."

"It'll be thoroughly analyzed by the lab, and as we speak detectives are hot on the trail of its origin, but I can tell you what they'll find. They'll find that it is decades old and that, when new, it could've been bought at any hardware store on the continent and probably beyond. Between then and now, God knows how many hands have come into contact with it. It won't be traced to anybody."

"The girl was shot. What about the gun?"

"Left at the scene and in our possession. But it'll be like the screwdriver. It's cheap and it's old and reliable only at close range. In this case, four to six inches. The user knew we couldn't trace it to him. We'll try, but it won't do any good."

"You know it was Lozada," she cried softly. "Wick can identify him."

"Can he? I don't question that Wick suspects him. He would be the number one suspect on anyone's list. He and Wick are bitter enemies."

Judging by Lozada's tone of voice whenever he spoke Wick's name, she had gathered as much. "What happened between them?"

"It's a police matter."

A matter he obviously chose not to divulge to her. "Can't you at least take Lozada into custody for questioning?"

He scoffed at that. "With no probable cause? He'd love that. It would virtually ensure he would never be tried. I'll only arrest him if Wick can positively identify him as his assailant. But I can almost promise you that Wick didn't see him.

"And just as I expected, that motel room is so chock-full of trace evidence it could belong to Lozada or to anyone else who's ever cleared the threshold of that room, me included. Anything we retrieve from there would never hold up in court.

"Even evidence we retrieved off the other victim, the girl, is no good to us. Dozens of people saw her having physical contact with several men in that bar, including Wick. We cleaned her fingernails and got only grit. There was nothing on her that she couldn't have picked up by casual contact."

"She was in the wrong place at the wrong time."

"Definitely, but that's not all. She had a connection to Lozada," Wesley said. "Her job was cleaning his penthouse and she bragged to her coworkers that they were intimate."

"Then what more proof do you need?"

"Oh, we've got lots of proof that she came into daily contact with Lozada's clothing, his bed linens, his carpet, his everything. That's more a liability than an advantage. All his defense lawyer would have to argue is that she could have picked up the evidence at any time, and he would be right. So much for our proof."

He gave her a wry look. "Why don't you tell me what kind of proof a jury would need to convict Lozada, Madam Forewoman?"

"What about blood on his clothing?"

"You know better than I do that all the significant bleeding was internal because he didn't withdraw the weapon. If Lozada got any on him, which is doubtful, by the time we got a search warrant he would have destroyed the clothing. There was blood from the victim's neck in the previous case. Was the prosecution able to produce it on any of Lozada's belongings?"

"No," she replied. "And his defense attorney made certain we jurors knew that." She was thoughtful for several seconds, then asked, "What about DNA? That would be virtually indisputable. What about semen? Saliva?"

He shook his head. "He would never be so careless. But even if he were, he and the girl could have been together earlier in the day, not necessarily in that motel room."

He didn't say whether they'd found Wick's DNA on the girl, and Rennie didn't ask. "It seems I've wasted your time."

She stood and pulled open the door, killing all chatter in the room beyond. Every head turned. She hesitated, but Wesley nudged her forward. "Before you go I'd like you to see something."

He directed her back to his desk, where he picked up a photograph. "The girl's name was Sally Horton. She was twenty-three."

She had to ask. "Had Wick known her long? Were they friends?"

"For about twenty minutes. The bartender saw her approach him and introduce herself. Wick left the bar with me. I'll have to ask him what happened after that. But whatever went down and regardless of the length of time she spent with Wick, Lozada disapproved." He passed her the photograph.

Rennie witnessed death on a routine basis. She had seen the havoc that disease or machine or a weapon could wreak on a human body. Often the damage defied belief and looked like something out of a gruesome horror movie made by a producer with a vivid and sick imagination.

She expected a photograph similar to the ones the jury had been shown during the trial. A bloated face, protruding tongue, bulging eyes. But Sally Horton appeared untouched except for two dark spots on her forehead.

Rennie returned the photograph to Wesley's desk. "If I had told you about Lozada earlier, he might have been in jail and she wouldn't have been killed. Is that why you showed me the picture?"

"That, yeah. But also to warn you."

"I already know that Lozada is dangerous."

"So is getting involved with Wick."

# Chapter 17

When Lozada first heard about it on TV news, he'd been furious.

How could Rennie have saved Wick Threadgill's life after he had gone to so much trouble and placed himself at such risk to rid her of him? Women! He would never understand them. Nothing you did for them was ever enough.

Whenever any cop was killed, it made news. Other cops rallied. The black armbands were brought out. Pictures of the widowed and the orphaned made the front page. The general public grieved as though they'd lost a friend. The fallen man was hailed a hero.

But to hear them tell it on TV this morning, Wick Threadgill could walk on water. The reports cited various crimes that Threadgill had solved, seemingly all by himself, Batman and Dick Tracy rolled into one. He had been all but drummed off the force, but that was downplayed.

Rennie was touted as the gifted surgeon who had worked valiantly to bring him back from the brink of death. She brought to the operating room at Tarrant General the trauma-treatment experience she had gained in war-torn countries while participating in international programs like Doctors Without Borders.

Lozada had been so upset by these blatantly biased news stories that he couldn't even enjoy playing with his scorpions. His worst enemy was receiving accolades. Rennie was working against him. He hadn't felt this frustrated since a paramedic had saved his baby brother after he'd shoved a ball down his throat.

It had been Christmas morning of his sixteenth year. His brother was thirteen but had the mind of a two-year-old. One of his gifts from Santa had been a foam baseball and a plastic bat. He was playing with them beneath the decorated tree. Their parents were in the kitchen checking on the Christmas ham.

Lozada had sat watching his brother for several minutes and decided that his world would be so much nicer without him in it. The idiot had thought it was a game when Lozada crammed the foam ball into his mouth. He hadn't uttered a sound. He put up no resistance whatsoever.

The life had almost gone out of his brother's trusting eyes when Lozada heard his parents returning from the kitchen. He started hollering for them to come quickly, that baby brother had put his new baseball in his mouth. Nine-one-one was called and the kid was spared. His parents had wept with relief, held the boy close all day, and said over and over again what a blessing he was.

It had been a rotten Christmas Day. Even the ham had burned.

Ironically, he could have saved himself the trouble of trying to kill his brother. A mere six months later, his parents had been flying the kid to Houston to consult with yet another witch doctor—didn't these people know when to quit?—when their commuter plane crashed into an East

Texas swamp during a thunderstorm. Everyone on board perished. How had he gotten so lucky?

But Lozada wouldn't leave Wick Threadgill to fate.

For one thing, he wouldn't deny himself the satisfaction of killing him. Already he'd had to sacrifice the leisurely planning of it. Only yesterday he had resolved to take his time and devise something special for Threadgill. But last night it had become clear that he must act without delay. He hated like hell having to accelerate his plans. You didn't drink a decanter of Louis XIII like a can of soda. He was being deprived of the savoring. But if it meant Threadgill would be dead sooner rather than later, he could accept that.

Although faced with a few tactical problems last night, he had planned quickly and acted swiftly. The would-be exotic dancer had been easy to entice. She had believed him without question when he told her he had a friend who liked threesomes—was she game? "If he's as cute as you, you bet!"

She had balked at taking her car instead of his, but she had consented quickly enough when he said, "On second thought, let's just forget about it."

He knew where Threadgill was staying. It was the rathole where the FWPD normally stashed paid trial witnesses, visiting law enforcement personnel, new recruits, and such. For verification all he'd had to do was call and ask to be connected to Wick Threadgill's room. He'd hung up while the phone was ringing, but he had confirmed Threadgill's lodging.

He had Sally park in a supermarket parking lot two blocks away from the motel, and they'd gone the rest of the way on foot. When she asked why, he told her he wanted to surprise his friend. She bought it.

Wick's pickup was parked outside Room 121. Lozada

scanned the parking lot to make certain no one else was about. Most of the rooms were dark. The few where lights were on had the drapes drawn.

He motioned the girl forward. "You go first. I want you to be the first thing he sees when he opens the door."

She knocked, but after waiting for several seconds, she pressed her ear to the door. "I think I hear the shower."

She'd been impressed when he opened the lock with his credit card. Signaling for her to be very quiet, he ushered her inside and told her to lie down on the bed. She obliged him and had been suppressing a fit of giggles when he shot her twice in the forehead. He considered cutting out her tongue as he had promised to do if she talked about him, but it would have been messy. Besides, the shower faucets were turned off.

In hindsight, he should have used the silenced pistol on Wick, too. One pop in the ear as he came out of the bathroom, another between the eyes to make sure. But where was the fun in that? He'd wanted Wick to realize that he was going to die.

On the other hand, the screwdriver was a good choice. He'd found it in an old toolbox in the rear storage room of his TV repair shop. Practical, rusty, antiquated, untraceable.

Another thing he might do differently: He would have made that jab fatal instead of recreational. Rather than making it instantaneous and stabbing Wick in the heart as he'd done Howell, he'd wanted to play with Threadgill. That turned out to be a bad call. He hadn't had time to finish the job, thanks to the motel maid. Who cleans rooms at 4:30 in the morning?

By the time she had dialed 911, he was back at the supermarket. He'd driven Sally's car to where they'd made the exchange. He had left the keys in it, retrieved his SUV, and parked it in the undesignated space of a garage, then walked to the hotel coffee shop for breakfast. He was having a last cup of coffee when the first reports of the murder appeared on the morning news shows.

All that work and nothing to show for it, he thought now. The bastard hadn't died. And Rennie had helped him survive. Why? Why had she saved him? She had been furious with him. She had told him she never wanted to see him again. She hated him.

Or did she?

He remained in his condo all day, too dispirited to go out. He called his ultra-private voicemail number and had a message that said a job was his for the asking. The contract was so important to the client that Lozada could name his own price. Ordinarily the prospect would have excited him, but even the promise of a lucrative job with a built-in bonus didn't lift him out of his doldrums.

He was superior to Wick Threadgill in every way. He had class. He doubted Threadgill could even spell it. He was a millionaire. Threadgill scraped by on a cop's salary. He wore designer clothes. Threadgill dressed like a saddle tramp. He wanted to place Rennie on a pedestal. Threadgill wanted to use her to get to him.

It simply didn't tabulate. How could she possibly prefer Threadgill to him?

He was still sulking when the early edition of the evening news came on. Nothing had happened that day to supplant the lead story of Sally Horton's murder and the near-fatal attack on Wick. After recapping the morning's events, the talking head said, "A press conference was held today at Tarrant General, where Dr. Rennie Newton answered the questions of reporters."

That segued into videotape of the press conference. Rennie was standing behind a podium and was flanked by two somber men in dark suits who were probably hospital administrators. She squinted against the glare of video lights as she acknowledged one of the eager reporters.

"Dr. Newton, what's Mr. Threadgill's current condition?"

"He's stable," she replied. "Which is encouraging. He was critical this morning. He had a penetration wound in his back that did a lot of damage to surrounding tissue."

*In the right hands, a Phillips screwdriver would do that to a person.* Lozada's lips curled into a smirk of gratification.

"Was the wound potentially fatal?"

"In my opinion, yes. Lifesaving measures were taken immediately. Our trauma team did an excellent job."

"Was this attack related to the unsolved murder of Mr. Threadgill's brother three years ago?"

"I don't know anything about that."

"Is Wick Threadgill still on leave from the police department?"

"That's a question for the police."

"Is he—"

She held up her hands for quiet. "I responded to an emergency call this morning. For a time, I didn't even know the patient's name. I don't know anything about Mr. Threadgill's career or his family history. I did my job. Beyond that, I can't tell you anything more."

The video ended there. The talking head returned with a brief summation and then moved on to the next story.

Lozada switched off the TV set but sat there and thought about Rennie's statement, "I did my job."

Of course! She hadn't saved Threadgill because she liked him. She had only been doing her job. He'd had nothing against most of the people he'd killed. He hadn't even known them, but that hadn't stopped him from doing what he was paid to do. Rennie had simply been going about her work with the same professional detachment he had when he went about his.

And wasn't she fantastic, the way she'd handled the media? Coolly professional, unfazed and unimpressed by the media exposure. She was extraordinary.

Oh, she was tired. He could tell that. He'd seen her looking better. But even disheveled and fatigued she was still beautiful and desirable. He wanted her. He would have her soon. Surely after this she would appreciate the depth of his devotion to her.

Suddenly he was ravenously hungry and felt like going out.

He poured himself a tequila and took it with him into the black marble shower. After showering and shaving his head and body, he let the water stream for another ten minutes. Following that thorough rinsing he disassembled the drain, cleaned every component of it with disposable wipes, then flushed them down the toilet.

He replaced the drain. He wiped the shower stall dry with a towel and placed it in a cloth bag. On his way out he would drop the bag into a chute that emptied into a bin in the building's basement. A laundry service collected the bags twice daily. He never left a used towel in his bathroom.

He finished his drink while dressing in a pair of hand-tailored linen slacks and a silk T-shirt. He liked the feel of the silk against his skin, liked the way it caressed his nipples, as soft and sensual as a woman's tongue. He hoped Rennie would like his tattoo.

He topped off the outfit with a contrasting sport coat. He was overdressing for the Mexican restaurant, but he felt like celebrating. He called down to the parking valet and asked that his Mercedes be brought from the garage.

Before leaving his condo he placed one more call.

The valet had the Mercedes waiting for him and was holding the driver's door open. "Have a good evening, Mr. Lozada."

"Thank you."

Knowing that he looked great and that the young man probably envied him, Lozada tipped him generously.

# Chapter 18

The instant she stepped off the elevator she saw the roses.

It would have been impossible for her to miss them. The bouquet had been placed on the ledge of the nurses' station. Nurses and aides had obviously been awaiting her arrival to see her reaction. All were wearing expectant smiles.

"They're for you, Dr. Newton."

"They were delivered about half an hour ago."

"You could barely see the delivery boy behind them. Aren't they gorgeous?"

"Who's your secret admirer?"

"He's not a cop." This from the policeman that Wesley had posted outside Wick's ICU. "No cop could afford them, that's for sure."

Rennie didn't give the bouquet another glance. "There must be some mistake. They're not for me."

"B-but there's a card," one of the nurses stammered. "It's got your name on it."

"Get rid of the roses and the card. The vase. All of it."

"You want us to throw them away?"

"Or distribute them among the patients. Take them to the lobby atrium, the chapel, put them on the dinner menu. I don't care. Just get them out of my sight. I need Mr. Threadgill's chart, please."

The group, no longer smiling, dispersed. The policeman slunk back to his post. One of the nurses carried away the heavy arrangement. Another passed Rennie the requested chart and bravely followed her into Wick's cubicle.

"He's been waking up for longer periods of time," the nurse told her. "He hates the spirometer." Patients were forced to blow into the machine periodically to keep their lungs clear.

His vitals were good. She checked the dressing covering his incision. He moaned in his sleep when she peeled the bandage off to take a look. After replacing the bandage, she asked the nurse if he'd had anything to drink.

"Just the ice chips."

"If he asks for something again, let him have sips of Sprite."

"Widschumburohn."

Rennie moved to the left side of the bed, the one he lay facing. "Come again?"

"Burohn. In the schpirte." Barely moving his head, he tried to locate her with his single eye. To make it easier on him, she sat on the edge of the chair beside the bed.

"Do bourbon and Sprite mix?"

"Don' care."

She smiled. "I think you're well medicated already."

"Not enough."

The nurse bustled out to get the Sprite. Wick readjusted his head so that his face wasn't half buried in the pillow. "Did you do this to me, Rennie?"

"Guilty."

"Then you're off"—he winced, sucked in his breath—"off my Christmas card list."

"If you can joke you must be feeling better."

"Like hammered shit."

"Well, that's what you look like."

"Ha-ha." His eye closed and it remained closed.

Rennie stood up and applied her stethoscope to several spots on his chest.

"Are you getting a beat?" he asked, which surprised her because she thought he had drifted off again.

"Loud and strong, Mr. Threadgill." She sat back down in the chair. "Your lungs sound clear, too, so keep blowing into the spirometer when the nurses ask you to."

"Sissy stuff."

"But pneumonia isn't."

"Rennie?"

"Yes?"

"Was I shot?"

"Stabbed."

He opened his eye again.

"With a screwdriver," she told him.

"Damage?"

"Considerable but reparable."

"Thanks."

"You're welcome."

"My balls hurt."

"I'll see that you get an ice pack for them."

It surprised her that a single eye could pack such malice into a dirty look.

"They're swollen," she explained. "Blood collects in the testicles after an injury like yours."

"But they're okay?"

"They're okay. This is a temporary condition."

"You swear?"

"Give them a few days. They'll return to normal."

"Good, good." He closed his eye. "Funny conversation."

"Not-so-funny pain, though. So I've been told."

"Rennie?" He reopened his eye. "Did they get him?"

She shook her head.

"Fuck."

Rennie remained where she was, seated beside the bed. Again she thought he had gone back to sleep when he mumbled, "My face. Hurts like hell. Wha'd he do to it?"

"Apparently he attacked you from behind."

"Right."

"You fell forward and landed hard on your cheek. Your chin was busted open, but it didn't require stitches. You're bruised and swollen, but no bones were broken."

"So I'll be as handsome as ever?"

"And as conceited, I'm sure."

He smiled but she could tell that any facial expression caused him discomfort.

The nurse returned with the soft drink in a foam cup and looked at Rennie strangely when she took it from her. Few surgeons ministered to patients this way. She pressed the bent straw against Wick's lips. He took several careful sips, then angled his head back slightly to signal that he was done.

"Is that it for now?" she asked.

"Don' wanna throw up."

Then he remained quiet and she was certain this time that he had gone back to sleep. Even after the nurse left the room, Rennie stayed. The next thing she knew, a soft voice was asking, "How's he doing?"

She looked up to find Grace Wesley standing just outside the door. Rennie hadn't heard her approach, hadn't noticed anything, hadn't been aware of the passage of time. How long had she been staring into Wick's battered face?

Quickly she came to her feet. "He's, uh, he's better, actually. Talking coherently when he wakes up. He had some sips of Sprite." She set the cup of soda on the rolling bed tray. It seemed incriminating somehow to be caught holding it. "He's sleeping now."

"Is it okay if I come in?"

"Of course."

"I don't want to disturb."

"I doubt you will. He's out of it."

Grace Wesley was attractive and slim. She wore her hair in a small chignon on the back of her head, a minimalist style that was flattering only to someone with her high cheekbones and delicate features. Her almond-shaped eyes bespoke intelligence and integrity. She had a quiet and gentle way about her. Earlier, Rennie had noticed that Grace's slightest touch had a calming effect on her brawny husband.

She moved to the foot of Wick's bed and for several moments watched him sleep. "It's hard for me to believe that's Wick," she said, smiling. "I've never seen him inert. He never even sits still for more than a few seconds at a time. The man's in constant motion."

"I've noticed that too." Grace turned and looked at her quizzically. "Of course, I don't know him well," Rennie was quick to qualify. "Not well at all. But I gather you do."

"Wick was a senior in high school when Oren, my husband..."

Rennie nodded.

"When Oren and Wick's brother Joe entered the police academy. We became good friends with Joe. He invited us to a high school basketball game 'to watch my kid brother play,' he said." She laughed softly. "Wick fouled out."

"He's an aggressive competitor?"

"And a hothead. Volatile, easily set off. But when he loses his temper he's usually just as quick to apologize."

They were quiet for a time, then Rennie said, "I didn't know about his brother until today when a reporter asked me about him."

"Joe died three years ago. None of us is over it. Especially Wick. He thought Joe could do no wrong and loved him very much."

The nurse came in to replace an IV bag. They suspended their conversation until they were once again alone. "I understand that Joe was..."

"Murdered," Grace said bluntly.

In one blinding instant of clarity, it connected. Rennie said, "Lozada."

"That's right. Lozada."

"How'd he get off?"

"He was never indicted."

"Why not?"

Grace hesitated, then took a step closer to Rennie and spoke more softly. "Dr. Newton, I asked my husband what was going on between the two of you this morning. I sensed the strong undercurrents."

"Two weeks ago I served on a jury that acquitted Lozada."

"Oren explained that."

"Your husband resents me for the outcome of that trial. Especially now. Lozada took one friend from him, and almost took another." She looked down at Wick. "If the jury had arrived at a different verdict, Wick wouldn't have been attacked and that young woman who was killed last night would be alive."

"May I ask you something?" Grace asked quietly. When Rennie turned back to her, she said, "If you could do it all over again, would you still vote to acquit Lozada?"

"Based on what I knew then, or on what I know now?"

"On what you knew then."

Rennie gave the question the same degree of consideration she had given that final and fateful vote. "Based strictly on what I knew then and the charge the judge gave us, I would be compelled to vote for acquittal again."

"Then your conscience should be clear, Dr. Newton. You can't be held responsible for Lozada's attack on Wick."

Ruefully she said, "Tell your husband that."

"I already did."

Rennie was taken aback. Grace smiled her gentle smile and reached out to press Rennie's hand. "I'll go now. But when Wick wakes up please tell him that I was here."

"I'll be going soon too, but I'll leave word with the nurses to be sure and tell him."

"Do you know when he'll be moved to a regular room?"

"In a day or two, if he continues to do well. I'm watching him closely for any sign of infection."

"What can I tell my girls?"

"You have daughters?"

"Two. Very lively ones."

"How nice for you."

"They begged to come with me tonight, but Oren didn't want them to leave the house."

Rennie didn't need to ask why. Wesley feared for their safety, feared Lozada might not be satisfied with an attempt on Wick's life. He had posted policemen at various places throughout the hospital, and now she noticed two more on the other side of the glass wall of Wick's ICU. No doubt they were Grace Wesley's bodyguards.

"My girls adore their Uncle Wick," she was saying. "If there were a poster of him, it would be on the wall of their room along with their other heartthrobs."

"Tell them their Uncle Wick is going to be all right."

"We have you to thank for that. The girls are dying to meet you."

"Me?"

"I told them all about you. Afterward, I overheard them

talking together. They've now decided to become surgeons. They want to save people as you saved Wick."

Rennie was so touched she didn't know what to say. Grace must have sensed that. She let her off with a quick good-bye. The two policemen flanked her as they walked to the elevator.

There was no trace of the roses when Rennie returned to the nurses' station. Inside the circular enclosure sat several desks, computer terminals, monitoring machines, file cabinets, and general clutter. She didn't know where to begin looking for what she needed, and apparently she looked at a loss.

"Can I help you find something, Dr. Newton?"

"Uh, yes."

Several drawers were searched before a tin of medicated lip balm was located. Rennie took it with her into Wick's ICU. He was still sleeping, breathing evenly. She sat down in the chair at his bedside, but it was at least a full minute before she uncapped the small tin and released a pleasant aroma that hinted of vanilla.

She had noticed earlier that Wick's lips were dry and cracked. This wasn't an unusual side effect of surgery and loss of fluids. In fact it was quite common. But Wick's lips had looked *exceptionally* dry. She had thought an application of lip balm might help. What was wrong with that?

Who was she arguing with?

She rubbed the surface of the salve with the pad of her index finger, making several tight circles in it, until the friction and her own body heat warmed and softened it. She dabbed the salve on his lower lip, then the upper one, barely making contact, touching him so gingerly it hardly counted as touching.

When both lips had been dotted with the fragrant salve, she withdrew her hand. Hesitated. Then she touched his lower lip again, except this time she didn't break contact. Slowly, she spread the balm from one corner of his mouth to the other, then back again. She did the same with the upper lip, following the masculine contour, staying within the shape of it with the painstaking care of a child who would be scolded if she colored outside the lines.

And just as she was about to retract her hand again, he woke up. The eye contact was electric.

Neither said anything. They remained perfectly still, with her index finger resting on the seam of his lips. Rennie held her breath, realizing that his deep and even breathing had also ceased. She strongly felt that if either one of them moved, something would happen. Something momentous. Exactly what, she didn't know. In any case, she didn't dare move. She wasn't certain she could. His blue gaze had an immobilizing effect on her.

They remained frozen in that tableau for... how long? Later she couldn't remember. It lasted until Wick's left eye closed against his pillow. She actually heard his eyelashes brush against the pillowcase. She didn't resume breathing until after he had.

Then she pulled back her hand, clumsily recapped the tin of lip balm, and left it on the bed tray. She didn't look at him again before leaving the ICU. "Call me if there's any change," she instructed brusquely as she returned his chart to the nurses' station.

At the elevator, the policeman on guard held open the door and addressed her shyly. "Dr. Newton, I just wanted to say... well, Wick's a great guy. A few years back, one of my kids got hurt. Wick was first in line to donate blood. Anyhow, I wanted to tell you thanks for pulling him through this morning."

Rennie attributed the tear to exhaustion. She hadn't realized how tired she was until the elevator began its descent.

She leaned against the rear wall of it and closed her eyes. That was when she felt the tear roll down her cheek. She wiped it away before reaching the ground floor.

As she moved through the hospital exit, another policeman surprised her by following her out. "Is something wrong?"

"Wesley's orders, ma'am. Doctor," he said, correcting himself.

"Why?"

"I didn't ask, and he didn't say. I figure it's something to do with Threadgill."

The officer walked her to her car, checked the backseat, looked beneath it. "Drive safely, Dr. Newton."

"Thank you, I will." He continued watching her until she had gone through the gate.

She had driven several blocks before she noticed the cassette. It was protruding from the audio player in the dashboard. She stared at it, mystified. She never played cassettes, always CDs.

At the next stoplight, she pulled it out to check the label. There was none. She could see the tiny spools of audiotape through clear plastic. Dismissing the sense of foreboding that came over her, she inserted the cassette and punched the arrow indicator for Play.

Strains of piano music filled the car, along with the husky tones of a female torch singer.

"I've got a crush..."

Rennie struck the controls with her fist, banging it against them repeatedly until the music stopped. She was trembling, primarily with anger, but also with fear. Having policemen posted around the hospital hadn't deterred Lozada from placing this tape in her car. How the hell had he managed it? Her car had been locked.

She groped inside her leather satchel in search of her cell

phone, but all she succeeded in doing was dumping the contents of her satchel onto the floor. She reasoned that by the time she stopped and found her phone she could be home. She would call Wesley from there.

She sped through two red lights after glancing right and left to check for oncoming traffic. She wheeled into her driveway at an imprudent speed. The garage door took an eternity to open. It had barely cleared the roof of her car when she drove under it. She used the transistor to reverse it, and it began to close behind her before she even cut her car's engine.

Leaving her spilled possessions on the floor, she clambered out and hit her back door at a dead run. She burst into her kitchen, then drew up short.

Flickering light shone through the connecting door to the living room. No light source in her living room produced that kind of light. So what was going on? Until she knew, the sensible thing to do would be to back out the door, reopen the garage, and run down the center of the street, waving her arms and yelling for help.

But she wasn't going to run screaming from her own house. To hell with that!

She left the back door standing open. She took a butcher knife from a drawer. Then she crossed the kitchen and entered the living room. Candles, hundreds, it seemed, but probably closer to dozens, flickered in clear-glass containers of every shape and size. They had been placed on every available surface, filling the air with a heady floral fragrance and making the room appear ablaze.

On her coffee table was another bouquet of red roses. And from the CD player, music in stereo. Another version. Another artist. But the same classic Gershwin tune. Lozada's theme song.

She was breathing hard through her mouth, and she

could hear the pounding of her heart above the music. She took a cautious step backward, rethinking the advisability of handling this herself. Maybe she should escape through the kitchen door after all.

She calculated the time it would take to get help. Back through the kitchen. Out the door. Punch the garage door switch on the wall. Duck beneath the door. Down the driveway and into the street. Or through the hedge to Mr. Williams's house. Calling for help. Involving other people. Involving the police.

No.

She walked to the sound system and turned off the music. "Come out and face me, why don't you?"

The shouted words echoed back to her. She listened closely, but it was difficult to distinguish any sound except those of her own harsh breathing and hammering heartbeat.

She moved toward the hallway, but paused at the end of it. It stretched before her, dark and ominous, seemingly much longer than it actually was. And because he had made her afraid in her own sanctuary she became even angrier. Anger propelled her forward.

She moved quickly down the hall and reached for the light switch in her home office. The room was empty, with nowhere to hide. She pulled open the closet door. Nothing in there but her stored luggage and travel gear. Again, there was nowhere for a grown man to hide.

From there she went into her bedroom, where more candles flickered. They cast wavering shadows on the walls and ceiling, against the window blinds that, because of him, she now kept closed at all hours of the day and night. She looked under the bed. She went to the closet and opened the door with a flourish. She thrashed through the hanging clothes.

The bathroom was also empty, but her shower curtain,

which she always kept open, was drawn. Too angry now to be afraid, she shoved it aside. Another arrangement of roses rested on the wire shelf spanning her tub.

She swung at the vase and sent it crashing into the porcelain tub. The racket was as loud as an explosion.

"You bastard! Why won't you leave me alone?"

She marched back into the bedroom and went around blowing out the candles until she feared the smoke would set off the alarm. She retraced her steps through the living room but left the candles burning for now. In the kitchen she closed the back door and locked it, returned the knife to the drawer.

She found a half-full bottle of Chardonnay in the fridge, poured most of it into a glass, then took a long drink. Closing her eyes, she pressed the cold glass against her forehead.

She debated whether to call Wesley. What would be the point? She couldn't prove that Lozada had broken into her home any more than Wesley could prove that he had murdered Sally Horton and attempted to kill Wick.

On the other hand, if she didn't report this and Wesley somehow found out about it...Right. Much as she dreaded doing it, he should be notified.

She raised her head, opened her eyes, and saw her reflection in the window above the sink. Standing behind her was Lozada.

She'd only *thought* she was too angry to be afraid.

# Chapter 19

He took her by the shoulders and turned her around to face him. His eyes were so dark the pupils were indistinguishable from the irises.

"You seem upset. I wanted to please you, Rennie, not upset you." His voice was soft. Like a lover's.

Her mind was racing down twin tracks of terror and fury. She wanted to lash out at him for disrupting her systematized life. Equally as much she wanted to cower in fear. But either reaction signaled weakness, which she didn't dare let him see. He was a predator who would sense his prey's weakness and take full advantage of it.

He took the wineglass from her and pressed the cup of it against her lips. "Drink."

She tried to turn her head aside, but he gripped her jaw with his other hand and held it in place while he tipped the glass. She felt the wine cold against her lips. The glass clinked against her teeth. Wine filled her mouth. She swallowed, but not all of it. Some dribbled over her chin. As he wiped it away with his thumb, he smiled at her.

Rennie had seen that kind of smile all over the world. It was an abuser's smile for the abused. It was the smile of a cruel husband for the wife he had beaten beyond recognition. The enemy warrior's smile for the girl he had raped. The father's smile for the virgin daughter he'd had castrated.

It was a possessive and condescending smile. It announced that the abused one's free will had been taken away, and that, through some perverse reasoning, she should be happy about it, even grateful for her abuser's tolerance.

That was Lozada's smile for her.

He tipped the wineglass toward her lips again, but she couldn't endure that smile any longer and swatted the glass away. The wine sloshed over his hand. His eyes narrowed dangerously. He raised his hand, and she thought he was about to strike her.

But instead he lifted his hand to his mouth and licked off the wine with obscenely suggestive strokes of his tongue.

His evil smile turned into a soft laugh. "No wonder you didn't want it, Rennie. It's cheap. A terrible vintage. One of my first projects will be to introduce you to really fine wines."

He reached around her to set the glass of wine on the counter. His body pressed against hers and held. His nearness smothered her. She couldn't breathe and she didn't want to. She didn't want his cologne to be recorded in her olfactory memory bank.

She willed herself not to push him away. A flashback to the photo of Sally Horton enabled her to remain still and endure the pressure of his body. Lozada probably wanted her to struggle. He would welcome an excuse to assert himself as the dominator. Abusers thrived on reasons to justify their cruelty.

"You're trembling, Rennie. Are you afraid of me?" He leaned even closer. His breath ghosted across her neck.

He was erect and rubbed himself against her suggestively. "Why would you be afraid of me when I want only to make you happy? Hmm?"

Finally he moved back and, with an air of amusement, took a long look at her, from the top of her head to her shoes and back up. "Maybe before we tackle wine education we should start with something more basic. Like your wardrobe." Placing his fingers on her collarbones, he stroked them lightly. "It's a sin to hide this figure."

His eyes lowered to her breasts and lingered there, and somehow that was worse than if he had actually touched them. "You should wear clothes that hug your body, Rennie. And the color black to offset your pale hair. I'll buy you something black and very sexy, something that shows off your breasts. Yes, definitely. Men will want to fondle you, but I'll be the only one who will."

Then his eyes returned to her face and his tone became teasing. "Of course you're not looking your best today. You've been working very hard." His fingertip traced the dark crescents beneath her eyes. "You're exhausted. Poor dear."

She swallowed the gorge that had filled her throat when he described his fantasy. "I am not your dear."

"Ah, the lady speaks. I was beginning to wonder if you'd lost the capacity."

"I want you to leave."

"But I just got here."

That was a lie, of course. It had taken him at least an hour to place all the lighted candles in her living room. Where had he been hiding when she searched the house?

As though reading her mind, he said, "I never give away trade secrets, Rennie. You should know that about me." He pinched her chin playfully. "We do, however, have a lot to talk about."

"You're right. We do."

Pleased, he smiled. "You go first."

"Lee Howell."

"Who?"

"You killed him, didn't you? You did it as a favor to me. And the attack on Wick Threadgill. That was you too, wasn't it?"

He moved like quicksilver. He raised her blouse with one hand and ran his hand over her breasts and around the inside of the waistband of her skirt. She shoved against his chest with all her strength. "Get your hands off me." She slapped at his searching hands.

"Stop that!" He grabbed her hands and pulled them hard against his chest. "Rennie, Rennie, stop fighting me." His voice was gentle; his grip wasn't. "Shh, shh. Relax."

She glared up at him.

In a deceptively soft and reasonable voice, he apologized. "I'm sorry I had to do that. A few years ago the police used an undercover policewoman to try and trap me. I had to make sure you weren't wearing a wire. Forgive me for getting a little rough. How's this? Better now?"

He let go of her hands and squeezed her shoulders, his strong fingers flexing and relaxing rhythmically, massaging her like an attentive husband who'd just learned that his wife had had a long and tiring day.

"I'm not working for the police."

"I would be terribly disappointed in you if you were." His hands squeezed a little harder. His expression turned malevolent. "Why is it you've been spending time with Wick Threadgill?"

She made a face of dislike. "I didn't know he was a cop. He deceived me to use me."

"So why did you work so hard to save his life?"

Wesley's words of warning came back to her. Sally Horton had been an innocent pawn in the blood rivalry between Wick and Lozada. She had died for the role she had unwittingly played. "That's what they pay me for," she said flippantly. "I don't always get to choose my patient. In this case, fate chose me. I drew the short straw. I couldn't let him bleed out there in the emergency room."

His eyes searched hers. He curved his hand around her throat. His thumb found her carotid and stroked it. "I would be very unhappy if you were to cheat on me with Wick Threadgill."

"There's nothing between us."

"Has he ever kissed you?"

"No."

"Touched you like this?" He caressed her breast.

Her throat was too tight to speak. She shook her head.

"That cop has never been this hard for you, Rennie," he whispered, pressing himself against her. "He never could be this hard for you."

"Hands in the air, Lozada!"

Oren Wesley barged in, followed by two other officers, service pistols drawn and aimed. The three fanned out into a semicircle around them.

"Hands up, I said! Now, move away from her!"

Rennie was dumbfounded. But as Lozada complied with the order his face became a placid mask. Within seconds he'd been transformed into an identical replica of himself, the kind of perfect effigy that would appear in a wax museum. He revealed no anger, surprise, or concern. "Detective Wesley, I didn't know you stayed up this late."

"Assume the position."

Shrugging negligently, Lozada leaned forward upon the kitchen table. His hands were splayed near a basket of fruit where the bananas were getting too ripe. It was a bizarre thought to register when a would-be rapist and reputed killer was being patted down in her kitchen, but Rennie found it a welcome distraction.

The policeman who had the honors retrieved a small handgun from Lozada's pants pocket. "It's registered," Lozada said.

"Handcuff him," Wesley instructed. "He'll have a knife in an ankle holster." While one of the policemen was dragging Lozada's hands to the small of his back for cuffing, the other knelt and raised his trousers leg. He slid a small, shiny knife from the sheath. Lozada's expression never changed.

Wesley looked across at her. "You all right?"

Still too astonished to speak, she nodded.

One of the policemen was reading Lozada his Miranda rights, but he was looking at Wesley over the cop's head. "What am I being arrested for?"

"Murder."

"Interesting. And who was the alleged victim?"

"Sally Horton."

"The chambermaid in my building?"

"Save the innocent act for the jury," Wesley said, giving Rennie a glance. "You also stabbed Wick Threadgill in attempted murder."

"This is a farce."

"Well, we'll see what turns up in our investigation, won't we? In the meantime, you'll be a guest of the county."

"I'll be out by morning."

"As I said, we'll see." Wesley motioned with his head for the other pair of policemen to escort him out.

Lozada smiled back at Rennie. "Good-bye, love. See you very soon. I'm sorry about this interruption. Detective Wesley loves to grandstand. It's compensation for other deficiencies." As he drew even with Wesley, he said, "I think your dick was buried with Joe Threadgill."

One of the policemen shoved him hard in the back. They

disappeared through the door into the living room. Rennie sagged against the counter.

"Thank you."

"Don't mention it."

"You said you wouldn't arrest him until you had solid evidence. Does that mean—"

"All this means is that I wore my sergeant down. He agreed to me bringing Lozada in while we're running our traps. If we get real lucky—and luck seems to be in short supply when we're trying to nail Lozada—something incriminating will turn up."

"I take it nothing has so far."

He gave a noncommittal shrug. "We can't hold him indefinitely without arraigning him, but we'll drag it out for as long as possible. Unless we can collect some hard evidence to support Wick's allegation, it would amount to a pissing contest in court. If the DA would even take it to court."

"He would have to, wouldn't he? If Wick identified Lozada as his attacker?"

"The DA's office might be reluctant to take only Wick's word for it to the grand jury. They would factor in the history between Wick and Lozada, which sorely reduces Wick's credibility. Besides, they're not too fond of him over there."

"The DA's office? How come?"

A cop poked his head though the door and spoke to Wesley. "He's on his way to lockup."

"I'm right behind you."

The policeman withdrew. Rennie followed Wesley into her living room, where the candles still burned. Their scent was cloying. She went to one of her front windows and opened it so the room could air out. Several patrol cars were pulling away from the curb in front of her house, strobes flashing.

Pajama-clad neighbors had congregated on the sidewalk and were talking among themselves. Mr. Williams was in the middle of them, holding center stage and gesturing theatrically.

"How did you know Lozada was here, Detective? Are you still watching my house?"

"No. We got a call. Your neighbor. A Mr. Williams. Said something weird was going on."

God, this was a nightmare.

Wesley stood in the center of the room, taking a slow look around. The roses didn't escape his notice. When he finally came back around to Rennie, he said, "I talked to a hospital board member today. He said you had accepted the position vacated by Dr. Howell."

Her chin went up a notch. "I gave them my decision this afternoon. After my meeting with you. I didn't see that accepting made any difference. You were going to continue believing that I hired Lozada to kill Lee whether I took it or not."

He gestured toward the roses. "Congratulations."

"This wasn't a celebration, if that's what you're thinking. All this was here when I arrived home from the hospital. He broke in again."

"You didn't call to report it."

"I didn't have a chance."

He looked down at her rumpled clothing. "He was terrorizing me," she exclaimed. "He has this... this mad notion that I'm going to become his lady love." She told him everything that Lozada had said to her, even the most embarrassing parts. "He manhandled me. He thought I might be wearing a wire."

"A wire?"

"When I mentioned Lee Howell's murder, he searched me. He was afraid I was working for you to try to trap him."

"Well, we both know how wrong that is."

Disliking his snide tone, she said, "Detective, I did not invite him here. Why would you automatically assume that I had?"

"Did you break something?"

"In the bathroom. He'd left another of those bouquets in my bathtub. I was so angry I knocked it over."

"Mr. Williams was in his backyard waiting for his dog to do his business. He heard the crash and tried to call you, see if you were okay." Wesley spied the cordless telephone on the end table.

Rennie picked it up, then held it out toward Wesley. There was no dial tone. It had been disconnected for so long that the obnoxious beeping alert had played itself out.

"I guess he didn't want to be disturbed," she said quietly.

"I guess not."

She returned the telephone to its usual place on the table, then drew her hand back quickly. "Should I have touched that?"

"He doesn't have fingerprints. Anyhow, it doesn't matter. We already know that Lozada was here, and this isn't a crime scene."

"Since when did breaking and entering stop being a crime? He came in and made himself at home."

"Yeah. Mr. Williams told the 911 dispatcher that he looked right at home. After reporting the disturbance, he said, 'Wait, never mind, I can see her and a man through the kitchen window. It appears that nothing's wrong, that she knows him very well.' Something like that. However, this dispatcher was on the ball. She recognized your name and address, knew I—"

"Had been spying on me."

"So she called me. Said she'd just had a curious

911 from your neighbor. You and a man were getting it on in the kitchen."

"Hardly how I would describe it. I was afraid if I resisted I would wind up like Sally Horton."

"You might have."

"Then why do you always put me on the defensive?"

He only looked at her before turning away. "I need to be on my way."

As he headed for the door she rushed after him, grabbed his arm, and brought him around. "I deserve an answer, Detective."

"Fine. Here's my answer," he said tightly. "You haven't given me any reason to trust you, Doctor, but you've given me a lot of reasons not to."

"What would convince you I'm telling the truth? Would you have been convinced if Lozada had killed me tonight?"

"Not really," he returned with a blasé shrug. "Before Sally Horton became his victim, she was his lover."

# Chapter 20

He wants only to make her happy."

"Are you kidding?"

"Stop looking at me like that, Wick," Oren complained. "*I* didn't say it. *She* said *he* said it."

Wick had stayed in ICU for two days. For the past five, he'd been in a private room that afforded a view of the downtown skyline. He was able to lie on his back now. It still hurt like hell, especially when he was forced to get up and walk around, which was at least twice a day.

Each of those hikes, as he called them, was an ordeal equivalent to climbing Everest. It took him five minutes just to get out of bed. At first he was able only to shuffle around his room, but earlier today he had managed to make it to the end of the hall and back, which the nursing staff claimed was a major breakthrough. Big woo. They commended his progress. He cursed and asked them where they stored their Nazi uniforms. When he returned to bed, he was sweating and feeling as helpless as a newborn.

He looked forward to the pain medication that was regularly dispensed. It didn't eliminate the pain but made it tolerable. He could live with it if he didn't think about it too much and focused on something else. Like Lozada.

This morning he'd been taken off the IV. He'd been glad to get rid of it, but then the nurses had begun bullying him to take in lots of fluids. They brought him fruit juice in little plastic cups with foil lids. He hadn't succeeded in opening one yet without spilling half of it.

"Are you eating?" Oren asked.

"Some. A little. I'm not hungry. Besides, you wouldn't believe the crap they try to pass off as food."

His cheek was still the color of an eggplant going bad, but the swelling had gone down enough for him to see out of both eyes. For instance, he could see that Oren's eyebrow was in its critical-arch position. "What?" he asked grouchily.

"How're your privates?"

"Fine thanks, how're yours?" For several uncomfortable days he had straddled an ice pack, but, as Rennie had promised, his balls had returned to their normal size.

"You know what I mean," Oren said.

"They're okay. Wanna check 'em out?"

"I'll take your word for it." Oren shifted his weight from one foot to the other. "I haven't had a chance to tell you. I'm sorry about your chin."

"Least of my problems."

"Yeah, but I shouldn't have hit you."

"I struck first."

"Stupid of both of us. I apologize."

"Noted and accepted. Now get back to what you were saying about Lozada and his fixation on Rennie."

"I've told you already," Oren complained.

"Tell me again."

"Jesus, you're cranky. They haven't taken the catheter out yet, have they?"

"This afternoon. If I can pee they'll leave it out."

"What if you can't?"

"I can. I will. If I have to squeeze it out, I'll pee. No way are they putting that thing back in while I'm conscious. I'd jump out the window first."

"You're such a crybaby."

"Are you going to tell me or what?"

"I've told you. I've repeated it word for word several times. The neighbor said they looked cozy with each other. Dr. Newton says that Lozada was terrorizing her, that she was afraid to fight him off for fear that he would do to her what he'd done to Sally Horton."

Wick sank back into his pillow and closed his eyes. The reminder of what had happened to that girl was painful. He would never forget seeing her lying dead. While he'd been enjoying a shower, she had been killed in cold blood.

Leaving his eyes closed, he said, "She makes sense, Oren. Lozada's a threat to her. Especially if he thinks it comes down to a choice between him and me, and she's favoring me."

"I don't suppose she's talked to you about it."

"No. If you hadn't told me what went down the other night, I wouldn't even know about it."

He couldn't figure Rennie's attitude, and that was the primary reason he was so grumpy. Yeah, he hurt. Yeah, the food was lousy. Yeah, he was ready to be peeing on his own. Yeah, he didn't like walking around bare-assed and feeble.

But what really had him bothered was Rennie's aloofness. She came in every morning and every evening, usually with her head down, her eyes on his chart rather than on him. "How are you, Mr. Threadgill?" Always the same ho-hum inflection.

She gave his incision a cursory inspection, asked how he was feeling, and nodded absently to whatever answer he gave her, like she wasn't really listening and didn't really give a damn. She told him that she was pleased with his progress, then smiled mechanically and left. He realized that he wasn't her one and only patient. He didn't really expect preferential treatment.

Well, maybe he did. A little.

He'd been heavily medicated when he was in the ICU, but he remembered her sitting near his bedside and giving him sips of Sprite. He remembered her applying the lip balm. He remembered the way they had looked at each other and how long that look had lasted and how significant it had seemed.

Or had any of that actually happened?

Maybe he'd been so drugged out he'd been hallucinating. Had it been a pleasant dream he'd mistaken for reality? Possibly. Because that was, after all, the night Oren had caught her and Lozada in a "cozy" clinch in her kitchen.

Damned if he knew what was going on with her.

"When she's on her rounds she's all business," he told Oren. "We haven't even talked about the weather."

"It's hot and dry."

"Looks it."

"She took that chief of surgery position."

"I heard," Wick said. "Good for her. She's earned it." Oren continued to look at him meaningfully. "That doesn't signify anything, Oren."

"I didn't say it did."

"You didn't have to."

A nurse came in with another container of juice. "I'll drink it later," he told her. "I promise." She didn't look convinced, but she set it on the bed tray and left. He offered the juice to Oren.

"No thanks."

"Cranberry apple."

"I'm fine."

"You sure? Forgive me for saying so, but you don't look too healthy yourself." Oren had arrived looking wilted not only from the summertime heat, but ragged out in spirit as well. "What's up?"

Oren shrugged, sighed, glanced out the window at the hazy view before coming back to Wick. "The DA called about an hour ago. The big cheese himself. Not an assistant."

Wick had guessed that Oren's glumness had something to do with their case against Lozada. If he'd had good news to impart, he would have imparted it before now.

Discomfort made getting bad news worse. He adjusted himself to a more comfortable position that favored his sore right side. "Let's hear it."

"He says that what we've got on Lozada is weak. Not enough to take to the grand jury. In any case, he refused to."

Wick had guessed as much. "He came to see me yesterday. A pillar of goodwill and good cheer right down to his Italian loafers. Brought those." He gestured at a tacky bouquet of red, white, and artificially blue carnations.

"He went all out."

"I gave him a full account of what happened the night I was stabbed. Told him that as sure as I was still breathing, it was Lozada."

"How'd he react?"

"Let's see, he tugged at his turkey wattle, scratched his temple, rubbed his gut, frowned, expelled his breath through his pursed lips, and winced several times. He looked like a guy who had gas and was trying to figure out a polite way to fart. He told me that I was making some serious allegations. 'Well, no shit,' says I. 'Murder and attempted murder are pretty fucking serious.' He had trouble looking me in the eye as he left. He didn't come right out and say it—"

"He's not a politician for nothing."

"But I gathered from all his seeming distress that he had problems with my story."

"He did."

"Such as?"

"I won't bore you with the details," Oren said. "God knows he bored me with them. For about thirty minutes he stammered and stuttered, and did that bellows bit with his cheeks, but basically..."

"No soap."

Oren fiddled with the tricolored satin ribbon tied around the ugly carnations. He glanced at Wick askance. "You gotta look at it from his standpoint, Wick."

"The hell I do! Until he has to have six units of blood, until his nuts swell to the size of bowling balls and he's got a tube shoved up his dick, don't talk to me about his standpoint."

"I know you're gonna be pissed when I say this—"

"So don't."

"When it comes right down to it, he's right."

"If I could slug you right now, I would."

"I knew you'd get pissed." Oren sighed. "Look, Wick, the DA plays it safe, yes, but—"

"He's a pussy!"

"Maybe, but he's justified this time. When you boil it down, we've got nothing hard on Lozada."

"Lozada," Wick sneered. "He's got everybody running scared, doesn't he? You think he's not laughing his ass off at us?"

Oren gave him several seconds to cool off before continuing. "Everything in our hopper is circumstantial. Lozada knows you. He knew Sally Horton. That's a link, but it doesn't provide motivation. If, by some weird fluke, the grand jury did indict him, we could never make a case out of that. I was given three days to come up with something. Same as always, he didn't leave a trace. I've got nothing."

"Except my word on it."

Oren looked pained. "The DA factored in your background with Lozada. He hasn't forgotten what happened. That reduces your credibility."

Arguing a point so blatantly valid would be futile.

Oren sat down on the green vinyl armchair and stared at the floor. "I've got no choice but to release him. It wasn't easy, but I got search warrants. We've tossed his place. Nothing. Clean as a freaking whistle. Even his scorpions look sanitary. His car, same thing. Not a trace of blood, fibers, anything. We've got the weapons, but they could belong to anybody. No eyewitnesses except you, and you've been discredited. Besides, by your own account, you didn't actually see him."

"I was too busy leaking blood into my gut."

"His lawyer is already making a hell of a racket about police harassment. He says—"

"I don't want to hear what he says. I don't want to hear a goddamn word about that son of a bitch's civil rights being violated, okay?"

A long silence ensued. After a time, Oren glanced toward the corner near the ceiling. "TV work all right?"

Wick had muted the sound when Oren came in. The picture was little more than colored snow, but images could be detected if you looked hard enough. "Sucks. No cable."

They stared at the silent program for several moments before Oren asked if it was a good show.

"Those two are mother and daughter," Wick explained. "The daughter slept with the mother's husband."

"Her father?"

"No, about her fourth stepfather. Her real father is the father. The parish priest. But nobody knows that except her mother and the priest. He hears his daughter's confession about boinking her mother's husband and freaks out. He blames the mother for being a bad influence, calls her a slut. But he's guilt-ridden because he hasn't been there for his daughter. As a father—I mean as a dad. He's been her priest since he christened her. It's sorta complicated. He went to her house, for christsake." Wick's last statement didn't relate to the soap opera, but Oren knew that.

"I can't rule out the possibility that she invited him there, Wick."

He didn't even honor that with a comeback. He let his hard stare say it all.

"I said it's only a possibility." Averting his head, Oren muttered something else that Wick didn't catch.

"What was that?"

"Nothing."

"What?"

"Nothing."

"*What?*"

"He was feeling her tit. Okay?"

He wished he hadn't asked, but he had. He'd pressured Oren into telling him, and Oren had, and now he was gauging Wick's reaction. He kept his expression as passive as possible. "She was afraid to fight him off."

"That's what Grace said too, but neither of you was there."

"Grace?"

"Oh, yeah." Oren gestured expansively. "My wife has become Dr. Newton's number one fan."

"I knew they had met. All Grace said to me was that she was glad I was in such capable hands."

"I get slightly more than that at home. I get an earful about how I'm judging the doctor too harshly and unfairly. Grace thinks I'm holding a grudge because she served on that jury."

For the first time since Oren walked into his room, Wick came close to smiling. He liked to think of Grace giving his partner an earful. If there was anyone on earth Oren would listen to, it was his wife, whom he not only loved but also respected for her insight. "Grace is a smart lady."

"Yeah, well, she didn't see the romantic setting that I did. She hasn't seen this, either."

From the breast pocket of his sport jacket, Oren withdrew several sheets of paper that had been folded together lengthwise. He laid them on the bed tray next to the untouched juice. Wick made no move to pick up the sheets.

"In all the excitement of recent days you might have forgotten that Dr. Newton fatally shot a man when she was sixteen."

"It didn't escape your memory, though, did it?"

"Don't you think it needs to be checked out before we submit her name for sainthood? I contacted Dalton PD, along with the county sheriff's office. It's all in there."

Wick resented the incriminating sheets on the bed tray and was reluctant to read them. "Why don't you summarize it for me."

"Ugly. Very ugly," Oren said. "Daddy walked in seconds after the two shots were fired. Raymond Collier was dead. Died instantly. T. Dan asserted that his big bad business partner had tried to seduce his sweet baby girl. She shot him to protect her virtue. Clear-cut self-defense."

"It could've gone down that way."

"It could've, but unlikely. Especially since she'd been going down on Collier."

"Oh, good segue, Detective."

Oren ignored the remark. "A good question for her would be why she chose to protect her virtue on that particular day."

"Did anyone ask her?"

"I don't know. I doubt it. Because here's where it gets really interesting. No one was formally questioned. There was no hearing, no inquest, no nothing. T. Dan had deep pockets. Apparently he threw enough money around to bury the thing quicker than it took for Collier's body to get cold. His death was ruled an accident...at the scene. Case closed. Everybody went home happy, including Collier's widow. She left Dalton for her new, completely furnished condo in Breckenridge, Colorado. She made the trip in her shiny new Jag."

Wick thought it through, then said, "You talk about reduced credibility. I don't believe any of it."

"Why not?"

"The police department and sheriff's office admitted to sweeping a fatal shooting under the rug?"

"No. Their reports were brief, but official. There was no evidence to support anything other than an accident. But I tracked down the former cop who was first on the scene."

"Former?"

"He left law enforcement to install satellite dishes. But he remembered driving out to the Newtons' house that day in response to the summons. He said it was the weirdest thing."

"What?"

"Their behavior. Whether it was accidental or intentional, if you'd just shot somebody stone-dead, wouldn't you be upset? A little rattled? Shed a few tears? Show some remorse? At the very least do a little nervous hand-wringing?

"He said Rennie Newton sat there cool as a cucumber. Those big green eyes of hers stayed dry. And she's sixteen, remember? Kids that age are usually excitable. He said she never faltered as she talked him through what had happened.

"T. Dan and Mrs. Newton sat on either side of her. T. Dan lambasted Collier for attempting to rape his daughter. Just went to show, he said, how you never really knew someone as well as you thought you did. The mother cried softly into a hanky. She had heard nothing, seen nothing, knew nothing, and would the officers care for something to drink. The ex-cop said it was downright spooky, like being in an episode of *The Twilight Zone.*"

Wick tried to imagine a sixteen-year-old Rennie giving a calm account of killing a man, even accidentally. He couldn't. He couldn't imagine the incorrigible teen Crystal had described either, or the nymphet who had enticed a married man. Nothing he had heard about her past life coincided with her present one.

Oren said, "I'd better be shoving off. Let you catch a nap. Can I get you anything before I go?"

Wick shook his head.

"I don't mind going down to the magazine shop and—"

"No thanks."

"Okay then. I'll come back with Grace tonight. Sometime after supper. Think you're up to a visit from the girls?"

"Sure, that'd be great."

"They've been bugging us to bring them to see you. I promise we won't stay long."

Wick forced a smile. "I'll look forward to it."

Oren nodded and headed for the door, but he paused with his hand on the handle. "No bullshit now, Wick. Fair enough?"

"Fair enough."

"Man to man, not partner to partner."

Wick frowned with impatience. "What is it?"

"You've got it bad for her, don't you?"

Wick turned his head toward the window and the familiar view. "I don't know."

Oren swore softly.

"Just go, why don't you?" Wick said. Suddenly he was very weary. "You've said what you came to say."

"Almost. I have a couple more things to say."

"Lucky me."

"Rennie Newton saved your life. No two ways about it. And I'll always be grateful to her for that."

Wick turned back to him. "What's the 'but'?"

"That ex-cop in Dalton? He said he couldn't believe that anybody could take a life, even the life of a bitter enemy, and be so emotionally detached from the act. She was so cold, he said, it still gives him chills to think about it."

# Chapter 21

Wick glared at the man with the white lab coat and white smile who breezed into his hospital room like he owned the place. "Who're you?"

"I'm Dr. Sugarman. How are you feeling this evening, Mr. Threadgill?"

"Where's Dr. Newton?"

"I'm making her rounds tonight."

"How come?"

"I understand the catheter came out today. How was that?"

"Oh, it was great. I hope I get to do it again tomorrow."

The doctor flashed another white smile. "Everything okay now?"

"I could out-pee you. Where's my regular doctor?"

"I'm a regular doctor."

*And a comedian too,* Wick thought sourly.

Dr. Sugarman nodded his approval over whatever he read on Wick's chart, then closed the cover. "I'm glad I'm finally getting to meet the hospital's celebrity patient. Saw you on TV. You had it rough there for a while, but you're making excellent progress."

"Glad to hear it. When can I get out of here?"

"Anxious to be leaving us?"

What kind of sappy question was that? Wick could have throttled him. He didn't like him or his big white smile. And where was Rennie? Why wasn't she making her rounds? She deserved a night off like everyone else, but why hadn't she mentioned to him that she wouldn't be here tonight? Did she not want him to know?

*Lozada is released from jail and Rennie takes the night off.* It was an unpleasant thought and he hated himself for thinking it.

His dark expression must have conveyed to Dr. Sugarman that he should practice his bedside manner on a more agreeable and appreciative patient. His Colgate smile faltered. "Dr. Newton will make the final decision on your release, but it shouldn't be more than a couple more days. Barring any unforeseen complications." The doctor shook hands with him and left.

"What a turkey," Wick muttered.

The Wesleys arrived. As promised, Oren limited the visit to fifteen minutes, but there was no limit to the girls' energy and exuberance.

They brought him chocolate-chip cookies that they had baked themselves and weren't satisfied until he ate two. Grace had arrived with a shopping bag. "Pajamas. I don't know if they'll let you wear them yet, but you'll have them just in case. I got slippers, too."

He grabbed her hand and kissed the back of it. "Marry me?"

Her daughters squealed with laughter and had to be admonished to settle down. They chattered nonstop, and they were wonderful, but they wore him out. He was ashamed for being relieved when they gave him hugs and said their good-byes.

Oren didn't talk business until after his family had

moved into the hallway, out of earshot. He told Wick that Lozada was again free. "Sarge wouldn't authorize surveillance on him. And after tonight he's pulling the guards from the hospital."

"You're putting me on alert."

Oren nodded solemnly. "Watch your back. After tonight you won't be protected by the FWPD."

That was fine and dandy with Wick. He didn't want police protection, because in exchange for it he would have to give up his freedom. After hearing the DA's decision today, he had concluded that the authorities were no contest for Lozada. Jurisprudence was carried out within moral boundaries, and Lozada operated under no such restraints.

If Wick wanted Lozada he would have to go after him alone. To level the playing field, he must go after him ruthlessly, with a mind-set like Lozada's. He couldn't do that if he were constantly monitored and guarded.

He asked about his pickup truck.

Oren's brow lowered suspiciously. "What about it?"

"I'd like to know where it is."

"Why?"

"Because it's my truck," Wick replied testily.

Reluctantly, Oren told him that it was at his house. "I took the liberty of checking you out of the motel. Once the CSU guys were finished with your room, I packed up everything and took it outta there."

Wick wanted to ask specifically about his pistol, but didn't. No sense in giving Oren more to worry about. "Thanks. I wasn't looking forward to going back into that room."

"I figured. All your stuff's locked up in your truck. It's parked in my driveway."

"Keys?"

"I've got them and your wallet in a safe place inside the house."

Safe from whom? Wick wondered. Safe from him? Again he didn't ask. "Thanks, partner." Oren didn't return Wick's guileless smile, probably guessing that it was disingenuous.

After that, Wick impatiently endured the long, boring evening hours. Eventually the traffic in the corridor outside his room subsided. Dinner trays were collected and placed on trolleys that were shuttled back to the kitchen. Doctors completed their rounds and left for home. Visitors departed. Personnel went through a shift change. The hospital settled down for the night.

At eleven o'clock a nurse came in to give him a pain pill. "You want your blinds drawn?"

"Please. Sun comes in through there in the morning."

As she moved to the window, he remarked offhandedly, "Too bad about Dr. Newton."

The nurse laughed. "Too bad? I wish I could take vacation at the drop of a hat."

"Vacation? Oh, I thought Dr. Sugarman said she was under the weather."

"No, she's taking some vacation days, that's all."

He twirled his finger near his temple. "This medication makes me goofy."

"It can do that."

"When will Dr. Newton be coming back?"

"She didn't clear her schedule with me," the nurse said around a wide grin. "But don't worry. Dr. Sugarman is a sweetheart."

While she fiddled with the blinds, Wick pretended to swallow the pill. He set the empty drinking cup on his bed tray and she rolled it away.

Readjusting his head on the pillow, he yawned. "Nighty-night."

"Good night, Mr. Threadgill. Rest well."

* * *

Darkness had fallen by the time Lozada let himself into his condo. He was pleased to see that his instructions had been carried out. His home was as quiet and serene as a church.

Upon hearing from his lawyer that it had been searched, he had known what to expect. He'd had residences searched before, as early as high school when narcs came into his house one night with a search warrant, hoping to find drugs. They had succeeded only in looking like fools and terrorizing his parents and idiot brother. Since then, he'd had other houses searched with the same storm-trooper enthusiasm.

So he had made arrangements from his jail cell through his lawyer for a cleaning service to put his condo back together, then to sanitize it against police contamination. He had also arranged to have it swept for electronic surveillance devices.

"It's clean," his lawyer had reported as they celebrated his release over drinks at the City Club. "In every sense of the word."

The attorney never inquired as to Lozada's guilt or innocence. Lozada paid him an exorbitant annual retainer, which enabled him to represent Lozada exclusively and play a lot of golf. He could also afford to live the lifestyle of a rich playboy. Lozada's culpability was last on his list of priorities.

"But it's clean only for the time being," he warned. "Be careful who goes in and out of your place from now on."

Lozada didn't need to be cautioned about that. Already he had notified the building's concierge that he would no longer be availing himself of the housekeeping services it provided. He had hired his own housekeeper, who came highly recommended by one of his former—and very satisfied—clients. He was assured that the young man brought excellent skills to the position and could be trusted implicitly.

Nor would he entertain women at home—except for Rennie, of course. He had used that stupid girl, that Sally Horton, because she was convenient, a careless indulgence, as it turned out. He would go out for sex until he had Rennie here with him.

He had been making such good progress with her until Wesley had come charging in, gun drawn like the main character in a silly detective show. What a laugh. Hadn't he realized how ridiculous he looked?

Rennie hadn't been amused. She had seemed mortified to have a group of clumsy cops invading her home, spoiling the surprise he had staged for her. No, she hadn't looked at all happy about the unannounced arrival of Wesley and company.

After spending a half hour of quality time with his scorpions, he took a long shower to wash away all remnants of jail. He shaved carefully, since he hadn't trusted his skin to the dull razor the county provided, then went through the ritual of cleaning out the drain and disposing of the towels.

He enjoyed a couple of tequilas and ate the dinner he ordered from his favorite restaurant. Delivery service wasn't extended to any other patrons, but it was included in Lozada's VIP treatment.

Over a nightcap, he dialed Rennie's number. Eventually her voicemail answered. "This is Dr. Newton. Please leave your name and number. If this is an emergency—"

He hung up. He wanted to see her urgently, but she might not think his desire qualified as an emergency. As he sipped his drink, he tried twice more to reach her, at the hospital and at home, with no success.

Ah well, he thought, tomorrow was soon enough. He would invite her to dinner. It would be their first official date. He smiled at the thought of walking into a fine restaurant with her. He would take her to Dallas. Someplace very upscale, elite. He would buy a sexy black dress for her tomorrow and surprise her with it. He would help her dress, from the skin out, so that everything would be perfect and to his liking. She would be gorgeous, breathtaking. He would wear his new suit. They would turn heads. Everyone would see what Lozada had done for himself.

After spending three nights on a cot with an odorous mattress, he looked forward to sleeping in his own wide bed. Naked, he slid between the silky sheets and luxuriated in their cool caress against his hairless skin. He fell asleep rubbing himself, thinking of the stirring sound Rennie had made when she felt the strength of his erection.

He slept like a baby until he was awakened by the insistent ringing of his doorbell.

* * *

Sneaking out of the hospital was much easier than Wick would have thought.

The hardest part was getting into the new pajamas Grace had brought him. By the time he got the damn things on, he was damp with perspiration and so weak he was trembling. He resisted the temptation to lie down and rest for a few minutes, afraid that if he did he wouldn't get up again.

The nurses were too busy performing clerical duties at the central desk to notice when he crept from his room. During his walk down the hall earlier, he had noted the location of the fire exit. Fortunately, it wasn't too far from his room. He made it into the stairwell undetected. Gripping the metal railing every step of the way, he walked down four flights. His knees were rubbery by the time he reached the ground floor.

No one accosted him. The cops posted as guards would have easily recognized him, but he slipped past them unseen. One was flirting with the nurses at the emergency-room admitting desk and the other was napping in his chair.

So much for security.

The nearest commercial area was two blocks from the hospital. He started walking but hadn't gone far when he realized that the two blocks might just as well have been the distance of a marathon. It was as difficult for him to cover that distance as it would have been for him to go twenty-six miles. He was wobbly and faint, and his back throbbed in protest of each step, but he pushed on.

When he entered the 7-Eleven, the turbaned man working the counter regarded him with unconcealed fright.

"I know I look ridiculous," Wick said quickly. "Can you believe it? The wife's pregnant. Got a craving for a Butterfinger fifteen minutes after I fell asleep. So I'm driving here in my PJs to get her a damned Butterfinger—I mean, hell, we have Snickers in the pantry, but, no, it *had* to be a Butterfinger. Anyhow, I ran out of gas up there on the freeway about fifty yards from the exit ramp. Had to walk down, and it's hotter than hell outside even at this time of night." Sweat had stuck the pajama jacket to his chest. He pulled it away from his skin and fanned himself. "Can I please use your Yellow Pages? I need to call a taxi."

Possibly the only words of the whole monologue that the foreign gentleman understood were "Yellow Pages." He slid a well-worn copy across the counter along with a soiled and sticky telephone.

After placing his call, Wick sat down to wait on a folding fishing stool and passed the time by perusing the wide selection of body-builder magazines. Only one other customer came in. He bought a pack of cigarettes and left without giving Wick a second glance.

When the taxi pulled into the parking lot, Wick said, "Much obliged," and waved good-bye. He didn't know who was more relieved to see the taxi: him or the nervous cashier. He left without a Butterfinger.

Luckily, the Wesleys' house was dark. What Oren didn't know was that he kept a spare key in a magnetized box on the underside of his pickup's fender. He retrieved it, although getting up and down was an effort that caused him to gasp in pain. Several times he was forced to pause for fear of passing out.

He unlocked his truck and rummaged through the pockets of his packed clothing in search of money. Finally he scrounged up enough to cover his cab fare. The series of delays hadn't set too well with the driver, who peeled away with an angry spate of obscenities and an even angrier squeal of tires.

Wick waited in the shadow of the house to see if the noise had awakened Oren. He gave it a full five minutes, but no one came out to investigate. Wick got into his truck and turned the ignition key. The engine growled to life. He got the hell out of there.

He drove to the empty parking lot of an elementary school, where he exchanged the pajamas for street clothes and the slippers for a pair of athletic shoes. He was constantly on the lookout for Oren's car, or a police patrol unit, but apparently he had made good his escape.

From the elementary school he drove straight to Rennie's house and parked at the curb. The front porch light was on, but the house was dark. "Too bad." She was about to be awakened. He eased himself from the cab of his truck with all the agility of an octogenarian invalid.

At her door, he leaned heavily on the bell, and, when that got no response, he banged the brass knocker. He waited thirty seconds before pressing his ear to the door and listening through the wood. Nothing but silence. "Dammit!"

But if he were in Rennie's situation, would he be answering the front door in the middle of the night?

He moved toward the garage and studied the horizontally sectioned door. Having followed Rennie home last Sunday, he knew she had an automatic opener. He tested the handle anyway. Without the programmed transmitter, the door was secure.

He slipped around the corner of the house—hoping that an insomniac neighbor didn't mistake him for a thief—and moved along the side of the garage toward the rear of the house. His exploration was rewarded. There was a door into the garage from the backyard. Miracle of miracles, it had a window.

Cupping his hands around his eyes, he peered inside. It was dark, but he knew that had her car been inside he would've been able to see it. The garage was empty. She wasn't at home.

Trembling with fatigue, he retraced his steps to his truck. The task of climbing inside seemed insurmountable, but he managed it—barely. His skin was clammy, and he feared he might toss his cookies. Literally. Stephanie and Laura's homemade chocolate chips. The headrest was tempting. He hurt too bad to sleep, but if he could just close his eyes and rest for a few minutes...

No, he had to move and keep moving until he found Rennie.

Second on his list of places to look: Trinity Tower.

* * *

Lozada's face was a mask of cold fury when he opened the door to his condo.

"I'm sorry to disturb you, Mr. Lozada, but I have an urgent message for you." The concierge extended to him a sealed envelope with the building's discreet logo embossed in gold in the upper-left corner.

Lozada had been having a delicious dream about Rennie. The first peal of his doorbell had jolted him awake. A handgun was weighting down the pocket of his robe. Shooting the messenger became a literal temptation.

He snatched the envelope from the man. "What kind of message? Who's it from?"

"He didn't give me his name, sir. I asked, but he said you would know him."

Lozada ripped open the envelope, removed a stiff note card, and read the so-called message. There was no question who had written the succinct poem.

"He was here?"

"Only a few minutes ago, Mr. Lozada. He left after writing that and asking that I hand-deliver it to you immediately. The man didn't look at all well. When he first came in, I thought he was intoxicated. He was certainly confused."

"In what way?"

"Initially he said he had a message for your guest."

"Guest?"

"That's what I said, Mr. Lozada. I told him that to my knowledge you had come in alone this evening and that no visitors had been announced except for the food delivery. I checked the log book to be sure."

Threadgill had played this moron like a fiddle.

"I offered to ring you, but he said no, then asked to borrow the stationery and a pen."

"All right, you've delivered the message." Lozada was about to close the door when the concierge raised his hand.

"One more thing, Mr. Lozada." He coughed lightly behind his fist. "You'll receive an official notice in writing, but I suppose this is as good a time as any to tell you."

"Tell me what?"

"I've been appointed to advise you that the building's homeowners' association convened earlier today and voted unanimously that you . . . that they . . ."

"What?"

"They want you out of the building, sir. In light of recent allegations, they're demanding that you vacate within thirty days."

Lozada wasn't about to demean himself by arguing with this nobody. "You can tell the other homeowners to go fuck themselves. I own this penthouse and will live here for as long as I fucking well please."

He slammed the door in the man's face. Striding angrily to the built-in slate bar, he poured himself a straight shot of tequila. He didn't know which had made him madder and insulted him more: being asked to move out of the prestigious address or Wick Threadgill's juvenile dare:

*The roses were red;*
*My blood, too.*
*Come get me, asshole.*
*I'm waiting for you.*

# Chapter 22

When Rennie arrived at her ranch, the first thing she did was saddle Beade and go for a long, galloping ride. Following that, she spent two hours in the barn grooming the horses. They didn't need grooming, but it was therapeutic for her.

Earlier in the day, Oren Wesley had made a courtesy call informing her of Lozada's imminent release from jail.

"You're releasing him?"

"I have no choice." He explained the district attorney's decision. "I warned you that the charge might not stick. Wick claims it was Lozada, but without hard evidence—"

"What about his breaking into my house?"

"There was no sign of forced entry, Dr. Newton."

"But he broke in," she insisted.

"If you wish, you could come down and file a complaint."

"What good would it do?"

What had become clear to her was that she couldn't rely on the judicial system to take care of Lozada for her. The problem was hers and she must solve it. But how?

Then there was the matter of Wick. She was still angry with Wick the cop, who deserved her scorn. But Wick the man was her patient who deserved the best medical care she could provide. How was she to reconcile the two?

Out of respect for Dr. Howell, the board had set a date two weeks hence for her formal assumption of the chief of surgery position. She wanted to move into that job with a clear slate, with her life in perfect order, free of problems. She needed time away to think things through and plot a course of action.

Her last-minute decision to take a few days off had required some deft maneuvering by her able office staff, but they juggled the schedule so that her patients were only moderately inconvenienced. Dr. Sugarman returned the favor she had done him a few months ago by agreeing to oversee the care of her post-op patients who were still in the hospital, Wick among them.

She had packed in a hurry and made good time driving. The horseback ride had provided a temporary reprieve from her troubling thoughts. Toby Robbins arrived shortly after she returned to the house. "You didn't have to come right away, Toby," she told him as soon as she answered the door. Earlier she had called him to report a loose board on the corral gate.

"I feel bad about overlooking it."

"It's no big deal. It'll keep."

"I'd just as soon get it fixed now. Unless this is a bad time for you."

"Now is fine."

He looked beyond her at the pieces of luggage still standing on her living room floor. "Staying for a while this time?"

"A few days. Let me show you that loose board." They went down the front steps together. On the way to the corral he retrieved a metal toolbox from the bed of his pickup truck. "How's Corinne?"

"Fine. She's giving the devotional at the church ladies' luncheon next Thursday. She's got butterflies."

"I'm sure she'll do fine."

He nodded, glanced at Rennie, then said, "We read about you in the paper this week."

"Don't believe everything you read, Toby."

"It was all good this time."

*This time.* She didn't know if the qualifier had been intentional. The old rancher remembered newspaper stories about her that hadn't been so flattering, the ones about the fatal shooting of Raymond Collier.

Before inheriting his ranch from his parents, Toby had lived in Dalton and occasionally had done odd jobs for T. Dan. When he took over the ranch, it had a modest herd of beef cattle, but, with careful management, he had increased it and prospered when other ranchers had succumbed to drought or economic recessions of one origin or another.

Through the years, he had stayed in touch with Rennie. He knew she was interested in having a weekend getaway, a place where she could keep horses, so he had notified her when the ranch neighboring his went on the market. She saw it only once before signing a contract for the asking price.

Toby no longer needed the additional income that came from doing odd jobs for her. She supposed he worked for her because he was a good neighbor, a nice man, or simply because he liked her.

Or maybe he was kind to her because he had known T. Dan so well.

"Here. See?" She showed him the gate, wiggling the loose slat, then stepping aside so he could get to it. He inspected it, then hunkered down and took a hammer from his toolbox. He used the forked end to pry the rusty nails out of the loose holes.

"That guy, the one whose life you saved..."

"Wick Threadgill."

"Wasn't he the fella I met out here?"

"That's right."

"What do you think of him?"

"I don't."

She had answered too quickly and defensively. Toby squinted up at her from beneath the brim of his hat.

"Uh, listen, Toby, if you'll excuse me, I think I'll go back inside and start putting things away. Come say good-bye before you leave."

"Will do."

She was busy in the kitchen an hour later when he approached the back door and knocked. "Come on in."

He stepped inside and removed his hat. "Some of the other boards had loose nails, too. I replaced them all. Solid as a rock now."

"Thank you. How about something cold to drink?"

"No, thanks. I best get going so Corinne won't have to hold supper for me. Next week sometime I could come over and give that gate a coat of fresh paint."

"That would be nice. Want me to buy the paint?"

"I'll bring it with me. Same white okay?"

"Perfect."

"Are you going to be okay here, Rennie?"

"Why wouldn't I be?"

"No reason."

He had his reasons, all right. She could tell by the way he nervously threaded the brim of his hat through his fingers and stared at the toes of his scuffed work boots.

"What's on your mind, Toby?"

Raising his head, he gave her a direct look. "You've been

mixed up lately with some pretty raunchy characters. If you don't mind my saying so."

"I don't mind. I agree. I think raunchy would be a mild adjective for Lozada."

"Wasn't talking about just him. That Threadgill was kicked off the police force, you know."

"He took a leave of absence."

Toby's shrug said *Same thing*. "Well, anyhow, me and Corinne have been worried about you."

"Needlessly, Toby, I assure you. I haven't been mixing with these people voluntarily. My path crossed with Lozada's by happenstance. My association with Mr. Threadgill is purely professional. His profession as well as mine. That's all."

His expression was skeptical.

"I've been protecting myself for a long time, Toby," she added softly. "Since I was sixteen."

He nodded, looking embarrassed for having resurrected bad memories. "It's just sort of a habit, you know, for me and Corinne to look out for you."

"And I can't tell you how much your concern means to me. Has always meant to me."

"Well," he said, replacing his hat, "I'm off. If you need anything give us a holler."

"I will. Thanks again for repairing the gate."

"Take care, Rennie."

She sipped a glass of wine as she cooked herself a meal of pasta and marinara. As she ate, she watched the sun sink into the western horizon. Afterward she carried her bags upstairs to unpack. Here in the country she wasn't persnickety. She tossed undies into drawers without folding them. She hung clothes in the closet willy-nilly, in no particular order. Out here she yielded to a rebellious streak—against her structured self.

These tasks completed, she went from room to room looking for something to do. Now that she had the desired free time, she didn't know how to fill it. TV had nothing interesting to offer. She wasn't inspired to watch a movie from her library of DVDs. She tried to read a new biography, but found the subject dull and the writing pretentious. She wandered into the kitchen, looking more for something to occupy her than for something to eat. Nothing looked appetizing, but because she was there she opened a box of cookies and nibbled on one.

A benefit of being in the country, far removed from city lights, was the panoply of stars. She ventured outside to gaze at the nighttime sky. She located the familiar constellations, then spotted a satellite and tracked its arc until she could no longer see it.

She crossed her yard and entered the corral through the gate Toby had repaired. Although she knew his intentions had been good, and that his concern was sincere, his caution had left her feeling restless and even a little jittery as she went into the dark barn.

Usually the familiar smells of hay and horseflesh comforted her. T. Dan had put her astride a pony about the time she had learned to walk. Ever since, horses had played an important role in her life. She had never experienced any fear of them and loved being in their environment.

Tonight, however, the cavernous barn seemed ominous. The shadows were abnormally dark and impenetrable. As she moved from stall to stall, the horses nickered and stamped skittishly. They had been groomed and fed. They were dry. There was no approaching storm. She spoke to them in a low and soothing voice, but it sounded counterfeit to her own ears and must have conveyed to them her own disquiet. Like her, they were unsettled for no apparent reason.

Rather than being comforted by the animals, they increased her uneasiness because they seemed to share it. Upon returning to the house, she did something she had never done before. She locked all the doors and windows, then double-checked to make certain she hadn't overlooked any. Upstairs, she showered, but she realized she was rushing through it.

She, who had waded through snake- and croc-infested African rivers, was now afraid to shower in her own tub? Annoyed with herself for buying into the spookiness, she turned out the light with a decisive *click* and got into bed.

She slept lightly, as though expecting the noises that eventually awakened her.

* * *

"What the . . . ?"

Wick gripped the steering wheel of his pickup. He acknowledged that his mind was sluggish from exhaustion. There were probably a few grains of pain medication still swimming around in his bloodstream, gumming up his thought processes. He was a little slow on the uptake, but it sure seemed to him that the steering wheel had frozen up in his hands.

For several seconds he was stumped. Then he looked at the gas gauge.

"Son of a bitch!"

He was out of gas. In the middle of frigging nowhere. In the freaking wee hours of the morning. He was out of gas.

It had never occurred to him to check the gauge before leaving Fort Worth. Once he'd left Trinity Tower reasonably certain that Rennie wasn't shacked up in the penthouse with Lozada, once he'd left the concierge with the envelope and a ten-dollar bill guaranteeing its speedy delivery, he'd wanted only to get clear of the city before Oren saw that his driveway was minus one pickup truck or a nurse discovered that the hospital bed was shy one patient.

During the drive he'd had a hell of a time keeping his eyes open. Usually he was an aggressive driver who cursed slowpokes. He thought radar traps were a violation of the Constitution. But tonight he had stayed in the outside lane, yielding the faster lanes to long-haul truckers and motorists who hadn't experienced a life-threatening assault barely a week ago.

It was a broad assumption that Rennie had gone to her ranch. She could be on her way to anywhere in the world, but if she was taking only a few days of vacation, the ranch would be his first guess, so that was where he was headed.

He didn't know exactly what he was going to say to her when he got there, but he would figure it out as he went along. Nor could he predict what her reaction would be to his unannounced arrival. She had saved his hide on the operating table, but she might still be inclined to flay it off him for his lying and spying.

Whatever, he would deal with it. The important thing was that he was almost there.

Or so he'd thought until he ran out of gas.

He twisted the wheel as hard as his diminished strength would let him and steered the truck onto the narrow shoulder. He let it roll to a complete stop. Without the air conditioner it was already getting uncomfortably warm in the cab. He rolled down the window for ventilation, but that only let in more hot air.

The interstate was at least eight miles behind him. He estimated he still had a good ten miles to go before he reached the cutoff to Rennie's place. If he could run, he could cover that much distance in an hour, say an hour and ten minutes max. But he couldn't run. He could barely walk. Hobbling, it would take him hours to go that far, if he didn't collapse first, which he surely would.

He supposed he could use his cell phone to call a service station on the interstate. But service stations on the interstate usually didn't provide roadside assistance, much less deliver gasoline. Getting a wrecker here would take forever. Besides, he had no money or credit cards because Oren had his wallet in a safe place inside his house. The road wasn't going to be well traveled until daybreak, and that was still a few hours away. Basically, he was stuck.

As soon as the sun came up, he could start walking to Rennie's ranch and hope that a Good Samaritan would come along and give him a lift. It was too dark to see his reflection in the rearview mirror, but if he looked anywhere near as bad as he felt, he looked like someone in dire need of mercy.

He could use the hours until dawn to rest. With that blessed thought in mind, he leaned back against the headrest and closed his eyes. But it didn't take long for him to realize that, until he got horizontal, his back was going to continue throbbing so badly he wouldn't even be able to doze. He cursed himself for choosing bucket seats over a bench seat.

Wearily he unlatched his door. Pushing it open required all his strength. He took several deep breaths before stepping out, unsure that his legs would support him. They did, but they were shaky. Leaning heavily against the side of the truck, he made his way to the rear of it and lowered the tailgate, which seemed to weigh a million pounds.

Besides being a heavy bastard, it was as hard as a slab of concrete. *Try getting comfortable on that,* he thought. "Shit." If he didn't lie down he was going to fall down.

He looked at his surroundings. Not a light to be seen in any direction. Across the road and beyond a barbed-wire fence was a cluster of trees. Ground was softer than metal, right? Definitely. And ground beneath trees might be softer than open ground because it would retain more moisture, right? Hell if he knew, but it sounded good.

Before leaving his truck he retrieved his duffel bag, another heavy bastard, and dragged it along behind him as he trudged across the road. He lay down on the ground and scooted beneath the bottom strand of barbed wire. He could never have bent double and stepped through it.

The darkness had been deceptive. The grove was farther away than it had appeared. The silence was total except for his own labored breathing, but if breaking a sweat were noise-producing, he would've been making a terrible racket. He was drenched. And he was afraid that the blackness advancing from his peripheral vision had nothing to do with it being nighttime.

When he finally reached the trees, he dropped the duffel bag against the trunk of one and sank to his knees beside it. Then he went down on all fours and hung his head between his shoulders. Sweat dripped off his nose, off his earlobes. He didn't care, he didn't care if he melted, he didn't care about anything except getting prone. He lay down in the dry grass. It pricked him through his shirt, but he could live with that as long as he could close his eyes.

He turned his cheek into the stiff canvas duffel and imagined that it was a woman's breast. Cool and soft and fragrant with good-smelling talc. Gold leaf and hydrangea maybe.

* * *

He was sleeping dreamlessly. Only something really startling could have pulled him out of a sleep that deep. Something *really* startling, like, "Move and you're a dead man."

He moved anyway, of course. First he opened his eyes, then he rolled onto his back to orient himself and locate the source of the warning.

Rennie was standing about twenty yards from him holding a rifle to her shoulder, looking into the scope. He sat bolt upright.

"I told you not to move."

Then she fired.

# Chapter 23

The bobcat fell dead from the tree.

It missed falling on Wick only by a couple of feet. Its hard landing sent up puffs of dust. There was a bloody hole in the center of its chest. Inside Wick's, his heart was thundering.

He swallowed with difficulty. "Nice shot."

Rennie came and knelt beside the carcass. "He was so pretty." Except for the lethal incisors, the animal did indeed look like an overgrown house cat with a beautiful pelt. Rennie stroked the soft tuft of white fur at the base of its ear. "I hated to shoot him, but he looked about to pounce. For months he's been killing lambs and pets. This morning he got into my stable."

"I didn't know he'd prey on something as large as a horse."

"He wouldn't. He was probably looking for something small, like mice, or a rabbit. But he spooked the horses and got as scared as they were, wound up scratching one. I heard the ruckus and reached the barn in time to see him scamper out. For the past hour I've been tracking him."

"And he tracked me."

For the first time, she looked across at him. "You were easy prey."

"The walking wounded."

"The nearly dead. What the hell are you doing here, Wick?"

"Sleeping. Or was." He nodded toward the rifle propped on her knee. "Do you ever miss?"

"Never. Are you going to answer me?"

"What am I doing here? It's a long story. But the punch line is that my truck ran out of gas. I hope you're not afoot."

She stood up and gave a shrill whistle. He was impressed. He'd never known a woman who could whistle worth a damn. But that wasn't the extent of her talents. A few seconds later, a mare trotted toward the grove.

"Wow, just like in the movies," he said. The horse stopped a cautious distance away from the dead bobcat and stamped nervously. "I'm not sure I can get on her without a saddle."

"You're not getting on her at all. I am." Rennie turned and started walking away toward the horse.

"You're going to abandon me here? With this animal carcass?"

"I didn't invite you."

Poetry in motion. That's what it was to see her sink her fingers into the mare's thick mane and pull herself up far enough to throw her right leg over. She accomplished this in one fluid motion, without dropping the twenty-two. She nudged the horse with her heels and the mare danced a dainty circle, head and tail held high.

"You're coming back for me, right?" He thought he saw Rennie smile, but the sun wasn't fully up yet, so he might have imagined it. With a movement of her knees that was almost undetectable, she nudged the mare into a gallop.

So sure was he that she would come back for him that

he was asleep before horse and rider disappeared over the horizon.

* * *

He didn't know how long he slept. It could have been fifteen minutes or fifteen hours. When he opened his eyes, Rennie was beside him again. She was wrapping the bobcat in a thick, quilted furniture pad. When she noticed him watching her, she said, "I'm not going to leave him for them to pick apart."

He looked up through the branches of the tree. Buzzards were circling overhead. "They might be waiting for me to croak."

"They might be."

She picked up the bundle and carried it to a pickup he'd never seen her drive. He figured it must be restricted to ranch usage because it showed signs of wear and tear. By the time she had placed the bobcat in the bed and closed the tailgate, he had managed to stand up, using the tree trunk for support. He leaned down to pick up his duffel.

"I'll get that," she said, and started back for it. "You get in the truck."

As they passed one another he thought of saluting her, but at the last second he thought better of it.

Of course, her getup offset her military bearing. She had on a red tank top, the kind she slept in, a pair of butt-snug blue jeans, and cowboy boots. Her hair was loose and tangled. He guessed that the disturbance in her stable had caused her to jump from bed and pull on the jeans and boots before racing outside. Whatever, it was a fashion statement that won his approval.

Sliding beneath the barbed-wire fence was only slightly easier to do in daylight than in darkness. By the time he reached the pickup and had managed to climb into the cab, he had broken out in a cold sweat and was trembling.

Rennie returned with his duffel and unceremoniously threw it into the bed of the truck with the dead bobcat. She climbed in and cranked the ignition. She noticed him looking through the rear window into the bed of the pickup.

"Something wrong?"

"No. I'm just glad you didn't toss me back there too."

"I thought about it."

"What about my truck?"

"I've got a gas can."

She didn't outline her plan of how and when they were going to get the gas from her gas can into his truck, but he didn't ask. She pulled out onto the road and drove for at least a mile before saying, "I know Dr. Sugarman didn't release you from the hospital."

"Where did he buy all those teeth?"

"Did you just walk out?"

"Hmm."

"What about the guards?"

"I wouldn't want to be in their shoes when Oren discovers I'm gone."

"He doesn't know?"

"He might by now."

"He'll be upset?"

"Volcanic."

"Because he knows you need another couple days in the hospital."

"Because he knows I'm going after Lozada on my own."

She looked at him sharply. "Then why'd you come here?"

"Find you, find him. He'll come after you, Rennie, and, like me, this is the first place he'll look."

"He doesn't know about this place."

"He will. Eventually. He'll find you. He won't stop until he does. He's got too much of himself, of his ego, invested in you. He'll come."

They said no more. When they reached the house, she parked the pickup close to the front steps. She came around and assisted Wick out of the truck and onto the porch, then opened the door and motioned him inside.

They stepped directly into a spacious living room that was furnished and decorated in Texas chic. Lots of leather and suede, all very tasteful and expensive. Thick rugs on the hardwood floors. Fringed throw pillows. The pieces were large and comfy, inviting one to sit and relax for hours in front of the fireplace, reading the magazines that were scattered—scattered?—on accent tables.

A Mexican saddle of black tooled leather with lots of silver detailing stood in one corner, displayed and spotlighted as a sculpture might be. A boldly striped horse blanket served as a wall hanging. Wick loved it. "This is nice."

"Thank you."

"It doesn't look like you."

She met his gaze. "It looks exactly like me. Are you hungry?"

"I thought about starting on the bobcat."

"This way."

She led him into the kitchen, which held even more surprises. In the center was a work island with open shelving underneath. On the surface was a small copper sink where red and green apples had been left to drain after being rinsed. Cooking pots hung from an iron rack overhead. An opened box of cookies had been left on the counter.

"Soup or oatmeal?"

Painfully, he lowered himself into a chair at the round wood table. "Those're my choices?"

"Unless you were serious about the bobcat. Then you're on your own."

"What kind of soup?"

It was cream of potato and might have been the best food he'd ever eaten in his life. Rennie had started with canned condensed, but she added half and half, butter, and seasonings, then topped off the crockery bowl with grated cheddar and put it in the microwave long enough for the cheese to melt. Her motions were economic and skilled. Like a surgeon's.

"That was haute cuisine after hospital food," he said as he polished off a second piece of toast. "What's for lunch?"

"You'll sleep through lunch."

"I can't rest yet, Rennie. I didn't bust out of the hospital, and then bust my ass to get here, just to go to sleep as soon as I arrived."

"Sorry. That's what you need and that's what you're going to do. I've never had a patient look as bad as you and survive. I should call 911 and have an ambulance take you to the county hospital immediately."

"I would immediately leave."

"That's why I haven't already called." She finished rinsing out his dishes and dried her hands. "Let's get you upstairs and undressed."

"I slept, Rennie. Under the tree."

"How long?"

"Long enough."

"Not near long enough."

"I'm not going to sleep."

"Yes you are."

"You'd have to drug me."

"I did."

"Huh?"

"When you went to the bathroom, I ground a strong

painkiller and a sleeping pill into your soup. Any minute now you'll catch quite a buzz."

"Goddammit! I'll fight it off."

She smiled. "You can't. It's going to knock you on your can. You'll be more comfortable if you let me get you into bed before it does."

"We've got to talk, Rennie."

"We will. After you've had some sleep."

She put her hand beneath his elbow and hauled him out of the chair. Or tried. His legs were already wobbly and there was a distinct tingling in his toes that he knew was induced by narcotics, not hyperventilation.

"Put your arm across my shoulders." He did as she instructed. She slipped her arm around his waist and lent support as she guided him back through the living room toward the open staircase along the far wall.

"I'm catching a buzz, all right," he said about midway up. "My ears are ringing. How long before this wears off?"

"Depends on the patient."

"That's not an answer."

On the second floor a wide gallery overlooked the living room. Several doors opened onto the gallery. She led him through one of them into a bedroom. The bed was unmade. "Is this your room?" he asked.

"It's the only bedroom that's furnished."

"I get to sleep in your bed?"

She propped him against an armoire. "Lift your arms." He did and she pulled his T-shirt over his head. Then she knelt and helped him out of his shoes. "Now take off your pants and lie down."

"Why, Dr. Newton, I would've thought you'd be more subtle. That you'd... What's that?" She'd taken something from the bottom drawer of the armoire.

"That is a syringe." Coming to her feet, she held it up

and tapped the clear plastic tube. "And you're about to get a butt-load of antibiotic."

"I don't need it."

"We aren't going to argue about this, Wick."

No, she didn't appear to be in any mood to argue. He couldn't have argued with her anyway. His tongue had become about as nimble as a walrus. His legs had turned to columns of jelly. It was a struggle to keep his eyes open.

He unbuttoned his fly, dropped his jeans, and stepped out of them. She probably had expected him to be wearing underwear. Well, too damn bad, Dr. Newton. He strutted—as much as he could strut in his drugged state—to the bed and lay down.

"On your stomach, please."

"You're no fun at all," he grumbled thickly.

Rennie swabbed a spot on his hip with alcohol, then jabbed the needle into his muscle.

*"Son of a—"*

"This might hurt."

"*—bitch!* Thanks for the damn warning." He clenched his teeth and waited out the injection, which seemed to take forever.

Laying the empty syringe on the nightstand, she said, "Stay where you are. I'm going to clean your incision."

He thought of something clever to say, but forgot it before he could form the words. The pillow was feeling awfully good.

He was vaguely aware of her bathing his incision with cold liquid, then applying a fresh bandage. It dimly registered when she covered him with a sheet and light blanket. The room seemed to grow gradually darker. He opened his eyes only long enough to see her at the windows where she was closing the shutters. For a millisecond before she shut the louvers, he saw her in silhouette against the bright outdoor light. It detailed her shape. She wasn't wearing a bra.

He groaned, "Sweet Jesus."

Or maybe he didn't.

* * *

When he woke up he was lying on his back, favoring his right side. The room was empty, but light was leaking from beneath the closed bathroom door. He checked the windows. The shutters were still drawn.

God, what had she given him? How long had he been asleep? All day? Two days? Three?

Just then the light went out beneath the bathroom door. It was eased open soundlessly. Rennie stepped through, bringing the smell of soap and shampoo with her. She looked toward the bed and saw that he was awake and watching her.

"I'm sorry. I shouldn't have used the hair dryer. I was afraid it might wake you up, but you were sleeping so soundly I took the chance."

"What time is it?"

"Going on six."

Her bare feet made whispering sounds on the hardwood floor as she moved to the edge of the bed. "How are you feeling?"

When she bent down to take a closer look at him, her hair fell forward to curtain both sides of her face. She swept it over one shoulder to keep it out of her way. "Can I bring you anything?"

Hair, eyes, skin, lips. She was a beautiful woman. He had thought so the first time he'd laid eyes on her in Oren's eight-by-tens. That's when the desire took root and the lying began. He had lied to Oren and to himself, first about his opinion of her, then about his objectivity. It had died when she turned to him at the wedding reception. He had known in that instant that his professionalism was done for. It sank right along with him into the depths of her green eyes.

During his career he had dealt with all types of women, from hookers to homemakers. Cheats and liars and thieves and saints. Women who dressed in power suits and made it their mission in life to symbolically de-ball every man with whom they came into contact, and women who undressed for the amusement and entertainment of men.

Oren had been right when he said that he'd never had an unremarkable encounter with a woman. All had been memorable for one reason or another, from his adoring kindergarten teacher, to the policewoman who had pronounced him the biggest asshole she'd ever had the displeasure of knowing, to Crystal the waitress. He never failed to make an impression.

Good or bad, he had an innate awareness of females that was reciprocated. It was just one of those things, a component of himself that he'd been born with and more or less took for granted, like his palm print or his crooked front tooth.

He had slept with some of those women—he had slept with a lot of them. But he had never desired one as much as he desired Rennie Newton. Nor had one ever been so forbidden. She had meant trouble to him from the start, and she would mean trouble to him from here on.

None of that mattered, though, when strands of her hair brushed against his bare chest. Common sense and conscience didn't stand a chance.

"Ah, hell," he growled. Curving his hand around the back of her neck, he drew her head down to his.

It was a full-blown kiss from the start. No sooner had his lips touched hers than he pressed his tongue between them. He probed her mouth lustily. Her breath was warm and rapid against his face, and that urged him on. He tilted her head, found more heat, more sweetness, wet delight.

His hand moved up from her neck and spread wide over the back of her head. His other hand settled on her rib cage. Against his thumb he could feel the soft weight of her breast. Then the center of it, growing firm at his touch, responding, becoming harder beneath his stroking.

"No!"

Backing away, she shook her head furiously. She stared at him for several ponderous seconds, then turned and fled—the only way to describe the speed with which she left the room.

# Chapter 24

He showered. He shaved with one of Rennie's pink razors. In the mirror above the bathroom sink, he didn't look quite as frightening as he had before the long sleep. The dark rings under his eyes had lightened and the sockets weren't as deep.

But he was no Prince Charming. His hospital pallor emphasized the discoloration on his cheekbone. And when was the last time he'd had a haircut? "Screw it," he said to his reflection as he left the bathroom.

Rennie was in the kitchen. She glanced over her shoulder when he walked in. "You found your duffel bag?"

"Yeah, thanks." She had placed it at the foot of the bed so he would have a change of clothes.

"How do you feel?"

"Better. Thanks. For everything. Except the shot. My butt's sore."

"I'm sure you're thirsty. Help yourself to anything in the fridge." She was dredging boneless chicken breasts in seasoned breading and placing them in a Pyrex dish.

He took a carton of orange juice from the refrigerator, shook it, and twisted off the cap. "Okay to drink from the carton?"

"Not in this house."

"I used your toothbrush."

"I have extras."

"Why am I not surprised?"

"Glasses are in the cabinet just behind you."

The juice tasted good. He drained the glass and refilled it. "What did you do with the bobcat?"

"Called the game warden. He came out and picked him up. He congratulated me."

"You provided a valuable community service."

She gazed into near space for a moment. "It didn't feel like that. It felt like killing." She washed her hands, moved to the oven and turned it on, then went to the vegetable sink and picked up a chopping knife. She used it to gesture toward a cell phone lying on the counter. "It's rung several times."

"Jeez, I don't even remember where I last had it."

"It was in your truck."

"Where's my truck?"

"In the garage out back."

He looked through the window and spotted the building. It was a smaller version of the barn. The double doors were closed. "How'd you manage to get it here?"

"I rode Beade over, carrying the gas can. Then I tied him to the tailgate and drove back slowly."

"It would have been easier if you'd waited on me to go with you."

"I didn't think you wanted anyone to know you were here."

He studied her for a moment. "That's not quite accurate, is it, Rennie?"

She stopped slicing tomatoes and looked across at him.

"*You* didn't want anyone to know I was here."

She returned to her task. "Do you like tomatoes in your salad?"

"Rennie."

"Some people don't."

"Rennie."

She dropped the knife and confronted him. "What?"

"It was only a kiss," he said softly.

"Let's not make a big deal of it, all right?"

"I'm not, you are. You're the one who went tearing out of the bedroom like it had caught fire."

"So you would stop mauling me."

"Mauling you?" he repeated in a raised voice. "*Mauling* you?"

"The night we met—no, the night you arranged for us to meet—I told you then, straight out and in language a child could understand that I wasn't interested in . . . all that."

Masculine pride kicked in. Wick rounded the work island so it would no longer be between them. "Well that's a switch for you, isn't it? One kiss and I'm mauling you, but back in Dalton you were quite the party girl. What did you call it then?"

She recoiled as though he'd struck her, but that initial reaction lasted only a second before her facial expression turned hard. "You must have had a locker-room chat with your pal Detective Wesley."

"Only after I heard all about you from folks in Dalton. You're remembered there, Sweetcheeks. Because you used to do a lot more than kiss the locals, didn't you?"

"You're so well informed—why ask me?"

"You did *considerably* more than kiss."

She backed down and looked away. "I'm not like that now."

"Why not? Seems to me like you were having one hell of a good time. Tongues in Dalton are still wagging about your topless cruise through town in your red Mustang convertible. But I get your nipple ripe and you freak out."

She tried to go around him, but he executed a quick sidestep and blocked her path. "You had all those horny cowboys at the rodeo panting after you. And their daddies, and their uncles, and probably even their grandpas."

"Stop it!"

"And you knew it, too, didn't you? You liked keeping 'em steaming in their jeans."

"You don't know—"

"Oh, yeah, I do. Guys know. We have ugly names for girls like you, Rennie. Doesn't stop us from wanting what you advertise, though. How many hearts were broken when you set your sights on Raymond Collier?"

"Don't—"

"Then when that affair went south, you shot and killed him. Is that what turned you off mauling?"

"*Yes!*"

Her shout was followed by a sudden, reverberating silence. She turned away from him and leaned forward against the counter. She put her hand to her mouth and kept it there for several moments. Then, very unsurgeon-like, she seemed at a loss what to do with her hands. She crossed her arms over her midsection and hugged her elbows; she wiped her palms on her thighs; she finally picked up the baking dish of chicken and placed it in the oven. After setting the timer, she returned to chopping tomatoes.

Wick continued to watch her with the single-mindedness of the buzzards that had circled the carcass of the bobcat. He refused to drop this subject. He felt entitled to peel away just one of her multiple layers. He wanted at least a glimpse of who she was and what had made her so compulsively neat, what had made her so disinclined to touch another human being except in the sterile security of an operating room. He wanted to see, if only for an instant, the real Rennie Newton.

"What happened in your father's study that day?"

The knife came down hard and angrily on the chopping block. "Didn't Wesley share the details with you?"

"Yes. And I read the police report."

"Well then."

"It didn't tell me shit. I want to hear what happened from you."

She finished with the tomatoes and rinsed off the knife. As she dried it on a tea towel, she looked at him sardonically. "Prurient curiosity, Wick?"

"Don't do that," he said, keeping a tight rein on his anger. "You know that's not why I'm asking."

She braced her arms on the countertop and leaned toward him. "Then why *are* you asking? Explain to me why it's so bloody important for you to know about that."

He leaned forward to narrow the space between them. "You know why, Rennie," he whispered. There was no way his meaning could have escaped her. But just in case it did, he covered the back of her hand with his palm and encircled her wrist with his fingers.

She lowered her head. It appeared to him that she was staring at their hands, but all he could see was the crown of her head, the natural part in her hair. Half a minute passed before she withdrew her hand from beneath his.

"Nothing good can come of this, Wick."

"*This* being the weird triangle we have going? You, me, and Lozada?"

"There's no such triangle."

"You know better, Rennie."

"The two of you had a score to settle before you ever heard of me."

"That's true, but you've added another dimension."

"I'm not involved in your feud," she said adamantly.

"Then why did you leave town?"

"I needed some time off."

"You heard Lozada was released from jail."

"Yes, but—"

"And you beat it here within hours of his release. Looks to me like you're hiding from him."

His cell phone rang. He picked it up and read the caller ID, then swore under his breath. "I might as well get this over with." He carried the phone with him through the living room and out onto the front porch. He answered as he sat down in the swing. "Hey."

"Where the hell are you?"

"No hello?"

"Wick—"

"Okay, okay." He sighed heavily. "I just couldn't take that hospital anymore, Oren. You know I don't handle inactivity well. Another day in that place and I'd've wigged out. So I left. Retrieved my truck from your house and drove most of the night. Reached Galveston this morning around, hmm, five or so, I guess. Been asleep most of the day and got a whole lot more rest listening to the surf than I would have in the hospital where real rest is impossible."

After a significant pause, Oren said, "Your place in Galveston is locked up tighter than a drum."

Oh, shit. "How do you know?"

"Because I asked the police there to check it."

"What for?"

"I'm waiting for an explanation, Wick."

"Okay, on my way home I took a little detour. What's the big deal?"

"You're with her, aren't you?"

"I'm a big boy, Oren. I don't have to account to you for my—"

"Because she's coincidentally flown the coop too. From the hospital. From her house. Her obliging neighbor told me that he saw a man who looked seriously ill and malnourished knocking on her door in the middle of the night."

"Does that guy keep vigil at his window or what?"

"He's become a valuable informant."

"My, my, Oren. Talking to Galveston police. Talking to nosy neighbors. You've been busy today."

"And so has Lozada."

"Oh yeah? Doing what?"

"Terrorizing my family."

* * *

His name was Weenie Sawyer. Only someone of Weenie's diminutive size would have tolerated such a derisive name. Weenie did so only because he had no choice. He was defenseless.

He had acquired the name in second grade when he'd wet himself in the classroom. During a geography lesson on Hawaii a seeming river of urine had charted a course down his leg. To the amusement of his classmates, what wasn't absorbed by his sock had formed a puddle beneath his desk. He'd wanted to die on the spot, but he had had the rotten luck of living through it. That afternoon he had been dubbed Weenie by a pack of bullies led by the scourge of the school yard, Ricky Roy Lozada.

The nickname had stuck to this day. And so had Lozada's bullying. Weenie audibly groaned when he opened his door and saw Lozada standing on the threshold.

"May I come in?"

The formality was a mockery. Lozada asked only in order to remind Weenie that he didn't need an invitation. He pushed past Weenie and entered the cramped, poorly ventilated apartment where Weenie sometimes confined himself for days without going out. For self-protection, Weenie existed in a universe of his own making.

"This isn't a good time, Lozada. I'm having dinner." On a TV tray next to the La-Z-Boy a bowl of Cap'n Crunch was growing soggy.

"I wouldn't interrupt, Weenie. Except that this is very important."

"You always say that."

"Because my business is always important."

Lozada's torture of his unfortunate classmate hadn't ended that afternoon in second grade, but had continued through their high school graduation. Weenie's size, his perpetual squint, and his meek personality were open invitations to torment and ridicule him. He was almost too easy a target. Consequently Lozada had treated him as a forgettable pet, one he could scold and neglect, or grace and praise, at whim.

Every class has a computer whiz, and in their class it had been Weenie. While computers and microchip technology bored Lozada, he was nevertheless aware of the advancements being made. As the viability of computer usage increased, so had Weenie's value to him.

Nowadays Weenie's livelihood was designing websites. He liked the work. It was a rewarding creative outlet. He could do it alone, at home, on his own schedule. He billed his clients four times the number of hours it required him to complete a job, but they were so pleased with the result that none ever questioned the amount of the invoice. It was a lucrative business.

But that income was paltry compared to what Lozada paid him.

Weenie's computer setup occupied one whole room of his apartment and rivaled NASA's in sophistication. He put most of his money back into his business, buying state-of-the-art equipment, upgrades, and gadgets. He could dissect a computer with the precision of a pathologist, then reassemble it with new and improved specifications. He'd never met one he didn't like. He knew how they worked. Furthermore, he understood how they worked.

With a minimum of mouse clicks, he could enter any secret chat room, generate a deadly virus, or crack any security code. If Weenie had possessed any imagination or larcenous impulses, he could potentially control the world from this old, ugly, smelly, cluttered apartment in a rundown neighborhood in the shadow of downtown Dallas.

Lozada thought it a woeful waste of talent. Weenie's level of know-how should belong to someone who would exploit it, someone with panache and style and *cojones*.

Had Lozada been in another field, he could have used Weenie's genius to steal huge quantities of money with little chance of getting caught. But where would be the challenge? He much preferred the personal involvement his occupation required. He relied on Weenie strictly to provide him with information on his clients and his targets.

He told Weenie that was what he was after tonight. "Information."

Weenie pushed up his slipping eyeglasses. "You always say that, too, Lozada. And then the person I get you information on winds up dead."

Lozada fixed a cold stare on him. "What's wrong with you tonight?"

"Nothing." He picked at a crusty scab on his elbow. "What makes you think something's wrong?"

"You don't seem very glad to see me. Didn't I pay you enough last time?"

"Yeah, but..." He sniffed back a nostril full of mucus. "I've got no quarrel with the money."

"Then what's the matter?"

"I don't want to get into trouble. With the law, I mean. You've been in the news a lot lately, or haven't you noticed?"

"Have you noticed that it's all been good news?"

"Yeah, but this time, I don't know, the police seem to be closing in tighter. That Threadgill's got it in for you."

"He's the least of my worries."

Weenie looked plenty worried. "He comes across as a man with a mission. What if they, you know, link us? You and me."

"How could they do that?"

"I don't know."

Lozada remembered that whining tone from elementary school. It had annoyed him then, and it annoyed him even more now. He was in a hurry, and this conversation was wasting precious time.

"What I mean is," Weenie continued, "I don't want to become an accessory. I was watching *Law & Order* the other night. And they charged this guy with being an accessory before the fact. He went down for almost as long as the guy who did the actual killing. I want no part of that."

"You're afraid?"

"Damn right I'm afraid. How long do you think a guy like me would last in prison?"

Lozada looked him up and down. He smiled. "I see your point. So you'll have to be doubly careful not to get caught, won't you?"

Weenie went through his routine of nervous twitches again with the eyeglasses, the scab, the snot in his nose. He avoided making eye contact. Lozada didn't like it.

"Sit down, Weenie. I'm in a hurry. Let's get started."

Weenie seemed to consider refusing, but then he reluctantly sat down in the rolling desk chair in front of the bank of computer terminals, all of which were oscillating with a variety of screen savers.

"Rennie Newton," Lozada told him. "Doctor Rennie Newton."

Again Weenie groaned. "I was afraid you were going to say that. I saw her being interviewed on the news about that cop. What do you want to know?"

"Everything."

Weenie went to work. His nose stayed within inches of the screen as he squinted into the glare. His fingers struck the keys with impressive speed. But Lozada wasn't fooled. He could tell Weenie was dillydallying. It went on for at least five minutes. Occasionally he mumbled with frustration.

Finally he sat back and said, "Bunch of dead ends. Truth is, Lozada, there's not much on her."

Lozada slipped his hand into his pants pocket and removed a glass vial with a perforated metal cap. He unscrewed it slowly, then upended the vial over Weenie.

The scorpion landed on Weenie's chest. He shrieked and reflexively tried to roll back on the chair's casters, but Lozada was standing behind it, trapping Weenie between him and the computer table. He clamped his hand to Weenie's forehead, pulled his head back, and held him still while the scorpion crawled over his chest.

"He's been mine only a short while. I've been waiting for the perfect time to show him off. Isn't he a beauty?"

Weenie emitted a high-pitched squeal.

"All the way from India, meet *Mesobuthus tamulus,* one of the rare species of scorpions whose venom is toxic enough to cause death in humans, although it may take days for a sting victim to die."

Weenie's glasses had been knocked askew. His eyes rolled wildly as they tried to focus on the vicious-looking scorpion crawling up his chest. "Lozada, for the love of God," he gasped.

Lozada calmly released him and chuckled. "You aren't going to pee on yourself again, are you?"

He calmly scooped the scorpion onto a sheet of paper, then formed a cone and funneled it back into the vial. "There now, enough fun, Weenie," he said as he replaced the perforated cap. "You've got work to do."

# Chapter 25

"You don't like it?"

Wick looked up from his plate. "Uh, yeah. It's great. Just... I think that potato-soup breakfast filled me up." He tried to smile but knew he failed.

They'd taken their dinner trays out onto the patio behind the house and had watched the sunset while they ate, in silence for the most part. In fact, they hadn't exchanged more than a few inconsequential sentences since Wick's telephone conversation with Oren.

She stood up with her tray and reached for his. "Finished, then?"

"I can carry in the tray."

"You shouldn't. Not with your back."

"It doesn't hurt anymore."

"Will you just give me the tray?"

He relinquished it and she took it into the house. He heard her moving around in the kitchen, water running, the fridge door being opened and closed. Background noise for his preoccupation.

When Rennie returned, she brought with her a bottle of

white wine and set it on the small table between their two teak chairs. He said, "That'll hit the spot."

"You don't get any." She poured wine for herself into the single glass she had brought out.

"Why not?"

"The medication."

"You slipped me another mickey in my chicken breast? Or was it in the wild rice?"

"Neither. Because I don't know what you take."

"What do you mean?"

"For the panic attacks."

He thought about playing dumb. He thought about flat-out denying it. But what would be the point? She knew. "I don't take anything. Not anymore." He turned away and stared across the landscape. "How'd you know?"

"I recognized the symptoms." His gaze moved back to her and she softly confessed, "Borderline compulsive obsessive. Back, years ago. I never counted each heartbeat, or every footstep, nothing that extreme. But everything had to be just so, and to a great extent still does. It's all about being in control."

The topic under discussion made him terribly uncomfortable. "I had a . . . a few . . . what you'd call episodes, I guess. Rapid heartbeat, shortness of breath. That's all. A lot of shit happened to me all at once. Major life changes." He gave an elaborate shrug. "The shrink seemed to think there was nothing to it."

"There's no reason to be ashamed, Wick."

"I'm not ashamed." His brusqueness implied just the opposite.

She gave him a long look, then said, "Well, anyway, the drugs I gave you today would be compatible with anything you happened to be taking. Just so you know."

"Thanks, but as I said, I'm off that stuff."

"Maybe you should go back on it."

"Why's that, *Doctor*?"

"Because if you weighed five pounds less, I don't think the earth's gravity could keep you in that chair."

He made a conscious effort to stop fidgeting.

"Why don't you just tell me what Wesley told you?" she said.

Again, he turned his head aside and gazed out across the rear of her property. It was a pretty spread, the kind of place he'd love to have if he could ever afford it, which he never could. He wasn't, nor had he ever been, materialistic. Greed wasn't one of his flaws. But a place like this...this would be nice to have.

The pasture beyond the near fence was dotted with mature trees, mostly pecan. A stream cutting diagonally across the pasture was lined with tall cottonwoods and willows that swayed in the south breeze. The breeze had cooled the evening off, making it comfortable to be outdoors.

After being cooped up in the hospital for a week, he had welcomed her suggestion that they take their dinner onto the patio. But he hadn't enjoyed the al fresco meal as much as he should have. Oren's news had spoiled his appetite.

"Grace Wesley left her school office today around 4:30," he began. "The last couple of weeks, she's been getting things ready for the upcoming term, same as the rest of the faculty. Except that Grace is extremely conscientious. She's usually the last one to leave the building, as she was today. When she got into her car, Lozada was sitting in the backseat."

Rennie sucked in a quick breath and held it.

"Yeah," he said. "Scared her half to death."

"Is she..."

"She's okay. He never lifted a finger to her. He just talked."

"Saying what?"

"He wanted to know where I was, where you were."

"Does she know?"

"No, and that's what she told him. But he must not have believed her." He looked over at Rennie. She folded her arms across her middle as though bracing for what was coming. "He told her it would be in her best interest to tell him what he wanted to know, and when she said she couldn't, he remarked on how pretty her daughters were."

Rennie bowed her head and supported it in her hand, her middle finger and thumb pressing hard against her temples. "Please, please don't tell me that—"

"No, the girls are all right too. It was a warning. A veiled threat. But a real one because he knew a lot about them. Their names, favorite activities, friends, places they like to go.

"Grace started crying. She's a strong lady but, like all of us, she has a breaking point, and her family is it. Oren says she didn't fold, didn't beg or plead. But somehow she must have persuaded him that she didn't know anything. He got out of her car and into his. He even waved her good-bye before driving off.

"Grace immediately called Oren on her cell. Within minutes the girls were collected and put under police guard. Grace, too. Oren was . . . well, you can imagine."

They were quiet for a time. Crickets were tuning up for the night.

"He wants Grace and the girls to go stay with her mother in Tennessee," he continued. "Even while he was talking to me he was packing their bags. Over their protests. I could hear the girls fussing in the background and Grace saying that if he thought she was going to leave him alone, he could just think again. Nor, she said, was she going to be frightened away from her home by a homicidal freak like Lozada."

"What do you think?"

"Oh, he's a freak, all right."

"You know what I mean. Should she leave?"

He shrugged. "I can see both sides."

"So can I. Having met Grace, seen them together, it doesn't surprise me that she would refuse to leave her husband in a time of crisis."

"Not only that, Rennie. If Lozada wants to hurt Oren's family, he will. A trip out of state would be only a minor inconvenience." They exchanged a long look.

Then suddenly Wick left his chair and began to pace the width of the flagstone patio. "Lozada. He really is the lowest turd in the shit pile. He's threatening women and children now? I mean, what kind of lowlife... You know what I think? I think he's got no balls, that's what I think. He attacks in the dark like those goddamn scorpions he keeps."

"Scorpions?"

"He gets his victims in the back. In the *back.* Think about it. He choked the banker to death from the back. He stabbed me in the back. The only one he's met face-to-face in daylight is a woman, and he threatened her children. He's never faced a man. I wish to God I could get a crack at him face-to-face."

"That could prove dangerous."

He shot her a bitter look. "You and Oren are reading from the same script. I was already out of your porch swing and on my way to the garage to get my truck and return to Fort Worth, but Oren told me if I so much as crossed the city line, he'd have me arrested."

"For what?"

"He didn't specify, but he meant it. He said the only thing he needed to make a bad situation worse was a hotheaded avenger. He said the only good thing about Lozada's terrorizing Grace was his choosing to do it when I was out of town."

"He did it *because* you were out of town."

He stopped pacing and turned to her. "Did you eavesdrop on our conversation? Because that's exactly what Oren said. He thinks Lozada threatened Grace in the hope of smoking me out."

"I'm sure he's right."

He raked his fingers through his hair. "I'm sure he is too," he mumbled. "Lozada would expect me to ride in like the cavalry."

"Making you a target that would be hard for him to miss."

"Especially if I was the aggressor. Lozada would love nothing better than for me to come after him. If I did, he could drop me and then claim self-defense."

Rennie agreed with a nod, which agitated him further. He resumed pacing. "Oren hoped I'd gone back to Galveston. He wasn't too happy to learn I was still this close to Fort Worth."

"With me."

"I've told him there's no way that you and Lozada are, or ever were, in cahoots."

"Does he believe you?" His hesitation in answering gave him away. She said, "Never mind. I know he thinks I'm shady."

Wick didn't belabor the point. He returned to his chair, picked up the bottle of wine, and took a drink from it. She didn't stop him. He then leaned toward her. "Lozada upped the ante today when he messed with Grace. Attacking me is one thing. Going after her, Oren's kids—that's another. I'm gonna get this son of a bitch, Rennie. For good.

"And it can't be done through legal channels. I've learned that lesson several times over. Now Oren realizes it too. We can't rely on the system. It's let us down. We've got to get him some other way. We've got to forget the law and start thinking like Lozada."

"I agree." He registered his surprise, and she continued, "You thought I left town to escape him. That I ran in fear when I learned that he'd been released from jail. You thought I had come here to hide. Well, you're wrong. I left because I needed time to plan how I was going to free myself from him. I refuse to live in fear, especially in fear of a man.

"Lozada has invaded my home. Twice. He killed my friend Lee Howell. He killed Sally Horton and tried to kill you, and, so far, he's gotten away with it. He got away with killing that banker, and I helped him do that."

"You were a juror. You voted according to your conscience."

"Thanks for the endorsement, but I regret that decision now. Lozada seems to be immune to the law, but he's not invincible, Wick. He's not bulletproof."

"And you're a damn good shot." His grin collapsed when he saw the drastic change in her expression. "I was referring to the bobcat, Rennie, not to what happened in Dalton."

She formed a half smile and nodded acknowledgment. "I have no intention of shooting anybody, even Lozada. I don't want to wind up in prison myself."

"I'd rather not either, although I'm committed to eliminating him no matter what it costs me."

"Because of your brother?" When he nodded, she added, "Was that one of the life-changing things that happened to you all at once?"

"That was the major one."

He leaned back and laid his head against the chair cushion. The sky had turned an inky purple. Already he could see stars. Thousands more than were visible in the city.

Even more than he could see on the Galveston beach where commercial lights reduced stars to dim reminders of what they should look like.

"Joe and Lozada had actually known each other in school. Or rather they knew *of* each other. They attended rival high schools but graduated the same year. Joe was a star athlete and student leader. Lozada was a hoodlum, hell raiser, drug dealer. They saw each other occasionally at places where teens hang out.

"They only clashed once, when Joe broke up a fight between Lozada and another guy. They exchanged words, but it amounted to no more than that. Joe became a cop. Lozada became a hired killer. Both excelled at what they did. They were destined to collide. It was only a matter of time."

He reached for the wine bottle and took another drink, hoping it would relieve the throbbing pain in his back, which had returned with a vengeance.

"Fast-forward a few years. Joe and Oren were working a high-profile homicide case. Typical Texas tale. Socialite wife of wealthy oilman whacked on terrace of mansion.

"The husband was conveniently out of town and had a long list of indisputable alibis. Since nothing had been disturbed, nothing stolen, it stunk of a murder-for-hire. Joe and Oren leaned heavily on the husband, who had a very demanding, very expensive twenty-two-year-old mistress in New York.

"Figuratively speaking, the murder had Lozada's fingerprints all over it, but they couldn't link him to the husband. Joe hammered the guy, and each time he questioned him, he cracked a little more. Joe was relentless, kept at him. He was this close to splitting the thing wide open."

He was quiet for a time before continuing. "The last time I saw Joe, we met for a cup of coffee. He told me he could taste the man's fear. 'I'm close, Wick. Close.' He predicted that the guy was gonna crash and burn soon, and when he did, Joe would have his ass as well as Lozada's. The oilman was a schmuck, he said. Pussy-whipped by this brat in New York. His dick had done him in. Joe said you could almost feel sorry for him.

" 'But that Lozada dude is bad news, little bro. I'm talking real bad news.' Joe's words exactly. He said Lozada killed for pleasure more than for money. He liked killing. Joe said he was gonna do the world a favor and put that heartless, hairless son of a bitch away for life.

"I remember us clinking our coffee cups in a toast to his success. Which, apparently, Lozada also thought was coming down soon. He must've sensed the oilman was close to ratting him out.

"That same evening, Oren left the office a few minutes behind Joe. When he got to the parking lot, he noticed that Joe's car was still there. The driver's door was standing open. Joe was just sitting there, staring through the windshield. Oren remembers walking toward the car and saying, 'Hey, what's up? I thought you'd be gone by now.' "

He paused to inhale a deep breath and let it out slowly. The darkness was now complete. The moon was a sliver hanging just above the horizon.

"Joe was already dead when Oren found him. I was hosting a party at our house that night. Oren and Grace came to tell me." He leaned forward, planted his elbows on his knees, and lightly tapped his lips with his clasped hands.

"You know what I wonder about most, Rennie?" Turning his head, he looked at her and realized that she hadn't moved since he began talking. "You know what really puzzles me?"

"What?"

"I wonder why Lozada didn't kill the oilman instead.

That would have shut him up. Why didn't he do him instead of Joe?"

"Joe posed the greater threat. Killing the oilman would have been a temporary fix to a long-range problem. Lozada knew Joe wouldn't give up until he had him."

"His twisted form of flattery, I guess."

"Why was he never charged and brought to trial for Joe's murder?" she asked.

But Wick's cell phone rang, sparing him from having to answer.

* * *

He opened the phone and put it to his ear. "Yeah?"

He listened for a few seconds, glanced at Rennie, then left his chair and moved to the edge of the patio, keeping his back to her. "No, we haven't talked about it yet," she heard him say as he stepped off the flagstones and moved even farther away from her.

Taking the hint that he wanted privacy, she went inside and finished cleaning the kitchen. She wondered what unpleasant developments Detective Wesley would tell them of this time.

Through the window above the kitchen sink, she could see Wick pacing along the fence line. She shared his restlessness. She felt she should be taking action, doing something, but she just didn't know what to do.

In the living room, she switched on an end-table lamp and took up her favorite spot in the corner of the sofa. She flipped through a magazine, but neither the pictures nor the text registered. She was preoccupied with thoughts of Wick.

He was in perpetual motion, just as Grace Wesley had said. Yet he had a habit of making his point by holding a stare for an interminable length of time. Once his blue eyes locked with yours, it was difficult to escape their intensity.

He was clever and glib and funny and had self-confidence to spare. But he wasn't superficial. He felt things deeply. He had loved his brother, and the loss was still a raw, open wound. Every hour Lozada went unpunished was like salt to that wound. He seemed to hate Lozada as much as he had loved Joe, and that was a perilous level of emotion to keep contained. Lozada should be very afraid of Wick Threadgill.

She identified with the rage that drove him to get even. Her vengeance had taken an altogether different form, but she understood Wick's compulsion to seek it. She also pitied him for it, because finding retribution is a lonely, all-consuming business.

She hadn't wanted to like Wick Threadgill, but she did. She hadn't wanted to forgive him for tricking her, but she had. She hadn't wanted to be attracted to him, but she was. She had known that if she ever kissed him once, she would want to again. She had, and she did. And if that kiss was any indication of how fervently he made love, she wanted to experience it.

"Rennie?"

She sat up straight and cleared her throat. "In here."

His boot heels made clomping sounds against the hardwood floor. He took the opposite end of the couch but perched on the very edge, as though he might spring off it at any moment. "What are you doing?"

She indicated the open magazine in her lap.

"Horse magazine?"

"Hmm."

"Anything new and interesting in the world of horses?"

"What did he say, Wick?"

He expelled a breath and ran his hand around the back of his neck. "I need a massage."

"It wouldn't be good for your wound."

"Just my shoulders. I've got a crick in my neck from sleeping under that tree last night. How 'bout some massage therapy for your favorite patient?"

"More bad news?"

"Not really. Where'd you get the saddle?"

"It was a prize."

"For barrel racing?"

"You know about my barrel racing?" Reading his guilty expression, she said, "Of course you know. Yes, I won the saddle for barrel racing."

"Good-looking saddle. But don't those silver studs make for an uncomfortable ride?"

"Wick, if Oren's news wasn't that bad, why are you stalling?"

"Okay," he said curtly. "I'll tell you what we talked about. But I want you to know up-front that it wasn't my idea."

"I'm not going to like it, am I?"

"I seriously doubt that you are."

She looked at him expectantly, but still he hesitated. "For heaven's sake, how bad can it be?"

"Oren thinks we should pretend to be lovers." He bobbed his head for additional punctuation.

She stared at him for several moments, then began to laugh. "That's it? That's the brilliant plan to snare Lozada?"

He took offense at her laughter. "What's the matter with it?"

"Nothing. As every dime novelist and C-movie producer will attest." She laughed harder, but he didn't join in. "Come on, Wick. Don't you think that idea is a trifle clichéd? We try and make Lozada jealous. He devises some horrible punishment, and when he attempts it, we nab him. Is that the gist of this grand scheme?"

"Basically," he said stiffly.

She shook her head in disbelief. "Lord help us."

"I'm glad you can laugh, Rennie, because I can't. Lozada's disappeared. His Mercedes is in the parking garage, so he's using an unknown means of transportation. He hasn't been spotted in his favorite restaurants, hasn't been seen at his place in Trinity Tower since last night. The concierge told Oren that the homeowners' association has asked him to vacate."

"Then maybe he just moved out."

"And maybe that bobcat you dropped this morning will resurrect tonight." He got up and began to roam the living room aimlessly. "Lozada wouldn't have complied with an eviction request from his neighbors. That place is one of his status symbols, like his hand-tailored suits and that hundred-thousand-dollar set of wheels.

"Being asked to leave would be the worst kind of affront and would make him mad as hell. And who's he going to blame for being undesirable to Fort Worth's elite? You guessed it. Me. Us. He's pissed at us for vanishing, especially if he knows we're together. He's pissed at us for making news and getting him kicked out of his building. Now nobody knows where he is. And all of that makes me real nervous."

When she was certain his outburst was over, she apologized. "I didn't mean to make light of the situation, Wick. I know how serious it is. I only have to think about Grace to be reminded. But let's be reasonable. Lozada wouldn't fall for a corny charade like that."

He came to stand directly in front of her, forcing her to tilt her head back to look at him. "Okay then, let's hear your idea. I assume you have a workable alternate plan. You said you came here to think of a way to get him out of your life. Has the fresh country air stimulated the gray matter?"

She lowered her head. "You don't need to be insulting."

"Considering your recent laughter, I can't believe you have the gall to look me in the eye—in the fly, rather—and say that."

He headed for the kitchen. Rennie went after him. By the time she got there he was downing a bottle of water.

"You're limping. Does your back hurt?"

"And then some."

"You said it didn't."

"I lied."

"Not for the first time."

They stared at each other in hostile silence. She was the first to break it. "All right, what are we supposed to do? Hold hands on the corner of Fourth and Main? Gaze at each other over candlelight dinners? Slow-dance till dawn? What?"

"Don't forget mauling," he said. "I could maul you some more."

Heat rushed to her face, but she remained where she was. To stalk away angrily would only give the incident the importance she had told him it didn't have.

Swearing softly, he set the bottle of water on the counter and rubbed his tired eyes. "I'm sorry. You're always making me say things that make me feel like shit after I say them."

"It's all right. I should never have used that term for what..."

He lowered his hand from his eyes and looked at her. "For what... What?"

"You weren't mauling me."

He fixed her with one of those immobilizing gazes until she willed herself to look away. "You'd better tell me more about Oren's plan."

"Uh, yeah." He shook his head as though to remind himself what they'd been talking about. "He said we might get

Lozada on a stalking charge. If we can put him away for that, even for a while, we'd have more time to build a case against him for the murder of Sally Horton and the attack on me. But—"

"I was afraid there would be one."

"No one else has heard these calls you claim he made." She was about to object when he held up his hands, palms out. "Bear with me. I'm thinking like our DA's office. I can hear some fresh-out-of-law-school ADA asking for the evidence of these calls, and we have none. True?"

"True. But I have that note that came with the roses."

"It didn't contain a threat."

"He broke into my house."

"Oren and two other cops saw you and Lozada in a clinch."

"I was afraid if I resisted I'd wind up like Sally Horton."

"There was no sign of forced entry at your house, Rennie."

"There was no sign of forced entry when you broke in either."

He was taken aback. "You know about that?"

"I guessed, and Wesley confirmed it with a stony silence."

"Oren didn't tell me you knew." He hung his head and rubbed the back of his neck again. "It's a wonder you didn't let me bleed out."

"I didn't know about the illegal search until after I'd saved your life."

His head came up quickly. She smiled wryly to let him know she was kidding. He returned the smile. "Lucky for me."

"Getting back to the stalking angle," she said, "how effectual is it if I can't prove Lozada's been harassing me?"

"We'd have a better chance of getting a charge to stick

if something happened in another locale. The allegation would have stronger legs if he followed you somewhere."

"Like here."

He shook his head. "He could say you had invited him. It would be his word against yours."

"Then where?"

"My place in Galveston. He sure as hell wouldn't be on any guest list of mine. How soon can you be packed?"

# Chapter 26

Oren answered on the first ring. Wick told him they had decided to go along with his plan.

"Dr. Newton is okay with it?"

"No," Wick said. "No more than I am. It's hackneyed and Lozada would have to be a moron to fall for it."

"But no one has a better idea."

"I do. Arm me to the teeth and let me hunt down the bastard and blow him away."

"That plan could sorely affect your quality of life in the future."

"Which is the only reason I'm agreeing to this one. Rennie is of the same mind. It's not an ideal strategy, but it's the only one we've got going. On the plus side, it smacks Lozada right where it'll hurt most—in his ego."

"That's why it just might work."

"What did you and Grace decide?"

"The girls went. Grace stayed."

Wick smiled into the telephone. "Good for Grace."

"Yeah, well...Listen up. By the time you get to your place in Galveston, there'll be men watching it around the clock. Don't look for them. You won't see them. I hope not, anyway."

"Will you be coming down?"

"Would you invite your best buddy to a lovefest with your new squeeze?"

"I don't know. How kinky are we gonna get?"

"Wick."

"Sorry. I got it." If Lozada spotted Oren, he would know it was a setup.

"I'll be in touch by phone 'round the clock," Oren continued. "Keep your eyes open and check in often. If you hear a seagull fart, I want to know about it."

"Are you sure? 'Cause if they fart as much as they shit—"

"Will you stop messing around? This isn't funny."

"I know. All joking aside." And he meant it.

"Lozada's gone underground, Wick. You know what usually happens when he disappears for a few days."

"A body turns up."

"I don't like it."

"Neither do I. However, I don't think he could find us this soon."

"But it's possible. I've got people all over town talking up your affair with the surgeon who saved your life. Word has probably reached him that you and Dr. Newton are a hot item."

"Oh, he'll turn up. I'm sure of that." He hadn't told Oren or Rennie about the red flag he'd waved in Lozada's face in the form of a nursery rhyme. Lozada wouldn't be able to resist the dare.

He signed off with Oren, then went outside to take a look around. He walked the perimeter of the house, around the barn and garage, checked inside both. Nothing seemed to be amiss. When he came back in, he and Rennie checked all the windows and doors to be certain they were locked. She wasn't overwrought, but she had the good sense to be cautious.

"Who would have thought my stint as a juror would result in this?"

"You didn't know the defendant was going to develop a crush on you."

"That word implies an innocent, almost childlike infatuation. This is far beyond that. This is..."

When she seemed at a loss for the right word, Wick summed it up. "Lozada."

"Even his name sounds menacing." In a subconscious gesture, she rubbed her arms as though she were chilled. "Did he honestly expect me to be flattered by his creepy attention?"

"Absolutely."

"How could he be that arrogant? He was on trial for murder. Capital murder that carried a death sentence. In that situation who could be thinking of romance?"

"No one who's rational. Only someone with Lozada's delusions of grandeur. He thinks of himself as the winning quarterback."

"In the Super Bowl for professional assassins."

"Something like that. He's one of the best at what he does. As far as we know he hasn't gone international, but why should he? He can make more money with less risk working out of Fort Worth, USA. Besides, most of the guys who do that kind of killing work deep undercover, which isn't Lozada's style. Why should he hassle with popping public officials and having entire governments and Interpol on his tail? He's a big fish in a relatively small pond."

"So what woman wouldn't welcome his attention. That's his thinking?"

"Exactly," he said. "Add to that his quest for the best. He grew up middle class. His only sibling was severely retarded and physically handicapped. His parents depleted their resources providing for him.

"So to Lozada, acquisitions are a big thing. He sees himself as a well-paid businessman who can recognize and afford the finest of everything. To complete the package, he wants a classy woman by his side."

"What about scorpions?"

"He collects them. Yeah, gives you the heebie-jeebies, doesn't it? They're sort of like his mascot. They're nocturnal; they kill their prey at night. He wouldn't collect anything like coins or stamps or even art because that would be too ordinary. He prides himself on being exceptional."

She tilted her head and regarded him thoughtfully. "You've analyzed him thoroughly, haven't you?"

"I haven't been idling my time away since leaving the department. Contrary to what Oren believes, I've been busy. I've collected everything on Lozada I could get my hands on."

"Such as?"

"Public-school records. He was psychologically profiled when he was in junior high school, roughly when his criminal career began. That's where I got most of the background stuff. His sociopathic behavior, the superiority complex, have been consistent throughout his life. I've studied him inside out. Psychologically speaking, I probably know him better than I know myself."

He paused, then said grimly, "One thing I didn't know was that he was sleeping with Sally Horton. If I had, I would have warned her to stay away from him, and from me, and I'd have been watching my back that night. If he thinks you and I are lovers..." He didn't need to say more. "Sally Horton wasn't even important to him. You're very important, Rennie."

"And I've betrayed him with another man."

"That's how he'll see it. Don't underestimate the danger you're in. Oren has got cops and informers spreading juicy gossip about us. Lozada won't be able to tolerate our being together. You've cheated on him, and I've stolen one of his play-pretties."

"But I'm not his anything, except an obsession."

"If he *thinks* you're his, you're his."

"Over my dead body."

"I'd like to avoid that." He tipped up her chin so that they were looking directly at one another. "Say the word and I'll call Oren back, tell him we'll get Lozada by some other means, some way that doesn't put you in danger. I came here last night to warn you, to urge you to get far away until Lozada is out of the picture one way or the other."

"That could take a long time."

"I don't think so," he said, thinking again of the note he'd sent to Lozada last night.

"I'm already in danger, Wick. With or without you, I spurned him. Besides, I can't just up and leave my responsibilities. No, let me put it another way. I *won't*."

"All right then, how soon can you be ready?"

"You aren't thinking of leaving tonight?"

"As soon as you get packed."

"Packing isn't the issue. You're less than twenty-four hours out of the hospital and you left days before you should have."

"I'm fine."

"You're not fine. Your back is stiff and sore. You can't walk across a room without grimacing. Imagine driving across the state. You have no stamina, and I'm still afraid of infection and pneumonia, both of which could be fatal. You might've popped some stitches."

"You said the incision looked fine."

"There are many more sutures inside than out. Promise

me that at the first sign of tenderness in your abdomen, you'll tell me."

"I'll tell you. If I start feeling really rotten between here and Galveston, I'll stop at the nearest hospital."

"We're not leaving tonight," she said stubbornly. "I've deferred to you and Wesley on the police matters. But your health is my domain. We're going nowhere until you've had more rest. End of argument."

* * *

They shared the bed since he refused to leave her downstairs alone to sleep on the couch. He said, "It's a police matter to which you should defer. End of argument."

Being a true-blue gentleman, he kept his pants on and lay outside the covers. He dozed, but falling into a deep sleep just wasn't going to happen tonight, partially because he had slept so long during the day, partially because he was alert to every sound, partially because he was trying to think with the guile of Lozada, and partially because he was acutely aware of Rennie sleeping beside him.

The features of her face and the contours of her body had relaxed in sleep. One hand rested outside the covers, near him. It lay palm up, the slender fingers curved inward. It looked susceptible and defenseless, not like the strong, skilled hand of a surgeon. She was the most self-reliant and capable woman he'd ever met. He admired her accomplishments. But he also felt protective of her.

And he wanted to make love to her.

God, did he. He wanted to because... well, because he was a man and that was what men wanted to do with women. But it wasn't just that. His humor, charm, even anger, had failed to pierce her hard shell of self-containment. Dented it perhaps, but hadn't broken through.

Would he be able to reach her if he penetrated her body? It was a provocative thought that left him agitated on several levels.

She shrank from his touch, but he didn't think it was because she disliked him. The reaction was a self-imposed conditioned reflex, part of that control she was so hung up on, a legacy of the Raymond Collier incident. Passion had landed her in a terrible fix. That didn't necessarily mean that she was any less passionate. She just no longer submitted to it.

In spite of her reserve, he could imagine her flushed with arousal. Today when he kissed her, for a few incredible seconds, it hadn't been all one-sided. She hadn't permitted herself to kiss him back, but she had wanted to. And that wasn't the pompous disclaimer of a braggart who'd kissed a lot of women.

He hadn't imagined that catch in her breath or that almost-but-not-quite surrendering of her tongue. Her skin had felt feverish even through her clothes. He hadn't had to coax a response from her, either. Two strokes of his thumb and her nipple was hard, ready to be drawn into his mouth.

He stifled a groan by pretending to clear his throat. Beside him, Rennie slept on, undisturbed and unaware of his misery. He rolled onto his side to face her. If she woke up and challenged him, he could truthfully claim that his back had begun to ache. He couldn't really see her anyway. It was too dark in the room.

But he could feel her soft breath, and he didn't need to see her in order to feed his fantasies. During those long nights of surveillance he'd had plenty of time to memorize the features of her face.

He summoned up the memory of her removing the dress she'd worn the night of the wedding. Were those inadequate patches of lavender lace the lingerie of a dispassionate woman? Hell no.

One by one, moving slowly, he undid the buttons of his fly. If she woke up now, she would raise the standard for freaking out, because his back wasn't all that was stiff. He was grateful that his sexual apparatus hadn't suffered permanent damage and had resumed full, operational capacity, but it seemed to be trying to prove itself better fit than before the injury.

That pressure having been relieved, he closed his eyes and willed himself, if not to sleep, at least to clear his mind and rest. He would not remember how good that kiss had tasted, or how perfectly her breast had molded to his hand. He would not think of her, warm and soft, under the light covers, or of that sweet place where she would be even warmer and softer. Taking him in. Enveloping him.

* * *

A horse nickered, waking him with the impact of a clanging alarm clock. He lay perfectly still, eyes open, holding a lungful of air he didn't dare exhale for fear of missing another sound. He didn't have to wait long before hearing another equine snuffle.

The noises hadn't awakened Rennie. She continued to sleep soundly. Despite the soreness in his back, he came off the bed with the alacrity of a cat and picked up his pistol where he'd left it within easy reach on the nightstand. He tiptoed to the window, pressed himself against the adjacent wall, and leaned forward only far enough to look out.

He watched for several moments but detected no movement in the yard or in the clearing between the rear of the house and the barn, but instinct told him something was going on inside that building. Maybe a mouse had spooked one of the horses. Maybe the bobcat had a mate who'd come looking for him. Or maybe Lozada was paying them a call.

He crept across the bedroom and, after checking first to see that Rennie was still asleep, slipped from the room and moved soundlessly across the gallery. At the top of the stairs he paused to listen. He waited for a full sixty seconds but heard nothing except his own pulse beating against his eardrums.

He took the stairs as rapidly as possible but was mindful of creaking treads that would give away his presence. The living room appeared just as they'd left it several hours ago. Nothing had been disturbed. The front door was locked and bolted.

His pistol was cradled between raised hands as he approached the door leading into the kitchen. He hesitated, then sprang into the room and swept it with his outstretched hands. It was empty, as was the walk-in pantry.

He unlocked the back door and slipped through, walking in a ninety-degree crouch but still feeling exposed. He took cover behind the patio chair in which he'd sat earlier. It wasn't very substantial cover, but darkness also provided concealment. He blessed the skinny moon.

He waited and listened. Soon the unmistakable sounds of movement came from within the barn. He slipped from behind the chair and covered the distance at a run. When he reached the barn, he flattened himself against the exterior wall, hoping to meld into its shadow. He also needed it for support. He was dizzy, out of breath, sweating profusely, and his back felt like he'd been impaled on a railroad spike.

That's what a few days in the hospital would do for you, he thought. Make you a weakling. Against any foe stronger than a pissant, he might be in trouble. But he had a pistol, and it was fully loaded, and, at the very least, he was going to give the bastard a fight.

He inched along the wall until he reached the wide door, where he stopped to listen. And what he heard bothered him, because he heard absolutely nothing. But the silence was heavy, not empty; he sensed another presence. He knew someone was in there. He knew it in his gut.

Whoever it was had stopped whatever he'd been doing. Something, maybe his own keen instinct, had alerted him to Wick's presence. He was now listening for Wick with the same intensity that Wick was listening for him.

The standoff stretched into its second minute. Nothing moved. There wasn't a sound. Even the horses had become completely still and silent inside their stalls. The atmosphere was thick with expectation. Wick felt the weight of it against his skin.

Acrid sweat ran into his eyes. It trickled down his rib cage and between his shoulder blades. It stung his incision. His hands, still gripping his pistol, were slippery with it. He reasoned he could either stand there and slowly dissolve or he could end it here, now.

"Lozada! Have you got balls enough to face me like a man? Or are we gonna continue this silly game of hide-and-seek?"

Following a short silence, a voice came to him from the other side of the wall. "Threadgill?"

It wasn't Lozada. Lozada had refined his voice into a low-pitched purr. This one had the nasal intonation of a Texas native. "Identify yourself."

The man stepped from behind the wall into the opening. Wick's hands tensed around the pistol and kept it aimed at head level. Toby Robbins raised his hands. "Whoa, cowboy."

His easygoing manner didn't faze Wick. Cops had died when fooled by that. "What the hell are you doing sneaking around in the dark?"

"I could ask you the same thing, couldn't I? But since you're the one with the firearm, I'll be pleased to answer first. If you'll direct that thing somewhere else."

"Not until I hear why you're in Rennie's barn."

"I was checking on things."

"You gotta do better than that."

"Heard one of her horses got a nasty scratch from a bobcat."

"Who told you?"

"Game warden. I came to check it out, see if I ought to call the vet."

"At this time of night?"

Toby Robbins glanced toward the eastern horizon where by now the sky was blushing pink. "It's practically lunchtime."

Wick glanced toward the gate. It was closed and locked, no vehicle parked beyond it. "How'd you get here?"

"Walked."

He looked down at the man's feet. He was wearing athletic shoes rather than cowboy boots.

Robbins tapped the left side of his chest. "The cardiologist recommends at least three miles a day. That's about a round-trip between our place and Rennie's. I like to get the miles in before it gets too hot."

Reluctantly Wick lowered the pistol and stuffed it into the waistband of his jeans. Or would have if they'd been buttoned. Hurriedly he did up his fly with one hand. "You know, Robbins, I ought to go ahead and shoot you just for being stupid. Why didn't you call first? Or turn on a light, for godsake?"

"The light switch is in the tack closet. It was locked. Rennie keeps an extra key above the door. I was looking for it when I heard you. Didn't know it was you. Thought it might be another bobcat."

Wick eyed the older man distrustfully. He didn't think he was lying, he just wasn't telling the whole truth. "Rennie told me she put antiseptic on the scratch and thought it would heal up in a day or two. If she had thought the horse needed a vet, she would have called one."

"Doesn't hurt to get a second opinion."

Robbins turned and reentered the barn. Despite his bare feet, Wick followed. As long as he stayed in the center aisle he would be okay. As stables went, Rennie's was as clean as an operating room.

Robbins went straight to the tack closet and ran his hand along the top of the doorjamb. He came away with a key. He unlocked the closet door, reached inside, and, an instant later, the overhead lights came on.

Paying no attention to Wick, he entered a stall, speaking softly to the mare as he moved in behind her. He located the scratch on the horse's rear leg, then hunkered down to examine it more closely.

When he'd finished, he left the stall, moving around Wick as though he were an inanimate object. He returned to the closet, switched off the lights, locked the closet door, and replaced the key where he'd found it.

Wick fell into step behind him. When they got outside, he said, "That scratched mare wasn't your only reason for coming over here this morning, was it?"

The older man stopped and turned. He gave Wick a look that could've scoured off paint, then he moved to the corral fence and leaned against it. For the longest time he kept his back to Wick and focused on the sunrise. Eventually he fished a small pouch of tobacco and rolling papers from the pocket of his plaid shirt that had white pearl snaps in lieu of buttons.

He spoke to Wick over his wide shoulder. "Smoke?"

"Sure."

# Chapter 27

Robbins shook tobacco from the cloth pouch onto the strip of paper and carefully passed it to Wick, who tapped the tobacco into a straight line down the center of the paper, moistened the edge of it with his tongue, then tightly rolled it into a cigarette.

Robbins watched him with interest. Wick figured that by knowing how to roll his own he had elevated the cattleman's opinion of him. In the older man's eyes he had adequately performed a rite of passage.

Wick silently thanked the high school friend who'd taught him the skill by rolling joints—until Joe found out. After the beating he'd taken from Joe, he had decided that smoking anything was bad for his health.

Robbins rolled his own smoke. He struck a match and lit Wick's first, then his own. Their eyes met above the glare of the match. "This another of your cardiologist's recommendations?"

Robbins inhaled deeply. "Don't tell my wife."

It was damn strong tobacco. It stung Wick's lips, tongue, and throat, but he smoked it anyway, pretending to be a pro at it. "You weren't surprised to see me here."

"The game warden told me Rennie had company. I figured it was you."

"Why?"

Robbins shrugged and concentrated on his smoking.

"You came here this morning to check on Rennie, didn't you? See if she was okay."

"Something like that."

"Why would you think I'd harm her?"

The older man looked off into the distance for a moment before his unnerving gaze resettled on Wick. "You might not mean to."

Wick still resented the man's implication. "Rennie's a grown woman. She doesn't need a guardian. She can take care of herself."

"She's fragile."

Wick laughed, which caused him to choke on the strong smoke. To hell with this. He ground out the cigarette against a fence post. "Fragile isn't a word I would free-associate with Rennie Newton."

"Goes to show how ignorant you are then, doesn't it?"

"Look, Robbins, you don't know me from shit. You don't know anything about me. So don't go making snap judgments about me, okay? Not that I give a flying—"

"I knew her daddy."

The curt interruption silenced Wick. Robbins was giving him a look that said *Shut up and listen.* He backed down.

Robbins said, "Before I inherited this place from my folks, I lived in Dalton and did some work for T. Dan. He was a mean cuss."

"That seems to be the general consensus."

"He could be a charmer. He had a smile that didn't stop. Came on to you like he was your best friend. A glad-hander and backslapper. But make no mistake, he was always looking out for number one."

"We've all known people like that."

Robbins shook his head. "Not like T. Dan. He was in a class by himself." He took a last greedy drag on his cigarette, then dropped it on the ground and crushed it out with the toe of his shoe. The cross-trainers looked incongruous with his cowboy attire, with him. John Wayne in Nikes.

He turned to face the corral and propped his forearms on the top rail of the fence. Wick, hoping to have some light shed on Rennie's secrets, moved to stand beside him and assumed a similar pose. Robbins didn't acknowledge him except to continue talking.

"Rennie was a happy little kid, which is a wonder. T. Dan being her daddy and all."

"What about her mother?"

"Mrs. Newton was a nice lady. She did a lot of charity work, was active in the church. Hosted a big party every Christmas and did the house up real pretty. A Santa Claus handing out candy to the kids. Stuff like that. She kept T. Dan's house running smooth, but she knew her place. She didn't interfere with his life."

Wick got the picture. "But you said Rennie was happy."

Robbins gave one of his rare smiles. "Me and Corinne always felt a little sorry for her. She tried so hard to please everybody. Skinny as a rail. Towheaded. Eyes bigger than the rest of her face."

*They still are,* Wick thought.

"Smart as a whip. Polite and knew her manners. Mrs. Newton had seen to that. And she could ride like a pro before she got to grade school." Robbins paused for several moments before saying, "The hell of it was, she thought her daddy hung the moon. She wanted so bad for him to pay attention to her. Everything she did, she did to win T. Dan's notice and approval."

He clasped his hands together and in the faint morning

light studied the calloused, rough skin on the knuckles of this thumbs. Wick saw that one of his thumbnails was completely dark from a recent bruise. He would likely lose the nail.

"Everybody in Dalton knew T. Dan messed around. It wasn't even a secret from Mrs. Newton. I figure she made her peace with his womanizing early in the marriage. She bore it with dignity, you might say. Ignored the gossip as best she could. Put up a good front.

"But Rennie was just a kid. She didn't understand the way it was supposed to be between a loving man and wife. She didn't know any different, because her parents' marriage had always been the way it was. They were pleasant to one another. Rennie wasn't old enough to realize that the intimacy was missing."

He glanced over at Wick, and Wick knew it was to make sure he was still paying attention. He was getting to the crux of the story.

"Rennie was about twelve, I think. A rough time for a girl, if my wife is any authority on the subject, and she seems to be. Anyhow, Rennie surprised T. Dan in his office one afternoon. Only she was the one who got the surprise."

"There was a woman with him."

"Under him, on the sofa in his office. Rennie's piano teacher." He paused and stared straight into the new sun. "That was the end of the happy childhood. Rennie wasn't a kid anymore."

Crystal, the waitress in Dalton, had told Wick that Rennie went hog wild about the time her female parts took form. But her emerging sexuality hadn't been the cause of her personality change at puberty. It had been the discovery of her father's adultery.

The rebellion made sense. Probably Mrs. Newton had been having mother-daughter talks with Rennie about sex and morality. Rennie had caught her father violating the principles her mother was trying to instill. The experience would have been disillusioning, especially since she worshipped her dad.

It was also a catalytic event. Her promiscuity as a teen had been a fitting punishment for her philandering father and for her mother who turned a blind eye to it. The innocent girl had discovered her father in flagrante delicto with her piano teacher, and, as a consequence, became the town slut.

As though following Wick's train of thought, Robbins said, "These days they call it 'acting out.' So Corinne tells me. I think she heard the term on TV. Whatever they call it, Rennie changed overnight. Became a holy terror. Grades went to the cellar. For the next several years she was out of control. Nothing in the way of punishment seemed to take. She defied teachers, anyone with the least bit of authority. T. Dan and Mrs. Newton revoked privileges, but it didn't do any good."

"Her father gave her a red Mustang convertible," Wick said. "I call that sending a child mixed signals."

"She probably blackmailed him into getting her that automobile. Rennie knew she had the upper hand and she exercised it. T. Dan lost his parental authority when she saw him humping her piano teacher. She was on a fast track to hell."

"Until she was sixteen."

Robbins turned his head and looked at him. "You know about Collier?"

"Some. I know Rennie fatally shot him. She was never charged with a crime. It was never even investigated as a crime. The whole thing was swept under the rug."

"T. Dan." Robbins said it as if the name alone summarized the explanation.

"I can't say my heart bleeds for Raymond Collier," Wick

said. "What kind of scumbag has an affair with a sixteen-year-old girl who obviously needed good parenting, strict discipline, and counseling?"

"Don't be too quick to judge him. If Rennie set her cap for a man, she was hard to resist."

Wick's eyes sharpened on Robbins, who shook his head wryly. "No, not me. I was a Dutch uncle to her. I wanted to scold her, knock some sense into her, not bed her. But it was another story with Raymond Collier."

"What was he like?"

"I didn't know him well, but most folks seemed to like him okay. Had a good head for business. That's why T. Dan was partnering with him on a big commercial real estate deal. But he had a weakness."

"Women."

"Not women. Only one. Rennie," the older man said grimly. "He was obsessed with her. Like that James Mason movie."

"*Lolita.*"

"Right. I guess she knew how Collier felt about her. Sensed it, you know, the way women can. She—"

"Why didn't I get the memo for this meeting?"

Wick and Robbins turned in unison. Rennie was crossing the yard toward them. Her hair was still damp from her shower, indicating that she had rushed to dress and join them. "I saw you from the bedroom window. You've had your heads together for a long time." Her eyes dropped to the pistol tucked into his waistband.

"I nearly shot him." Wick tried to smile convincingly, but his mind was still on everything Robbins had told him.

Robbins gave her one of his typically laconic explanations for why he was there. "Heard you got that cat with one shot straight through the heart. Folks around here who've lost livestock will be thanking you."

"Do you think I should have called the vet to look at Spats?"

"No," Robbins replied. "You were right. The wound isn't deep, and it's clean. Should be closed up in no time."

Her eyes cut to Wick, then back to Robbins. "I'm going to be away for a couple of days. Would you mind looking after things until I get back?"

The old man hesitated long enough for it to be noticeable. Finally he said, "Happy to. Can I reach you at the Fort Worth number if something comes up?"

"Galveston," Wick said. "I have a place down there. I'll leave you the number." Rennie didn't seem too pleased with him for sharing that.

"I'm going to check on Spats," she said. "I think she should probably stay in her stall one more day, but I'll let the others out into the corral."

"I'll be over this evening to put them up," Robbins told her.

She headed toward the open door of the barn, then glanced back as though expecting Robbins to follow her. "Be right there," he told her. "I need to get that phone number."

"You can always reach me on my cell."

"Doesn't hurt to have two numbers. Just to be on the safe side."

She seemed reluctant to leave them alone again, but she turned and went into the barn. Wick looked at Robbins, but he wasn't sure he wanted to hear any more about Rennie's fatal seduction of Raymond Collier. "You've got something to add?"

"Yeah, I do," Robbins said. "There's something maybe you should know. It may not matter to you, but I hope it will."

When he hesitated, Wick gave an inquisitive shrug.

Robbins glanced over his shoulder toward the barn, then

said in a low voice, "After that business with Collier, Rennie didn't pick up where she left off. She didn't go back to being the way she was before."

Wick didn't comment and waited him out.

"You're right, Threadgill, I don't know you from shit, but I know you're trouble. I read the newspapers. I watch TV. I don't much like you hanging around Rennie."

"Too bad. You don't get a vote."

"Especially with this character Lozada being involved."

"It's because of him that I'm hanging around."

"That the only reason?" His eyes bored into Wick's. "Me and Corinne have been looking after Rennie for a long time. We don't plan to stop now." He inclined his head, moving in closer. "You've got a big gun and a big mouth, but you're dumber than this fence post here if you don't get what I'm telling you."

"I'd get it if you'd say it straight out."

"All right. Rennie's worked hard to get where she's at in her career. I've seen her take chances on horseback that seasoned cowboys and stunt riders wouldn't take. She flies off to the other side of the world, goes to places where there's fighting and God knows what kind of pestilence, and she never shows an ounce of fear.

"But," he said, taking a step closer, "I've never seen her in the company of a man. She's certainly never let one spend the night." He took in Wick's bare chest and made a point of looking down at the fly he had hurriedly buttoned. "I hope you're decent enough, man enough, to handle that responsibility."

* * *

When Rennie came in from the corral, Wick was watching coffee drip from the filter basket into the carafe. Bare-chested and barefoot, he was wearing only blue jeans. His handgun was lying on the counter next to the Mr. Coffee. None of this was compatible with her safe, familiar kitchen, and all of it was disconcerting.

"Is there something wrong with the coffeemaker?"

He shook his head with chagrin. "I'm just so anxious for it I've been counting the drips."

"Sounds good to me, too." She took two mugs from the cabinet.

"Spats okay?" he asked.

"Just as Toby said."

"He hates my guts."

She passed him a mug. "Don't be silly."

"I'm not. And my feelings aren't hurt. I'm just stating a fact. Did he go home?"

"He just left."

The last of the coffee gurgled into the carafe. Wick filled her mug, warning, "It's cops' coffee. Strong."

"Doctors have the same kind." She sipped and gave him a thumbs-up.

"Robbins makes a very serious business out of looking after you. He warned me to keep my grubby paws off you."

"He said no such thing. I know he didn't."

"Not in so many words."

She took another few sips of her coffee, then set her mug on the counter. "Turn around and let me check your incision."

He turned, set the heels of his hands on the edge of the counter, and leaned forward. "Can't fool me. You just want to look at my ass."

"I've seen it."

"And?"

"I've seen better."

"Now *that* hurts my feelings."

The human body held few mysteries for Rennie. She had studied it, learned it, seen it in every condition, size, color, and shape. But yesterday when she saw all of Wick's body stretched out on her bed, it had made an impression. And not from a medical standpoint. His torso was long and lean, his limbs well proportioned. No body she had ever seen had the appeal of his, and she had struggled for professional detachment when she touched it.

She removed the old bandage and gently probed his incision. "Tender?"

"Only when you poke it. It's starting to itch."

"A sign of healing. A medical miracle considering your shortage of bed rest."

"When will you remove the stitches?"

"A few more days. Stay put and finish your coffee. I might just as well clean it during one of your rare periods of immobility."

"No more shots," he called to her as she left the room.

She retrieved the supplies from upstairs and was actually surprised to find him still in place when she returned. She told him so.

"Doctor's orders."

"Yes, but I can't believe you followed them. You're not exactly an ideal patient, Mr. Threadgill."

"Why are Toby and Corinne Robbins so protective of you?"

"They've known me since I was a little girl."

"So have a lot of other people in Dalton. I don't see anyone else hovering around you and warding off satyrs like me."

"I doubt Toby Robbins knows what a satyr is."

"But you do, don't you, Rennie?"

"You're not a satyr."

"Was Raymond Collier?"

He was baiting her, trying to get her to talk about it. She wasn't ready to talk about it. She doubted she would ever be ready to talk about it with Wick. Where would she even begin? With the day she had discovered her father's adultery? Could she make Wick understand how shattering it had been to realize the hypocrisy she'd been living with and stupidly accepting?

Or would she begin with Raymond? How he used to follow her. How his longing gaze had never strayed from her if they were in the same gathering of people, including his wife. How she had loathed his calf eyes and moist hands before she realized that she could use his obsession to punish her father. No, she couldn't talk about that with Wick.

"There," she said as she placed a new bandage over the incision. "All done, and actually you were fairly cooperative this time."

Before she could move away, he took one of her hands in each of his and pulled them around him, to the front of his body, so that she was hugging him from behind.

"What are you doing, Wick?"

"Who was your ideal patient?"

She dismissed the question with a light laugh, something not easily accomplished with her breasts flattened against his back, her hands splayed over the crisp hair on his chest, and her center growing warm from the contact with his rump.

He had covered her hands with his, holding them captive against him. His skin—not his epidermis, but his skin—felt warm and vital against her palms. Beneath her left hand she could feel the strong beating of his heart. For someone accustomed to listening to hearts beat every day, the rhythm of his had a strange effect on her. It was making her own beat faster against the strong muscles of his back.

"Shouldn't we be preparing to leave, Wick? I thought you were in a hurry to get away."

"Your ideal patient. I want to hear about him or her, or we'll stand here until I do, and you know that I'm just stubborn enough to mean it." For emphasis he pressed down on her arms at his sides, forcing a tighter hug.

In surrender, she rested her forehead in the shallow depression between his shoulder blades. But it was far too comfortable, far too nice, so it lasted for only a few brief seconds before she raised her head.

"It was a she. A thirty-four-year-old woman. She was a victim of the World Trade Center attack. I was in Philadelphia on September the eleventh, attending a conference. I drove straight to New York and arrived late that evening.

"She was one of the few who'd been pulled from the rubble still alive, but her injuries were severe and numerous. I worked on her internal injuries. A specialist amputated her leg. For twenty-four hours we didn't even know her name. She had no identification on her and wasn't lucid enough to tell us who she was. But subconsciously she knew she was being helped. Every time I took her hand, trying to let her know that she was safe, that someone was taking care of her, she would squeeze my hand.

"Finally, she regained consciousness enough to give us her name, which we matched with a family, one of thousands desperately seeking information. She was from Ohio and had been on a business trip. Her husband and three children had an emotional reunion with her in the hospital. In the midst of it, she looked at me. Her eyes spoke with such eloquence she didn't have to say anything."

At some point during the telling, she had rested her cheek against Wick's back. He was stroking the backs of her hands where they still rested on his chest. "You saved her life, Rennie."

"No," she said thickly. "I couldn't. She died two days later. She knew she was going to die. We had told her it was doubtful she could survive such massive damage. She was thanking me for extending her life long enough for her to see her family. She wanted to tell them good-bye. It took an act of will and tremendous courage for her to live even that long. Her love for them was stronger than her pain. So when you asked who my ideal patient was, she immediately came to mind."

Several moments elapsed before he said, "I think you're incredible, Dr. Newton. No wonder the Robbinses think so highly of you."

She recognized the statement as a transition. He wanted to know about her relationship with Toby and Corinne, and this was his roundabout way of asking. What would be the harm in telling him that much? He probably knew anyway. It was possible that Toby had told him during their extended conversation at the corral fence and Wick wanted to hear her version of it.

This time when her forehead came to rest between his shoulder blades, she kept it there. "After Raymond Collier, my parents enrolled me in a boarding school in Dallas. The first Christmas I was there, they went to Europe. Mother didn't want to go, or so she claimed. But there was no arguing with T. Dan. As part of my punishment for the trouble I'd caused, I was left at school to spend the holiday alone.

"Somehow, Toby and Corinne found out. They showed up on Christmas morning. They brought their children, goodies, presents, and tried to make me happy. They've been seeing to my happiness ever since. If he comes across as overly protective, I think it's because he still sees me as a lonely abandoned girl on Christmas."

"What happened in your father's study that day, Rennie?"

She raised her head and withdrew her hands from beneath his. "If we're going to Galveston, we should be going."

He came around and took her by the shoulders. "What happened, Rennie?"

"Wesley will blame me for any delay" was her only answer.

"Did he rape you? Try?"

Angered by his tenacity, she flung off his hands. "God, you never give up!"

"Did he?"

"Isn't that what my father told the police?"

"Yes. And from what little I know of T. Dan Newton, lying would be the least of his sins. He'd lie to the police and smile while doing it. Now, what caused you to shoot Raymond Collier?"

"What does it matter?"

"It matters because I want to know, dammit! It matters because you're so damned and determined to keep the secret your daddy's money got buried. And it matters because I'm working on a two-day hard-on that I can't do anything about. Not without you accusing me of mauling you and getting death threats from your neighbor Toby."

He had backed her into a corner, literally—she was wedged into the right angle formed by intersecting cabinetry—and he had backed her into a corner emotionally. She came out fighting.

"Raymond never forced me to do anything. Not that afternoon. Not ever. If you want to invent a myth about attempted rape because that somehow sanitizes it in your mind and makes you feel better about me, then fine. But that's not the way it was.

"Raymond and T. Dan became partners on a land deal when I was fourteen. He started coming around a lot, spending time with us. I knew the impact I had on him. I teased him unmercifully. Under the guise of an affectionate older man, he seized every opportunity to touch me. I encouraged it and laughed about it later. He had this . . . this naked yearning that I thought was hilarious." She paused to take a breath. "Still think I'm 'incredible,' Wick? Just wait. There's more."

"Stop it, Rennie."

"Oh no, you wanted to know. You wanted relief for your hard-on. Well, this ought to cure it. For two years I tormented that poor man. Then, about a week before that wretched day, I had a quarrel with my father. I don't even remember what I'd done, but he took away the keys to my car and grounded me for a month.

"So I got back at him by sleeping with his business partner. That's right, Wick. I called Raymond from a motel and told him that if he wanted me he could have me, but that he had to come right then. I was waiting for him."

She brushed tears of shame off her hot cheeks, but it was too late to stop now. The words continued to bubble out of her. "Raymond came to the motel and I went to bed with him. Just like I went to bed with all of them. Everything you've heard about Rennie Newton is true. You probably haven't heard a fraction of what there is to tell. Sometime when I haven't got a killer breathing down my neck, we'll get together and split a bottle of wine, and I'll detail for you all my sexual escapades. It'll be like telling ghost stories, only better.

"But this is the one story that seems to have you itching for the lowdown. And rightly so, because it was the worst thing I ever did. Daddy punished me, but I showed him, didn't I? I showed him but good."

# Chapter 28

Reportedly, Wesley had been relieved to hear that she and Wick had passed the night safely and that there'd been no trace of Lozada. But since they'd left the ranch he had called Wick at half-hour intervals even though Wick had assured him he would be notified immediately if they spotted Lozada at any point on the long drive to Galveston.

Wick had insisted on taking his pickup, and he had insisted on driving. It would be a difficult and exhausting trip for him as a passenger. Driving would add more stress and strain, but she hadn't quarreled with him about it.

They avoided talking at all.

The tension between them since their last conversation was pulled so taut that one cross word could cause it to snap like an overextended rubber band. And Wick had resumed wearing one around his wrist.

She was staring out the passenger window looking disinterestedly at the scenery speeding by when his cell phone rang for the umpteenth time. "Jesus, Oren, give it a rest," he said.

"Extend to the detective my warmest regards," she said drolly.

"Yeah?"

Rennie sensed the change in Wick instantly. She turned away from the window and saw that his free hand had tightened around the steering wheel and his lips were set in a thin, straight line.

His voice, however, was incongruently pleasant. "Well, well, well, Ricky Roy. Haven't seen you in a while. Of course the last time we shared space I didn't exactly see you, did I?"

Just knowing that Lozada was on the other end of the call caused Rennie to shudder. The fear she'd felt that evening in her kitchen was still a fresh memory. Had he been brutal or raving, he wouldn't have frightened her nearly as much, but his complacency had been terrifying.

Wick steered the pickup off the highway. "I hate to be the one to break it to you, Ricky Roy, but backstabbing someone is really a chickenshit thing to do." When the truck came to a full stop, he pushed the gear stick into Park. "But I'm as good as new now. Pity I can't say the same for Sally Horton. Sally Horton, asshole. You remember. The girl you killed the night you tried to kill me."

Rennie could hear Lozada's silky laughter coming through the phone. She unfastened her seat belt, moved closer to Wick, and motioned for him to hold the phone away from his ear so she could listen in.

"You must still be on mind-altering painkillers, Threadgill," he said. "I don't know what you're talking about."

"Then let me clarify it. You're a cowardly woman killer."

Lozada was too clever to fall for such obvious baiting. "I read that you had barely survived an assault of some kind, and that you would have died if you hadn't received excellent emergency care."

"Rennie Newton is an excellent surgeon."

"A good fuck, too."

Rennie reacted as though she'd been struck. She looked at Wick but could only see herself reflected in the lenses of his sunglasses.

"Is she there with you now?" Lozada asked.

"If she weren't you wouldn't be calling me, would you?"

"Strange, isn't it? You and I sharing a woman. Although," he continued smoothly, "it's not surprising that Rennie is attracted to both of us. Danger turns her on. Like when her friend Dr. Howell died. She described to me the violent way he died, and during the telling, she got wet."

Rennie made a lunging grab for the telephone, but Wick caught her wrist and pushed her hand away. He shook his head furiously.

"That was only the second time we were together," Lozada said. "She was a wild one that night. Even I could barely keep up with her."

"That doesn't surprise me," Wick said as though bored. "I always figured your murder weapons were substitutes for physical shortcomings."

Lozada tsked. "That was a cheap shot. Unworthy of even you."

"You're right. I should have come right out and called you an impotent slug-dick."

Lozada laughed. "It really bothers you that I had her first, doesn't it? I bet you wonder how you compare. I once made her come just by licking her nipples. Can you do that?"

Rennie covered her ears, but she could still hear Wick say, "You know, Ricky Roy, I'm beginning to think you're trying to come on to me with all this dirty talk. What's the point of this call, anyway?"

She didn't hear what Lozada said, but Wick's response to it was, "Wrong. If you were finished with her, you wouldn't be making this call. You're jealous and can't stand it that she's with me now. Eat your heart out, asshole."

He clicked off, practically threw the phone up onto the dashboard, and cursed viciously.

"He's lying," she said gruffly.

He shifted the pickup into Drive and checked for oncoming traffic, then pulled back onto the highway.

"He's lying, Wick."

He still didn't acknowledge her.

"He's manipulating you, and you're letting him!"

He turned to her then and she could feel his eyes probing hers from behind the sunglasses. But all he said was, "Buckle your seat belt."

* * *

Although he disliked Wick Threadgill hanging up on him, Lozada was chuckling as he clicked off his cell phone. The call had accomplished what he'd wanted. The only thing more gratifying would be to hear the conversation going on between them now. He would love to know if the seeds of doubt he'd planted had taken root in Threadgill's mind.

Rennie had probably been listening in. She would be denying everything and Threadgill would be finding her denials hard to believe. Especially since he knew all, if not more, of what Lozada's own investigation had uncovered about the young Rennie Newton.

In another life he might have been a cop, he thought philosophically. He definitely had the instincts of an undercover detective. He had turned these intuitive skills one hundred eighty degrees to serve his own needs, but he would have made as good an investigator as Oren Wesley or Joe Threadgill or little brother Wick. And, unlike them, he wasn't constrained by conscience or legality.

For instance, had the waitress at the Wagon Wheel Café in Dalton not been so cooperative, he might have followed her home and tortured answers out of her before killing her.

As it turned out, however, Crystal had been a gushing fountain of information. At first she had thought it curious that he was the second man in so many weeks to inquire about Rennie Newton.

"Funny that you're askin' 'bout her."

Lozada had picked at his plate of greasy enchiladas and said nonchalantly, "How so?"

"There was another fellow in here not long ago. I think it was a Sunday. He'd known her in college, he said. He was a real cutie pie." She winked. "Rennie missed out on him, same as she did on you, Mr. Tall, Dark, and Handsome."

"Thank you. What did the other guy look like?"

She had described Wick Threadgill from his mop of blond hair to his scuffed cowboy boots. When he told Crystal that this dreamboat was a cop, she had been miffed. "Now *that* pisses me off," she exclaimed. "I fell for every word of his BS!"

He told her that Wick was an investigator for a sleazy medical malpractice lawyer. "His sole job is to dig up dirt on defending doctors." Crystal fell for the story just as she'd fallen for whatever line Threadgill had given her. "Don't blame yourself, Crystal. He can be very convincing."

"Dadgum right. Must've been those big blue eyes of his." Her gaze turned wary. "You some kind of investigator too?"

He gave her his best smile. "I'm a freelance writer. I'm doing an article on Dr. Newton. About her volunteer work in underprivileged countries."

"Well, if you ask me, all her volunteering won't make up for her past shenanigans," she said with a righteous sniff. Then for the next half hour she had regaled him with stories about the licentious Rennie Newton. "Don't guess we should've been surprised when she shot poor ol' Raymond."

Oh, yes, his trip to Dalton yesterday had been very worthwhile and informative. He had even come away with a complimentary piece of chocolate meringue pie, packed up for carry-out.

Weenie Sawyer had come through for him. The threat with the scorpion had rendered all kinds of information, such as new and useful facts regarding Wick Threadgill, including the place of his last credit-card charge, which happened to be located in the town where, according to other computer data, Rennie Newton had been born and reared.

He had also learned how much property tax she paid on her ranch in a neighboring county, that she was quite a horsewoman, and that she had competed in rodeo barrel racing in her hometown. That is, when she wasn't fucking for sport.

Now, feeling flush with the success of his phone call to the former cop, he turned up the volume on the CD player in his SUV and inhaled deeply, wondering when he would catch the first whiff of coastal air.

* * *

Wick unlocked the door and it swung open on rusty hinges. He motioned her inside. "Don't expect too much."

"It'll be fine."

"I don't earn a six-figure surgeon's salary."

"I said it's *fine*."

"Kitchen's there. Bedroom and bath through there. Make yourself at home."

"I'd like to shower."

"I don't guarantee hot water. Clean towels—if there are any—will be in the cabinet above the commode."

Without another word she went through the door into the bedroom, closing it behind her. "Never mind, Your Highness, I'll bring in the bags by myself," he muttered.

He returned to the pickup, consciously telling himself to act naturally and not to look around for the police personnel posted to watch them. He hauled the two bags from the bed of the pickup, wincing at the pinching pain in his back.

Twice Rennie had offered to drive. The first time he had declined the offer and politely thanked her for the courtesy. The second time he had snapped at her. That was after Lozada's call, when their strained silence had turned into hostile coexistence. The last three hours of the trip had seemed like thirty. The tension had found his weak spot and settled in. Every time he felt so much as a twinge, he cursed Lozada.

With no regard for his guest's privacy, he pushed open the bedroom door and went in. He could hear the water pipes knocking in the bathroom. A naked and soapy Rennie would be the best thing ever to grace that sorry shower, but he'd be doing himself a favor not to think about Rennie either naked or soapy or at all.

He tossed the bags onto the bed, then went to the bureau and opened the bottom drawer. Beneath a jumbled pile of his oldest and most comfortable shorts he located the mike and transmitter that had been planted there for him. Wesley had told him where they would be hidden. They would keep him in constant communication with the surveillance team.

He inserted the earpiece and spoke into the minuscule microphone. "We're here."

"Ten-four. We see you."

"Who's this?"

"Peterson. I'm heading the operation."

"Threadgill."

"Pleased to meet you."

"Where are you?"

"Best you don't know," Peterson said. "Don't want to tempt you into looking for me and giving us away."

"Hey, Wick, how was your trip?"

"Long. Who's this?"

"Plum."

"Hey, Plum. I didn't know Oren had sent down any of his guys."

"It's a coordinated effort between Fort Worth and Galveston PDs. Lozada was a suspect in a murder case here. Organized-crime bigwig who was trying to get legalized gambling in here. Some said a church group hired Lozada."

"I'd vote for a competing organized-crime bigwig."

"Me too," Plum said. "No church group could afford Lozada. Anyhow, it's an unsolved murder on their books down here, so they were willing to help us out."

"Glad to have you, Plum. Thank God it's you and not Thigpen."

"Kiss my ass, Threadgill."

"Oh, Jesus," Wick groaned. "Tell me no."

"And, while you're at it, kiss the doctor's sweet ass for me."

"I'd volunteer for that," said an anonymous voice.

"Animals," growled a distinctly female voice, obviously a policewoman.

Thigpen said, "Hey, Threadgill, leave the mike on. We want to hear everything."

"Okay, that's it," Peterson cut in sharply. "Shut up, all of you, unless you've got something to report."

"Bye-bye, boys and girls. Have fun," Wick taunted.

"Up yours," he heard Thigpen whisper.

He kept the earpiece in so he could hear their warnings, but he turned off the mike. Rennie emerged from the bathroom, wrapped in a towel. When she saw him, she pulled up short. "I forgot that my bag is still—" He motioned toward the bed. "Oh. Thank you."

He could have taken it to her. He didn't. He could have excused himself and left the room. He didn't. Instead, he let her cross the room and get her bag and carry it into the bathroom with her, which she did with amazing dignity for a woman who was wet from head to toe and covered only by one of his skimpy towels.

The rear view was just as good as the front, and he enjoyed the hell out of it, although he wondered uneasily if he was turning into a slimmer, cleaner version of Pigpen.

* * *

Wick was in the kitchen when Rennie rejoined him. "Did something die in here?"

He glanced at her over his shoulder. "An opened package of bologna. Found it in the bottom drawer of the fridge. Real slimy. Do you want to eat out or in, honey?"

"Whatever."

"No, you decide, sweetheart."

"All right, since you asked, I'd rather eat in so I don't have to dress up."

"Do you like steak?"

"Filet mignons."

"Naturally," he said as he added filets to what she had determined was a grocery list. "Only the best for you."

"Is this how you're going to be, Wick?"

He looked over at her and asked innocently, "How am I being?"

"Sarcastic. Snide. Because if so, I'm leaving. You, Wesley, and Lozada can go to the devil. I don't know why I consented to this. Lozada probably won't even show."

Wick turned away from her and stared through the salt-encrusted window. "You're wrong, Rennie. He'll show. I don't know how or when, but he'll show. You can count on it."

The dark conviction with which he spoke made her wish for a return of his sarcasm.

At least the solemn reminder of why they were there leveled the chip on his shoulder that had been there since the call from Lozada. He insisted that she go with him to the supermarket. As he ushered her to his pickup, he said, "Lovers on a getaway do chores and run errands together."

She was glad he had insisted she go along. The house was a dreary place, and she hadn't relished the thought of being there alone, anticipating an appearance by Lozada and knowing that she was under constant observation by undercover officers.

Even sitting in the passenger seat of Wick's truck she felt conspicuous. When they stopped for a traffic light she said, "I haven't noticed anyone watching us."

"They're there."

"Can they hear us?"

"Not if I don't engage the mike."

He had explained the tiny, clear earpiece he was wearing. "Are they saying anything now?"

"The blue van two cars back just passed us off to the gray Taurus over there signaling to turn left."

She forced herself not to look and instead leaned forward to change the station on the radio.

"Very good, Rennie."

"I'm trying." As she sat back she smiled at him. He surprised her by reaching across the seats and stroking her cheek with the backs of his fingers.

"What's that for?"

"For show. Just in case the cops aren't the only ones who have us in their sights."

That was an unnerving possibility, so she didn't protest when Wick threw an arm across her shoulders and stayed close as they walked from the parking lot into the store where he played the role of attentive and affectionate lover. He smiled at her a lot, and nudged her shoulder playfully, and asked her opinion about everything he placed in the basket, and showed off for her by juggling a trio of oranges.

They shared a cone of frozen yogurt, and when they were in line to check out, he held a *Sports Illustrated* in one hand and read an article while his other hand massaged her neck with the absentmindedness of someone accustomed to doing it. Had she been observing them, she would have been convinced that they were two people in love and comfortable with the relationship.

The sun was going down by the time they returned to the house. "I'll start the charcoal. While it's smoldering, let's go down to the water."

"I didn't think to bring a suit."

"Then I guess you'll have to skinny-dip."

She shot him a retiring look and headed for the bedroom. "I brought some shorts. They'll do."

When she came out a few minutes later, Wick had exchanged his jeans for a pair of baggy shorts with a stringy hem. The low-slung shorts made his chest look even wider, his waist more tapered. She made a point of not looking at his tanned, muscled calves.

He, on the other hand, took one look at her and said a soft but emphatic, "Damn."

Her face turned warm. She had changed into a black knit top with thin straps and a pair of faded denim shorts. The outfit—or perhaps Wick's reaction to it—made her feel more self-conscious than she had wearing only the towel.

"Let's go." He turned and headed for the door.

"What about those?" She pointed to the communication

apparatus he'd left lying on the coffee table alongside his pistol.

"Shit. Almost forgot."

He had to put his shirt back on so he could clip the mike inside the collar and hide the thin cable to the earpiece. He stuck his handgun into the waistband of the shorts. It was covered by his long shirttail.

Holding hands, they walked to the shore and waded into the strong tide of the Gulf. It was twilight. Only a few stragglers were on the beach. "Afraid of sharks?" he asked.

"In water this shallow?"

"That's where most attacks occur."

"Don't we have a better chance of getting struck by lightning?"

"Or getting popped by Lozada."

She tugged on his hand, pulling him to a stop. When he was facing her, she said, "He was lying, Wick. Those things he said were not true."

"Shh." Apparently someone was speaking to him through the earpiece. He pulled her into a close embrace and nuzzled her neck. "There's a man moving at seven o'clock, but don't turn around. Keep up the act. But if something happens, if all hell breaks loose, you hit the surf, Rennie. Got that?"

She nodded.

He angled back, but kept his hands loosely on her waist. The current surged against their legs. Their bodies swayed together. For balance, he assumed a wider stance, placing her feet between his. He kissed her cheek just beneath her ear. His hands moved down to her hips. Another wave caught them just behind the knees. Reflexively she reached for him so she wouldn't lose her balance. She could feel the tension in his biceps. He was playing his role well, but he was primed for action.

Then he said, "Not our man."

It had been a false alarm, but they remained as they were, with her hands resting on his upper arms and his on her bottom. Beneath her feet, the sand shifted with the current. She felt like she was losing ground and that the only solid thing in the universe at the moment was Wick's blue stare.

"He was lying, Wick."

"I know. I—"

"*Do* you?"

"For a few minutes there—"

"You believed him."

"Not really. Okay, for maybe half a second he had me going. He probably guessed that you were listening and said those things to embarrass you. But even if you weren't listening, he knew they would rile me. And they did. He got to me, and I acted like a jackass. I realized it about ninety seconds later, but was—"

"Too bullheaded to admit it."

"Am I allowed to complete a sentence here?"

"I'm sorry. What did you want to say?"

"I wanted to say that the way he talked about you is reason enough for me to want to kill him. And that..."

"What?"

"That I'm going to kiss you now and make it look like I mean it."

He dipped his head and settled his mouth on hers. His tongue slipped easily past her lips and moved against hers in what felt like a mating ritual, ancient and elemental. A wave took her unawares from behind and pushed her against him. Middles bumped together. And stayed.

"Oh man," he groaned. His fingers flexed tighter on her hips, held her firmly against him.

A burst of heat spread through her center. It all felt too

good. So she pulled back. "Wick, I can't..." The words stuck in her throat. "I can't keep my balance."

He set her away from him. "That's enough for now, anyway."

But as they walked back toward the house, his face was hard and set, his stride was long and angry, and she didn't believe for an instant that it had been enough.

# Chapter 29

They were so ridiculously transparent.

Did those undercover yahoos think he wouldn't spot them? They might just as well be wearing neon vests. The stocky bitch and her hairy companion sweeping their metal detector across the sand. Please. And the fat guy fishing from the pier. His hat was too new and his technique too clumsy. The three guys and a girl having a tailgate cookout were working way too hard at having a good time. The others were just as obvious.

Lozada had spotted them all from the passenger seat of the realtor's van. She was fiftyish, friendly, and eager to please. He had seen the billboard advertising her as Galveston Island's most successful real-estate broker. He had called her from his car.

Thanks to Weenie Sawyer's research, he knew the location of Wick's house. He mentioned the vicinity to the realtor as an area where he was interested in buying a lot on which to build a beach house for his wife and four children. He had requested a late evening appointment. They had met at her office and she had driven him here in one of the company's vans. The logo painted on the side was a familiar sight; it was plastered all over the island. Police wouldn't give the van a second glance.

Now, while she prattled on about the excellent investment opportunities of beachfront property, Lozada picked out the cops on the beach.

He dismissed them as insignificant amateurs and focused on Rennie and Wick. Walking in the surf. Holding hands. How sweet. How romantic. All staged to draw him out and slap him with some trumped-up charge.

But what really rankled was that this newfound romance of theirs wasn't just a futile police operation, as he had originally thought. It was real and, as such, it was an affront. His blood pressure soared when he saw Wick groping her. Even from this distance he could tell their kiss wasn't play-acting. Which only affirmed that Rennie was a whore.

She had been a whore from her youth. She had spread her legs for every lout in that miserable little town where she'd grown up, and now she was spreading them for Wick Threadgill, days after Lozada had professed his affection. He sorely regretted that now. Why hadn't he realized sooner that she was a whore, undeserving of him and his attention?

He had been tricked by her. During his trial she had noticed his attraction and had played games with him. She had used her cool, aloof demeanor to taunt him and make herself desirable.

Well he didn't want her anymore. She had proved herself unworthy.

Oh, he still wanted to fuck her. And when he did, he would make it hurt. By the time he got through with her she would understand that nobody toyed with Lozada and got away with it. Maybe he would force Threadgill to watch. Oh, yes. Threadgill would pay dearly for taking what Lozada had claimed as his.

"Mr. Smith?"

"Yes?"

"I asked if you had prearranged financing."

He'd almost forgotten that the realtor was there. He turned to her and thought seriously about snapping her neck. Quickly and painlessly, she would be dead and he would have let off some steam. But he had never let spontaneity overrule sound judgment. He was better disciplined than that.

Answering as the mild-mannered Mr. Smith, he said, "Financing would be no problem."

"Excellent." She launched into the next phase of her sales pitch.

He would have to wrap up this appointment soon. From the safety of the van he had seen everything he needed to see. Twilight had turned into full-blown darkness, his favorite time. He looked forward to the busy night ahead.

* * *

"How was your steak?"

"Perfect."

"Glad you liked it." Wick propped his forearms on the edge of the table and rolled the glass of wine between his palms. "The Merlot was a good choice."

"Yes, it was."

"Can't say much for the glass." His collection of mismatched glassware hadn't included wine balloons, so they'd drunk from juice glasses.

"I didn't mind."

He swirled the ruby liquid in the glass. "Know what I think?"

"What?"

"If this were a blind date, it would be a bust."

She smiled ruefully. "It's hard to make casual conversation when you're on display. I feel like a goldfish."

They had sat out on the deck while the steaks were grilling and the potatoes were baking on the coals. They had sipped wine, said little, listened to the swish of the surf.

The glider had squeaked each time Rennie's bare foot gave it a gentle push. Those shorts made her legs look about nine miles long. There were small dots of salt on her thighs where splashes of seawater had dried. Wick's attention had often strayed there.

A young dog had wandered up to the deck, no doubt attracted by the aroma of the cooking meat. She got down on his level, scratched him behind the ears, and laughed the laugh of a child when he tried to lick her face. She played with him until his master whistled sharply. He charged off obediently, but then stopped and looked back at her wistfully, as though he hated to leave her, before disappearing into the darkness to rejoin his owner.

About every five minutes the undercovers would check in with Peterson, one by one. He could hear them in his earpiece. If Lozada was anywhere on Galveston Island, he was remaining invisible. He wasn't registered at any hotel, motel, or bed-and-breakfast. Wick wasn't surprised.

Peterson gave him signals to send them. "If y'all are okay in there, scratch your nose." Put your right hand in your pocket. Stretch. Stuff like that. But it reached the point where he could tune out the voices in his ear. If an emergency arose, he would react appropriately, but for the time being he minded the bacon-wrapped filets and spent the rest of the time looking at Rennie.

When the steaks were done, they brought the meal indoors. Once while they were eating, her bare foot had made contact with his calf beneath the table. She hadn't excused herself for the accidental touch, which was progress of a sort. But she hadn't acknowledged it either. She pretended it hadn't happened.

She had discovered a yellowed candle in a drawer and had placed it on a saucer in the center of the table to create a romantic atmosphere and help obscure the ugliness of his kitchen. But the only thing the candlelight really enhanced and made look good was Rennie.

When her hair was loose, like now, she had a habit of combing her fingers through it. She wasn't even conscious of doing it, but he was conscious of it because he liked watching it sift through her fingers and fall back onto her shoulders. *Liquid moonlight,* he thought, and wondered when he'd become a poet.

The candlelight deepened the triangular shadow at the base of her throat and the cleft between her breasts. Throughout the evening he had tried to ignore the shape they gave the fitted black knit top, but some things were beyond human endurance, and for him, that was one.

The meal had been satisfying and tasty. His stomach was full, but another hunger gnawed at him. He should have known better than to kiss her again. It had been unnecessary. It had been overkill. Their little sunset stroll in the surf would have been just as romantic a scene without the kiss. The only thing it had accomplished was to make him want her with an ache that was damn near killing him.

She drained the wine from her juice glass and looked across at him. "You're staring."

"I'm trying to get my fill."

"Your fill?"

"Of you," he said. "Of looking at you. Because once this is over, however it comes down, you're going to return to your life, and I'm not going to be in it. Am I, Rennie?"

Slowly, she shook her head no.

"That's why I'm staring."

She pushed back her chair and picked up her place setting, but as she passed him on her way to the sink he reached out and caught her arm.

"Relax, Rennie. You may get lucky. Lozada could kill me."

She yanked her arm free, carried the dishes to the sink, and set them down hard. "That was a horrible thing to say."

"You'd care?"

"Of course I'd care!"

"Oh, right, right. You're in the lifesaving business, aren't you? Which I find odd... since you court death."

She laughed shortly. "I court death?"

"All the time. You're reckless. You take unnecessary risks."

"What in the hell are you talking about?"

"No alarm system in either of your houses. Downright foolish for a woman who lives alone. Riding bareback and jumping fences. Dangerous no matter how skilled an equestrian you are. Going to places in the world where every day is a field day to the Grim Reaper. You flirt with him, Rennie."

"You've had too much wine."

He stood and joined her near the sink. "You don't live life, Rennie, you defy it."

"You're either drunk or crazy."

"No, I'm *right.* Self-sufficient Rennie, that's you. No friends or confidantes. No socializing. No nothing except those goddamn invisible walls you erect every time someone gets too close.

"You even keep your patients at arm's length. Isn't that why you chose surgery over another field of medicine? Because your patients are unconscious? You can treat them, heal them, without any emotional involvement on your part."

Peterson asked into the earpiece, "Hey, Threadgill, everything all right in there?"

"He's famous for losing it," Thigpen said.

"I'd like to know what he's saying to her," the policewoman said. "I don't like his stance."

Wick ignored them. "You shower affection on your horses. You turn to mush over a puppy dog. You mourn a wild animal you were forced to put down. But if you make skin contact with another human being, you either ignore it or run from it."

"That's not true."

"Oh, it's not?"

"No."

"Prove it."

He bent over the table and blew out the candle, pitching the kitchen into darkness. He yanked out the earpiece, then, curving an arm around her waist, pulled her against him.

"Wick, no."

"Prove me wrong." His lips hovered above hers, giving her an opportunity to protest again. When she didn't, he kissed her. Tempering his anger, he gently rubbed her lips apart then went seeking her tongue with his. When they touched, he deepened the kiss. He fit himself into the vee of her thighs.

She pulled her mouth free and turned her face away. "Wick…"

He trailed kisses down the column of her throat, lightly nipping her skin with his teeth.

She placed her hands on his shoulders and dug her fingers in. "Please."

"I could say the same thing, Rennie."

He lowered his head and kissed the swell of her breast above her neckline.

"No." She pushed him hard.

Wick's arms fell to his sides. He backed away from her. Their harsh breathing soughed through the darkness. He heard Peterson cursing him through the earpiece where it dangled on his chest.

He tried to keep his anger in check, but arousal had fueled it and there was no putting it down yet. With a distinct edge, he said, "I just don't get it."

"What don't you get?"

"Why you keep saying no."

"I have the option of saying no."

A growl of frustration rose out of his throat. "It's so goddamn good, Rennie. What's not to like?"

"I do like it."

Thinking he hadn't heard her correctly, he reached for the wall switch and turned on the lights. "What?"

She blinked against the sudden glare, then met his bewildered gaze. She said huskily, "I never said I didn't like it."

He stared at her with such profound incomprehension that it didn't even register with him that a cell phone was ringing until she asked, "Is that yours?"

He groped for the phone clipped to his waistband and then shook his head. "Must be yours."

She went to get her phone. Wick reinserted the earpiece and caught the tail end of a blistering condemnation. He switched on the microphone. "Calm down, Peterson. We're fine."

"What's going on, Threadgill?"

"Nothing. A little electrical problem when we tried to turn on the lights. A fuse or something."

"Everything's all right?"

"Yeah, I'm about to wash the dishes and Rennie's talking on her—"

He broke off when he turned and read the expression on her face. "Hold on, guys. Someone just called her on her cell."

She was holding on to the small phone with both hands.

She listened for possibly fifteen seconds more, then slowly lowered it and disconnected.

"Lozada?" Wick asked. She nodded. "Son of a—what did he say?"

"He's here."

"He told you that?"

She raised her hand to her throat in a subconsciously self-protective gesture. "He didn't have to. He let me know that he had seen us."

"Are you guys getting this?" Wick asked into the mike. After receiving acknowledgments through the earpiece, he motioned for Rennie to proceed.

"He said that I should wear black more often. That it was a good color for me. He asked if you could cook a decent steak."

"He's that close?"

"Apparently."

"What else?"

She looked at him meaningfully, with appeal. Slowly he raised his hand and switched off the mike. There would be hell to pay later, but he was more concerned about Rennie than he was about having the Galveston PD miffed at him.

"They're raising bloody hell in my ear, but they can't hear you. Go ahead. Tell me what he said."

"He said…vulgar things. About you and me. Us. Together."

"Like the things he said earlier today?"

"Worse. He said that before I…before I…" She crossed her arms over her middle and hugged her elbows. "Paraphrasing, he said that before I become too enamored of you, I should ask how you fucked up the investigation of your brother's murder."

* * *

"She was too embarrassed to give it to me word for word. I imagine it was awfully crude."

Oren was so tired his eyeballs hurt. He massaged them as he listened to Wick's account of Lozada's most recent contact with them.

"He brought up the investigation of Joe's murder and how I botched it because, like earlier today when he lied about Rennie and him being lovers, he's trying to cause a rift between us."

"Is it working?"

"Not in that sense, but we're both a little frayed around the edges. She's in the shower now. Her second since we got here. She's clean, I'll give her that."

"I'm more interested in Lozada's whereabouts than in Dr. Newton's hygiene. None of those undercovers spotted him?"

"Neither hide nor hair."

"How could he get close enough to watch you cooking steaks without them seeing him? Binoculars, I guess."

"Or he could be buried in sand up to his eyeballs ten feet from the front door. With Lozada you can't rule out anything. He's not going to be caught by following procedure. Peterson seems competent enough, but—"

"You're not cooperating."

"He said I'm not cooperating?"

"You're taking offense?"

"I don't like being tattled on like I'm a kid."

"Then stop acting like one. He said you rarely leave the mike on and only have the earpiece in about half the time."

"I have it in *at least* half the time."

"You joke? Those people down there have put their lives on the line for you," Oren said angrily. "Keep in mind that if Lozada's that close to you, he's probably marked them."

Oren heard him sigh heavily. "I know, I thought about

that. And I'm not joking. Really. I appreciate what they're doing, and that's no bullshit."

"It wouldn't hurt to tell them that."

"I'll make it a priority."

"It may be that Lozada has spotted them and they're the only reason he hasn't attempted something."

"I thought of that too," Wick said.

"One thing puzzles me."

"Just one?"

"Why the phone calls? This isn't Lozada's MO. It seems out of character for him, almost careless. He's never warned a victim before."

Wick thought about it for a moment. "This time he isn't doing it for the money. It's not a job, it's personal."

Grace stuck her head through the door and looked at him inquisitively. He motioned her in. She sat near him on the sofa and laid her head on his shoulder. He lifted her hand to his lips and kissed it. He died a little every time he thought of what Lozada could have done to her had he chosen to.

Into the phone he said, "Well, at least we know he's in Galveston. An APB has already been issued."

"I hope they've been warned to approach with caution. What will he be arrested for?"

"Since he made that call today and it was obscene, both you and Dr. Newton can testify to his stalking her. If we can find him, we can bring him in on that."

"It's a flimsy charge, Oren."

"But it's all we've got."

"Okay, I'm gonna go smooth Peterson's feathers now," Wick said. "Over and out."

After hanging up, Oren filled Grace in on the latest development.

"How's Dr. Newton handling it?"

"He says she's okay. Clean."

"He likes her."

"He likes her looks."

"More than that. I think he might have really fallen this time."

"In love?" he scoffed. "What else is new? Wick's been in love with every woman he's ever taken to bed. His love affairs begin with an erection and end with a climax."

"And that makes him unique?" she said, laughing. "That speaks for most men."

"Not me."

"You're not most men."

He kissed her hand again. "I miss the girls."

"Me too. I talked to them this afternoon. They're having a great time. Mom's keeping them entertained, but they miss their friends and are already asking how many more days until they can come home."

"No time soon, Grace. If there's a chance in hell that Lozada—"

"I know," she said, patting his chest. "And I agree completely. I explained it to them."

"Did they understand?"

"Maybe not completely, but when they're parents they will. Now come to bed."

"I can't sleep now. I gotta go back to the office."

She stood up and tugged on his hand. "Since when is sleep all we do in bed?"

"Sorry, hon. I'm too tired to be any good in that department."

She leaned down and kissed him, saying sexily, "Leave everything to me."

"The policewoman's in the kitchen."

"She and I had a heart-to-heart. We won't be disturbed unless it's an emergency."

He was tempted, but he checked his wristwatch and frowned. "I promised to be back in half an hour."

Grace smiled and reached for him. "Hmm, I do love a challenge."

It was forty-five minutes before he returned to his desk at headquarters, and, although he hadn't even napped, he felt considerably refreshed after thirty minutes in bed with Grace. God, he loved that woman.

He knew before asking that there had been no further word from Galveston. Had there been, he would have been called or paged. But he asked anyway. "Nothing," another detective reported. "But there's a guy been waiting here to see you."

"What guy?"

"Over there."

The unkempt, bespectacled individual sitting in the chair in the corner with his shoulders hunched was gnawing on his index finger cuticle as though it were going to be his last meal.

"What's he want?" Oren asked.

"Wouldn't say."

"Why me?"

"Wouldn't say that either. Insisted on talking to you and only you."

Oren looked at the man again, but he was certain he'd never seen him before. Surely he would have remembered. "What's his name?"

"Get this. Weenie Sawyer."

# Chapter 30

Rennie came up on one elbow. For the past half hour Wick had been standing at the bedroom window, looking out. Motionless, he stood with one arm propped just above his head on the window frame, the other hanging loosely at his side. In that hand he held his pistol. His weight was shifted to his left foot, favoring his right side. His shorts rode low on his hips. The bandage over his incision showed up very white in the dark room.

"Is something wrong?" she whispered.

He looked at her over his shoulder. "No. Sorry I disturbed you."

"Did you hear—"

"No, nothing." He walked back to the bed and set his pistol on the table. "Other than the periodic check-ins by the undercovers, it's been quiet."

"No word about Lozada?"

"No word. I wish the son of a bitch would show himself and get it over with. This waiting is driving me nuts." He lay down beside her and stacked his hands behind his head.

"What time is it?" she asked.

"Still an hour before sunrise. Were you able to sleep?"

"I dozed."

"That was about it for me, too."

For the sake of the microphone that hung loosely on his chest, he was lying, just as she was. They had lain side by side all night, silent and tense, each fully aware that the other was awake but, for their individual reasons, not daring to acknowledge it.

"You should get some sleep, Rennie."

"I learned to live on very little my first year of internship. It scares me now to think of how many patients I treated while virtually asleep on my feet."

"Did you always know you wanted to be a doctor?"

"No. Actually it wasn't until my second year in college that I decided to go pre-med."

"Why then?"

"It sounds banal."

"You wanted to help your fellow man?"

"I told you it sounded banal."

"Only if you're a beauty-pageant contestant."

She laughed softly.

"I don't think it's a trite explanation at all," he continued. "That's the reason I wanted to be a cop."

"I would have thought you wanted to follow in your big brother's footsteps."

"That too."

"It was a good career choice, Wick."

"You think?"

"I can't see you sitting behind a desk for eight hours a day. Eight minutes a day. I should have known you were lying when you tried to pass yourself off as a computer-software salesman."

"Sorry about that."

"You had a job to do."

"I still do."

Which brought them around to the subject of Lozada again. She rolled onto her side to face him. "What do you think he'll do?"

"Honestly?"

"Please."

"I don't have the slightest idea."

"What about Detective Wesley?"

"Oren doesn't know either. I've been studying Lozada for years, but the only thing I know with any certainty is that when he strikes, we won't see it coming. It'll be like the sting from one of his scorpions. We won't see it coming."

"Chilling thought."

"Damn right it is. That's what makes him so good." They were quiet for a time, then he turned his head and looked across at her. "Did he sexually abuse you, Rennie?"

"He tore my shirt open to see if I was wearing a wire. He thought—"

"Not Lozada." With a deliberate motion, he switched off the mike. "T. Dan."

"What? No! Never."

"Anyone?"

"No. What made you think that?"

"Sometimes when girls turn promiscuous in their teens it's because they've been abused as children."

She smiled sadly. "Stop trying to find justification for my misdeeds, Wick. There is none."

"I'm not trying to justify them, Rennie. Any more than I'd try to justify why I attempted to nail every girl I possibly could. And did."

"The rules are different for boys."

"They shouldn't be."

"No, but they are."

"Not in my rule book. Believe me, I'm in no position to cast the first stone, or even to visit the rock pile." He slid his hand from beneath his head and reached for one of hers. "What I'm having trouble understanding is why you're punishing yourself for things you did twenty years ago."

"What's the statute of limitations on self-chastisement?"

"Pardon?"

"How long since Joe's murder?"

He released her hand and bounded off the bed. "Not the same."

"No, it's not. But it's relevant."

He propped his hands on his hips. "Lozada sparked your curiosity. Is that it? He warned that before you . . . how was it you paraphrased? Before you become too enamored of me, you—"

"Before I take it up the ass. That's what he said."

He dropped the belligerent pose, sighed, and raked his fingers through his hair. He sat down on the edge of the mattress with his back to her and propped his forearms on his knees. Head lowered, he massaged his forehead. "I'm sorry, Rennie. You shouldn't have had to listen to that." He added quietly, "And I shouldn't have made you repeat it."

"Doesn't matter. My reason for asking about Joe has nothing to do with Lozada."

"I know."

"What happened when he was killed?"

He took a deep breath, releasing it on a long, slow exhalation. "At first I was too stunned to think. I couldn't take it in, you know? Joe was dead. My brother was gone. Forever. He'd been there all my life. And suddenly he was a body in the morgue with a tag on his toe. It seemed"—he spread his hands as though trying to grasp the right word—"unreal."

He stood up and began pacing the length of the bed. "It didn't really sink in until the funeral two days later. In the meantime, Oren was working around the clock, despite his own grief, trying to build a case against Lozada. He had the

CSU turn over every pebble in that parking lot, look under every blade of grass in the adjacent lawn, in a search to find anything that could remotely be tied to Lozada. Before Oren could obtain a search warrant or have just cause even to bring him in for questioning, he needed something, a shred of evidence that would place Lozada at the scene.

"Then just before the funeral, Oren told me they'd finally found something. A silk thread. A single thread, maroon in color, no more than two inches long, had been found at the scene. The lab had already analyzed it and determined that it came from very expensive goods, the kind sold in this area only in the most exclusive stores. The kind Lozada wore. If they could find a garment made of that fabric in his wardrobe, they'd have him.

"The turnout for the funeral was incredible. Cops show up to honor fallen cops, you know. There wasn't enough room in the church to accommodate the crowd. The church choir sang, and angels couldn't have done it better. The eulogies were unbelievably moving. The minister's message was comforting.

"But I didn't hear a word of it. None of it. Not the songs, the eulogies, the message about eternal life. All I could think about was that incriminating silk thread."

He had made his way back to the window and resumed his original pose, staring out toward the ocean. "I lasted through the graveside service, the final prayer, the twenty-one-gun salute. Grace and Oren hosted the wake. More than a hundred people crowded into their house, so it wasn't hard for me to slip out unnoticed. This was before Trinity Tower. Lozada lived in a house near the TCU campus. I busted in, even though he was there at the time.

"You can probably guess what happened. I tore his place to pieces. Ripped through his closet like a madman. Upended drawers. Ransacked the whole house. And you know what he was doing all that time? Laughing. Laughing his ass off because he knew I was destroying any chance we had of bringing him to trial for Joe's murder.

"When I didn't turn up the piece of clothing I had hoped to find, I went after him. That scar above his eye? Courtesy of me. He wears it proudly because it signifies his biggest victory. To me it represents my lowest point. I honestly believe I would have killed him if Oren hadn't shown up and physically pulled me off him. I owe Oren my thanks—and my life—for that. And the only reason Lozada didn't kill me and claim self-defense is because he knew the torture it was going to be for me to live with this."

He came around slowly and his eyes connected with hers through the darkness. "You have me to thank for all the trouble Lozada's caused you. If I hadn't lost my temper along with my sanity, he would be on death row and you wouldn't be in this mess."

He chuckled softly and spread his arms to encompass the small room. "And I wouldn't be in this one. I wouldn't be living in a hovel, licking my wounds and wearing a rubber band around my wrist to ward off panic attacks like a—"

"Human being," she said, interrupting. "You said it yourself, Wick. A lot of shit happened to you all at once. Everything you felt, everything you feel now, is human."

"Well, sometimes I'm a little too human for my own good." He gave her a weak smile and she returned it. Then he grimaced and swore softly. Reaching for the microphone, he switched it on. "Yes, I hear you. Jesus, do you think I'm deaf? What's up?" He listened for a moment, then said, "Nothing here either. I'm coming out to get some air. Don't shoot me."

He moved past her to retrieve his pistol and cell phone, then headed for the door. "I'll be right outside. If you hear or see anything, holler."

Sleep was out of the question, so she dressed and was in the kitchen making coffee when he came back in. He was moving quickly. His expression was purposeful.

"What's the matter?"

"We're leaving, Rennie. Now. Get dressed." Then he saw that she was already dressed. "Get your things together. Hurry."

"Where are we going? What's happened?"

He kept moving, through the kitchen, through the living room and into the bedroom where he began stuffing discarded clothing back into his duffel. "Wick! Tell me. What's going on? Has Lozada done something?"

"Yeah. But not in Galveston."

* * *

He told her nothing more because he didn't know anything more.

Oren had called him on his cell phone while he was outside breathing in sea air in an attempt to clear his head and his conscience. Telling Rennie about his fuckup had left him with a mixed bag of feelings.

On the one hand, it had been cathartic to talk about it. She was a damn good listener. On the other, talking about it had reminded him that he was the idiot who had secured Lozada's freedom. He would carry the guilt of that until Lozada was behind bars. Or, better, dead.

Knowing that Lozada was out there mocking his futility made him feel incompetent. Oren's call had left him feeling powerless.

"We don't believe Lozada's still in Galveston," Oren had said.

"Why not?"

"We have good reason to believe he's no longer there."

"What's with the prepared speech and double talk? This isn't a press conference. What's up?"

"Do you have access to Dr. Newton's cell phone?"

"Why?"

"For the next few hours, it might be best if she didn't receive any phone calls."

"Why?"

"Let me sort this out and I'll get back to you."

"Sort what out?"

"I can't tell you until I sort it out."

"What do you mean you can't tell me? Where are you?"

"Ever heard of a Weenie Sawyer?"

"Who the devil—"

"Ever heard of him?"

"No! Who is he?"

"Never mind that now. It can keep. You stay put. Keep the doctor occupied. Have a picnic on the beach or something. Peterson's going to keep his people in place just in case we're wrong. I've got to go now, but I'll be in touch."

"Oren—"

He had hung up and when Wick tried to dial him back, his line was busy. He called the Homicide Division and was told that Oren couldn't be reached but he would be given a message.

He had deliberated for maybe ten full seconds before he returned to the house and alerted Rennie that they were leaving immediately. *Picnic on the beach, my ass,* he thought. If the FWPD was closing in on Lozada, he wanted to be in on the action, although he couldn't blame Oren for wanting to keep him away until it was a done deal.

Maybe it wasn't so smart to drag Rennie along, but what if Oren *were* wrong and Lozada was still in Galveston? It was possible that Lozada had duped them into thinking he'd left Galveston for just that purpose: to lure Wick back to

Fort Worth and clear his way to Rennie. Wick didn't have enough confidence in Peterson and his crew to protect her. He certainly wouldn't entrust her to Thigpen. Which left him no alternative but to take her back with him.

Why had Oren suggested that he confiscate her cell phone? Knowing his partner must have a good reason for such a strange request, Wick had placed it in his duffel bag while she was in the bathroom. She didn't miss it until they were on the far side of Houston and heading north up I-45.

"I think you had it with you in the kitchen," he lied.

"I'm always so conscientious about keeping it with me. How could I have left it?"

"It's too late now to go back for it."

About every ten miles, she questioned him about the phone call that had prompted them to leave so abruptly. "Wesley didn't tell you anything else?"

"Nothing else."

"Only that he doesn't think Lozada is still in Galveston."

"That's what he said."

"We know he was there last night."

"I guess he could have made a quick round-trip. He could have left sometime after calling you."

"And Wesley said nothing else?"

"Rennie, what he said to me hasn't changed since the last ninety-nine times you've asked."

"So where are we going?"

"To your ranch. I'll drop you there. Make sure Toby Robbins is available to keep an eye on you. Then I'll go into Fort Worth and find out what the hell is going on."

"You can take me to the ranch, but only so I can get my Jeep. I'll drive myself to Fort Worth."

"No way. You stay where—"

"I have work to do."

"Bullshit. You're on vacation, remember?"

"I'm going back."

"We'll argue about it when we get there."

The argument never took place.

When they arrived at her ranch a little before noon, they were shocked to see several vehicles, including a sheriff's squad car, parked inside her gate. Wick recognized Toby Robbins's pickup among them.

"What in the world is going on?"

"Stay in the truck, Rennie."

Of course she didn't. Before he could stop her, she was out of the pickup and running toward the gaping barn door.

"Rennie!" He bolted out his own door. But when his feet hit the ground, a pain knifed through his back. It took his breath for a second, but he struck out after Rennie in a hobbling run. She had too much of a head start for him to catch her. He watched her disappear into the barn.

Then he heard her screams.

# Chapter 31

She didn't remember it ever raining this hard in August. Today's aberrant weather would probably set state records. The clouds had rolled in from the northwest at about two o'clock, providing unexpected and welcome relief from the sun and heat. But it wasn't a passing thundershower. It had begun as a hard, steady rain and hadn't let up.

Rennie sat on a hay bale with her back propped against the door of Beade's empty stall. Beyond the barn door, the rainfall looked like a gray curtain. Gullies had been gouged into the hard, dry earth. Channels of rainwater filled puddles that had formed in natural depressions. Rain had washed away the tire tracks left by the cattle truck that Toby had arranged to haul off the carcasses.

Carcasses. Her beautiful horses. All that magnificent power, beauty, and grace reduced to carcasses.

She wept without restraint, sobbing audibly, shoulders shaking. Her heart was broken. Not only for her loss, which was enormous, but for the sheer cruelty of the act. She wept over the wanton waste of those five beautiful, living creatures.

She wept to the point of exhaustion. When her weeping

subsided, she remained as she was, listless, eyes closed, tears drying on her cheeks, listening to the hypnotic patter of raindrops striking the roof.

Sounds of his approach were eclipsed by the rainfall, but she sensed his presence. She opened her eyes and saw him standing in the open doorway of the barn, seemingly impervious to the torrent beating down on him.

He had offered to assist with the removal of the carcasses but had been reluctant to leave her alone. Toby had suggested calling Corinne to sit with her, but she had declined. She'd wanted to be alone for a while. He had seemed to understand that and had honored her wishes.

Nevertheless, he had asked a sheriff's deputy to remain parked at her gate until his return and had told her to stay inside the house, rifle nearby, with the door bolted. And for a while she had complied. But the barn had seemed the only appropriate place in which to mourn. Taking a throw from the sofa, she had used it as protection from the rain as she ran to the barn. Either the deputy hadn't seen her or had elected to leave her undisturbed.

Taking advantage of the solitude, she had grieved for each of the animals individually, then as a group. They had been her family. She had loved them as children. And now they were gone. Destroyed maliciously.

She didn't know how long she'd been here in the barn alone, but Wick would consider any amount of time too long. He would be angry at her for leaving herself unprotected.

He stepped inside and started down the center aisle. His boots squished rainwater. It had plastered the old T-shirt to his skin, making a mold of his torso. His blue jeans were soaked through, too, and clung to his legs. His hair was dripping rainwater and lay flat against his skull.

He stopped a few feet away from her. Contrary to

what she had expected, his expression wasn't angry, but anguished. His eyes weren't hard with annoyance, but soft with compassion. He stretched out his hand, clasped hers, and pulled her to her feet. Before her next heartbeat, she was in his arms and his mouth was possessively taking hers.

This time she gave herself over to it. She went with what had been her inclination the first time he'd kissed her. Mouth, hands, body—all responded. She pushed her fingers up through his wet hair and clutched his head, kissing him back hotly and hungrily, with desire finally unleashed.

She worked the clinging T-shirt up his chest and ran her hands over his wet skin, enmeshing her fingers in the curled hair, brushing his nipples. Then she dipped her head and kissed his chest, her lips skipping over it lightly, greedily. Hissing swear words of surprise and arousal, his large hand closed around her jaw, lifted her mouth back up to his, and made love to it.

When at last they broke apart, she clawed at his T-shirt until, together, they had it off. "Get close to me, Wick. Please. Be close to me."

He peeled her top over her head and brought her up against his bare chest. His skin was wet, cool; hers felt very hot against it, an erotic contrast.

He buried his face in her neck. His arms enveloped her. She felt the imprint of all ten of his fingers on her back as he held her hard and flush against him. She worked her hands between their bodies. It was difficult to unfasten the metal buttons of his jeans because the wet fabric was stubborn, but she stayed with the task until they were all undone and she was touching him.

His breathing was harsh and loud in her ear as he walked her backward until she was pinned between him and the door of the stall. They kissed ravenously while he dealt with the zipper of her slacks. He pushed them down, along with her underpants. When her legs were free, he lifted her up.

With one thrust he was inside her. "My God, Rennie," he gasped and was about to withdraw.

"No!" She slid her hands over his butt and drew him deeper into her, rocking her hips against him. He rasped her name again and began to move. He stroked them toward a climax that seized them quickly and simultaneously.

Supporting her on his thighs, he gradually lay her on the throw she had brought from the house and stretched out above her. He brushed loose strands of hair off her face and lowered his head to kiss her. "Wick—"

"Hush."

His lips moved over her face delicately, caressing each feature in turn. She tried to follow them, to capture them with her own for a kiss. But they were elusive, moving from ear to eyelid to temple to cheek to mouth. His breath was warm and sweet on her skin as he traced a slow path to her breasts.

He touched her nipple with his lips, sipped at it tenderly, then tugged it into his mouth. The other was reshaped by his hand, the nipple fanned with feather-light strokes until it was stiff and flushed and even then he continued to fondle her.

She moved restlessly beneath him, but when she reached for him, he stretched her arms high above her head and traced kisses on the underside of her arm from her wrist to her armpit. By the time he returned to kissing her breasts, she was aching to have him inside her again.

But he withheld. Sliding his hand between her thighs, he found her center. He drew small circles on it with his fingertip. The lightest of touches, yet it created an exquisite pressure inside her.

Darkness closed in around her. Her limbs began to tingle. There was a quickening in her middle. "Wick..."

He timed it perfectly and was nestled deep inside her when she climaxed. Wave after wave of sensation pulsed through her, each more pleasurable than the one before it, until she heard, as from a great distance, her own choppy cries of ultimate release.

Eventually, when she opened her eyes, Wick was smiling down at her. He kissed her softly on the lips, whispering, "Welcome back."

Feeling him still full and firm inside her, she squeezed him from within. He winced with pleasure. "Again." And then, almost inaudibly, "Jesus. Again."

He bridged her head with his arms. His deep blue eyes held hers as he began thrusting into her smoothly and powerfully. She ran her hands over his back, loving the feel of his skin. It emanated vitality. Her fingertips felt the currents of energy that made him unable to remain still, that made him Wick.

She was careful not to caress his incision because she didn't want to detract from his pleasure, even with an unpleasant reminder. Her hands skimmed over it to the small of his back, which dipped gracefully before swelling into his hips. She pressed his buttocks with her palms, and when he came, she held him tightly within the cradle of her thighs. Drawing his head down beside hers, she held it fast until his body relaxed.

The rain had decreased to a sprinkle. They dodged puddles on their way back to the house. "The sheriff's car is no longer there," she observed.

"When I saw you in the barn, you were crying but you were all right. I sent him away."

"Why?"

"I wanted to be alone with you."

"So you thought it might happen?"

He placed his arm across her shoulders and hugged her close. "A guy can hope."

The phone was ringing when they entered the house. It was Toby Robbins asking after Rennie. Wick assured him that she was all right. "Still upset but holding up."

"Can I speak to her?"

Wick passed her the telephone. "Hello, Toby. I'm sorry you had to be the one to find them. It must have been horrible."

Earlier she had been too traumatized to talk about it. Wick could hear only one side of the conversation now, but he knew Toby was giving her his account of finding the horses dead in their stalls when he arrived to let them into the corral.

Rennie listened for several minutes in silence, then said, "I can't thank you enough for making all the arrangements. No, the authorities haven't made an arrest. Yes," she said quietly, "Lozada is definitely a suspect." Then Wick heard her say "Sandwiches?"

He pointed to the Tupperware container on the table and whispered, "Corinne sent them back with me."

"We were just about to sit down to them," Rennie said into the telephone. "Please thank Corinne for me."

After she hung up, Wick said, "I forgot about the sandwiches during my mad search through the house looking for you."

"I'm sorry I alarmed you."

"Alarmed me? Scared me shitless is more like it." He motioned her into a kitchen chair. "Hungry?"

"No."

"Eat anyway."

He coaxed her into half a ham sandwich and a glass of milk. After their meal he went around the house checking doors. "A locked door won't stop him," Rennie said.

"I'm only checking out of habit. Lozada won't come back here."

"How can you be sure?"

"Criminals often return to the scene, whether to gloat or to see if they overlooked something, whatever. But as you know, Lozada isn't a common criminal. He's too smart to return to the scene. He did what he wanted to do here."

"Punish me for being away with you."

"I told you that when he struck we wouldn't see it coming."

"But my horses," she said, her voice cracking. "He knew what would hurt me most, didn't he?"

Wick nodded. "He's done the deed. If I thought he would come back, I wouldn't have left you here with only a sheriff's deputy posted at the gate."

"Then why were you so frightened when you couldn't find me in the house?"

Grimly he said, "I've been known to be wrong."

They went upstairs. He switched on the nightstand lamp. The pale light cast deep shadows on her face, emphasizing her weariness. "How 'bout a hot shower?"

"You read my mind."

The shower was a time for leisurely exploration. He was delighted and surprised by her lack of modesty and the access she gave him. Nor was she shy about caressing him.

He asked her if she liked hairy chests, and she showed him how much she liked his.

She apologized for one breast being slightly larger than the other, which gave him an opportunity to weigh and measure them with his hands and mouth.

She ran her tongue across his crooked front tooth and told him she really got off on that.

They kissed often, sometimes playfully with the water splashing on their faces, sometimes deeply and with feeling. They caressed each other with slick, soapy hands. And once, after she'd had her way with him, he knelt in front of her, nuzzled her thighs until they parted, and then made provocative use of his tongue.

The foreplay was stimulating and left their bodies buzzing, but they didn't take it too far. It resulted only with their holding each other very close.

Afterward, they got into bed and were lying spooned together when she said, "At least they didn't suffer. Lozada didn't torture them."

"Try not to think about it." He pushed aside a handful of her hair and kissed the back of her neck.

Lozada had killed the horses using the same efficiency, and probably the same detachment, with which he'd killed Sally Horton—a couple of bullets through the brain. Wick didn't have to wonder why Lozada hadn't dispatched him that neatly. He'd wanted him to suffer. He had probably planned to stab him more than once with that screwdriver, let him die slowly and painfully.

Lying next to Rennie like this, he was very glad to be alive, and he knew that he was alive only because Lozada had unwisely decided that for Wick Threadgill only a protracted execution would do.

"Rennie?"

"Hmm?"

"You…" He searched for a tactful way of putting it. "You were so…"

"It almost stopped you."

She lay facing away from him, her hands beneath her cheek. He stroked her arm. "I'm not registering a complaint." He laid a soft kiss on her shoulder. "It was like a…a fantasy. A gift. Like you'd never—"

"I haven't been with anyone since the tragedy with Raymond Collier."

That's what he had surmised, but hearing her say it lent this moment, this day, even more significance. Had she told him before he'd made love to her, he would have been astonished. He probably wouldn't have believed her.

"That's a hell of a long time to pay penance, Rennie."

"Not penance. It was a conscious decision. I felt that after what happened, I didn't deserve to have a normal and fulfilling sex life."

"That's nuts. Collier got what he had coming. You were a child."

She laughed dryly. "With my track record? Hardly. No way could I be called a child."

"Maybe a child in desperate need of guidance."

She gave a small shrug of concession.

"Collier was the grown-up. He had no business messing with you. If he did have this sexual obsession for you, he should have stayed away from you, got his own counseling, something. He made a conscious decision too, Rennie, and the consequences of it were his own fault. Whatever caused you to pull that trigger—"

"I didn't."

Wick's heart jumped. "What?"

"I didn't shoot him. I never even touched the pistol. Not until afterward, that is. When the police were already on their way. I held the pistol then, but it didn't make any difference because they never tested it for fingerprints. They never looked for gunpowder residue on anyone's hands. Nothing."

"Who would have had gunpowder residue, Rennie?" When she didn't say anything, he spoke the name that was blaring inside his head. "T. Dan."

She hesitated, then gave a quick nod.

"Son of a bitch!" Wick sat up so he could look down at her, but she kept her head on the pillow, staring straight ahead, giving him nothing except her profile. "He shot Collier and let you take the blame?"

"I was a minor. T. Dan said there would be less mess if I admitted to shooting Raymond in self-defense."

"*Did* he try to rape you?"

"I had been avoiding him since that one time I met him at the motel. I was disgusted with him, and more so with myself. I wouldn't agree to see him, wouldn't even talk to him on the telephone. He showed up at the house that afternoon. I wasn't happy to see him. I don't know why I took him into T. Dan's study. Maybe subconsciously I wanted him to catch us together. I don't know. Anyhow, when my father walked in on us, Raymond was trying to kiss me. He was crying, pleading with me not to refuse him."

"T. Dan fired and asked questions later, is that it? He walked in, read the scene wrong, and thought he was protecting you from being raped?" She didn't answer. "Rennie?"

"No, Wick, protecting me wasn't his reason for firing. Raymond was a savvy businessman. My father was in partnership with him because he was smart. He was relying on Raymond to make them a lot of money on a real-estate deal. So when he came in and saw Raymond clinging to me, he was furious. He told him he was making a fool of himself by crying like a baby over 'a piece of tail.' "

Wick's jaw bunched with anger. "He said that? About his sixteen-year-old daughter?"

"He said much worse than that," she said quietly. "Then he went to his desk and took the revolver from the drawer. When the smoke cleared, literally, Raymond lay dead on the floor."

"He murdered him," Wick said in disbelief. "In cold blood. And got away with it."

"T. Dan forced the gun into my hand and told me what

to tell the police when they arrived. I went along because... because at first I was too stunned to do otherwise. Later, I realized that it was, ultimately, my fault."

"No one ever contested T. Dan's story? Your mother?"

"She never knew the truth. Or if she did, she never let on that she did. She never questioned anything T. Dan told her. No matter what happened, she kept up appearances and pretended that all was well and harmonious in our household."

"Un-fucking-believable. All this time you've assumed the blame and guilt for T. Dan's crime."

"His crime, Wick, but my blame. If not for me, Raymond wouldn't have died. I think about that every day of my life."

Wick expelled a heavy breath and lay back down. She had carried this burden just as he had borne the guilt for letting Lozada escape prosecution. Both of them had suffered severe consequences for behaving irresponsibly. Maybe they should learn to forgive themselves. Maybe they could help each other to forgive themselves.

He placed his arm around her but, unlike before, she held her body stiff and didn't adjust to the contours of his.

"Are you flattered that you're my first lover in twenty years?"

Softly he said, "I'd be lying if I said I wasn't."

"Well, you shouldn't be. There were so many others."

"It doesn't matter, Rennie."

Turning only her head, she looked at him over her shoulder. Her expression was nakedly vulnerable. He was reminded of what Toby Robbins had said about her eyes being larger than the rest of her face when she was a child.

"Doesn't it, Wick?"

He shook his head. "What matters to me," he whispered, "is that you're with me now. That you trust me enough to be here with me like this."

She turned and took his face between her hands. "I was

afraid of you. No, not of you. Of the way you made me feel."

"I know."

"I fought it."

"Like a tigress."

"I'm glad you didn't give up on me." She touched his hair, his cheek, his chin, his chest.

They continued nuzzling until they fell asleep.

When he woke up hours later, he was very hard. Rennie must have sensed it because her eyes opened seconds after his. They gazed at each other across the width of the pillow.

He reached for her hand and drew it down to his lap. She closed her fingers around him and rolled her thumb across the glans, discovering a bead of moisture. One nudge of his knee and she separated her thighs. Moving closer, he propped her thigh on his hip, opening her. She was wet, but knowing that she was probably tender, he held back and didn't enter her.

Instead he covered her hand that was holding his penis and, guiding her, positioned it so she could caress herself with the tip. Connecting in that most intimate way, her eyes conveyed to him an immensity of feeling. And it was incredible. The sensations were new and novel, and holding back was a delicious agony in itself.

He was almost past the point of endurance when she slipped only the tip of his penis within the lips of her sex and came around it warmly and wetly while her hand milked him. He wouldn't have thought it was possible to have a more satisfying climax than the ones they had already shared. He'd been wrong.

He hugged her close and breathed in the scent of her hair, her skin, their lovemaking. He wished for the honor of killing T. Dan Newton for sentencing this beautiful, talented woman to twenty years of self-sacrifice and loneliness for a crime she hadn't even committed. He wanted to give her enough happiness to make up for all that lost time. He wanted to be with her every day for the rest of their lives.

But first they had to survive Lozada.

# Chapter 32

"That's him. Do you recognize him?"

Wick looked into the interrogation room. "Never seen him before."

"I hadn't either," Oren said. "Not until he came in here the other night ready to hand over the goods on Ricky Roy Lozada."

"*I've* got the goods on Ricky Roy Lozada. My great-aunt Betsy's got the goods on Ricky Roy Lozada. Where Lozada is concerned, 'the goods' have been got for a long time. Trouble is, they're worthless."

"Calm down," Oren said. "I know you're upset about Dr. Newton's horses."

"Damn right I am."

"Nobody could've predicted he would do that."

"Why wasn't someone watching her house?"

"It's not in our city, not even our county."

"Don't give me any bullshit about jurisdiction, Oren. You staked out Galveston cops at my house there."

Oren dragged his hand down his tired face. "Okay, maybe it was an oversight. How is Dr. Newton bearing up?"

"She insisted on going back to work today. Said that's

what keeps her grounded. We drove in early from her ranch. I dropped her at the hospital just before coming here."

"Hmm."

Wick gave him a sharp look. "What?"

"Nothing."

"So okay, let's see what this bozo has to say."

As he reached for the doorknob Oren caught him by the arm. "Hold up. Don't go charging in there with steam coming out your ears."

"I'm cool."

"You're anything but cool, Wick."

Everyone in the FWPD Criminal Investigation Division knew that Wick Threadgill was among them that morning. Everybody, at least all the homicide detectives, knew that Oren Wesley's scheme to attract Lozada to Galveston had been a dismal failure. While Threadgill and the lady surgeon were playing footsie on the beach, Lozada had doubled back and killed her stable of fine horses. That's why Wesley had egg on his face, and you could fry one on Threadgill's ass.

Wick was aware of the attention he had attracted. If he'd had a bull's-eye painted on the back of his shirt, he couldn't have felt more conspicuous. It hadn't been easy for him to enter the CID or even to walk into police headquarters. He had felt right at home and ill at ease at the same time.

Since his departure, the turnover of personnel hadn't been that considerable, so he knew many. Some spoke to him and even shook his hand as though genuinely glad to see him. Others looked at him askance and kept their hellos low-key. Wick understood. A police department was as political as any other bureaucracy. Everyone watched his own back. A friendly greeting to an officer on indefinite leave might be misinterpreted by those who recommended advancement. Anyone concerned about his next promotion wouldn't jeopardize his chances by mingling with a persona non grata like Wick Threadgill.

As though validating his paranoia and self-consciousness, it seemed that everyone on the entire third floor, upon hearing his and Oren's raised voices, had stopped what they were doing and were watching with frank interest to see how this scene between the former partners was going to play out.

Wick threw off Oren's hand. "I said I'm cool."

"I just don't want—"

"Are we gonna do this or not?"

Oren glanced over his shoulder at their attentive audience, then opened the door to the interrogation room and waved Wick in. Weenie Sawyer was seated at the far end of the small table. He was jiggling both legs, his bony knees bobbing up and down as rapidly as synchronized sewing-machine needles. His teeth were doing a number on a fingernail.

When he saw Wick he paled, which was remarkable considering that his complexion was already the pasty color of a toad's belly. "What's he doing here?"

"You know Mr. Threadgill?" Oren asked pleasantly.

The man's eyes darted from Wick to Oren then back to Wick. "I recognize him from the pictures in the newspaper."

"Good. Then there's no need to make formal introductions." Oren sat down next to Weenie.

Wick pulled out a chair at the opposite end of the table, turned it around, and straddled it backward. He glared at the little man. "So you're the sniveling little shit who's been doing Lozada's research."

The diminutive man seemed to shrivel even smaller. He looked over at Oren. "Why's he here?"

"He's here because I invited him."

"What for?"

"So he could hear what you have to tell us."

Weenie swallowed hard. He squirmed in his seat. "I...I've been thinking about it. It's not too smart for me to be here and talking to you without a lawyer."

"Come to think of it, you're right," Oren said. "Maybe you'd better go hire you one. When you do, give us a call." He made to stand.

"Wait, wait!" Weenie divided another nervous glance between them. "If I get a lawyer is the deal still on?"

Wick practically came out of his chair. "Deal?" He looked at Oren. "You made a deal with this dickhead?"

"Remember, Wick, you're only here because you promised not to interfere."

"Well *you* promised that this asshole was our ticket to getting Lozada."

"I think he is. But not without—"

"A deal," Wick said, fuming. "What did you offer him?"

"Immunity from prosecution."

He swore under his breath. "That's bullshit. That's what that is."

"Then what's your idea?"

Wick gave Weenie a scornful once-over. "He's a little too big to throw back. Why don't we bread him in cornmeal and deep-fry him?"

Sweat popped out on Weenie's face. He looked wildly at Oren. "He's crazy! Everybody says so. Lozada says so. Lozada says he went 'round the bend when his brother died."

In a blur of motion, Wick practically vaulted the length of the table. He lifted Weenie out of his chair by his scrawny neck and pushed him backward, hard up against the wall, and held him there. The little man squealed like a trapped mouse.

"My brother didn't *die*."

"Wick, have you lost your mind? Let him go!"

"He was *murdered,* you puny little cocksucker."

"Wick, I'm warning you."

"Murdered by your pal Lozada."

Weenie's face had turned beet red. His feet danced uselessly a few inches above the floor. He rolled terrified eyes toward Oren. The detective had hold of Wick's arm, trying to break his grip on Weenie's neck.

"Wick, you're going to kill him. Let him go," he said, straining the words through clenched teeth. He literally tried to peel Wick's fingers from around Weenie's neck. When that didn't work, when Weenie's eyes began to bug out of his head, Oren rammed his elbow into Wick's ribs.

His breath whooshed out. Immediately he released Weenie, who sank to the floor. Cursing expansively and holding his injured right side, Wick bent double.

Oren was breathing hard. "I'm sorry I had to hurt you, but goddammit, you just never learn, do you?"

Weenie remained crouched on the floor, whimpering, but their attention was on each other, not on him.

Wick straightened up, gasping with the effort. "You do that again and I'll—"

"Shut up and listen, Wick. For once. *Listen.*" Oren took several breaths to control his own temper. "You're still having issues with anger management."

Wick laughed. "Issues? Anger management? Where'd you hear that? On *Oprah*?"

Oren shouted over him. "Has your rage blinded you to the fact that you're making the same mistake you made before? You want Lozada to escape prosecution again, you go right on doing what you're doing."

Thigpen opened the door and cautiously poked his head inside. "Everything okay in here?"

"None of your goddamn business!" Wick roared.

Oren told him everything was fine.

"What's the matter with him?" The detective was looking at Weenie, who was still on the floor, mewling and wiping his nose on his sleeve.

"He's okay."

Thigpen gave a dubious shrug, then withdrew and pulled the door closed after him.

Wick continued as though there'd been no interruption. "I've got a temper. I admit it. What you refuse to admit is that when it comes to Lozada, you've got no balls, Oren."

"Speaking of balls, yours should be good and blue by now."

Sparks shot from Wick's eyes. His hands formed fists at his sides. "What are you getting at?"

"Nothing."

"No. Oh, no. We're way past insinuations. Why don't you come right out and say what's on your mind?"

"Okay. You're sleeping with a suspect. Aren't you?"

"If you're referring to Rennie Newton, yes. I am. And loving every second of it. But she's not a suspect."

"I haven't eliminated her as a suspect in the murder of Dr. Howell. Have you forgotten about that?"

"It was Lozada."

"Who could have been hired by her."

"He wasn't."

"Did she ever tell you about that card that she kept in her nightstand?"

"The enclosure card? I found it, remember?"

"Right, right. It came with the roses that Lozada sent her."

Wick spread his arms wide and shrugged. "What's your point?"

"I'm curious is all. When she discovered that Lozada

was the sender of those roses, why didn't she tear up the card? Destroy it along with the flowers? Throw it away?"

"She was saving it as evidence."

"Or as a keepsake. See, after I dismissed it as evidence, she took it back. Far as I know she still has it."

Wick thought about that for maybe a split second, then shook his head emphatically. "She despises Lozada. He gives her the creeps."

"Yeah, so she's said. Tell me, Wick, did you start believing her before or after she screwed your brains out?"

Wick advanced a step. "I warned you once, Oren. Now I'm telling you for the last time, if you ever want to call yourself my friend again, if you ever called my brother your friend, you won't make remarks like that about Rennie. Ever."

Oren didn't back down. "Funny you should mention Joe. Because if he were here, he'd be telling you the same thing. He'd be the first to tell you that you're over the line. You can't be both cop and lover boy to a suspect."

"She's not a suspect," Wick repeated loudly. "She's a victim."

"You sure? You seem to have forgotten that she shot a man."

"She didn't."

"What?" Oren exclaimed.

"She didn't shoot Raymond Collier. Her father killed him. She took the blame."

"Why?"

"Because T. Dan told her to."

Oren barked a laugh. "You believe that?" He laughed again. "She gives you this sob story that nobody can corroborate and you believe her?"

"That's right."

"Uh-huh. And when she told you this, was she blowing in your ear? Or just plain blowing you?"

Wick launched himself at Oren and both flew backward onto the floor. Weenie shrieked. Wick landed a few punches, but he wasn't anywhere near up to full strength and Oren had always been the heavier and stronger of the two. He fought back with a vengeance and without deference to Wick's injury.

When he had Wick somewhat subdued, he struggled to his knees and pulled his service revolver from his shoulder holster. He pointed it down at Wick. Tears of pain smarted in his eyes, but he could see the bore of Oren's handgun clearly enough.

Upon hearing the commotion, several other plainclothesmen rushed into the room. "Back out!" Oren ordered. "Everything's under control."

"What happened?"

"Just a little misunderstanding. It stays in this department, understood?" When no one said anything, he shouted, "*Understood?*"

There were murmurs of consent.

Oren motioned with his pistol. "Get up, Wick."

"I'm not believing this. You pulled a goddamn gun on me?"

"Come on. Up. It might be a good idea if you went in the tank for a while. Cool off." Oren glanced toward the door. "Thigpen, you got a pair of cuffs handy?"

"Not fucking hardly," Wick growled. He surged to his feet and head-butted Oren's belly. He heard the scuffle of feet behind him and knew the other officers were scrambling to assist Oren. Wick had the momentum, however, and succeeded in backing Oren into the wall. He placed a forearm across his throat while with the other hand, he tried to wrest the pistol away from Oren.

"Take back what you said about Rennie."

Oren struggled just as hard as he.

The other cops were trying to pull Wick off, but he had adrenaline working for him. "Take it back!" His shout reverberated off the walls of the small room.

But it wasn't as loud as the gunshot. That deafened him.

# Chapter 33

Weenie had wet himself. It was the definitive humiliation. The second-grade nightmare had been revisited to validate his cruel nickname. There was only one variation—today no one had noticed the dark stain on the front of his trousers. They'd been too busy trying to control the pandemonium.

Following the gunshot all hell had broken loose, and that was how Weenie had managed to escape. There were advantages to being small in stature and easily forgettable. In the aftermath of the shooting he'd been the last thing on anyone's mind.

When he saw an opportunity to slip out of the interrogation room, he had seized it. He'd used the fire-escape stairs rather than taking the elevator. It wasn't until he had exited the building that he realized he'd peed himself.

What had he been thinking when he decided to go to Fort Worth? Dallas had the more colorful reputation, but Fort Worth was wilder and woollier by far. The people over there thought they were still living in the wild, wild West. He'd barely survived thirteen years of its public school system and he should have known better than to cross into that testosterone-charged territory again.

All the way home—and the thirty-mile distance between the two cities had never seemed so far—he'd expected a squadron of police cars to come screaming after him.

But the FWPD had much bigger problems to deal with than one missing would-be confessor who had come to his senses. A bleeding cop was a major event, especially since it had been another cop who'd made him bleed. Probably no one in that room would even remember that Weenie Sawyer had been there to witness the shooting.

Even so, he was taking no chances. He figured he was long overdue a relocation. He would start looking for another place. All he needed was space for his lounger, TV, and bed, and enough electricity to support his computer setup. When he moved he wouldn't leave a forwarding address.

In the meantime, a vacation to a tropical Mexican clime sounded good. Acapulco. Cancún. Someplace where he needed more sunscreen than *pesos*. He'd go out to DFW Airport and hop terminals until he found an available flight to a destination where he could enjoy peace and obscurity until things settled down.

With unsteady hands he unlocked his front door. He tossed his keys onto his TV tray and entered his bedroom in a rush. He groped beneath his bed for his suitcase. It was covered by a thick layer of dust, but he set it on his bed, unlatched the top and raised it, then turned toward his narrow closet.

He screamed in fright.

"Hello, Weenie." Lozada was leaning against the opposite wall, arms and ankles crossed, looking perfectly relaxed. And deadly. Noticing the stain on the front of Weenie's trousers, he grinned. "Did I startle you?"

"H-hi, Lozada. How's it going? I was just—"

"About to pack." He gestured toward the suitcase. "Going somewhere? But then you've already been somewhere, haven't you, Weenie?"

"Been somewhere? No." He was trying very hard to keep his teeth from chattering.

"I've been calling you for a day and a half."

"Oh, I was, uh . . . my phone's out of order."

Indolently Lozada unfolded his arms and legs and crossed to the rickety table beside Weenie's bed. He lifted the receiver of the telephone. The dial tone buzzed loudly.

Weenie swallowed. "Son of a gun. They must've got it working again."

Lozada replaced the receiver and came to stand close to him. "I was getting worried about you, Weenie. You rarely leave this dump of yours. So where have you been?"

Weenie had to crane his neck to look up into Lozada's face. He didn't like what he saw. "I-I'm sorry I wasn't around. Did you need me for something?"

Lozada ran his index finger along Weenie's hairline. "You're sweating, Weenie."

"Uh, listen, whatever you wanted me to do, I'll do it for free. No charge. You know, because I wasn't here when you—"

"You've peed your pants, Weenie. What made you nervous enough to lose bladder control?"

Lozada removed a switchblade from his pocket. With a flick of his wrist and a deadly *click,* he opened it inches from Weenie's face. The small man whimpered in terror.

"You'd better tell me what's got you so shaken." Lozada began to clean beneath his fingernails with the knife. "I'd hate to hear it from somebody else. If you withheld information from me, I'd be very disappointed in you."

Weenie considered his options, which were, basically, life or death. His life wasn't much, but it beat the alternative. "Th-that Threadgill?"

"What about him?"

"He shot what's-his-name. The black guy. Wesley."

Lozada's eyes narrowed to slits of mistrust.

Weenie's head bobbed on his skinny neck. "He did. He shot him. I saw it. I was there."

"Where?"

"At the police station in Fort Worth. The big one downtown. They hauled me in for questioning," he lied. "But don't worry. I didn't tell them anything. Honest, Lozada. They tried several tactics to get me to talk, but—"

"Skip that. What about Threadgill shooting Wesley? I don't believe you."

"I swear," Weenie said, his voice going shrill. "First he went for me. Nearly choked me to death and would have if Wesley hadn't pulled him off. Then they got into an argument over that doctor."

He recounted their quarrel almost word for word. "Wesley said some things about her that didn't sit well with Threadgill. He attacked Wesley. Wesley pulled his pistol and threatened to have Threadgill locked up until he cooled off. Threadgill was having none of it and went for Wesley again. They were in a struggle for the pistol when it went off.

"Cops came running in, all trying to figure out what had happened. There's blood all over Wesley. Threadgill's going berserk, yelling, 'No, no, Jesus, no!' Stuff like that. He was trying to get to Wesley, but other cops were holding him back." Weenie paused to push up his slipping eyeglasses.

"I don't think Threadgill meant to shoot him. It was an accident. But the other cops heard a heated argument before the gunshot, so they figured, you know, it was intentional. And Threadgill was a wildman. It took several men to handcuff him and haul him outta there."

"Wesley's dead?"

"I don't know. I sneaked out before the ambulance got there, but somebody had a handkerchief stuffed into the wound and it looked bad. He was gutshot, I heard somebody say."

Lozada backed up a bit, and Weenie relaxed considerably when he retracted the blade of the knife. But Lozada's stare was still activating his sweat glands.

"A shooting at police headquarters is big news, Weenie. How come I haven't heard any bulletins?"

"They talked about that. Even during all the hullabaloo, everybody kept saying, 'This is contained, understand? Contained. It's a department matter.' They want a tight lid kept on it. Makes sense. A cop shooting a cop. They don't want the public to know about it. They'll probably tell the people at the hospital that Wesley's gun accidentally fired while he was cleaning it. Or something."

Weenie nervously cracked his knuckles. He wondered about the departure time of the last plane to Mexico. Did you need a passport to enter Mexico or would a driver's license do?

"She kept my card?"

"Huh?"

Irritably Lozada snapped his fingers in front of Weenie's face as though to wake him up, then repeated the question.

"Oh yeah, a card you sent with some roses? Wesley thinks the lady has a thing for you. That's what pissed off Threadgill. Wesley said she was playing him like a fiddle. Not in those words, but—"

"Do you masturbate?"

"Beg pardon?"

Before Weenie could blink, his male parts were suspended over the razor-sharp blade of Lozada's knife. "Do you—"

"What are you talking about?" Weenie screeched.

"You might not miss it for sex, but you'll be pissing like a woman if you don't tell me what you were doing in an interrogation room being questioned by Wesley and Threadgill."

Weenie was up on tiptoes, trying to maintain his balance. If he faltered, he'd be a eunuch and any chance he had of fulfilling his fantasies with an amiable señorita would be dashed. "I was afraid of getting into trouble."

"So you ratted me out."

"No, I swear. God as my witness."

"There is no God." Lozada raised the knife blade another centimeter and Weenie squealed. "There is only Lozada and the laws of physics, one of which is the law of gravity. If I cut off your balls, Weenie, they'll drop like marbles."

"I went there to see what kind of deal I could make," he sobbed. "You know, in case they ever linked me to you. But then, Wesley got all worked up over some phone call you had made to Dr. Newton's cell phone. They thought you were in Galveston."

"I was."

"Then he got word that her horses had been shot. Miles from Galveston. Confused the hell outta them all. Anyhow, Wesley slapped me in a holding cell and sorta forgot about me, I guess. Until this morning. He let me shower. Gave me breakfast. Put me in this room and told me to wait.

"When he came back, Threadgill was with him. I told them I had changed my mind, that I wanted a lawyer. You know the rest. I swear I didn't tell them anything." He was crying now, blubbering like a baby, but he couldn't help it.

Lozada withdrew the knife. "The only reason I'm not killing you is because I don't know how to destroy your computers and be certain I'm also destroying all the data they contain."

Weenie wiped his nose with the back of his hand. "Huh?"

"Get to it, Weenie," Lozada said softly.

Weenie swallowed convulsively. "You want me to destroy my computers?" Lozada might just as well have asked a mother to smother her child. Weenie had been prepared to take a vacation from his computers for a while, but to destroy them was beyond his imagining. He couldn't do it.

Lozada's hand barely moved, but Weenie felt a slight tug at his crotch and a sudden draft. When he looked down he saw that his pants had been split open from inseam to waistband. The knife was poised just below his crotch. The blade gleamed wickedly.

"Get to work, Weenie, or your foreskin is next."

Weenie had been circumcised, but, at the moment, that seemed a rather insignificant detail.

* * *

As soon as Rennie alighted from the elevator on the ground floor of the hospital, she heard her name.

Grace Wesley was entering the atrium lobby through the revolving doors. Rennie tried to catch the elevator and hold it for her, but the doors had closed and it had already begun its ascent.

Grace rushed up to her. "Please don't tell me he's dead."

"No, he's still with us." Grace's knees buckled and she might have collapsed had Rennie not been there to lend support. "He's still listed as critical, but they think he's going to make it."

Grace covered her mouth to stifle a sob of relief. "Thank God, thank God. You're sure?"

"I talked to them just now as they were wheeling him out of surgery."

Grace blotted her eyes with a tissue. "I was so afraid that by the time I got here..." She was unable to speak aloud the horrible thought.

Rennie reached for her hand and squeezed it tightly. "I heard you'd gone to Tennessee to see your daughters."

"A Nashville policewoman met my flight and told me what had happened. I never even left the airport. Took the next flight back. Oren's supervisor met me at DFW and drove me straight here." She paused. "You said 'they.' "

"What?"

"You said 'they' think Oren's going to make it."

"I was referring to the surgical team."

"I thought you—"

"I wasn't even allowed to observe, much less perform the surgery. Under the circumstances that would have been very awkward. But he had an excellent team working on him."

"I would have requested you."

"Thanks for that." Moved to tears, Rennie turned away and punched the elevator button again.

"Is it true, Rennie? Wick did this?"

Sadly she lowered her head, nodding.

Grace said, "That's what I was told, but I thought there must be some mistake. I can't believe it."

"Neither can I. It's...incomprehensible. What could have driven him to do this? The two of them have been through so much together, been such good friends. Wick thinks the world of your husband." Head still down, she rubbed her eyes. "Detective Wesley is in ICU and Wick's in jail."

"He's in love with you."

Rennie's head came up quickly.

"He is." Grace held Rennie's astonished stare until an elevator arrived and the doors slid open. "I've got to go."

"Yes. By all means."

Grace quickly boarded the elevator. Rennie waited until the doors had closed before she turned to go. Yesterday's unseasonable rain was a memory. It was blistering hot on the doctors' parking lot. She would never again traverse it without thinking of Lee Howell. His murder had been cataclysmic, but this tragic chain of events had really begun when she'd announced the jury's verdict. "We find the defendant not guilty."

Her house was dark when she arrived. As always, she drove her Jeep into her garage and entered through the kitchen door. She went straight to the refrigerator and got a bottle of water. She stood at the kitchen sink until she had drunk all of it.

She passed through her living room, went down the dark hallway and into her bedroom. She switched on the nightstand lamp and undressed. When she was down to her underwear, she went into the bathroom and turned on the tub faucets. She chose a scented gel and took a long shower.

Wrapped in her favorite, most comfortable robe, she went back into the kitchen and poured herself a glass of wine. She carried it with her into the living room and sat down in her favorite spot in the corner of the sofa.

She sipped her wine and thought back to the night she'd fallen asleep here and later had been called to an emergency at the hospital. The patient had had a critical stab wound to the back.

Wick. She had caused him so much pain. Wesley, too. He and his whole family. And now... God, now.

Her head fell back against the sofa cushions. She closed her eyes, but tears slid through her eyelids and rolled down her cheeks. They had all suffered because of her and that damned verdict.

She sat there for a long while, with her head back and her eyes closed. That was how he found her.

Or rather, that was how she was when she sat up, turned, and said, "Hello, Lozada." He was standing behind the sofa, inches away, looking down at her. "I've been expecting you."

He smiled, pleased. "Have you, Rennie?"

Hearing him say her name, seeing that reptilian smile, almost made her throw up the wine. Placing the glass on the coffee table, she stood up and came around the end of the sofa to face him. "I knew you'd come when you heard about what happened to Oren Wesley."

"Your boyfriend can't control his temper. An unfortunate character trait. It was only a matter of time before he self-destructed. Wesley?" He shrugged. "His problem is choosing the wrong friends."

"How'd you find out? It hasn't been on the news. Security was so tight at the hospital that only a handful of staff knew Wesley's identity and the nature of his injury. You must have an informant in the FWPD. Who told you?"

"A little birdy," he whispered. "He's a cowardly little birdy. I didn't believe him at first, but I've checked out the sad tale, and, alas, it's true."

He reached out to finger a strand of hair that lay against her chest. She forced herself not to recoil, but he must have sensed her revulsion because he smiled that smile again. "You look lovely tonight."

"I don't look lovely at all. I'm tired. Weary, actually. Of everything."

"Your trip must've been exhausting."

"How'd you do it?"

"Do what, my dear?"

"How'd you get from Galveston to my ranch before daybreak?"

"I told you before, Rennie, I don't reveal trade secrets. If I did, I'd soon be out of business."

"It was quite a feat."

He laughed. "I don't have wings, if that's what you're thinking."

When her palm connected with his cheek, it made a sound as emphatic as an exploding firecracker.

"That's for killing my horses."

No longer laughing or smiling, he gripped her wrist so hard she cried out in pain. He whipped her around and thrust her hand up between her shoulder blades. His breath was hot against her ear. "I ought to kill you right now for doing that."

"You're going to kill me anyway, aren't you?"

"How could I possibly let you live, Rennie? You have only yourself to blame. You should have allowed me to cherish you the way I wanted. Instead you chose to be manhandled by that crude cowboy ex-cop." He drew her tighter against him and pushed her hand up higher. "After an insult like that, you leave me no choice but to kill you both. I'm only sorry he's in jail so he won't get to watch you die. But one can't have everything."

The pain was considerable, but she didn't struggle. She didn't even whimper. "They should've locked you up years ago, Lozada. Not for being a killer, but for being insanely delusional. Don't you get it? I wouldn't have had you near me even if Wick Threadgill didn't exist. You're a creep."

He clicked open the switchblade and placed it across her throat. "Before I finish with you, you'll be begging me to spare your life."

"I'll never beg you for a damn thing. I might have pleaded with you to spare my horses, but you didn't give me a chance. When you killed them, you played your trump card as far as I'm concerned. I'm over you, Lozada. I'm over being afraid of you."

"Oh, I doubt that." Lowering the knife, he patted the flat side of the blade against her nipple.

Reflexively she sucked in a quick breath.

"See?" he chuckled. "You're very afraid, Rennie."

It was true. She was terrified, but still she refused to show it. "I won't fight you, Lozada. For twenty years, every day of my life has been a bonus. I won't beg you to let me live. If that's what you're waiting for, you're only wasting your time."

"Such courage. And for that, I hate to kill you, Rennie, I really do. You're a remarkable woman. I hope you understand how badly I feel about the way our affair must end."

"We never had an affair, Lozada. As for understanding, I understand that the only way you can get a woman's attention is to terrorize her."

He drew her tighter against him and ground his crotch against her bottom. "Feel that? That's what gets women's attention. Plenty of women."

She remained silent.

"Say pretty please, Rennie." He slid his tongue down the length of her neck. "Say pretty please and I may let you suck it before I kill you."

"Oh, Lo-za-da."

At Wick's singsong voice, Rennie felt him start.

"Yeah, that's right. That's the barrel of my three-fifty-seven in your ear. Blink and you're history."

"Please blink, Lozada. Pretty please," Oren Wesley taunted from the connecting kitchen door. His handgun was aimed directly at Lozada's head.

"Drop the blade!" Wick ordered.

Lozada chuckled and raised the razor edge back to Rennie's throat. "Go ahead and pull the trigger, Threadgill. If you want to see her blood gush, shoot me."

"That's just like you, you chicken-livered son of a bitch. Using a woman to save your ass. Attacking her from behind, too. Another of your—what you'd call it?—unfortunate character traits.

"But if that's the way you want it, Ricky Roy, fine by me," he said easily. "When I fire, Oren will, too. See, we've been practicing all day. Ever since we staged that little scene for your pal Weenie. Messy as hell, all that fake blood and all, but obviously convincing.

"Now, here's what'll happen. Our bullets will enter your skull. His may be a thousandth of a second behind mine. But pretty damn near simultaneous, wouldn't you say, Oren?"

"That's what I'd say."

"They might even intersect at some point, Ricky Roy, but in any case, your brains will spatter like shit from a tall goose."

"She'll be dead by then," Lozada said.

"Let her go, Lozada."

"Not a chance."

"What do you think, Oren?" Wick said. "Are you tired of this crap?"

"I'm tired of this crap."

"Me too." And with his left hand, Wick fired a small pistol into Lozada's right elbow, point blank. Bone shattered. Nerves and blood vessels were severed. The switchblade fell from useless fingers. Rennie dropped to the floor, as she had been instructed to do. Lozada spun around, left hand raised, thumb extended, jabbing toward Wick's eye socket. Wick fired the .357 directly into his chest.

Lozada's eyes widened with astonishment. Then Wick said, "This is for Joe," and fired a second time.

Lozada fell backward onto the floor.

Rennie crawled over to him and immediately checked his neck for a pulse.

"His heart's still beating." She ripped open his shirt.

"Leave him."

She looked up at Wick. "I can't."

Then she turned back to Lozada and set about trying to save his life.

# Chapter 34

It was eight o'clock the following morning before Rennie left the hospital. Wick was outside waiting for her in his pickup truck with the engine running. He leaned over and opened the passenger door for her.

They had timed her departure to coincide with Oren's press conference so the media would be occupied and she could make a clean getaway. As they pulled away from the hospital, they saw news vans lining the street and a cluster of reporters and cameramen surrounding the lobby entrance.

"What's he telling them?" she asked.

"That the FWPD pulled off a flawless sting operation, with the cooperation of Tarrant General Hospital personnel. One of the city's most notorious criminals, one Ricky Roy Lozada, died from gunshot wounds he received while resisting arrest."

Before turning him over to paramedics, Rennie had heroically worked to keep his heart beating. She had ridden in the ambulance with him to the emergency room, but upon their arrival he was pronounced dead. Wick had personally escorted his body to the morgue.

Rennie had then insisted on examining Wick, even ordering a CAT scan to check for internal bleeding. He'd told Oren not to hold back, to make their fight look authentic. Oren had taken him at his word. He felt like a punching bag, but Rennie's examination had turned up nothing worrisome.

"Oren's going to try and keep your name out of the story," Wick told her.

"I will appreciate that."

"But it might be unavoidable, Rennie."

"If it's unavoidable, then I'll deal with it."

Their destination had been predetermined. She wouldn't be returning to the house in which Lozada had died. Once they were headed west on the interstate, Wick reached for her hand. "I died a thousand deaths while he was holding that knife on you."

"I was afraid that something had happened to detain you, that you and Oren wouldn't be in place. When I got home I was tempted to look in the kitchen pantry and under the bed to make sure you were there."

"Hell couldn't have kept me away."

"It was a daring plan, Wick."

"I just thank God it worked."

He had resolved that he and Rennie had no hope of a future until the problem of Lozada was resolved. In other words, until he was taken out of the picture. And that had been the key phrase: out of the picture. His mind had snagged on those four words. It occurred to him that if Lozada thought he was out of the picture, and Oren was out of the picture, he would make a move on Rennie.

"The toughest part of the plan for me was the necessity of placing you in danger."

"But I was already in danger."

"That's the conclusion I finally drew. And you were going to remain in danger unless and until I forced Lozada's hand." Yesterday morning, he had got up well before dawn, called Oren, and outlined the plan. Oren had liked the idea, made a few suggestions of his own, and put things into motion.

"How did you convince Oren that I wasn't the femme fatale he believed me to be?" Rennie asked.

"I didn't have to. Lozada did that when he killed your horses. Actually, I think Oren had made up his mind long before that and was just being mule-headed. Believe me, Rennie. If he hadn't been totally convinced of your innocence and his misjudgment, he would never have pulled this sting. And by the way, he sends his apology for all the ugly things he had to say about you in order to convince Weenie Sawyer.

"Who, by the way, was a lucky break for us. If not for him, we might have had to wait for days, me in jail, Oren in the hospital pretending to be gravely wounded, before Lozada got the news and acted on it.

"We had Sawyer tailed to his place in Dallas, and when the stakeout team saw Lozada there, they called in a heads-up. After Lozada left, they moved in and arrested Weenie. He was lying on his bed crying because Lozada had forced him to hammer his computers to bits. He started confessing his complicity even before they got the cuffs on."

"Will there be any repercussions for you?"

"For shooting Lozada? No. Oren had me reinstated before we went in to question Weenie."

She turned to him with surprise. "So you're officially a cop again?"

"I'm thinking about it."

"What's there to think about?"

"All the shit that goes with it."

"There's shit with every job, Wick."

"Not a very encouraging maxim," he said wryly.

"It boils down to one question." He looked across at her. "Do you love the work more than you hate the shit?"

He didn't have to think about it for long. "I love the work."

"There's your answer."

He nodded thoughtfully. "Now that I'm finally able to bury Joe, really bury him, it'll be different, I think."

"I'm sure it will be. It's your calling." She laughed softly, "And speaking of callings, Grace may have missed hers. She should have been an actress. She put on quite a performance at the hospital."

"I heard you both did."

"I don't know if Lozada saw it or not."

"I don't know either, but every scene had to be staged and played out as though it were real. If Lozada had been watching the hospital and Grace hadn't rushed to Oren's bedside, he would have smelled a rat."

Noticing her yawn, he said, "You've been up all night. Why don't you try and sleep the rest of the way?"

"What about you?"

"I napped between all those unnecessary tests my doctor put me through."

Smiling, she closed her eyes. She woke up when he stopped the truck at the gate and got out to open it. After driving through, he parked at the front steps.

Rennie looked toward the barn. "That was always my first stop."

He stroked her cheek. "Try not to think about it."

"I'll always think about it."

He got out and came around to open her door, but he blocked her from getting out. "What?" she asked.

"When I was in your bedroom, waiting to make my move on Lozada…"

"Yes?"

"I heard you say something to him that I thought was strange. You said that every day of your life for the past twenty years had been a bonus." He removed her sunglasses so he could see into her eyes. "And I just wondered what you meant by that, Rennie." She lowered her head, but he placed his finger beneath her chin and raised it, forcing her to look at him. "You didn't finish the story, did you?"

He could see she wrestled with lying about it, but his will won out. She took a deep breath. "When T. Dan fired?"

"Yes?"

"He wasn't aiming at Raymond."

He stared at her for a moment, and then when misapprehension cleared and he understood what she was saying, he expelled his breath slowly. "Jesus."

"My father was much angrier at me than he was at Raymond. Raymond had lost interest in their business deal, had lost his edge. When T. Dan saw us together and realized that I was the reason for Raymond's preoccupation, he regarded me only as an obstacle that had to be eliminated."

She paused for a moment and stared vacantly into near space. "He was my father and I had adored him. He'd broken my heart with his infidelity. He had betrayed my mother, our family. He was a selfish, self-serving scoundrel."

She laughed bitterly and shook her head. "But, Wick, you know what's really funny? Or tragic? I still loved him. In spite of everything. If I hadn't, I wouldn't have tried so hard to anger and upset him by doing the very things he did. I wouldn't have seduced his business partner. I loved him," she repeated sadly.

"But his land deal meant more to him than I did. He whipped himself into a froth and was angry enough to kill me. He would have if Raymond hadn't jumped in front of me just as T. Dan fired. So, you see, I meant it literally when

I told you if not for me, Raymond wouldn't have died. He died saving me from my own father.

"Afterward, I was in shock. I went along with everything T. Dan told me to do, said everything he told me to say. Soon after the incident he sent me away. Maybe the sight of me pricked his conscience, or maybe I was an unhappy reminder of the land deal that got away. I don't know. But until the day he died, we never spoke of that afternoon again."

Wick pulled her toward him and when she resisted he said, "Uh-huh. No way. You're not going to retreat, withdraw, and pull on your hair shirt." He tucked her face into his neck and stroked her head. "It happened twenty years ago. It's long past, you've atoned for it a thousand times over, and T. Dan is frying in hell. He can't hurt you anymore, Rennie. I won't let him."

He held her close for several moments before setting her away. "I'm glad you told me. It explains a lot. The need to be in control. The thumbing your nose at danger because you could have died at sixteen. I just hope that you'll cut back on some of that daredevil bullshit. I can't be running around all the time covering your ass. Speaking metaphorically, of course."

She laughed. Or sobbed. It was difficult to tell because there were tears in her eyes but she was smiling. He helped her out of the truck and together they climbed the steps. As he pushed open the front door, he said, "How 'bout breakfast?"

"Sounds good."

He reached around her to close the door and trapped her between it and him. "Breakfast. Every morning for the rest of our lives."

She smiled at him sadly. "Wick—"

"Now wait. Before you start raising objections, hear me

out." He cupped her cheek with his hand. "I'll be your best friend for the rest of your life. I'll try my damnedest to heal that part of you that still hurts. I'll be an ardent and faithful lover. I'd father your children, gladly. And I would protect you with my life."

"You already have."

"You saved me, too, Rennie. And not just on the operating table. I was in a wretched state when Oren came to Galveston. Being lured into a case involving a mysterious lady surgeon was the best thing that ever happened to me."

She smiled, but her eyes were still clouded with doubt. "I don't see how we could ever work."

"Come to think of it, you may be right," he sighed. His hand moved to the top button of her blouse and undid it. "I throw temper tantrums and you're cool under pressure. I'm a slob; you insert the tabs on your cereal boxes. I'm poor; you're rich."

By the time he had enumerated those fundamental differences, all the buttons were undone and so were her slacks. Leaning into her, he kissed the side of her mouth. "We make no sense at all."

She tilted her head to give his lips access to her throat. "Except what Grace said."

He pulled her earlobe gently through his teeth. "What did Grace say?"

She tugged the shirttail from his waistband and ran her hands up over his chest. "That you're in love with me."

"Smart Grace."

"So you are?"

"I are." Her soft laugh became a low moan when he unclasped her bra and took her breasts in his hands.

"Then there's my work."

"There is that." His tongue stroked her nipple.

"It's very demanding."

He caressed her tummy with the backs of his fingers, down past her navel. "I guess you're right." He turned his hand and slid it into her underpants. "We've got nothing going for us." She was wet and receptive, and as he slipped his fingers into her, he captured her mouth in a searing kiss.

A few minutes later, Rennie lay sprawled on top of him on the sofa. The clothes that hadn't been removed in time were damp, wrinkled, and twisted around them. Strands of her hair were wrapped around his neck. He was balancing with one foot on the floor. They were flushed and breathless, and excitement still pulsed where their bodies remained joined.

He panted a few breaths. "You were saying?"

He felt her smile against his chest as she asked drowsily, "Pancakes or eggs?"

# About the Author

Sandra Brown is the author of sixty-eight *New York Times* bestsellers. There are more than eighty million copies of her books in print worldwide, and her work has been translated into thirty-four languages. In 2008, the International Thriller Writers Association named Brown its Thriller Master, the organization's highest honor. She has served as president of Mystery Writers of America and holds an honorary doctorate of humane letters from Texas Christian University. She lives in Texas.

For more information you can visit:
SandraBrown.net
Facebook.com/AuthorSandraBrown
@Sandra_BrownNYT